"FANS OF ROBERT B. PARKER'S SPENSER WILL LOVE McMORROW, a quintessential male who's tough, funny, macho, and intelligent."

—*Booklist*

Lifeline

"Jack Morrow, seen before in *Bloodline* and *Deadline*, is a former *New York Times* reporter now working for a small paper in Maine. Covering the courthouse, he senses a good story in Donna Marchant, a young woman complaining of domestic abuse but ignored by the autocratic assistant district attorney . . . McMorrow writes about Donna's plight, arousing the wrath of her loutish boyfriend, Jeff Tanner. When Donna is murdered, suspicion falls not only on Tanner but also on McMorrow . . . Boyle, a Maine newspaper writer himself, makes McMorrow a credible crusader, equally comfortable in the quiet woods and small-town courthouses. The narrative moves briskly as McMorrow eliminates several suspects on his way to a surprise solution."

—*Publishers Weekly*

Deadline

"The rhythms of the weekly newspaper work a wonderful counterpoint to the building tension of McMorrow's investigation, and the writing is sharp and evocative without being showy."

—*Washington Post Book World*

"There's a steel backbone in his lean plot, and the clipped prose and flinty characterizations are to this rugged literary landscape what the black woods and craggy cliffs are to the contours of Maine—a daunting kind of beauty."

—*New York Times Book Review*

continued on next page . . .

MORE MYSTERIES FROM THE
BERKLEY PUBLISHING GROUP ...

FORREST EVERS MYSTERIES: A former race-car driver solves the high-speed crimes of world-class racing ... "A Dick Francis on wheels!"
—Jackie Stewart

by Bob Judd
BURN   SPIN
CURVE

THE REVEREND LUCAS HOLT MYSTERIES: They call him "The Rev," a name he earned as pastor of a Texas prison. Now he solves crimes with a group of reformed ex-cons ...

by Charles Meyer
THE SAINTS OF GOD MURDERS   BLESSED ARE THE MERCILESS

FRED VICKERY MYSTERIES: Senior sleuth Fred Vickery has been around long enough to know where the bodies are buried in the small town of Cutler, Colorado ...

by Sherry Lewis
NO PLACE FOR SECRETS   NO PLACE LIKE HOME
NO PLACE FOR DEATH   NO PLACE FOR TEARS
NO PLACE FOR SIN

INSPECTOR BANKS MYSTERIES: Award-winning British detective fiction at its finest ... "Robinson's novels are habit-forming!"
—*West Coast Review of Books*

by Peter Robinson
THE HANGING VALLEY   PAST REASON HATED
WEDNESDAY'S CHILD   FINAL ACCOUNT
GALLOWS VIEW   INNOCENT GRAVES

JACK McMORROW MYSTERIES: The highly acclaimed series set in a Maine mill town and starring a newspaperman with a knack for crime solving ... "Gerry Boyle is the genuine article."   —Robert B. Parker

by Gerry Boyle
DEADLINE   BLOODLINE
LIFELINE   POTSHOT
BORDERLINE

SCOTLAND YARD MYSTERIES: Featuring Detective Superintendent Duncan Kincaid and his partner, Sergeant Gemma James ... "Charming!"   —*New York Times Book Review*

by Deborah Crombie
A SHARE IN DEATH   ALL SHALL BE WELL
LEAVE THE GRAVE GREEN   MOURN NOT YOUR DEAD

POTSHOT

Gerry Boyle

BERKLEY PRIME CRIME, NEW YORK

POTSHOT

A Berkley Prime Crime Book / published by arrangement with
the author

PRINTING HISTORY
G. P. Putnam's Sons hardcover edition / 1997
Berkley Prime Crime mass market edition / July 1998

The Penguin Putnam Inc. World Wide Web site address is
http://www.penguinputnam.com

ISBN: 0-425-16233-8

Berkley Prime Crime Books are published
by The Berkley Publishing Group,
a member of Penguin Putnam Inc.,
200 Madison Avenue, New York, NY 10016.
The name BERKLEY PRIME CRIME and the BERKLEY PRIME CRIME
design are trademarks belonging to Berkley Publishing Corporation.

PRINTED IN THE UNITED STATES OF AMERICA

10 9 8 7 6 5 4 3 2 1

Thanks go to the news staff of the *Lowell Sun*, to acquaintances on both sides of the marijuana debate, to the people of western Maine, a wild and welcoming place, and especially to Brent Smith, who graciously and patiently drove me in circles.

For

JEANNE CAREW McGOWAN BOYLE:

a bright light, always

POTSHOT

One

IT WAS RAINING, not a deluge, but a cold, resolute drizzle that turned the pathways at the Country Life Fair into muck and drove the fairgoers into the animal barns, where they looked with wonder at cows and goats and strange fluffy chickens.

"This one's for sale," I said, peering into a cage where a white snow-shoed hen peered back. "We could have chicken salad tonight."

"Jack," Roxanne said. "Please."

"You're right. She's small. I guess we'd better buy two. Which job do you want? Lopping off the heads or pulling out all the feathers?"

Roxanne rolled her eyes and chewed. She was eating an eggplant sandwich, which looked as good as it sounded. The cold autumn air had rouged her cheeks and the mist had waved her hair.

"You're beautiful when you're chewing," I said.

Roxanne swallowed. She was beautiful when she was swallowing, too.

"God, I hope you didn't try that line on anybody over dinner," Roxanne said.

"You don't like it?"

She rolled her eyes and shook her head.

"I'll go find a hippie who appreciates me," I said.

"Tell him I said hello."

"No, I mean a woman hippie. You know. With low-cut Birkenstocks. Underwear made out of natural fibers. I miss the free-love days, you know?"

"They weren't what they're cracked up to be," Roxanne said.

"How do you know? You weren't born," I said.

Roxanne gave her best imitation of a lascivious leer.

"I'm living proof of the wonder of monogamy."

"You win," I said.

Roxanne smiled.

She finished her eggplant and walked over to a recycling bin and tossed her paper napkin in. I walked over with her and looked out at the rain. People in expensive mountaineering gear trooped by triumphantly, knowing their five-hundred-dollar all-weather outfits, field-tested on K-2, would keep them safe and dry on their trek to the craft tent across the fairgrounds.

"What'd you do with your french fries?" Roxanne said.

"I couldn't eat 'em. The ketchup was weird."

"That's because it doesn't have sugar."

"What's so bad about sugar?" I said. "I think these people ought to lighten up."

"You tell them, then," Roxanne said. "You hear that drumming? What's that?"

"West African drums. Down behind the grandstand. I was down there before. There was a tribe of upper-middle-class white people, dancing up a storm."

"What for?"

"I don't know. I think they're getting back to their roots."

"What roots are those?" Roxanne said.

"Toms River, New Jersey. Pound Ridge, New York. Ridgefield, Connecticut. A lot of big heartless corporations put these people through college."

Roxanne smiled at me.

"You're being too hard on them," she said. "They're like you. They like Maine and living in the country and all that."

I thought for a moment. Watched a guy who had his hair in a long braid and a ring through his upper lip.

"I know," I said. "But you know what gets me a little? I guess it's the idea that they're biting the hands that raised and fed them. They should, I don't know, show some appreciation, don't you think? Their parents didn't like to go to the office every day, but they did it anyway. How are these people going to put their kids through college?"

Roxanne put her arm around my waist, her hand on my hip.

"Financial aid. But I saw some beautiful sweaters, hand-knit by your hypocritical hippies. I'm going to go back."

"Don't try to pay with plastic."

"What are you going to do?" Roxanne said.

"I don't know. Wander around. There was a guy selling yurts over by the ox-pulling. I think I'll check them out."

"You mean those tent-looking things?"

"Yeah. I think they come with yaks. You know. Mongols and the steppes and all that."

"What would you do with a yurt?"

I stepped closer to her.

"I don't know, but I know what we could do in one."

I raised my eyebrows knowingly.

"Oh, Jack, you are sick."

Roxanne grinned. She was beautiful when she grinned. She was just plain beautiful. I grinned, too.

"I'll meet you in a half hour," she said. "Where do you want to meet?"

I gave her the look again.

"Oh, Lord," Roxanne said. "Just meet me at the front gate. I want lots of people around in case you get any ideas."

"I'm full of ideas."

"Front gate. Half hour," Roxanne said, grinning at me. "You're lucky I love you."

"Very," I said.

Roxanne walked one way and I walked the other. The path was slick with mud and people were picking their way around the puddles. Even with the rain, the place was teeming, both with the hippies, who worked here, and with fairgoers, who were more mainstream; handsome, healthy, prosperous looking couples herding handsome, healthy kids. The kids wore yellow slickers and tall rubber rain boots. The fathers wore baseball hats that advertised programs on public radio or universities with industrial-sized sports teams. The mothers were attractive and outwardly well adjusted, the kind who made sure everyone wore seat belts in the Volvo.

They were here to give their children the opportunity to see a cow, close up.

And there were cows. Lots of them. I cut through one of the livestock barns, where the cows reclined in stalls bedecked with the banners of their respective farms. The names of the farms were meant to sound idyllic: Pumpkin Hill, Salt Marsh, Windy Hollow. The cows were big and placid. Like kids these days, they were identified by stuff worn on rings through their ears and noses.

I walked out of the back side of the barn and continued on, my boots sticking in the mire. Beyond the barn I saw men standing beside pickups that cost half as much as a house. The pickups pulled matching trailers that carried oxen to the fair. When all of the machinery was parked and the oxen unloaded, the men and oxen would move massive loads of wood and stone, in the manner of the desperate, dirt-scraping pioneers who, if they'd had a four-wheel-drive truck, would have eaten their oxen for supper.

The fair was billed as a celebration of rural life, and tens of thousands of people joined the party every fall, linked by the common bond of being able to come home from work every day without being shot, stabbed or terrorized by the threat of either or both. This was a legitimate reason for celebration, I thought, but not a reason for smugness.

"Lighten up, McMorrow," I said aloud to myself.

"I'll try," myself said back.

So I continued on. I saw booths where people were selling honey and dry beans and giant squash. A kid selling towels purportedly made by the indigenous people of Guatemala wore a sweatshirt that said, "Princeton Lacrosse." A preppie-looking guy with gold-rimmed glasses stood and watched the judging of Percheron horses, their manes and tails braided with ribbons.

"Bizarre," he said.

"Why's that?" I said, standing beside him.

He looked over at me, startled.

"You into this?" the guy said.

"No, but it probably beats staying home and polishing your BMW."

I looked at him and grinned. He looked back, then walked away.

No social graces.

In the next row was the political wing. A banner proclaimed, "Extinction is forever." Another said, "Peace is Patriotic." I strolled along, eyeing the literature, listening to the boom box music, which was obscure reggae and ska.

"Hey, man," a voice said. "You like the music of the islands?"

I looked over. He was on the small side, lithe and dark, but white. More Brooklyn than Barbados. He stopped and put a clipboard down in front of him and me.

"If it wasn't for this herb, that music would never have been created, man," the guy said.

"If it weren't," I said.

"Exactly right. We're putting the question to the people. Legalize hemp. You registered to vote in Maine?"

"Yeah," I said.

"Then put yourself on the list, man. End the double standard that has beer companies sponsoring sports on TV while people who use hemp get locked up, have their houses seized, their cars taken away. If the people have a say, all that'll end."

He held out a pen. I gave him a quick glance. Early thirties. Dark curly hair. A gold stud in his left ear. A confident, bemused look about him, especially around the eyes. An accent that said Boston or points south.

"Bobby Mullaney," he said. "Florence, Maine."

"Jack McMorrow. Prosperity, Maine."

"Prosperity? I've never been to Prosperity."

"I've never been to Florence."

"Man, nobody's been to Florence. That's why we're there. It'd be God's country if God could find it, you know what I'm saying? It's beautiful. No tourists. No jobs. No money. No nothing."

He grinned at me, cocky and disarming, in a big-city, fast-talking sort of way.

"Paradise," Mullaney said.

"So there must be something up there."

"Woods. Beauteous hardwood hills, man. Trout streams. You spent much time in western Maine?"

"Some," I said. "Place called Androscoggin."

"Oh, that's the other western Maine. Industrialized. I'm talking about the end of the earth, the sleepy hollows. Reminds me of West Virginia. Been to West Virginia?"

"Been through it."

"That's what Florence is like. Me and the old lady, we came up from Valley, man. Valley, Mass. Old beat-to-shit pickup. Didn't have a pot to piss in. But we'd saved up thirty-five hundred bucks, and the ad in the *Globe* said we could get a hundred acres for twelve thousand. They'd finance. I said, 'Shit. Why the hell not?' We drove up—her kid was just a rug rat—and we seen this land, I mean, trees as far as you could see. Man, we were renting four rooms with a view of an alley where there were skaggy old hookers and crackheads. It was the walking dead, no shit. And man, we saw all those woods and trees and we said—it was this old guy who owned it—we said, 'We'll take it. Here's the down payment. Where do we sign?' You know what I'm saying? We felt like the friggin' settlers, you know? Forty acres and a mule."

"That was ex-slaves, I think," I said. "President Andrew Johnson."

"Right. 'Cause, man, we were slaves down there in the city. Slaving away. Getting nowhere. Barely surviving. The old lady, her name's Mel. For Melanie. She said she felt like she'd been emancipated. No shit. She said that."

I listened and couldn't help but smile. Bobby Mullaney had one mark of the city still on him: the gift of gab.

"So Jack, you gonna help us with the cause here? 'Cause, man, it's a grave injustice that's going down. This state has goddamn Gestapo and they are doing terrible things to innocent people. I mean, I know people who have lost everything for growing pot. You grow a few plants for your own use, in the privacy of your own home, you get called a drug trafficker, like you're some sort of Colombian drug lord. These are peaceful, gentle, law-abiding people and they're getting treated like vicious criminals."

"Well, it *is* against the law," I said.

"And the law is friggin' obscene. But even that, they bend it. They stretch it. They lie in court. They lie to get warrants. They lie about what they find. I mean, it's a goddamn police state. And the only way to stop it is to put it to the people, once and for all. Legalize it. Take the cops out of it. Take the crime out of it. You want to smoke pot, plant a plant next to your tomatoes. You don't want to smoke pot, don't."

Mullaney took a breath. A couple of teenage boys eased up and he moved over toward them. "You guys registered to vote? . . ."

There was a brashness to his pitch, but at the same time, a naiveté that was almost endearing. He could have been behind a carnival booth, selling vacuum cleaners door to door, used cars in a seedy lot, fake Rolexes to tourists in Times Square. The guy drew you in with his openness. He'd fill a lot of petitions. He'd make great copy.

He came back.

"So what do you do in Prosperity, Jack?" he said.

"I write stories. For newspapers. Magazines."

"What kind of stories?"

"News stories. Feature stories. I'm freelance now. I was a reporter."

"No shit, man," Mullaney said.

He looked at me, a sharper interest in his eyes.

"Where'd you do that?" he said. "Here in Maine?"

"Some. Mostly New York."

"New York City?"

"Yeah," I said.

"Where at?"

"The *Times*."

For a moment, Mullaney considered me and said nothing.

"I was wondering," I began. "Maybe there's a story here. About the legalization movement in Maine. It's probably been covered for papers here, but not in Boston or New York."

He thought.

"Yeah," Mullaney said slowly, his grin returning. "Yeah. We could use some big-time press. Especially by somebody who isn't in the cops' pocket. I could introduce you to some people."

"That'd be good," I said.

"Hey, here's another one of us now."

He looked to his right, my left. A guy was approaching carrying two paper cups from the cider booth. He was tall and very lean, with a dark stubble of beard and long hair that was tied back. He wasn't smiling.

"Hey, man," Mullaney said, as the guy set the cups down on the counter. "Somebody I'd like you to meet."

The guy looked up but his expression didn't change. His eyes were deep-set and black. His hair was black, too, falling almost to his waist, held back with what appeared to be a piece of bone and a leather thong.

"Jack, this is Coyote," Mullaney said, the only one of us grinning.

"Coyote, this is Jack. He's a reporter. He's gonna do a story on us for the *Boston Globe* or the *New York Times*."

Coyote looked at me and I looked back. Our eyes met. Locked. There was a flicker of something, some sort of challenge. It was a look I'd seen in very tough guys. Prison inmates. Gang members. Riker's Island. East New York. I didn't expect to see it here.

"Nice to meet you," I said, still meeting Coyote's gaze. He waited, then nodded. Slowly.

Two

MULLANEY DID THE talking for a few minutes and then turned his attention to the teenagers, who were undecided. That left Coyote and me. Coyote hadn't said anything yet, and I didn't help him out.

"Jack what?" he began.

"Jack McMorrow."

"What'd you cover in New York?"

"Metro stuff. Cops. Courts. A little local politics, but it wasn't my thing."

Coyote looked at me.

"You got a *Times* ID?"

"Hey, man," Mullaney put in, turning back to us. "We've been talking. He's good people."

"Could be," Coyote said. "But we've got to be sure. He understands. He's from New York. Probably not the first time he's been asked. Nothing personal."

I looked at him, considered his odd mix of organic and tough. Add a little leather and he could be an outlaw biker. Cut his hair and he could be doing four to six for assaulting a cop. But here he was in the land of sugar-free ketchup and spiritual healing.

"Coyote," I said, digging in my back pocket for my wallet. "Is that Native American or something?"

"I'm one-quarter Oglala Sioux," Coyote said.

Baloney, I thought.

"That's interesting," I said. "Red Cloud and all that."

"We're related. Distantly."

Give me a break, I thought.

Our eyes locked again. I handed him my old *Times* ID, my face in the photo full of ambition. When that picture was taken, I was headed for the top. Unstoppable. Somehow I came up a little short, like making it to Wimbledon but never getting past the second round.

"So you quit, or get fired?" Coyote said.

"Quit," I said.

"Why?"

"To run my own paper in Maine."

"So what happened?" Coyote asked.

"It's a long story."

"I got time."

"I don't," I said.

Coyote looked at the ID, then up at me. His face relaxed just a bit. A little bit. Mullaney moved over to talk to a man and woman at the counter. Coyote handed me my ID and I put it back in my wallet.

"Maybe this isn't worth the trouble," I said.

"I don't know about that," Coyote said. "We just have to be careful. Drug cops will stoop to anything. Even impersonating a member of the press."

The faintest of smiles flickered across his face.

"But there's nothing illegal about lobbying for legalizing pot," I said. "What are you so worried about?"

Coyote gave me a long look, then, for the first time, reached for his cup of cider.

"Like I said, drug cops will stoop to anything," he said.

I waited for Mullaney to finish making his pitch. The man and woman, fortyish and trying not to show it, had signed the petition and were chatting before going on their way. While I waited, Coyote saw no need to engage in small talk. I was leaning on the counter when I felt a nudge behind me.

"Hi," Roxanne said. "I got sick of waiting."

I turned to her. She stood close.

"Sorry," I said.

"You ready?"

"Will be in a minute," I said.

Roxanne looked up at the sign, which said, "Legalize Hemp Now!" She looked at Mullaney, then at Coyote. He looked at her and she looked away.

"What are you waiting for?" Roxanne asked me.

"To talk to this guy. I might do a story on their effort to legalize marijuana. Maybe the *Globe*. New England page kind of thing, if they'll go for it."

As I talked, Coyote listened and watched. Roxanne, not me. I decided I didn't like the guy. Maybe I'd leave him out of the story. The best revenge. Or maybe I'd put him in. Something told me there was an outstanding warrant for him somewhere. A photo would be nice. Better yet, a nice clear fingerprint.

"Hey, man," Mullaney said, as the man and woman went on their way. "Another voter. Step right up."

He slid the clipboard with the petition in front of Roxanne. She scanned it, then slid it back.

"No, thanks," she said.

"No, thanks?" Mullaney said. "Don't you realize the damage that is being done by this drug war? Don't you realize that families are falling victim to the police state right here in Maine?"

"Families fall victim to themselves," Roxanne murmured.

"Well, excuse me, sister."

"I'm not your sister. I don't agree with what you're doing. Let's leave it at that."

"But don't you understand that this country is steeped in hypocrisy?" Mullaney went on. "It's soaked in alcohol. Alcohol is the cause of more problems in this country than marijuana could ever be. Ask any cop which drug they'd prefer to see legal. They'll tell you that it's alcohol that causes domestic abuse. Child abuse—''

"Uh-uh. Abuse is caused by people who can't face their own lives and responsibilities. This is just one more way out. When your baby's crying and you're stoned, zonked out, who goes and picks her up?''

"Would you rather have that person drunk on alcohol?''

"No,'' Roxanne said. "I'd rather that person wasn't stoned or drunk. And I'm sick of irresponsible adults, adults who won't grow up, who are so goddamn weak they won't even take care of their own kids.''

She turned to me.

"I'll meet you at the gate,'' she said, and she walked away.

Mullaney watched, openmouthed. He had very white teeth. Coyote watched, too, following Roxanne's backside with his eyes.

"Jeez,'' Mullaney said. "She a friend of yours?''

"Yeah,'' I said.

"What's her problem?''

"She doesn't have one.''

"Went up one side of me and down the other, didn't she?''

"That's her right,'' I said. "She works all day protecting children from their parents, their parents' friends. She sees more than most people.''

"Well, Jesus. Alcohol is the pisser there.''

"She wishes there weren't any pisser at all,'' I said. "Give me your phone number. If they bite on the story, I'll give you a call.''

Mullaney wrote it on a pamphlet. Coyote was still looking down the row, toward where Roxanne had disappeared.

"Hey,'' I said.

He turned, startled, then understood.

"Maybe I'll see you again,'' I said.

And I gave him the same look he'd given me, or as close as I could come, not having spent time in San Quentin.

• • •

Roxanne was at the main gate, leaning against the chain-link fence with her arms folded against her chest.

"Hey, baby," I said. "Need a lift?"

She looked at me and forced a smile, then fell in beside me as I went through the turnstile and out onto the road.

"You okay?" I said.

"Yeah. They just, I don't know, touched a nerve I guess."

"Sorry."

"Oh, it's no big deal. It's just sometimes I can't just let it go by. When people are like that."

"Why this one so much?"

Roxanne sighed as she walked, then slipped her arm through mine.

"I spent yesterday morning, all morning, with these kids in South Portland. Two gorgeous little kids. Towheads with these glowing blue eyes. A girl and a boy, six and nine. Father disappeared, last seen in Georgia. Mother keeps forgetting to come home. Last time, the baby-sitter, who was no brain surgeon herself, said to hell with it and left. We got called 'cause the cops found the older one, the boy, trying to walk to the store at six in the morning, down Broadway, this busy street. No jacket, sneakers untied, all by himself, to get his sister some Cheerios. Six-year-old, home alone. Cops had to break the door down 'cause the boy had locked her in and lost the key."

We waited for a break in the traffic, then crossed to the pasture where the cars were parked.

"At least somebody was thinking of her," I said. "Where was the mother?"

"Passed out," Roxanne said flatly. "At a party. She'd go to a party and she'd get so drunk and stoned that she'd pass out in a chair or on a couch and nobody else would be much better, so she'd just stay there all night."

"What'd she have to say for herself?"

"Oh, she was sorry and oh, it wouldn't happen again and oh, 'Please don't take my children away, they're all I have, they're my whole life.' "

"So what are you going to do?"

"We have them temporarily. We're going to try to make it permanent. Take them," she said.

We were at the truck. I opened the door for Roxanne.

"Well, that's good."

"No, Jack, it isn't. Those little kids don't get it. They want their mommy. They don't want these strange grown-ups."

"So what will you tell them?"

"Nothing they'll understand," Roxanne said. "And they'll sob and sob and you just try to hold them and then you get people like this bunch out there preaching like pot is the cure for cancer and the common cold. I just, I don't know, I just lost it."

I pulled the truck out of the pasture and headed east, toward home. The maples made a golden canopy over the road, and underneath it, the line of fair-going cars inched along. A caravan of registered voters. Roxanne looked out the window and let out a long breath.

"Hope I didn't foul up your story," she said.

"No. I understand. I just figured I might be able to make three or four hundred bucks in two or three days. A day up there, a morning on the phone, an afternoon to write it. I'll see what Tom says at the *Globe*."

"Well, if you need a social worker, I know where you can find one."

"I always need my social worker," I said.

Roxanne smiled and took my hand.

"After all that, I don't suppose you'd offer one a glass of red wine," she said.

"But what if you consume an entire glass and are unable to make it home to Portland and therefore have to stay the night at my house, where the guest room isn't finished, or even started, for that matter?"

"What if?" Roxanne said, and as we drove onto Route 3, headed for the coast, she lifted my hand to her lips and kissed it.

Ten miles east, as the road lowered itself into the shadowed hills of Waldo County, I turned off and drove north toward Prosperity. The road was twisting and black, and

the hills were steep and thick with trees, glowing orange
and yellow even in the rain. Roxanne was quiet for several
miles and then I turned off the two-lane road onto the dump
road and she suddenly turned to me.

"That guy scared me," Roxanne said. "The one with
the long hair and the dark eyes. I don't usually say this but
something about him . . ."

"I know," I said. "I don't usually say this, but he scared
me, too. A little."

Three

IN THE MORNING, I woke up and smelled wine, saw the glasses on the table beside the bed. I remembered holding Roxanne close to me, her bare back against my chest, my arms across her breasts. We had been quiet and then we'd been moving slowly and time passed and we'd twisted and rolled and had been not so quiet, and then everything was dark and warm and still.

Roxanne was still asleep, her dark hair strewn across the white skin of her back. I slid out of bed and pulled the sheet and blanket over her shoulders, then reached for shorts and jeans and a T-shirt. Picking up the wineglasses, too, I eased my way down the loft stairs. I put the glasses beside the sink and pulled on my clothes. The cork went back in the wine bottle. The kettle went on the stove. I took the atlas off the bookshelf.

Florence was on map 23, one grid south of the Sugarloaf mountain range, one grid southeast of Rangeley Lake. There were two ways into the town: Route 4 from Farmington and Route 156 from Wilton. It was a good twenty miles from either town and there was very little in between.

Of human design, that is.

There were lakes and ponds and mountains and hills, and on the map each little hill had a name, awarded it by some intrepid trapper or settler, now long dead. I pictured it as a part of Maine where the towns were forgotten hamlets, the people mostly poor and the only tourists hunters who came up from down south every fall, baited bear with apples and bacon grease, went a week without bathing and drank too much.

God's country.

I studied the page, the chicken scratchings that showed the hills and ridges, the expanse of roadless white that made it look like the map had been drawn in the dead of winter. The kettle rattled. There was a creak in the loft and Roxanne appeared at the head of the stairs. Naked.

"The casual look?" I said.

She smiled sleepily and disappeared, then came downstairs wearing one of my plaid flannel shirts. I got up and poured her a mug of coffee. She dumped sugar in and stirred and yawned.

"Somebody wore me out," Roxanne said.

"I was about to say the same."

"But it looks like you're raring to go."

"I guess," I said.

"But you haven't gotten an okay from the *Globe* yet."

"I'll live dangerously."

"You going today?" Roxanne asked, raising her mug to her lips.

"I don't know. What are your plans? Want to come?"

"And risk a scene with your marijuana buddies?"

"They're not my buddies," I said. "It's work."

"And you're happiest when you're working," Roxanne said.

I looked at her, her hair still mussed, her soft white skin.

"Not happiest," I said.

Roxanne smiled.

"Well, happiest with the exception of that. I need to head home early anyway. I'm back in court tomorrow morning."

"Another happy home?"

"Of course," Roxanne said. "I've got some more work to do on it. You going there this morning?"

"I told Clair I might cut wood with him, but I might call and tell him another day."

"You are raring to go, aren't you?"

"It's been a while. The ale cupboard is getting bare. You don't mind, do you?"

"Not if I can take a quick shower," Roxanne said, stretching appetizingly.

"We could take a quick shower."

"With you, that's an oxymoron."

"I love it when you talk dirty grammar," I said. "But your parts aren't like any grammar I've ever seen."

"I certainly hope not," Roxanne said, getting up and taking her coffee with her and, as she walked away, pulling the back of her shirt up, just for a teasing moment.

Clair was up at the store getting the paper and talking but I told Mary, his wife, that I couldn't cut wood that day but I'd see him when I got back. Mary said that was just as well, and maybe she could keep him out of the barn, too, on a Sunday morning.

"Day of rest, you know, Jack," she said, standing at her back door, still in her church dress.

"I rest all the other days, Mary," I said, and I was back in the Toyota and on my way.

But I didn't really rest. That summer I'd built the house, with Clair along to supply advice, instruction, tools and nearly all of the expertise. The house replaced one that had burned, thanks to a couple of fellows now confined to smallish rooms in the state prison at Thomaston. My house was small, too, and it was heavily insulated. Most of the windows faced south, where the fields and woods were. The fields and woods were full of birds and there was ale in the refrigerator, and Roxanne most weekends.

Life was good.

But Roxanne was right. I was happiest, almost, when I was working. It was a strange state of affairs for someone who had stepped off the pinnacle of the kind of work I did,

as a metro reporter at the *New York Times*. I'd stepped off
when the even hotter hotshots had started blowing by me.
I hadn't realized that a reporter walking out that door was
like an astronaut cutting the tether on a space walk. You
spin out of that orbit and into another and there really is
no easy way of going back. But then, at that time, I had
no intention of returning.

But I could still go about my business, which on this
gray September morning meant driving west, down the long
slope of the Kennebec Valley. After fifteen miles of woods
and pasture and corner stores, I crossed the river into Waterville, a brick mill city stubbornly fixed to the shore of
the Kennebec River. I cut through the little city, past the
shopping malls, and out the other side, still headed west.
The road climbed the valley, passing meager used-car lots
and tired farms, with barns and sheds sinking slowly into
the ground. There were houses plunked where rectangular
chunks had been hewn out of the woods, and many of the
houses had stuff piled on tables in the front yards, For Sale
signs on the cars and trucks and old aluminum rowboats.

The signs, like the cars and trucks and boats, were old
and weathered and faded.

I continued northwest, deeper into Somerset County, and
the houses were fewer and farther between. Some were
small and temporary-looking, like something put up for mi-
grant workers. In fact, everything had a temporal feel to it,
except the woods that lined the road like the wall of a steep
russet-colored canyon. Maples and alders and oaks, they
were like an army that couldn't be defeated, as if you could
knock them down and they'd keep coming, keep growing.
People could live out their little lives up here, farm their
farms, build their houses, and the relentless woods would
be waiting somewhere out back for the barns and houses
to fall vacant and the fields to grow back.

It was like the woods were laughing.

After a half hour or so, I passed through a couple of
small yard-sale towns, then a bigger one with a wood-
turning mill at its center along the river, three pizza shops
and a gas station owned by an out-of-state chain. The gas

station marked the end of civilization, as most people know it.

Across the green metal bridge over the river, there was a sign that said the town of Farmington was to the west. I turned and the truck whined its way up a grade and past the last of the houses and down a long roller-coaster hill, past a cemetery encircled with wire fence like a sheep pasture. I wondered if the fence was electrified to keep the dead from roaming.

The road vaulted up and then down, twisting and turning past a couple of abandoned barns and a stubbled field where cows stood behind barbed wire like prisoners of war. For miles, everything was green and orange, with slashes of tan, where someone had cut into an esker and hauled off the gravel. There were signs jabbed into the ground and nailed to trees saying the land was for sale, which seemed like trying to sell sand at the beach. And then there were more miles of woods and the Mount Blue range hunched darkly against the horizon to the northwest and then an intersection with a state sign, leaning crazily, that said Florence was to the right, eight miles north. I drove the eight miles and another sign, this one homemade, told me I had just crossed the Florence town limits.

I felt like I had reached the end of the earth.

In Florence, even the limits were limited. About five hundred yards from the first sign, I came over the crest of a hill and plunged down into the downtown area, which was really a cluster of about eight houses and a store.

I coasted through and looked. The houses were gathered around the remains of a some sort of old wooden mill building. The mill was falling down onto the banks of a stream and the houses were falling down in place. The one across from the store had plywood on the windows, which appeared to be some indication of disuse. But then again, the store had plywood on its windows, too, but the flashing beer sign in the one window in which glass remained said the place was open.

I pulled the truck into the dirt patch that was the store's parking lot. There were two other trucks parked there, in-

cluding another old four-wheel-drive Toyota like mine. Its
bumper stickers said, "Just say no to pesticides" and "Solar Power."

Bobby Mullaney's kind of people?

I shut off the motor and sat. A grim-faced man appeared
in the doorway, stared me and the truck up and down and
went back inside. A moment later another man, older and
shorter, came to the door and did the same thing. The Welcome Wagon was on its way, no doubt. I sat there with
newfound respect for any undercover drug cop who could
come within five miles of this place undetected, much less
make an arrest.

When the first guy had come to the door for a second
look, I decided it was time to go in and make friends. I got
out and walked to the door. There was no sign to say push
or pull. I guessed wrong and pushed, then pulled the door
open and went inside.

The store was one room with a low ceiling and very
understated lighting. When my eyes had adjusted to the
dark, I made out a few shelves of dusty groceries, a beer
locker and the two guys from the hostess committee leaning
against a low, white cooler. The sign on the cooler said,
"Crawlers." The two guys said nothing.

"How you doing?" I said, and the more gregarious of
the two almost nodded.

"Glad to hear it," I said. "I'm wondering if you could
tell me how I could find a guy named Bobby Mullaney."

The two guys, done up in matching green work clothes,
looked at me as if I were talking on the wrong frequency
and nothing was coming out of my mouth.

"Parlez anglais?" I said. *"Cómo está? Nein?"*

They stared. I smiled.

Something rustled out back and a door slammed and a
woman appeared behind a counter to a right. I switched
back to English and said hello.

"Hi," the woman said.

It wasn't much but it was a start.

She was in her fifties, with a smoke-weathered face and
long yellowish hair parted in the middle and tied in the
back. She and Coyote used the same stylist.

"I'm looking for a guy named Bobby Mullaney," I said. "He told me he lives in town but I never asked him where."

The woman started to say something, then hesitated.

"Whatcha looking for Bobby for?" she said, folding her arms across her chest.

"I'm a reporter. My name's Jack McMorrow. I met Bobby and a guy named Coyote yesterday at the Country Life Fair. We talked about doing a story on their group and I decided to take a ride up and talk to them some more."

She looked at me. Reached behind the counter for a pack of generic cigarettes and took one out and lit it with a purple butane lighter. She puffed.

"They wanted the story, if that's what you're worried about," I said.

The woman puffed again. One of the guys cleared his throat and looked like he was about to spit on the floor but remembered he wasn't at home. All three of them looked at me some more.

"I'm not a cop, if that's what you're thinking," I said.

I pulled my jacket open and the shorter guy flinched.

"See. No wire. No nine-millimeter in a shoulder holster. I'd let you search me but we're in mixed company."

I grinned. They didn't. The woman considered me some more.

"You see this road out here," she said suddenly, smoke billowing from her mouth as she spoke.

"Yup."

"You go up here and you take a left. And you drive out past Harrison's place, keep going till you come to a log house. There's a road after that, gravel, and you take that road about four miles down until you get to a fork. Take the left side of the fork and you'll see a cemetery and just a stone's throw up on the right you come to another dirt road. That's theirs."

"Their road?"

"Their driveway."

"How far in is their house?"

"About a mile," the woman said. "And you best be ready to put that truck in four-wheel."

"Mud?" I said.

"Rocks," the short guy said, almost startling me. "Size of a basketball. Discontinued road. Ain't plowed."

"All washed out," the woman said.

"How do they get in and out?"

"Slow," the bigger guy said.

The shorter guy snorted. I grinned. The big guy stared and the woman blew smoke. I felt like family.

"Well, thanks," I said.

I felt a sudden obligation to buy something but then I looked around. It was too early for beer and I didn't need any worms. I moved toward the door, then stopped.

"Oh, yeah. What about Coyote? Where can I find him?"

"Right there," the woman said.

"He has a house on that road, too?"

"He has the same house," she said. "They live together."

"All three of them?"

"Four, with the kid," the woman said.

"Oh," I said. "That's nice."

She looked doubtful and then she looked away at the two guys and when her gaze came back to me, the doubt was gone, replaced by an impassive screen that said nothing at all.

Four

THE BOYS IN the store had exaggerated. The rocks in the road weren't the size of basketballs. Most were the size of softballs, so that the road was no rougher than your average rocky streambed. As I lurched along in first gear, it occurred to me that I'd hate to be in a hurry to get in there.

I'd hate even more to be in a hurry to get out.

I followed the road, reassured by the phone line strung fifteen feet up on the trees to my right. Beyond the big roadside trees, the woods were mostly second-growth poplar and birch and maple, with occasional slash piles still showing in the brambles. The Mullaneys' acreage had been cheap for a reason. It was cut over, and up here, where woods meant timber and pulp, and timber and pulp meant cash money, cut-over land wasn't worth much.

But there were things other than trees that you could grow as a cash crop and I wondered whether the Mullaneys and their live-in buddy had adopted marijuana as more than a cause.

High-grade pot, all resin-filled buds, went for more than two hundred dollars an ounce, two to three thousand dollars a pound. A single, well-tended plant could yield ten ounces or more. A slash in the woods could support a family for

months. A bigger operation, with plants scattered in patches
over miles of remote woods, could make somebody rich,
or put them in prison. It was a gamble but up in these
forgotten faraway hills, any occupation beyond welfare and
food stamps was a gamble. And of all the ways you could
gamble in a place like Florence, Maine, growing marijuana
had the best odds and the biggest payoffs.

So what did Bobby Mullaney do? And Coyote? Whatever it was, I thought, bumping up a rise, it was a hell of
a commute.

The phone wire kept going and so did I. Just when I was
beginning to wonder if the pounding would ever end, the
road went uphill steeply and turned to the left, and there
was a hand-painted sign that said, "Notrespassing." I tres-
passed anyway and a truck came into view, an old black
four-wheel-drive Ford, backed into a clearing fringed by
wild blackberries. Then there was another truck, a red
Chevy four-wheel-drive with a wood body and copper-
colored doors. Beside the Chevy was a Subaru station
wagon. It was white and spattered with rust. Fifty yards
farther was home sweet home.

It was a funky sort of house, all unpainted wood and
odd-sized windows, built around a blue and white travel
trailer that showed at the core of the building like a suitcase
from which the rest of the place had been unfolded. There
was a big vegetable garden to the right, fenced with chicken
wire, and beyond that, dome-shaped stacks of firewood,
neatly piled. I heard a rustle behind me and a dark red
chicken scurried along the garden fence. Behind the garden
was a weathered-wood chicken coop sort of thing and another chicken showed in the door. Next to the chicken
house there was a black tablelike contraption that looked
like some sort of photoelectric equipment. Green-and-white
wires ran from the black thing to the back door, which
eased open as I sat and watched.

A woman looked out.

She was short and slight, dressed in jeans and a black
sweater and boots. She was halfway out the door and I gave
her a little wave from the truck seat, then popped the door

open. When I did, she stepped the rest of the way out of
the door, showing that she was holding a gun, the long
barrel pointed down.

Maybe I should have called first.

I stepped out of the truck but stood behind the open door.
The gun appeared to be a shotgun, and if it was loaded
with bird shot, the door would protect my vital organs. One
of the things they don't teach in Journalism 101.

"Hi," I called, forcing a smile. "I'm Jack McMorrow.
Looking for Bobby Mullaney. Is this the right house?"

"What are you looking for him for?" the woman called.

"I'm a reporter. The guy he met yesterday at the fair. I
told him I'd come see him about a story."

"What's your name?"

"Jack McMorrow. I met Coyote, too."

She eyed me for a long moment.

"Come on in," she said, and she and her gun went back
inside. I grabbed a notebook off of the seat of the truck,
and holding it in front of me like a white flag, followed.

I stepped into the room and felt the warmth of a woodstove
and the smell of some sort of herbs. There were bunches
of them hanging from the rafters and squash and potatoes
spread on newspapers in the corner of the room. The wall
art was posters of photographs of wilderness places. The
shotgun, an over-and-under model, leaned against the wall
beside the door. A place for everything and everything in
its place.

The woman wasn't in sight and I stood there awkwardly
for a moment. Maybe she'd gone to slip on something more
comfortable, like a nice .357. I waited and suddenly she
came from behind a big cinder-block chimney and walked
toward me. Unarmed.

"I'm Melanie," she said, her hand held out.

"Jack McMorrow."

She shook my hand firmly and glanced toward the shotgun.

"Sorry about that but you never know out here. And the
cops might as well be in Boston, if you try to call 'em.
Would you like a cup of tea?"

"Sure," I said. "Tea would be great."

No shots fired. No hard feelings.

Melanie turned and went back behind the chimney. She was fair-skinned, with red curly hair pulled back, and looked more like a Mullaney than her husband did. She was nice-looking enough, in a handsome sort of way, but with the telltale sign of an unprivileged upbringing: slightly crooked teeth.

Dishes rattled and Melanie came back holding a mug, a small earthenware pitcher, a wicker strainer and a jar that matched the pitcher. She set the stuff on the overturned packing crate that served as a table, and then she pulled up an old metal folding chair. I sat down on the chair, with my knees sticking out, and felt like a dad at a little girl's tea party. Melanie went and got her mug from behind the chimney and came back and sat down on an old brown couch, against the wall, next to the door—and the gun.

"He's not here," she said brightly. "They're working in the woods. You want me to do that for you?"

I was fumbling with the wicker thing and the spoon.

"Sure," I said.

Melanie got up and leaned over the table. She was very close to me, but very matter-of-fact about it, like she could have been cleaning my teeth. She scooped green tea into the strainer, then poured hot water through it and into the mug. She waited while the water ran through, then poured some more.

"It's green tea. Japanese," she said.

"Oh. Do you have some sort of specialty store where you can get it?"

"The health food store in Farmington. That's the only place I shop. The rest of the stuff we grow or barter for. I just traded twenty pumpkins for some steaks. I'm a vegetarian but the boys still like their red meat."

"I'm sure," I said.

I couldn't picture Coyote biting into a patty of soy substitute.

Melanie sat back down and I sipped the tea. It was hot but tasted like mown grass. She sipped hers.

"Mmmm, that's good," she said.

"Yeah," I said. "Hits the spot. Do you expect Bobby back soon?"

"I'm not sure. They didn't say."

"I guess I should have called first. Their crew works on Sunday?"

Melanie crossed her legs. Her boots were worn. The knees of her pants were faded.

"Oh, they're not working on a crew. They're working themselves. With the army truck. It's not an army truck now. It used to be. Now it's a wood-hauler thing."

"They cut on your land?"

"Firewood. There's a shitload of dead stuff out there. That's how we heat this place."

I looked around.

"Pretty cozy. Build it yourselves?"

"Me and Bobby."

"Not Coyote?"

"He hadn't come up here yet. This was back, I don't know, ten years ago."

"Coyote from Massachusetts, too?"

Melanie paused. Her eyes narrowed over her mug.

"You can tell you're a reporter," she said.

"Oh, yeah? How's that?"

"Everything you ask has a reason. Some piece of information you want. Are you a good reporter?"

I hesitated.

"Pretty good."

"Bobby told me you worked for the *New York Times*."

"Among others."

"So you must be pretty good."

"It's all relative," I said.

"So who would you write this story for?"

"The *Boston Globe* maybe. I haven't pitched it yet, but I don't think they'll turn it down."

"The *Boston Globe*. Front page?"

I smiled.

"On a very slow news day. I doubt it. I'd hope for it to make the split page. The New England section."

She eyed me some more over her mug.

"You seem pretty sure of yourself."

"Sometimes," I said.

"The *Boston Globe*. Getting a story in there would give us a boost, don't you think?"

"What kind of boost?"

"I don't know," Melanie said. "Credibility. Like this thing is for real. I would think that anything you'd read about in a paper like that would have a lot more credibility."

She was thinking. It seemed like she was thinking about something else.

"So you're involved in the legalization movement, too?"

"Oh, yeah. I think it's outrageous what this government does to people. It's a police state, it really is. Anyone who really thinks about it agrees with us. They do. Anybody who cares about other people and things being unfair. Do you care about that, McMorrow?"

The name came to her easily, as if she had thought about it, as if she wasn't totally surprised to see me.

"Yeah, I do," I said carefully, setting my mug down on the table. "That's one of the reasons I do this."

Melanie looked at me just as carefully. My eyes met hers and then I looked over her, out the window to where a figure had appeared, moving between the trees. Melanie turned.

"Oh, that's Stephen," she said, oozing motherly pride. "My son. He'll want to meet you."

Stephen did a good job of disguising his enthusiasm. First he gave my truck a careful inspection, as if he thought he might find a police-issue homing device under the rear bumper. Then he strode up to the house, pushed open the door and glared.

"Stephen, this is Jack McMorrow. He's a reporter. You heard your dad talking about him last night."

"Hi," I said. I smiled.

"Hey," Stephen said. He was fourteen or fifteen, tall like Coyote but his hair was shorn, like five o'clock shadow all

over his head. He had his mother's coloring and a small
hoop in his left ear, which made him look like a street tough
from Barrytown, in Dublin. His jeans were ragged, his
boots were black and his sweatshirt was camouflage green.
He didn't smile. He didn't say another word. He walked
by me and past the chimney into the kitchen. I heard a
refrigerator door open, then close.

"He's hungry," Melanie explained.

Boys will be boys.

"Stevie," she called. "Do you know where Bobby and
Coyote are working today?"

"Nope."

"You didn't hear saws when you came across?"

"Nope."

"Or the truck?"

"Nope."

The refrigerator door opened and closed again. I took a
sip of compost tea. As I put my mug down, Stephen came
through the room again, this time carrying a rifle, a .22.
That he didn't point it at me and pull the trigger probably
was due to his deep respect for me and my profession.

"Where are you going?" his mother asked.

Where could he go? There wasn't a paved road for three
miles, another house for five. To find another human, he'd
have to take a compass and rations.

"Out," Stephen said.

"Nice to meet you," I said.

Stephen paused at the door, took a box of cartridges off
of a wooden shelf and shoved them into his pocket.

"Yeah," he said.

Stephen opened the door and left.

"Squirrels for dinner?" I said.

"Oh, he just likes to have it with him," Melanie said,
getting up from her chair.

"Like a teddy bear?"

"Well, you never know what you're going to run into
in these woods."

"You could get a dog," I said.

"Bobby's allergic. Cats, dogs. Dogs are the worst."

She got up and headed for the kitchen.

"More tea?"

"No, thanks," I said. "This is fine."

Melanie refilled and came out and sat back down on the couch. She looked like she was ready to settle in for a long chat. Out here in the woods, people probably didn't just drop in. Probably once or twice. A year.

"So are you as involved in this hemp movement as your husband?" I asked, going to work.

"Yeah, I guess. He's the talker, though. As you probably noticed, he likes to talk."

"I did."

She smiled apologetically.

"That's Bobby. When we were in Valley, he knew lots of people. I mean, I couldn't walk down the street with him without him stopping to talk to this guy and that guy."

"So do you guys really like it up here? Florence is the end of the earth. And this is the end of Florence. Don't you miss, I don't know, traffic? And crowds of people and noise?"

Melanie stopped cold and looked at me. It was like she was a motor and it had stalled. Then it started again.

"No, I don't miss it," she said. "I mean, jeez, we had a guy killed right in front of the building next to ours. They shot him. Bang, bang, bang, bang. Right in the middle of the day. The schools had just gotten out and all the kids on the block, little kids three years old, older kids, are standing there watching the blood run out of this guy onto the sidewalk. How can you miss that?"

She stopped, as if she'd said enough to convince herself, yet again.

"I guess you can't," I said.

I thought for a moment.

"Isn't it awful tough to make a living up here?"

Melanie looked out the window.

"No," she said. "Not at all. I mean, we grow a lot of what we eat. We heat our house for nothing. We don't have a mortgage or anything. A little payment on the land and we can usually scrape that together. When we need cash,

Bobby cuts wood for Harold Bouchard for a few days. Makes two, three hundred bucks and we're good for a month or so.''

"You don't miss just walking into a Kmart and buying stuff? Slap down the old Visa card?''

Melanie looked at me, her face hardening.

"You go right for the jugular, don't you, McMorrow?''

"I don't know about that. I'm just curious. I don't mean to offend you and I'm sorry if I did.''

She looked some more.

"No, I don't, Mr. McMorrow. Because that's what's wrong with this country. We've lost our independence. We're sucked into the corporate industrial complex. Buy a new car. Buy a new TV. Watch this show that tells you you're shit because you don't have a new car. If only people understood that . . .''

She paused to take a breath. I looked into my tea. It looked like algae on a pond. I put it down and reached to my back pocket and took out a notebook, slipped a pen from my shirt.

"So where does getting high fit into all of this?'' I asked.

Melanie looked at the notebook. It was the moment. Would she talk for the record? Would this story be easy or hard?

"Well, Bobby's the one you should really talk to, but I think it's a natural, self-sufficient way to, you know, it's from nature. The Native Americans used nature to be spiritual and worship their gods and the earth and stuff and it's time we got back to that. Bobby explains this better than me but you see, corporate America is against marijuana because they can't control it. What happens to Budweiser if you can grow marijuana in your own garden? It's like this country wouldn't be depending on corporations anymore. Corporations are destroying this country, you know what I'm saying?''

"Yeah,'' I said, scribbling in my notebook. "I guess I do. Now, does your son smoke pot?''

Melanie looked chagrined for a moment, then put her PR face back on.

"He chooses not to. That's his choice. And that's what's so beautiful about this movement. Freedom of choice."

"Would you let him if he wanted to?"

"I'd want him to take a hit of pot instead of riding around drinking beer."

"So you really don't see anything wrong with it?" I pressed.

"I don't know, McMorrow," Melanie said, her Massachusetts accent slipping back to the surface. "Nothing's simple, you know? You ought to talk to Bobby, really. He's the talker of the family."

She got up from the couch and put her mug on the table. I got up, too, and we both walked to the door. Melanie opened it and went down the stairs into the yard.

"I know Bobby would like to talk to you."

"I should have called first. It was just a nice day for a ride and I thought I'd come check out the area. I haven't spent much time up this way."

"Well, I'd tell you to go out and try to find him but I don't know where he is. And you can get lost in these woods pretty easy if you don't know what you're doing. Down below is all bog and up on the hill is a lot of blowdowns. Bobby says it disorientates you."

"What about Stephen?"

"Oh, he knows every square inch of this place. He's got a tree house he built himself and a cabin and everything else. I don't even know where the cabin is."

She looked off toward the woods, where a tote road wound up a hill and disappeared into the trees. I stood there and listened. I heard blue jays and chickadees and, off in the distance, the hacking of crows. I stole a sideways glance at Melanie and she seemed a little nervous.

"I'll come back," I said. "Maybe tomorrow. I'll call tonight and make sure everybody will be around."

Melanie looked relieved.

"That would be better," she said.

She turned to me and held out her hand again. We shook and I walked to my truck, while she went back to the house.

By the time I hit the driver's seat, Melanie was gone. I sat for a minute.

There was something strange going on and it wasn't just a bunch of old hippies living out in the boonies. There was tension in both Melanie and her son. And where was Bobby? And Coyote? Why did this family live with a psycho with a phony name? Why did they live here?

I started the truck and took another look. Solar power. A mammoth garden. Decapitated sunflowers hanging from the eaves to dry. Two four-wheel-drive trucks with gun racks. A moody kid in the woods with a rifle, and Dad and his buddy off cutting firewood. A mother with more undercurrents than the Bermuda Triangle.

Maine—as the saying went—the way life should be.

I backed around and eased down the grade to the rocky path home. The truck lurched and bumped down the hill, the transmission whining in first gear. I negotiated the other side of the hill and back down again, both hands on the wheel, one foot on the clutch, the other tap-dancing from brake to gas.

In this tunnel in the trees, the light was dim and dappled and I had to concentrate to see the bigger rocks. The truck rattled and jounced and the jack and spare tire banged in the bed. I turned the radio on but got static and turned it off. As I reached, I let go of the steering wheel with one hand and at the same time bounced off a big rock.

There was a pop. And a snap.

A spring, I thought. I stopped, put the brake on and got out. The motor ticked. The woods were quiet. I lay down on the rocks behind the back left wheel and looked.

The spring was fine. So was the one on the right side. I looked for anything else that might have snapped but couldn't see anything. Relieved, I rolled away from the truck and jumped up.

And there it was. A small hole in the side of the bed. Perfectly round.

A bullet hole.

Five

"TWENTY-TWO," CLAIR SAID. "Didn't even dent the inner wall of the bed. Probably shot from a pretty good distance."

"Somebody who can shoot?"

"Unless he was aiming for your head. Then it was a bad shot."

"Is the glass half full or is the glass half empty?"

"Whichever makes you feel better," Clair said.

We were standing by my truck outside the front door of his barn, down the road from my house. I'd stopped there before going home to stare at the hole in my truck some more.

"The little bastard," I said.

"Friend of yours?"

"Fifteen-year-old kid with a bad attitude. I was talking to his mother for a story. This marijuana legalization thing. Way out in the boonies in Somerset County."

"He doesn't want you doing the story?"

"I don't know."

"Well, it is a pretty small-caliber gun," Clair said. "Maybe he can't make up his mind."

"Small-caliber ambivalence?"

"Right. He's reaching out to you. All confused inside."

"Thank you, Dr. Varney," I said.

Clair pushed his John Deere hat back and grinned.

"And to think I spent twenty years in the military when I could've been on talk shows, making real money."

"Never too late," I said.

I felt the hole in the truck with my index finger.

"It was only the one shot," I said. "I stopped and got down on the ground and looked 'cause I thought I'd broken a spring or something. It made this crack. Worst road you've ever seen. All rocks and boulders. I was a sitting duck, inching along."

"See, there was no second shot. The kid is just having trouble expressing his feelings. Maybe this is his way of saying he'd like to have somebody like you around. Toss a football on a Saturday. He just has trouble putting it into words."

Clair smiled.

"He has a dad," I said. "Lives with him and everything, but something isn't right."

"Evidently."

I opened the truck door.

"Well, I guess I'll go home and call his mommy and tell her what Junior's been up to. Want to cut tomorrow?"

"If the weather permits," Clair said. "Seven?"

I nodded, then slid onto the seat and started the truck.

"Hey, Jack," Clair said, putting his big hands on the edge of the door and leaning toward me. "You know a twenty-two will kill you just as dead as a fifty-caliber machine gun. It just takes a little more precision, that's all."

"So you're saying I should be careful?"

"I'd give it some thought."

I put the truck into reverse and gunned the motor.

"That's the trouble with you Marines," I said. "You're such worrywarts."

When I got home, the house was cold but so was the ale. It was after three o'clock, which was close to five, which was the time I felt morally and ethically justified in having a drink, so I opened a can of Ballantine and went and stood by the back window and took a long swallow. Then another. When the pint was a third gone I turned from the window and the woods and went to the desk. I hit the button on the computer and the answering machine, in that order. The computer whirred, the tape hissed and Roxanne told me she loved me.

Life was good.

Almost.

Roxanne said she was calling from her office to tell me and would talk to me very soon. I couldn't call the office on a Sunday so I would have to wait. We did a lot of that, Roxanne and me, but the reunions were worth the wait.

Almost.

I would have liked to talk to her now, in person, but we'd tried that arrangement and it hadn't worked out. Roxanne needed me but she needed other things, too. I needed Roxanne but I needed other things and our other things weren't the same. So we had settled for tumultuous weekends that were more like joyous collisions. We would drown in each other's arms and then we would talk. Have dinner. Talk some more.

Sitting there at the computer, I brought myself back. Drank some ale. Began typing my impressions of my visit to Florence, of Melanie and Stephen and their homemade house in the woods. My notes were barely legible but barely was good enough. If I met fast-talking Bobby Mullaney again, I'd bring a tape recorder. If I met his son or his buddy, I'd bring my rifle.

If . . .

I sorted through the junk on the desk and found the pot pamphlet with the Mullaneys' number on it. Took a sip of ale and dialed. The phone rang several times but I waited. Finally, a breathless Melanie Mullaney answered.

"This is Jack McMorrow. Did I bring you in from the garden?"

"Oh. Yeah. But that's okay, I needed a break anyway. Bobby still isn't back."

I told her that was all right. And then I told her why I was calling.

"Stephen?" Melanie gasped. "He wouldn't do that. You must be wrong. It must have been a rock or something. Stephen wouldn't—"

"Well, it wasn't a rock. It was a twenty-two. If there was somebody else out in your woods with a rifle, then maybe it wasn't Stephen. But you'd know that better than I would."

Melanie said she didn't know what to say. She said she was sorry. She said she would talk to Stephen. She said she would have Bobby call me. I said that was fine and I gave her my number. Then I hung up and thought that mothers, organic or otherwise, were all the same.

I went to the refrigerator and got another ale. Then I went to my seat by the window and opened the can and sipped, and watched the light begin to fade beyond the woods. Sometimes, at this time of day, I would sit and wait past dusk before turning on a light. The house would be still and dark and the woods would loom, all branches and shadows. And if I was lucky, a deer, or even two or three, would tiptoe out of the edge and over to the old apple trees. They would browse and I would watch, feeling the inner calm that came when I was in the woods with the birds, or in a field watching the searing stars, and knew, at least for the moment, that I was in the right place.

The feeling wasn't fleeting but it wasn't permanent, either. What could have been? I still could have been working for the *Times.* I still could have been living on the West Side, or moved down to Soho. I could have been writing about kids killing each other, covering the gang funerals, listening to the politicians preach about peace in a city that, for so many, meant anything but. I could have been living for the daily fix that was my byline, the indescribable rush I'd felt every time I'd said, "Hi. I'm Jack McMorrow from the *Times.*" I could have been hitting the clubs, meeting women, listening to jazz, walking the back halls at my late father's haunt, the Museum of Natural History. I could have

been feeling the pang that came with the knowledge that
I'd voluntarily traded that life for this one.

But I wasn't. Much.

Instead of all that, I had my good friend Clair and a new
chain saw. I had a hideaway in the hills of Waldo County,
Maine. I had built my own house, sort of, and could shoot
a rifle straighter than most. I could write the same stories
but in small towns instead of big housing projects. I knew
the woods and the birds. I read my books, listened to my
music, and I bowed to no one, played nobody's game.

On top of all that, I had Roxanne.

I sat and sipped and weighed it all and, of course, it never
quite balanced. But then it was getting darker and colder
and I got up to start a fire in the Jotul. I was on my knees,
crumpling newspaper, when the phone rang. I got up and
grabbed it.

"McMorrow," the voice said. "Bobby Mullaney."

"Hi."

"Hey, man. I don't know what to say. If it was Stevie,
I'm sorry. I mean, I'm sorry anyway, but if it was Stevie, I'm
really sorry. I just don't understand it. He's been going
through some tough times, you know what it's like to be fifteen, but nothing like this. Nothing anything like this."

"You haven't talked to him?"

"He ain't home yet. But man, I just had to call you as
soon as Mel told me. I mean, we'll pay for your truck or
whatever. And if this happened, it won't happen again. I'm
telling you right now. I thought I'd taught him a gun wasn't
a toy. I still can't friggin' believe it. Was it definitely a
bullet? A twenty-two?"

"Yup. Right into the bed, above the back wheel. I was
about halfway up your road there, coming down a rise. I
heard the pop and I thought I heard a crack, too. I got out
and looked and there it was. It went through the outer metal
but not the inner wall."

I paused.

"Was he probably the only one out there?"

"I don't know. We get hunters but not usually by the
road. This time of year, it'd be birds. It wasn't a shotgun
pellet, was it?"

"A friend of mine says no. He knows guns."

"Well shit, man, I don't know what else to say. I wish I'd been at the house when you got here. I really wanted to talk to you some more. About the story, I mean."

"Yeah, well, I don't know about—"

"Oh, man. I hope we can still do business. This is very important to a lot of people."

"My life's important to a lot of people. Including me."

"Well, how 'bout we meet in a neutral place or something, if you're nervous about coming back here. Madison, maybe. The restaurant in Madison. Around noon. And I'll talk to Stephen. If it was him, he'll tell me. If it wasn't, he'll tell me that, too."

"I don't know," I said.

"Come on, whaddaya say? I'll buy you lunch. Even if you don't write anything, at least let me do that. And pay for the truck."

"There's nothing to pay for. It's an old Toyota four-wheel-drive. One more hole doesn't make any difference."

"Lunch then."

"I don't—"

"It can't hurt, can it?"

I hesitated.

"Well . . ."

"Okay. I'll see you there. And I *am* sorry. But I gotta tell you. If it was Stevie, he didn't try to hurt you or nothin'. The kid can shoot the eye out of a woodchuck at fifty yards with that gun."

"Great," I said. "I feel better."

Six

"THERE'S EVEN A good Massachusetts connection," I told Tom Wellington at the *Globe* the next morning. "One of the leaders of this thing is a transplant from Valley. He's living in this tiny town called Florence, tucked away way up in Somerset County."

"What's his name?" Wellington asked.

"Mullaney."

"Well, no wonder he left. Dominicans run Valley now. The Irish mob's ancient history."

"He ran far enough then," I said.

"You think he's hiding from something?"

"I don't know. Probably no more than anybody else up here. But he's pretty public about this pot stuff. Unless he's changed his name and his face, you know, made up his past, then he doesn't act like he's got a contract out on him or anything."

"Maybe he's not even from Valley," Wellington said. "What's some wise guy from the Merrimack Valley doing up in the boonies in Maine? You can't tell me he took up bird-watching or something."

"Careful there. Some of my best friends are birds. Did I tell you I saw a red-eyed vireo last week?"

"I'm happy for you both."

"And I bought a new chain saw. A Husqvarna. With heated handles."

"Isn't that kind of a contradiction, McMorrow?" Wellington said. "Watch the birdies and then go out and chop down the forest?"

"One of many. Let me tell you about my new deer rifle."

"You shoot deer?"

"Of course not," I said. "I just fondle the thing."

"Don't tell me it's one of those inflatable rifles."

"Let the air out and it fits in the glove box of your car. Of course, you need your concealed inflatable-weapon permit."

"You've been in the woods too long, Jack."

"*Au contraire, mon ami.* Not long enough. So how 'bout it?"

Wellington thought for a moment. In the background, I could hear the old newsroom murmur that computers had quieted but hadn't silenced.

"Eight, nine hundred words. Two hundred fifty bucks."

"You won't go three hundred?" I said. "This isn't gonna be handed to me in a press release. Mullaney's a fast talker and he's got this buddy who looks like he's done hard time someplace. Probably Walpole. And I've gotta cover a lot of ground for this one. You don't jump on the 'T' and get off in Florence, Maine."

"Only on *The Twilight Zone.* Three hundred and that's it, Jack. The bean counters down here went over my budget with a scalpel. I mean, it's liposuction city. You know that."

"All right, it's a deal."

"When can you have it?"

"A week," I said.

"I'd like it better on Friday so I can use it for Sunday."

"Pushy, pushy."

"That's what they pay me the big bucks for," Wellington said.

"I wish I could say the same. Maybe I'll hang up and call the *Herald*. Maybe the Valley paper would want a story on hometown boys making good."

"Are they good guys?"

Someone shouted in the background.

"For hippies, they're very well armed."

"An ounce of prevention," he said.

"And they wear sensible shoes," I said.

"Take care of yourself, McMorrow. We're short-staffed on the obit desk."

"If you make it three-fifty, you might not feel so guilty if something happens to me."

"I'll risk it," Wellington said.

And so did I.

At ten-thirty I was on my way to Madison, classical music on the radio, notebooks and a palm-sized tape recorder on the passenger seat of the truck. The tape recorder had fresh batteries. I did not do things halfway.

The skies had cleared overnight but the roads were still damp and dark, with colored leaves glued to the pavement in a long abstract mosaic. I drove at the speed limit, easing over in Albion to let a loaded pulp truck hurtle past like something plummeting from space, the tree trunks bunched between steel posts and fastened with steel cables. The truck probably was headed for the mill in Skowhegan. Within a few weeks, people in Pennsylvania or Illinois or Arizona would be wiping their noses—or worse—with that central Maine spruce and larch. If they didn't, these towns would have one less reason to exist.

And there weren't all that many reasons left, except for an odd combination of momentum and inertia. People lived in these hard-bitten little towns because other people had lived here before them. That was the momentum; the inertia kept them from leaving.

Some of the towns still bustled, one or two were big enough to call themselves cities. Others, thrown up alongside a stream that ran a sawmill a century ago, were simply unlikely. Their populations dwindled, people flowing out like the water over the long-breached dam. The remaining residents were a mix of settlers' descendants and big-city refugees, with different quirks, different histories, linked only by happenstance and geography.

An odd collection.

Which is what greeted me when I walked through the door of Mandy's Lunch in downtown Madison.

Mullaney and Melanie and Coyote were sitting at the counter, which was red Formica with metal holders set out for the salt and pepper, sugar and creamer. The specials were scrawled on a blackboard—pork cutlet, mac and cheese—and the waitress behind the counter was a fiftyish woman wearing jeans and a black turtleneck and dragging on a cigarette.

Nobody asked me if I wanted smoking or non.

"Hey," Mullaney said, sliding off his red vinyl stool. "I knew you'd show. I told Mel, 'He'll show. He's a man of his word.' "

"Most of the time," I said, half smiling.

Melanie got off her stool, too, and nodded, a little sheepishly. Coyote was on the far side and he didn't nod and there was nothing sheepish about him. The kid wasn't there. Probably out by the road, winging passing cars.

I reached for a stool but Mullaney touched my shoulder and motioned toward a table. When I looked over, I saw five or six faces looking at me expectantly.

They'd brought the board of directors.

Oh, man, I thought.

It always happened when the subject of a story had too much time to prepare. When somebody agreed to talk to me, I wanted them right then, not the next day or the next week. I didn't want to give them time for their feet to chill. Or to write a statement or make notes. Or to invite their lawyer, mother or little brother.

As I approached the table, I wasn't sure which I'd gotten this time. There was a thin fortyish guy with dark curly hair and round gold-rimmed glasses, a preppie gone to seed. A hunched woman in her late fifties who'd parked an aluminum walker beside her chair. A kid, maybe nineteen or twenty, with a scraggly beard and hair hugged back with a blue bandanna, printed with tiny marijuana leaves. A slight albino-looking guy with long blond hair and a very pink face. Two plain short-haired women in their thirties, who seemed to be together.

"Hi," I said.

"Hi," they all said back.

"This is the reporter," Mullaney said. "He's gonna do the story on the truth about marijuana, and about us trying to legalize it. Where's the story going to be printed?"

"The *Boston Globe*, but it might not be—"

"The friggin' *Boston Globe*, folks," Mullaney boomed.

"It's about time," the hunched woman said. "The Maine press hasn't given this story shit for coverage. Did you know that only eight people in this entire country can use marijuana legally for medical purposes? I mean, I'm talking about chemotherapy. It is the only thing that helps people feel better. The nausea, you know? AIDS patients. I mean, I got MS. I tried all the drugs these goddamn doctors give you and they didn't do shit. Marijuana keeps my muscles from spasming—you ought to feel what that feels like, your whole back, legs going at once—but when I tried to buy pot, you know what happened to—"

"She got busted," the seedy preppie said. "I got busted, too. Story in the paper said we got arrested in a drug sweep. I can go down to the supermarket and buy a fifth of tequila and drink it all and literally kill myself. But if I choose to grow hemp in my own garden, for my own use, I get my name in the paper—"

"But you didn't get your truck took," the bandanna kid said. "They took my truck—1989 Nissan four-wheel-drive. New rear end, I just put in. They took my dad's hunting rifles. Four friggin' plants. They say if I don't plead to trafficking I'll get, like, friggin' six months. This country is so friggin'—"

"It's a disgrace," the hunched woman said, slapping the table. "They did this survey, they asked, like, a thousand cancer doctors if they'd told patients they should try marijuana to help them get through that chemo shit and forty-four percent said they did. I mean, come on. What is wrong with—''

''I'm no criminal. My son, they put my picture in the paper like I'm—''

''My father doesn't smoke pot. They bust down the door, scare my mother to friggin' death. Find these rifles up in a closet covered with dust—''

''And the press eats it up. Drug dealer this. Drug trafficker that. I mean, do I look like a drug trafficker person?''

''People should be able to get medical relief without being pursued like criminals, while the real criminals—''

I held my hands up to quiet the din. It did.

''I'm Jack McMorrow,'' I said. ''May I sit down?''

I put the tape recorder on the table and turned it on. I asked their names and ages and the towns where they lived. Then I asked them to go around the table and briefly tell me why they thought pot should be legal, what their interest in the issue was.

Fiddling with their coffee cups, they did. Roberta with the walker. Darrin with the bandanna. Sue and Kathy, the women who resembled each other. J. C., the pale fellow with the irritated skin. Sam, with the gold-rimmed glasses.

J.C., Darrin and Sue had been arrested; J. C. and Sue were awaiting trial, Darrin had been convicted. Darrin had lost the truck and rifles, too, and $537 in cash. Sam said the worst thing was that his seven-year-old son thought he was a criminal. Kathy said she believed marijuana was a sacred Christian herb, placed on the earth by God and used by Jesus.

''Genesis One,'' she said, looking down at the table. ''See, 'I give you every seed-bearing plant all over the earth . . . I give all green plants for food.' ''

Kathy smiled serenely. Coyote stared at her but didn't say a word.

When they finally petered out, Mullaney looked at me triumphantly.

''Well,'' he said. ''You gonna print it?''

They stared at me and waited for my answer.

"Probably. Some of it. In some form."

"Oh, jeez," Roberta said. "Here we go again. The press is so in bed with the medical establishment in this country—"

"I'm going to need some more," I interrupted. "The drug cops up here, that sort of thing. The DA. I'd like to talk to some of you individually. I'll talk to other people. I need to talk to you, Bobby, some more. And Melanie. I might like to see some of you at your homes. I need to know a little more about you."

I looked at Coyote. He stared back, his dark eyes unblinking, his face a black-eyed totem. I looked away.

"Hey, friggin' call me anytime," Darrin, the bandanna kid, said. "After November, you can find me in the Somerset County Jail. Doing time with all the other friggin' major outlaws. Hazard to society. That's me, man. Rasta outlaw, man. Friggin' cops."

Mullaney said he had their phone numbers. They heaved themselves out of the chairs, Roberta with help from Kathy, who wore the same calm smile, still enraptured by Scripture. Roberta had a nylon pouch attached to the front of her walker and she opened it and took out some papers and handed them to me. The top page was a copy of a newspaper story about activists in Boston pushing for legal medicinal use of marijuana.

"Read that stuff, if you dare," Roberta said. "This is a gross injustice if there's ever been one. I hope you're man enough to do something about it."

Ah, yes. If you can't appeal to the reporter's journalistic instincts, threaten his manhood.

With mine intact, more or less, I waited as they made their way to the door, stopping at the cash register to pay for six cups of coffee on six separate checks. For suspected drug dealers, they didn't flash much cash.

They all left and Mullaney, Melanie and Coyote stayed.

"How 'bout that lunch, man?" Mullaney said.

Groovy, I thought.

"Okay," I said.

"But let's go out to the house. You got time? We can talk more, show you around. And the kid's got something to say to you."

I considered it. I had no other assignments, nothing else to do. Why not? After all, Stephen had shot only the tail end of my truck, when he could shoot the eye out of a woodchuck.

"Fine," I said.

Coyote said nothing.

Seven

THE MULLANEYS AND Coyote—Melanie in the middle and Bobby driving—were in the red Chevy pickup with the oak bed and copper-colored doors. The truck rumbled over the Madison-Anson bridge and out of town to the west. I followed, digging a pair of aviators out from the tray between the seats as we turned into the sun. Bobby Mullaney drove slowly, like a man in no particular hurry. This activist business wasn't raising his blood pressure.

Outside of town and into the countryside, we were the only vehicles on the road. The sky was blue with high, hurrying clouds and the fields and woods were brightly colored but empty. It seemed strange that the place was so deserted on a beautiful autumn afternoon. Where was everybody?

Our little convoy traversed the hills and rolled down into Florence village, past the abandoned mill and the beer-and-crawlers store and out of town again. When we came to the Mullaneys' road, Bobby got out and gave a little wave and bent down to lock in the hubs on his front wheels. I got out and did the same and he called "Hidey-ho" as he climbed back in the cab, revved the motor once and ground the Chevy into gear.

We lurched and jolted our way down the rocky path, their heads snapping left and right like masts on rocking boats. Bobby Mullaney followed a course down the road that avoided the worst of the rocks and I followed behind him. When we got to the place where my truck had been shot, I stopped for a moment and looked up the slope to the right. I saw trees and brush and overgrown slash piles and countless places where Stephen could fire, prone or sitting or in a crouch. I didn't see Stephen.

Mullaney pulled up to the house and backed into the beaten-down space next to the garden. I pulled ahead of him and parked in front of the house. They dropped out of the Chevy and Melanie and Bobby walked over toward me. Coyote went and looked at the garden over the wire fence.

"Welcome to Green Acres," Bobby Mullaney said, grinning. "Come on in. Take your shoes off. Set a spell."

I followed them up the little steps and into the room where the potatoes were still spread on the newspaper on the floor. The woodstove was ticking cozily and the shotgun was leaning against the wall next to the door.

A place for everything and everything in its place.

"Would you like tea?" Melanie asked me, taking off her heavy sweater.

I remembered the last cup.

"No, thanks," I said.

"How 'bout a beer?" Bobby called from the kitchen.

"Sure," I said.

There was a rattle of bottles. The door eased open behind me and Coyote sidled in. Bobby came in with two beers in unlabeled brown pint bottles.

"Unfiltered wheat ale. Buddy of mine makes it. We supply him with vegetables."

I took one.

"I thought you were down on alcohol," I said.

"Everything in moderation," Bobby said. "And this is direct. No industrial corporation complex putting poison in it, bombarding the public with friggin' propaganda, you know what I'm saying?"

"Cheers," I said.

The ale wasn't bad. A little yeasty but not bad. I took
another sip and Bobby went back toward the kitchen.

"Rustle up some grub," he boomed.

I stood there and sipped and looked around the room,
the posters of the Brooks Range in Alaska, the flyers from
food co-ops. A sign for a pro-pot rally in Corvallis, Oregon.
As I stood, I watched Coyote out of the corner of my eye.
He had a bottle of ale but he hadn't taken a drink yet. He
went to a door at the far end of the room and opened it
and listened, then shut the door again. Then he went to the
old black telephone next to the couch and picked up the
receiver, listened for a moment, then hung up. Finally, he
sat down at a rickety table by the big window at the end
of the room, sat down with his back to the wall and took
a small sip.

Maybe I'd plunk down beside him and say, "How 'bout
those Patriots."

Maybe not.

Lunch was home-baked anadama bread and a big salad
filled with plants that looked like roadside weeds but turned
out to be pretty tasty. Melanie served from a worn wooden
bowl and we ate sitting in the old easy chairs. Stephen
hadn't shown up but that didn't mean he wasn't out there
in the woods, watching through an eight-power scope.

It was awkward once the eating began and silence fell
over the room. I complimented Melanie for the salad but
Bobby and Coyote just kept munching, leaves and stems
disappearing inch by inch inside their mouths like grass
huffed up by grazing cows. Finally, Bobby remembered his
manners.

"So, Jack," he said, buttering a chunk of bread. "What's
your angle gonna be?"

"Angle?" I said.

"For your story. You need an angle, right? A pitch. A
hook. A play. A spin."

He bit into the bread and chewed.

"I don't know," I said. "Maybe that in places like Florence, Maine, the marijuana movement is alive and well."

"And getting bigger," Melanie said. "At the fair we got, like, nine hundred and fifty signatures and that's just—"

"Everywhere you go it's like that," Bobby interrupted. "We had some people down at the Maine Mall a couple Saturdays ago. They got, like, a hundred signatures in two hours. I mean, people are ready for these friggin' police-state laws to go. We're gonna hold this massive rally at the statehouse at the end of October, and man, we're gonna friggin' pack that place. I mean occupy the goddamn building, you know what I'm saying? We already talked to Channel Nine. They're gonna cover it."

"This is not just a few people from the backwoods," Melanie said. "This is people all over, everywhere. We've got teachers, nurses—"

"College professors," Bobby interrupted again.

"And what comes after teachers and nurses?" I asked Melanie.

She looked perplexed. And then she smiled.

Dessert was homemade ice cream with blackberries in syrup. Bobby filled a soup bowl. Melanie had one hefty helping and even Coyote, who had only nibbled a piece of bread as he watched me warily, had a bowl with extra blackberries. Bobby finished his and had seconds. I'd hate to be in his way when he got the munchies.

We finished and Melanie took the bowls and plates to the kitchen. In this progressive household, a woman's place still was in the home.

Melanie brought a pot of green tea but she was the only one partaking. I watched her and wondered just how much of this retreat to the woods had been her idea. Probably not much. For all their earrings and braids, the Mullaney men had Neanderthal blood.

Outside, the sun had dipped into the trees. I stood and looked out the window at the path that wound up into the woods above the house. Dishes clattered in the sink and when I turned, Bobby and Coyote were standing behind me, one on each side.

"So Jack," Bobby said, more quietly than before. "Tell me true, man. Where do you stand on this?"

"Where do I stand?"

"Yeah. You for us or agin' us, man?"

Coyote watched me closely.

"To do the story, it shouldn't matter," I said.

"Come on," Bobby Mullaney said. "You're a smart guy. You gotta have an opinion."

I thought for a moment.

"Well, the laws are definitely out of whack. You've got the state selling rotgut vodka but putting people away for growing a little pot. That's not right."

"It's outrageous," Bobby said. "People going to jail for friggin' years. Losing everything they own. For growing a weed. You know how many people die in this country from tobacco every year?"

I shook my head no. And took out my notebook.

"Like four hundred thousand. Booze, another hundred thousand. No, maybe it's a hundred and fifty. I'd have to look that up. Friggin' caffeine, man. I mean friggin' caffeine. As many as ten thousand people die from caffeine, rotting out their stomachs and having heart attacks."

I scribbled, not as much for the numbers as the spirit of the message.

"Now, you guess how many people die in this country in a year from marijuana."

I didn't guess but Mullaney didn't notice.

"Zero, Jack. None. Nada. Not one, and that's a fact. I mean, what is the friggin' threat here? I mean, we got cops in choppers buzzing this part of the country. Last fall, I mean, not right now, but last fall last year, it was like friggin' Vietnam out here. We got guys who are vets and they're having, like, flashbacks 'cause these Hueys are buzzing the woods. Scaring the shit out of little kids."

"And the cow," Melanie put in.

"The cow," Bobby Mullaney said, gesturing with his ale bottle. "This guy has this cow and it's pregnant, you know? Chopper buzzes the cow and it calves right there on the spot."

"It miscarried," Melanie said.

"Right," her husband said. "Guy goes to the cops and complains and they tell him to take a friggin' hike."

He took a swallow of ale. I stopped writing and took one, too.

"Craziness, man," Bobby said. "It's gotta stop. People have to wake up in this country. This is turning into a friggin' police state."

"That's right," Coyote murmured.

"You think so, too, Coyote?" I asked.

"It's a sacred herb," he said.

I looked at him.

"Oh, you mean for your Native American religions."

"For a lot of religions. Mexican. Jamaican."

"Oglala Sioux, wasn't it?"

Coyote looked like it bothered him that I'd remembered.

"Yeah," he said.

"Hey, man," Mullaney said. "Come with me."

He turned and headed for the door. I followed. Coyote followed me. Melanie still was in the kitchen, clanging pans. When we got outside, Mullaney walked up into the woods from the house and stopped and turned to me. I stopped and he took two steps toward me, until he was a foot from my face. Coyote was somewhere behind me.

"I'm an up-front kind of guy," Mullaney said. He was close enough for me to see the hair in his nostrils. "So I'm gonna tell you straight out."

My deodorant's quit, I thought.

"I trust you, Jack. I know people and I think you're good people."

I tried not to blush.

"Thanks," I said.

"So I want to show you something. But it's gotta be off the record. Can you promise me that?"

"Depends on what it is. If it's a couple of dead bodies, I might feel an obligation to tell somebody."

He paused. Coyote pricked up.

"Just kidding," I said.

"Oh, well, listen. It ain't dead bodies. Off the record, man. I just want to show you what we're talking about."

"Hey—" Coyote began.

But Mullaney had already turned and was walking up the tote road. I followed. Coyote brought up the rear. We walked Indian file. Of course.

Mullaney walked thirty yards and turned off, though there didn't appear to be a path. He picked his way around brambles and maple saplings, holding the branches for me so I wouldn't get whipped in the face. The sun was skimming the tops of the trees to the west and the light was shimmering but fading. There still didn't appear to be any path, just damp leaves and viny undergrowth that Mullaney picked his way around and over, rather than through.

Coyote moved silently behind me.

We moved deeper into the woods, walking for what seemed like a mile but probably was a little less. I heard a wood thrush somewhere off to my right and then just the placing of our feet. The second growth seemed to open, barely, and suddenly Mullaney stopped. He turned back to me.

"Bend over," he said.

I looked at him and he reached out and grasped something in his fingers. I looked closer.

Black thread. Tied between two branches.

"Security," Mullaney said. "There'll be a lot of that from here on. I'll tell you when to duck."

I could see some sort of path now, not a track but a discernible opening between the trees, like a deer trail. Mullaney told me to duck a dozen times, and when I got closer I'd see the thread across the opening, neck-high. Then Mullaney told me to duck, and step. The threads crossed at the neck and knees. Once. Twice. Three times. Coyote followed twenty feet behind, moving easily in the woods. For a hood from Valley, Mass.

With Oglala blood.

And then Mullaney stopped. I did, too. He held his arm out to his left and smiled.

"Jack McMorrow," he said, grinning. "Meet *Cannabis sativa.*"

The plants were about six feet tall. There were six of them, with trademark marijuana leaves like something off a T-shirt. They were growing in a tiny hole cut in the woods, with birch and small maples on its fringes. The pot plants seemed frilly and tropical next to their wild neighbors.

"Look at this, McMorrow," Mullaney said, motioning for me to come closer.

"You notice anything?"

He was fondling the buds that grew head-high on the plants. The proud papa.

"I don't know. They look healthy."

"No, McMorrow. Look closer. The buds, man. Look at the buds."

I looked, then glanced up at Coyote, watching from the edge of the opening. His face was expressionless. For this game show, I was on my own.

"Are they special buds or something?" I said.

"Man, look at those buds," Mullaney exclaimed, unable to contain himself any longer. "They're huge. No pollination, man. No boys. These plants are all girls. Cloned from one female plant."

He looked at me like I should do cartwheels. Coyote looked at me like I knew too much.

"Great," I said.

"No seeds, just buds," Mullaney said. "All resin."

I searched back twenty years for the right word.

"Primo?" I said. "Maui zowee? Killer weed?"

"This is no weed, McMorrow," Mullaney said. "This is a natural wonder. A gift from Mother Nature."

Standing there in the little clearing, he showed me the dark green hose buried under the leaves. It ran uphill to a stream. Gravity pulled the water down to the pot patch. They started the flow with a plastic siphon hose, like you'd use to siphon gasoline. When the hose wasn't in use, it was plugged with a cork and buried.

The soil was full of compost from the bin near their garden, hauled up in camouflage-painted five-gallon buckets. The plants were dried and bagged, somewhere, and the marijuana was traded within a small network of kindred spirits, Bobby Mullaney said.

"It's the barter system, like before it was corrupted by capitalism," Mullaney said. "Milk. Beef. Chickens. Kerosene. Parts for the trucks. A guy's time to fix 'em. I traded two ounces for a ring job, once."

"How much would those plants be worth on the street?" I asked.

"Four or five thousand," Mullaney said.

"That's a lot of chickens."

"Yeah, well, it has to last a whole year. And we keep some for our use. So that takes a chunk."

"I'll bet."

"So what we're doing is bypassing the goddamn centralized government, the booze and tobacco cartels that have been running this country for so long. That's why they want this stopped, McMorrow. It's a revolution. And we're winning."

"What if you get caught?"

"No revolution is without risks," Coyote said suddenly, startling me.

"Opening yourself up with this petition stuff, aren't you?"

"They've got to find it first," Mullaney said. "It'll be gone next week. And next time it won't be here."

"Why'd you show me?"

"You're covering a war, McMorrow," he said. "I wanted to show you the front lines."

There was a method to their madness, and I thought about it as we walked back to the house, but not using the route by which we had come.

By letting me in on their little—and illegal—secret, I became an accomplice of sorts. Chances were I wasn't going to run to the cops anyway. They'd decided that before we went for our walk. Showing me the plot in the woods, which could be gone tomorrow anyway, was added insurance. By accepting their confidence, I was sucked in.

And I did find myself becoming more sympathetic. Mullaney was growing on me, with his cocksure naïveté. Coyote was intriguing, if nothing else. And I liked Melanie, though I felt sorry for her. I got the feeling her life wasn't turning out as she had once hoped, that as a young girl, a younger woman, she hadn't dreamed of living in remote western Maine, at the end of an almost impassable road, with her son and these two guys, so deep in the woods that no one would ever hear her scream.

So I thought about all of this as we slipped back down the hill, across a little ravine with the stream dodging through it. Eventually, we emerged higher up on the tote road and it was almost dark when we finally reached the house.

Mullaney asked me to come in but I said no, I had to go but I'd be in touch. I asked him how off-the-record our outing was supposed to be and he said no names, no location, just somewhere in the county. I said that was fine and stuck my notebook in my pocket and shook his hand. It was very strong and hard. From Coyote I got a nod, and that seemed hard, too.

The notebook went on the passenger seat. The truck started and I looked back at the house, which now had kerosene lamps burning, casting a soft, yellow light in this black expanse of woods. What did they do now? Play Parcheesi?

I pulled out and, in first gear, high-range, four-wheel drive, started up the rocky road. The transmission grated and I made a mental note to check the fluid. Even Toyotas needed some attention. And a new transmission was several ounces.

The truck lurched and bumped. The radio got country and western, with static. I was tired and needed a fix of Roxanne, even if only on the phone. I was considering calling her from a pay phone in the hinterlands, just for fun, when I saw it.

A glint of light.

In the woods ahead and to my left.

It went out but it had been there, glowing like a firefly but fixed. I watched the spot, drove another twenty feet, then turned the truck hard to the left so the lights pierced the blackness.

I saw woods but nothing else. Leaving the lights on but shutting off the motor, I eased the door open and dropped to the ground, letting the door swing closed. In a crouch, I moved past the back of the truck and into the woods on the opposite side of the road. I slid deep into the brush on my belly.

And waited.

Eight

THE LEAVES WERE damp and cold on my bare belly where my jacket and shirt had pulled up. I eased a hand down slowly and tucked my shirt back in, then eased the hand back up and was still.

I watched. I listened. My Marine friend, Clair, had once told me that kids could be turned into tough soldiers and they even could be turned into brave soldiers but patient soldiers were rare indeed. It was an exceptional man who could sit in the dark in the jungle for three hours with the bugs and the snakes, and not move a muscle.

It had been thirty seconds, maybe, and I was doing fine. I watched the area illuminated by the lights, saw moths veer in and out of the glare like tracers. I waited and listened.

If it had been Stephen, I figured he wouldn't approach the front of the truck. But from the uphill side, he would see only the high beams and wouldn't know that I wasn't in the cab. He would swing wide coming down and come up on the truck from the rear.

If it had been Stephen.

I waited. Heard the nebulous murmur of the night woods. The breeze in the leaves. Trees moving. Branches rubbing together. I listened for the sound of someone moving.

Nothing.

I wondered if I was deep enough in the brush but I didn't dare to move. I lowered my head and listened. Heard the woods whisper. Listened some more.

And something cracked.

A branch, to my right, up the road above the truck. I turned my head slowly and then was still. Watched. Listened. Heard the faintest of rustles. Then another. A footstep in the leaves. Something moving. Then nothing.

I waited. Listened hard. Watched the darkness. And heard it again. To my right. Behind me.

I lay still. Didn't breathe. Waited and listened. Didn't dare turn my head to look.

And then I saw him.

Stephen was coming up through the woods to my right, fifty feet away. He moved slowly, like a good hunter. Three steps and stop. Wait. Three more steps and stop. Listen.

He was moving more toward the center of my field of vision. I could see the rifle in his right hand, barrel pointed down. He was in a half-crouch, easing his way up through the trees. When he came to the edge of the woods, he stopped. Listened. I lay still.

Stephen was above me now. He eased along the edge of the woods, working his way closer to the road. I could see his camouflage sweatshirt, his jeans and boots. He was almost in front of me now, fifteen feet away, watching the truck. Stephen stopped and waited and listened. He seemed to think I would be in the truck, but seemed puzzled that he couldn't see my head, that I wasn't standing anywhere around the truck.

I waited until he was directly in front of me, rifle hanging down at his side. He bent down and looked under the truck, then popped back up. As he took a step toward the truck, then another, I eased myself up, first to my elbows, then on my hands and knees. Stephen was on the driver's side, near the back bumper. As he peered into the truck bed, I got to my feet. He moved toward the driver's door, very slowly. I moved after him, picking my feet straight up and easing them back down in the wet leaves. I was at the edge of the road when I saw his back stiffen.

"You from Triple A?" I said. "Took you long enough to get here."

Stephen turned slowly, like he thought I might have a gun pointed at his back. When he finished turning, I grinned.

"It runs fine but there's a small hole in the back, on the left. From a twenty-two. You haven't seen anybody tromping around these woods with a rifle, have you?"

Stephen glowered at me. I let my grin drain away and walked closer.

"So what's your problem?"

He looked at me.

"Hard of hearing? What's your problem?"

"No problem," Stephen said, barely moving his lips.

"Your dad said you had something to say to me."

"He isn't my dad."

"Okay. The guy who lives in your house with you and your mother and phony Chief Running Water also known as Joe Schmo from Valley, there. That guy said you had something to say to me."

I stepped closer so we were face-to-face. Stephen looked away. The rifle hung at his side limply, or at least as limply as a rifle can hang.

"If the mental telepathy doesn't work you can try talking with your mouth."

"Yeah, well . . ." Stephen began.

"Yeah, well what?"

"Yeah, well, it was a dumb thing to do."

"Yup," I said.

"So it was a dumb thing to do. What do you want me to do? Kiss your ass?"

"Heaven forbid."

I went to the door, opened it and shut off the headlights, but left the parking lights on. Then I stepped back and stared at him. The eyes with their permanent glare. The shaved head. The bottled-up anger that trickled out of the end of the barrel of his gun.

"So what is it? Got something against Toyotas?"

Stephen snorted.

"Got something against me?"

He didn't snort.

"So what is it? Here's your chance. Say it."

"Yeah, well."

"You already said that."

"Jeez, give me a chance, will ya?"

He almost looked at me.

"That's what I'm trying to do, Stephen."

"Yeah, well . . ."

I waited. We stood there in the glow of the parking lights. I waited some more.

"I don't want any goddamn pot story," he said, more quietly.

"But your parents do."

"He's not my—"

"Okay. Your stepfather or whatever you call him."

"I don't call him anything."

"Fine. But they want the story. They're all gung ho about it."

"Yeah, right," Stephen said. "They make themselves look like idiots. I take all the shit for it."

"You don't agree with them?"

"I hate it."

"Hate what?"

"Marijuana. Sitting around talking this crap, doesn't mean anything, laughing like he's the funniest guy in the world, eyes all shut up and red and you can't even talk to him, not that you'd want to. House friggin' stinks. I hate that smell. I hate all of it. That's why I live in the woods. Except when it's, like, zero out."

He looked away. His eyes were moist like he might cry. He wasn't as tough as he'd seemed. But then, very few people were.

"What about your mother?"

He shrugged.

"She goes along with him. She's always gone along with him. You think he's this funny guy, right? But he's not.

He bosses her around. His way or the highway."

"And the highway's a long way from here."

"That's how he wants it. She's a prisoner here, practically. Me, too."

"Where would you like to live?" I asked.

"I don't know. In town. Like everybody else. You know, a house with a driveway. Play hoops in the driveway."

"You like basketball?"

"I suck at it. 'Cause everybody else plays it all the time. I play at gym class, that's about it."

I looked out at the black woods, then back at him.

"Have many friends?"

Stephen shrugged, which answered the question.

"They call me Stoney. The teachers used to, like, send me to the office all the time 'cause they smelled pot on me. I'd say, 'It isn't me.' They'd say, 'Right.' Last year I got suspended, like, three times. They called my mom and shit."

"So what happened?"

"Bobby went in and made, like, this massive deal out of it. Brought in all these papers and waved 'em around and talked about his constitutional rights and all this crap. Got in the principal's face. Threatened to sue her."

"So what happened?"

"They backed down. They didn't want him parked there for the rest of the year. I mean, he was ready to bring in all his buddies and picket the place."

"Was he mad at you?"

"Shit no. He thought it was great. Gave him another chance to spout. That's what he does best. Talk, talk, talk."

"And what happened to you?"

"I got shit. The druggies thought I was one of them and I blew 'em off and the jocks think I'm a freak so what the hell. I don't need 'em."

"You've got your woods and your gun, huh?"

"Yup."

"What kind of gun is it?"

"Remington. Twenty-two. It's nothing special but it's accurate. I want a Ruger ten. Semiautomatic."

"I've got a Remington thirty-ought-six," I said.

"You deer-hunt?"

"No."

"Then what do you have it for?"

"I don't know," I said. "It's come in handy some-times."

"Too big," Stephen said. "Shoot it and you hear it for miles."

"You like it quiet?"

"I'd have a silencer if I could find one."

"They're illegal."

"I know," he said.

We stood. Stephen scuffed his boots on the rocks and looked off into the woods but didn't seem to want to leave.

"So what happens if I write this story?" I asked him.

He breathed in deeply, then exhaled, long and slow.

"Just more of it. Bobby gets all pumped up and thinks he's this big deal and I get more shit at school. Situation normal, you know?"

"And your mom?"

"She goes along."

I thought for a moment.

"Don't the cops have it in for Bobby? All this talk. I mean, it *is* illegal."

"He don't care. What are they gonna get him for? A couple plants, if they're lucky. And oh, man, the trial would be a friggin' circus. I don't think they think it'd be worth it."

"They ever come out here and look around?"

"A couple times."

"Pound around like a herd of elephants?"

Stephen looked thoughtful and almost smiled.

"No," he said. "Not really. There was this one guy. He was pretty good. I was, like, stalking him, you know? He moved pretty good in the woods. Musta hunted a lot or something. I followed him for, like, a mile."

"He ever spot you?" I asked.

This time Stephen did look at me.

"Nope," he said, and he smiled.

"Then why'd you let me spot you? What was it, a penlight?"

Stephen reached inside his sweatshirt and pulled it out. It was a magnesium flashlight, a small one.

"You wanted to talk to me, didn't you?"

"Yeah."

"To try to keep me from writing this story?"

He shrugged.

"It'd run in Boston, not Maine. Maybe the kids at school wouldn't see it."

"It only takes one," Stephen said. "I think some kids read the *Boston Globe*. For the sports."

"It's my job," I said.

"You could write about something else."

"I don't think so."

"Whatever." Stephen sighed.

He turned, as if to go.

"Something I wanted to ask you," I said.

He turned back.

"What's the deal with this Coyote guy?"

Stephen looked at me but as I watched him, he slipped away, somewhere behind his eyes.

"Friend of Bobby's," he said.

"Does he have another name?" I said.

"I don't know. I don't want to know."

"What's he doing here?"

"He's just here," Stephen said quickly, and then he turned and headed off, not down the rocky road, but up into the woods, where he slipped silently between the saplings, and in just moments, had disappeared into the blackness and left me alone.

I drove back to Prosperity in silence, no radio or tapes, and thought about Stephen and his short unhappy life. The problem was that nobody put Stephen first. Not before marijuana. Not before roaming around the countryside, wheeling and dealing. Not before whatever relationship it was that kept Melanie and Bobby together.

It wasn't the first time a child had been relegated to second place. But still it was sad and unnecessary and he seemed like a pretty good kid in spite of it all. It was cruel what fate handed children in the random crapshoot of birth. Stephen had been handed these people, this life, one for which he seemed so ill suited. But then, few kids are really cut out for loneliness and neglect. There still was hope for him, as long as that rifle didn't drag him into a hole so deep he couldn't climb back out.

But his mother and Bobby had already dug him a bit of a hole, and a strange one it was. Gun-toting hippies with an organic garden. Herbal remedies and shotgun shells. Inner-city con men turned backwoods pot activists. It was an odd mix, but then, my few years in Maine had taught me not to try to fit the people into pigeonholes.

People found their way to places like Florence, places like Prosperity, because they didn't fit in those little holes. Or wouldn't.

And there was something likable about the Mullaney clan, with the exception of Coyote. But at the same time, none of it seemed to add up. Stephen didn't fit with Bobby and Bobby didn't fit with Melanie. Coyote didn't fit with any of them, except perhaps with the side of Bobby that I hadn't fully seen. When I did, something told me it would show more than a happy-go-lucky guy who traded a little reefer for truck parts.

Much more.

Nine

IT WAS MONDAY night and Roxanne was working late. She worked late Tuesdays through Thursdays, too, a dedication that I balanced by knocking off as early as possible.

The house was dark when I swung open the door. It was lit when I opened the refrigerator and grabbed a can of ale, and then I closed the refrigerator and it was dark again. I opened the ale, took a sip and dialed Roxanne's direct line at the office by touch.

"Hey, baby," I said, when I heard the always reassuring sound of her voice.

"Hey, baby yourself," she said. "What's up?"

"I don't know. I spent the day with your buddies from the fair."

"My sympathies. How was it?"

"Great. We got really stoned and listened to music and I told these really funny stories. At least they seemed funny."

"I'm sure," Roxanne said.

"And we've all decided to quit our jobs and follow, well, who do you follow now that Jerry Garcia's gone?"

"I don't know. There must be somebody."

"Right," I said. "All those Deadheads can't just stay home. So we'll get a VW bus and hit the road."

"Send me a postcard."

"You're not coming? I thought you could wear tie-dye, have a new name. How 'bout 'Hummus Girl'?"

"I'm washing my hair that month," Roxanne said.

"Hey, you can wash it in a rest area. A communal shower. Maybe a farm pond full of muck. Weren't you at Woodstock?"

"I was two," Roxanne said.

"Oh, yeah," I said.

"You would have been about twelve."

"Don't tell the guys. I told them I met Janis Joplin back-stage."

"They won't remember."

"Who won't remember?"

I wanted to talk but Roxanne sounded harried and hur-ried. I asked her what she was working on and she said they were going to court in the morning to try to pull a ten-year-old girl.

"What's the problem?" I asked.

"It's confidential."

"It's me."

"Well, she's being physically abused at home. The mother is a sadist who gives her impossible chores to do, then punishes her when she can't do them. She goes to school with black eyes, cut lips, bruises on her arms. She was given this thing called the Thematic Apperception Test—"

"What's that mean?"

"They show them pictures and ask them what they're pictures of. She said a mother and daughter hugging was a woman choking a girl's neck because the girl hadn't put her laundry away. A man talking to a boy was a dad saying he was going to punch the boy's teeth out if he didn't eat all his supper."

"So what did that tell you?"

"That the girl is seriously screwed up."

"What does the mother say?"

"She says the girl is accident-prone. Won't have anything to do with us."

"No dad?"

"He's drunk most of the time."

"God almighty. What's the good news?"

"Well, he doesn't come home much. And they don't have any other kids."

"And about to have none at all?"

"I hope so. That depends on the judge," Roxanne said.

"And you."

"And me."

"The girl's in good hands," I said.

"Not yet," Roxanne said.

I thought for a moment.

"I've got one for you. This kid Stephen. Son of the woman who's married to the guy who you met at the fair. High school kid. Kind of a loner. Wanders around the woods by himself with a twenty-two rifle. These people live in the absolute middle of nowhere. The kid's dream is to live in town with a basketball hoop on the garage."

"To be like everybody else."

"Right. But he can't because Bobby and Melanie—Bobby mostly, I think—have decided to hide out in the hills."

"And smoke pot."

"Well, it isn't like they just sit around and get stoned all the time. But when they kick back, it's probably with a pipe instead of a bourbon. The kid hates it. The smell. The legalization stuff. The talk. He doesn't want me to write anything because the publicity gets him all this flak at school. The jock kids think he's a freak. The freak kids don't like him because he's not one of them, either."

"The poor kid."

"Yeah. I feel bad for him. He's really not a bad kid."

"He talked to you?"

"Yeah. I think he sort of wanted to apologize."

"For what?" Roxanne asked.

"Oh, I didn't tell you that. For shooting my truck."

"What?"

"But it was only in the back end."

"So I'm supposed to feel better?"

"Well, he *is* a crack shot," I said.

So I wished Roxanne luck, said I wanted to see her soon. She said she wanted to see me, too, so we could talk. And other things. I asked her which other things those were. She said I knew. She was right.

That night I fixed dinner, a tuna sandwich and tomato soup. Campbell's. Opening the can, I felt a little like I was selling out. I would have made salad but it was too dark to be foraging on the roadside.

I ate and finished another pint of ale and then made a pot of tea. Then I took the pot and a mug and went to the computer and sat down and sipped and typed. Everything I could remember of my conversation with Stephen. All of my notes from my conversation with the Mullaneys and Coyote. Notes on our visit to the marijuana patch. All female plants. Buds that don't go to seed.

After a couple of hours, I found myself sitting in the blue light of the computer screen and just staring. I thought about the odd places people end up, the random turns lives can take, the fact that so much of what we are is dictated by circumstances beyond our control.

And I thought of the power that these parents have to mold their kids in whatever shape they choose, how kids like Stephen stay in that shape until they grow strong enough to break free, like something that has come alive and smashed its way out of a tomb.

I slept well, though not as well as I did when Roxanne was wrapped around me. When I got up, the sun was creeping up, backlighting the trees so that they glowed yellow and orange like stained glass. I eased my way down the loft stairs, put water on the stove and took a shower. The tea steeped while I got dressed, and then I drank a cup with toast and thought of Roxanne in court, my beautiful, if not virginal, Jeanne d'Arc. I hoped it went well.

Pouring a second cup of tea, I went to the table and the phone. I got out my list of names and numbers from the restaurant in Madison and started calling.

I didn't need a lot, just enough to fill the holes. For three hundred bucks, they weren't going to be filled to the brim. After all, I may have been a freelancer, but I was a professional. And I had my pride, even if all else failed.

But it didn't. In fact, the morning went smoothly. I called Sam with the gold glasses first and he was home, even answered the phone. He told me he grew up in Colorado, had a master's degree in English literature and had taught in high school and colleges. Now he stayed home while his wife worked as a nurse in Waterville. She worked and he took care of their son, who was seven and thought his father was a criminal.

I asked Sam if he could recall exactly what his son had said.

"I remember every word," Sam said. "I'd been arrested for trafficking, a few little plants in the woods, and it had been in the paper that morning but he'd heard us talking about it, anyway. He'd been crying, you could tell, and he didn't want to talk at first but I sat with him and I remember I had this book on my lap, one of his books. He was leaning over and he started to cry again and a couple of tears ran down his face and landed on the page. And it was a library book. And he looked up at me and he said, 'But Dad, I thought you were one of the good guys.' "

"Do you consider yourself one of the good guys?" I asked, my voice soft and calm as I scribbled madly off camera.

"Yeah, I do, Mr. McMorrow," Sam said. "I'm really trying to right a wrong. I really think that. I think a terrible injustice is being done in the name of fighting this so-called 'war on drugs.' But sometimes I wonder if it's worth it. Fighting back, I mean."

"And this was one of those times?"

"This was one of those times. Yes."

It was all I needed, or almost all.

"Sam," I said, knowing it would be an awkward transition. "Could you tell me again how you spell your last name?"

It was good stuff and it kept on coming. I called Darrin and he went on at great length about how his truck had been confiscated and that left him with no way to get to work at the tannery in Farmington so he'd had to hitchhike and even if he got up at four in the morning, he sometimes had trouble getting rides, so he was late.

"So they canned my ass," Darrin said. "Now me and the old lady are on welfare and food stamps. All for a stupid little plant."

"You mean you only had one?" I asked.

"Well, no. I had . . . Well, they charged me with, like, seventeen or eighteen. But they weren't mine."

"Whose were they?"

"No comment," Darrin said.

Kathy commented, mostly by reading from the Book of Genesis. She said religious use of marijuana had given her insights into the spiritual world and enhanced her ability to pray to the Lord our God.

"Marijuana laws in this country are a clear infringement on religious freedoms guaranteed by the Constitution," she said.

I thanked Kathy for her time. She said she'd pray for me.

"And the sinners, too?" I asked.

She didn't answer.

"Just a joke," I said.

I was on a roll, reporting in the zone, as they say in sports. Roberta was home and she described her illness in great detail, and said that before she bought a small amount of marijuana to try to ease her pain, she had never broken a law, never had a traffic ticket, never been late on a car payment.

"When they arrested me, the two policeman said they were very sorry. One of them called me the next day to make sure I was okay."

"But they have to enforce the law."

"And the law needs to be changed," Roberta said. "My medication is two hundred eighty-three dollars a month. All I need is a little plant out in the garden."

And on it went the rest of the sunny morning. People were home. People were talking. Even when I made calls to get the police side, I scored.

At the Somerset County Sheriff's Department, there was a sergeant named Johnston who seemed to pop up in all the drug-bust anecdotes. I called the number in the book, a dispatcher answered and then Sergeant Johnston was on the phone.

I made my pitch. He apparently listened.

"I'd rather talk to you in person," Johnston said.

"I live in Prosperity. It's kind of hard to get over there."

He didn't say anything for a moment. In the background, a police radio crackled.

"Okay, Mr. McMorrow," Johnston began suddenly. "Here's the short version. Number one, I get paid to enforce the law. Marijuana is illegal. Possessing small amounts is a misdemeanor. Growing it for profit is a felony. That's the law. I didn't write it."

He paused. Writing on a legal pad, I caught up.

"Number two, and this is my personal opinion, you start legalizing drugs like this, where does it stop? All this stuff about it being a natural herb and all that, well, mushrooms are natural and they can put a fourteen-year-old kid on another planet. Cocaine comes from a plant. Grows all over South America. Coca plant. LSD comes from mold spores. Natural as hell. You have kids, McMorrow?"

"No," I said.

"Well, when you do, it changes the way you feel about this stuff. Hey, my kid smokes marijuana, it's not the end of the world. He drives into a tree while he's stoned and drunk, it could be. Hey, I know what alcohol can do. I've seen it in my own family. But bottom line is this. I can't arrest you for buying a case of Bud. I have to arrest you for buying marijuana."

"Or growing it."

"Or growing it," Johnston said.

"I've been up to Florence, around the area. Must be a tough place to infiltrate. At least in New York or some-place, there are people."

"We have our ways. You from New York or some-place?"

"I've worked there."

"What brings you up here?"

"Needed a change."

There was a pause, as if Johnston had processed that answer and filed it under crap.

"Thanks for your help," I said. "I appreciate it."

"No problem. Hey, so you've been around Florence. Let me guess. Bobby Mullaney and his wife, there. And his sidekick, there."

"Coyote."

"Yeah. I knew it was something like that."

"What's his real name?" I said.

"We don't know," Johnston said.

"But you've inquired?"

"No comment. Hey, I got a call, Mr. McMorrow. But if you're around Florence, we'll meet."

He didn't say maybe.

I hung up the phone and wrote. Next to Johnston's name I put "tough and smart." The Mullaneys had picked a for-midable foe.

Next I tried the Drug Enforcement Agency in Augusta. An answering machine hissed. I left a message, and five minutes later the phone rang. The guy on the line identified himself as Martin Jones. He had a radio voice and was pretty slick, for a cop. But he gave me only a couple of things worth using.

The Florence area had been targeted for special attention after informants said marijuana grown there was making its way to cities in southern Maine, New Hampshire and Mas-sachusetts, Jones said.

"These aren't all hippies drying a couple of ounces for sitting around the woodstove in the winter," he said, in a practiced tone that made me think he'd said the same thing many times before. "Money attracts serious criminals. And there's a lot of money to be made in marijuana.''

And there was, at least by my increasingly modest standards. Three hundred bucks, to be exact. If I kept my nose to the grindstone, I could knock this story off by two o'clock, zap it into the *Globe*'s computer and spend the rest of the beautiful autumn afternoon tromping around the woods with my binoculars, finishing with cocktails at the Varneys', or at least a beer with Clair in the barn.

All rewards weren't monetary.

So that's what I did, typing away at my little keyboard, eyeing my notes, underlining the best quotes, puzzling over different leads.

FLORENCE, MAINE—Accused marijuana trafficker Sam Sheedy says he can accept the fact that Maine drug agents think he's a criminal. What shook him, Sheedy says, was his seven-year-old son coming to the same conclusion.

"He was leaning over and he started to cry again and a couple of tears ran down his face and landed on the page," Sheedy said, at his home here recently. "And it was a library book. And he looked up at me and he said, 'But Dad, I thought you were one of the good guys.' "

Not bad.

FLORENCE, MAINE—Some people might say that when Bobby and Melanie Mullaney fled Valley, Mass., for the woods of this tiny hamlet in northern Somerset County, they were simply trading one drug scene for another.

The Mullaneys wouldn't agree. They say there's no comparison between the cocaine-fueled crime they left behind and the marijuana legalization movement they've joined in rural Maine.

A little flat, but it had a good Massachusetts hook.

FLORENCE, MAINE—Roberta Florio was arrested recently when she attempted to buy an ounce of marijuana from an undercover police officer outside a Waterville bar. The officer came to her car because Florio, 48, suffers from multiple sclerosis and finds walking difficult.

"I wasn't trying to buy drugs," said Florio, a fervent supporter of the growing marijuana movement in this corner of western Maine. "I was trying to buy medicine."

The quote was good but Florio wasn't really typical of the movement. And then there was another lead, one that had been skulking in the back of my mind all morning.

FLORENCE, MAINE—When 15-year-old Stephen———— was sent home from school because he smelled of marijuana, his mother and stepfather??? went right over to talk to the principal.

And threatened to picket the school.

Welcome to the world of the marijuana legalization movement, a growing presence in this corner of western Maine. . . .

That one would require some more work. I didn't know Stephen's last name, for one thing. I'd have to corroborate the incident with the school people. And last but not least, I'd have to clear it with Stephen.

But only if I wanted to sleep at night.

I leaned back in my chair, and eyed the screen. It had been the same at the *Times,* at the *Providence Journal,* the *Hartford Courant.* Some of my best work had been lost to the red pen of my nagging conscience.

So I went with the Sheedy lead, deciding against putting Roberta up there because the medicinal-use angle was important but not really representative and the drug-buy anecdote wasn't all that compelling. But you'd have to be illiterate not to be hooked by the recounting of the moment a father realized he had lost the the respect of his son.

I read it and reread it, and then plunged in. The inches flew by, the way they did when a news story had some meat to it. Describing the town, the unsettling remoteness of that corner of Maine. The Mullaneys and their petitions, their contention that marijuana users were being persecuted on behalf of the big corporations that sell beer and cigarettes.

The eclectic band of supporters, from Darrin to Roberta to Kathy. Johnston's counterpoint to their legalization arguments. The DEA guy's admonition that people should not be lulled into thinking marijuana growers were all harmless hippies.

It was 2:25. I was behind schedule.

I reread the story and there still were holes. I needed to know the year the Mullaneys came to Maine. How long they'd lived in Valley. Stephen's last name, maybe. How many acres they owned. Their ages and past occupations.

The phone rang. I picked it up.

"Jack McMorrow?"

"Yes."

"This is Melanie. Melanie Mullaney."

"Oh, hi. I was just about to call you. This very minute. I had a couple more questions, little things. Like how long you've lived in Florence, that kind of stuff."

"Yeah, well—"

She faltered.

"Okay, but the reason I'm calling, I mean, I'm calling because, it's about Bobby."

"What about him?"

"Well, um, I'm not sure how . . . Well, he's gone."

Ten

I SAT THERE, a little confused.

"Gone where?" I said.

"Just gone. Gone to, uh, oh God, gone to Lewiston. I mean, oh my God."

Melanie's voice broke. She breathed heavily, holding off a sob.

"Well, I don't really understand. What does that—"

"He went last night. Right after you left. Coyote went, too. In Bobby's Subaru."

"And he didn't come back?"

"No, and he hasn't called and he said he'd call and he'd be back late. I mean late last night. Now it's almost three and he hasn't called or anything."

"What was he going to do in Lewiston?"

Melanie hesitated.

"He had business," she said.

"So, I guess I'm not sure . . . Have you called the police? I mean, if you're that worried, they could spot that Subaru down there, I'm sure. You know where he was going? You think he had an accident on the way home or something? I don't mean to be rude, Melanie, but I don't get what you're—"

"I can't call the police. Mr. McMorrow, Jack, I think we need to talk. Something's wrong here."

"You don't want to talk on the phone? Is that it?"

"I can't. I mean, oh God, you must think I'm crazy. I don't know what to do. I'm all alone here and—"

"Well, I'd be glad to talk to you."

"How 'bout the restaurant in Madison? I can be there in an hour. I know this sounds nuts but you'll understand when I explain it more."

"It'll take me an hour to get there. I've got to file this story. Um, does this change the story, do you think?"

"The story," Melanie said. "Oh, yeah. I don't know. It, uh, I don't know. Oh, God, I don't know. Maybe you'll know. I'll see you there in an hour. Okay? An hour?"

I looked at my watch. I said okay. I hung up the phone and looked at the computer screen, humming away as if everything were just fine, the deluded contraption.

Something told me I'd been right to keep the Mullaneys out of the lead.

Melanie was sitting at the counter by the cash register when I came through the door, but she swung off the stool with her mug in her hand and, without speaking, walked to a table on the far wall. The table was halfway between the front window and the kitchen door, underneath a painting of a deer vaulting a fallen tree.

Melanie pulled out a chair and sat down without saying hello. I sat down across from her. We both kept our jackets on. Melanie looked over toward the counter so that I saw her in profile. Her hair looked like it had been pulled back hurriedly and her skin was taut.

She looked haggard. Finally she looked at me.

"You must think I'm nuts," Melanie said.

"Not yet," I said.

I smiled. She didn't. A young woman in jeans and a University of Maine sweatshirt banged out of the swinging metal doors, coffeepot in hand, and swooped down on the table. She asked how we were doing that day. I said we were doing all right. Melanie said nothing.

The coffee was strong and Melanie took a swallow from her refilled cup. She drank it black. No green tea this time.

I sipped my coffee and waited.

"This has to be off the record," Melanie began, both hands wrapped around her mug.

"Okay," I said. I was easy.

"Bobby didn't come home last night. And I know you've probably heard this before, but he doesn't do that. I mean, ever."

"Where'd he go?"

"He went to Lewiston."

I must have looked unimpressed.

"It isn't what it sounds like," Melanie said.

"It doesn't sound like anything yet."

"Yeah, well, what is it in these things most of the time? The guy goes to some bar and gets drunk and goes off with some barfly."

"And then doesn't dare to come home," I said.

"He wasn't going to a bar. Not to drink, I mean."

"Oh?"

"He was going on, I guess you'd call it business."

"Selling life insurance on the side?"

Melanie blanched.

"Sorry," I said. "Didn't mean to upset you."

She swallowed coffee. I noticed her fingernails were cracked and a little dirty.

"Well, Bobby was going down there on business. We have this, well, sort of business enterprise thing, I guess you'd call it."

"You sell pot," I said.

"You figured that out?"

"I can't picture Bobby and Coyote selling Amway. Is he gone, too?"

"Yeah."

"So what's the deal?"

Melanie looked around. The waitress had disappeared behind the swinging doors again. Somewhere back there, dishes clattered.

"This guy owed us some money. A couple thousand dollars. We fronted it for him. For a week. He was supposed to sell the pot and make his money and pay us back."

"Trusting souls," I said.

"It was the second time. He came through fine last time."

"What kind of volume are we talking about here?"

Melanie shrugged.

"Not huge. I mean, enough to support us. We make, I don't know, six or seven thousand every fall."

"A nice Christmas Club."

"It pays the bills."

"And beats really working in the woods."

"Hey, it's not easy. You've got to grow the stuff. And processing. That's practically a full-time job. You ought to try it if you don't think so. And people are very demanding these days. You can't deliver ragweed."

"Unless you want your legs broken."

Melanie flinched.

"Sorry," I said.

"Yeah, well, I don't know what happened. But this is the thing. Bobby was supposed to be back because this other customer was going to call and Bobby really didn't want to miss him. Well, he did call. I had to say Bobby wasn't around. This guy was gonna pay up front so we didn't want to lose him. No more of this chasing people for it."

"Is that was Bobby was doing? Chasing somebody?"

"Not like he was out to hurt the guy. He was just going down to talk about when the guy could come up with the money."

"With Coyote just going to keep him company?"

Melanie looked at me but didn't answer.

"So who's the guy they were going to see?" I asked.

"Some kid we called Paco."

"Is that his only name?"

"It may just be his name for this deal. These guys change names all the time."

"You don't even know the guy's name but you fronted him two thousand dollars. For drug dealers, you guys are sure unsuspecting."

"But we're not drug dealers," Melanie said. "This is an herb. It grows in the woods."

"Right. Like truffles. And it goes for three grand a pound. God, how could you be selling that much and go on with this public legalization thing?"

"We believe in that."

"Legalization would put you out of business, wouldn't it?"

"It would be worth it."

"And in the meantime, it's a pretty good cover."

Melanie shrugged.

"That's what Bobby said. Who would think we'd dare, you know? It doesn't hurt anybody. It's not like we're selling whiskey or vodka or something. It's a victimless crime."

"That sounds like Bobby talking."

"Yeah, well, you spend all these years with the guy, you're bound to sound a little alike. And it's true, don't you think? Who does this hurt?"

"I don't know. Maybe the guy above Paco sells more than pot. Maybe he uses his profits to buy crack. Downtown Lewiston isn't the Country Life Fair. Where'd they go? Lisbon Street?"

"I don't know. I just have an address. Poplar Street. A number and an apartment. I almost didn't have that. Bobby crumpled it up and threw it in the woodstove."

"And you fished it out of the flames?"

"The stove wasn't going," Melanie said. "I was, I don't know, I had a funny feeling about this one."

There was a clatter and the doors swung open and the woman in the sweatshirt swooped in again. She asked again and I said we were doing fine. Melanie looked like she could use a cigarette.

"Oh, shit," she said, and swallowed more coffee instead.

"So they just didn't come back?"

"Nope. Nothing. Not last night. Not today."

"And when they go off to put the muscle on nonpaying customers, they usually call so you can remind them to wear their galoshes?"

"Come on, McMorrow. I thought you could help me."

"Help you? How?"

"I'll pay you to go down there and see if there's any sign of them. I don't know, ask around. It's what you do, right?"

I looked at her and shook my head.

"I ask around with a notebook in my hand. I don't know who this Paco is, but something tells me he won't be impressed with a press pass."

"I'll pay you a thousand dollars just to go and check. I mean, what am I supposed to do? I can't call the—"

"Police," I said.

"Well, I can't," Melanie said. "I just don't know what to do. You could do it. I know you could."

"What about all your pot buddies?"

"Who am I going to call? Roberta? Kathy? Sam? He could bring his son. Darrin could do it but you know what he'd do? He's facing these drug charges. He'd turn us in in a second. That's what I've got. The people I can trust can't do it. The people who could do it I can't trust. And God almighty, I don't know where my husband is."

"Occupational hazard," I said.

"Goddamn it, I love him," Melanie said, and she looked like she was going to cry, but caught herself. She gave her eyes a quick wipe. As she did, three guys came in and gave us a once-over on the way to their stools.

"Cops?" I said.

Melanie looked.

"Too old," she said. "They don't use anybody over thirty-five."

"Don't they watch you pretty closely?"

"And Bobby lets them see what he wants them to see. A couple of plants. It isn't worth the hassle for them to have him in a courtroom for little stuff. He'd turn it into a three-ring circus."

"Kind of a strong personality, isn't he?" I asked.

Melanie knew what I really meant. That he was domineering. Didn't let her finish a sentence.

"Hey, I signed on for the duration, you know? And he did, too, warts and all."

"Till death do you—"

I caught myself.

"I've got to know what's going on," she said.

"What about Stephen?"

"I can't send him down there."

"No," I said. "I mean, is he worried?"

Melanie looked away.

"They never clicked. I don't know why. Stephen was two. Just never liked Bobby, even back then."

"He wants to be like everybody else," I said. "Most kids do."

"Yeah, well, there's only so much I can do," Melanie said. "And I've done it."

"In this thing here, there's only so much *I* can do."

"Couldn't you just ask around, sort of?"

"I'm not a detective. You could hire somebody who finds people for a living."

"Isn't that what reporters do?"

"Sort of, I guess. Sometimes."

I shifted in my chair. Fiddled with the place mat, which had a maze printed on it for kids.

"I feel like I already know you, Jack," Melanie said, her gaze direct this time. "And this sounds weird but I feel like I can trust you. I could try to find somebody else but it would be a completely new person. And it's been, it'll be twenty-four hours tonight. I mean, he's out there somewhere."

"They are, you mean."

"I only care about one. I only care about Bobby."

"So why does this Coyote guy live with you?"

Melanie pursed her lips, tugged at her red hair.

"Because Bobby said he was a good friend. He showed up and he needed a place to stay."

"For the rest of his life?"

"Bobby said if Coyote went back to Massachusetts he'd be killed."

I thought about that for a moment.

"You people aren't what you're cracked up to be, are you?" I said.

"I am," Melanie said. "Bobby is, pretty much. Coyote . . . I don't know. He can be very nice. Thoughtful, sometimes. He just doesn't say much. I think he got kicked around a lot as a kid. I mean bad."

"He isn't a kid anymore," I said.

We sat there for one more cup of coffee. The guys at the counter looked us over on the way out, and then the bell on the door jingled and we were alone again.

"So what do you want me to do? Find out if he ever got there? Find out if this place exists? Make sure he didn't wind up in a topless bar?"

"Anything's better than nothing," Melanie said.

I looked into my coffee.

"I don't know. It's going to be hard for me to be there, as a reporter I mean."

"What about as a friend?"

"That's when things get dangerous," I said. "A press pass is kind of like a shield. Without that . . ."

I thought about it while Melanie fingered her empty cup.

"How's this for a deal?" I said. "You keep your money. I write the story. But the whole story, including what I find in Lewiston. I'll write it without your names. Different names. Not use the town of Florence."

Melanie considered it.

"That's the only way you'll do it?"

"Yup."

She considered some more.

"Sounds okay to me, but Bobby isn't here to say yes or no."

"We'll cross that bridge later."

She took a sip of stone-cold black coffee.

"Okay."

"I need the address."

Melanie bent down and came up with a bag that probably was made of hemp. She dug in the bag and came up with a small rough cotton sack with a drawstring. She probably brought water in a goat's bladder.

In the sack was a wrinkled piece of paper, torn off a spiral-bound pad. Melanie unfolded it.

"Seventeen Poplar Street. Third. That's all it says."

"How do you know it's Lewiston?"

"Bobby said he was going to Lewiston."

"Maybe he was lying."

"He doesn't lie," Melanie said.

My eyebrows must have jumped.

"To me," she said.

On that ringing note of endorsement, I stood up. I left two dollars on the table and Melanie left one. The woman in the sweatshirt came out from the kitchen and told us to have a nice day. I told her to do the same. Her chances seemed better than mine.

Outside, log trucks and pickups rumbled by. The sun had skidded down behind the hills to the west and it was getting colder. The main street seemed like something out of the Wild West. Spruce trees instead of sagebrush. We stood at the curb.

"I've got to go into Skowhegan and get Stephen at school," Melanie said, digging into her bag for keys.

"What, he stayed late for target practice?"

"Detention," she said. "He got in a fight."

"Over what?"

"He wouldn't tell me. I'll take him to Burger King and try again."

"Ply him with french fries."

"Right," Melanie said. "So when will you go down there?"

"I don't know. Maybe tomorrow. I'll call you tomorrow night."

She nodded and walked up the street toward where the Chevy with the wooden bed was parked. I watched as she hoisted herself up into the cab, kicked the motor to life.

There was a puff of blue smoke, as if starting the thing were some sort of magic trick. Voilà.

The truck rumbled toward me and Melanie slowed as she rolled down her window.

"That's another thing," she said. "He's got my car. I hate this tank."

And with a rueful frown, she went on her way. The truck went straight at the next light, heading for Skowhegan. I walked across the street and got in the Toyota.

And proceeded directly to Florence. Not once—well, maybe once—did I wonder what the hell I had gotten into.

Eleven

I PULLED INTO the Mullaneys' road, drove fifty feet or so and then backed the truck into an overgrown tote road that ended fifty feet into the woods. When the truck was out of sight, I shut it off and opened the glove box. I dug around and took out a yellow plastic flashlight and a small compass, the kind that pins to your jacket. I stuck it in my pocket instead and got out and started off down the driveway. The driveway ran almost due east, perpendicular to the main road. That meant the way out, even if I was bushwhacking, was roughly due west.

Natty Bumppo. On assignment.

In the woods, it was almost dark. The trees had receded into deep shadows, and stood like a watchful, swaying army that had parted to let me pass. I stopped and listened. Heard snaps. Cracks. The creak of branches rubbing together. A scuffling in the leaves.

I walked on.

Every hundred yards or so I stopped and stood by the side of the road and listened. The sound of the woods seemed like a din. I heard the rustling quickstep of a deer, somewhere above me. A loud crack in the trees to my left.

I waited. Listened. Kept walking. As I started up the rise that led to the house, I slowed.

The house was dark. The Ford truck was still next to the garden. I stopped and listened and heard only the chickens making a muffled clucking in their coop. A couple of Rottweilers would have complicated things. I was grateful for Bobby's allergies.

Without them, it was simple. I'd go in the house and find Bobby sacked out on the couch. He'd tell me he'd had car trouble and he'd tried to call home but the phone must have been off the hook, because the line was busy. All night and all day. I'd tell him his wife was worried sick and he'd thank me for my concern and I'd go home, having saved myself a trip to Lewiston.

"In your dreams," I said.

I moved slowly toward the door and stopped. If the paths in the woods were rigged with thread, how did the Mullaneys protect their house? I stepped to the door and turned on the flashlight, playing it up and down the jamb. There was nothing sticking out. No paper. No thread. I turned the light off and moved to the front of the house and looked through the big windows. Inside, the place was dark and still. I went back to the door, stepped on the back stair and slid the metal latch up.

The door swung open.

I waited.

It was quieter in the house than in the woods. I went up the stairs and into the house and shut the door behind me. Listened. Walked into the room. Listened some more. Took another step and kicked a potato, which rolled across the floor like a bowling ball.

I froze. Listened. Nothing.

Nobody here but us chickens.

I went to the kitchen first and played the light across the shelves. There were glass jars of dry beans, big and small, light and dark. Jars of spices and little seeds. Jars of honey. Jars of flour and sugar. Brown, of course.

I opened the refrigerator and there were more jars and bowls in there. Nothing that could possibly have come from a supermarket. It looked like leftovers from the first Thanksgiving. I shut the door.

Maybe Bobby had gone on a junk food binge.

From the kitchen, a narrow hall led somewhere. I followed it and it came out in a very small room with a mattress on the floor, a couple of pairs of boots lined up and a frame-pack leaning against the wall. There were books lined up beside the pack and I played the light over the titles. Edward Abbey. Thoreau. Something about living alone in Alaska. One about rafting the Amazon.

The library of someone who liked to be alone in the woods. Stephen.

I looked some more but the room was spartan. There was a metal foot locker on the floor, lid open, stacked with clothes. The clothes felt coarse, from years of drying on a line, washing who knows where. On the floor next to the foot locker was a stack of issues of *Guns and Ammo* magazine. I looked on the address labels for a clue. The magazines were sent to Stephen Corso, General Delivery, Florence, Maine. So he hadn't taken the Mullaney name.

That didn't surprise me, and didn't help me, either. With the beam of the flashlight playing on the rough wood floor, I walked slowly back to the kitchen. Another narrow hall-way led from the rear of the kitchen straight back. I followed it and came to a door. Eased the latch up and gave it a small shove. I stepped back as the door fell open.

No gunshot. No crossbow. I played the light across the entrance. No thread across the doorway.

I walked into the room gingerly. This time the mattress was on a piece of plywood. The plywood was up on cement blocks. If they wanted to get rid of somebody, they tied them to Coyote's bed and tossed them in a swamp.

There was a dark blue sleeping bag on the mattress, which was covered with a blue sheet. The sleeping bag looked like an expensive one. Maybe Coyote was a charter member of the Valley Outing Club.

On the floor next to the mattress was a pile of newspa-pers. I flipped through it. It was mostly *Boston Herald*s, a

couple of *Globe*s, all from the last month. There were no
Maine newspapers. There were no magazines. There was a
beat-up bureau against the wall at the foot of the bed. On
top of the bureau there were a kerosene lamp and six books,
three hardcovers. They were all by Stephen King. They
looked well read.

I opened the top drawer of the bureau. There were match-
books, a supermarket brand that told me nothing. There
were a couple of pens. A pencil with a broken lead. An old
black penknife. Two tape cassettes, both early Rolling
Stones. Good taste but no clues.

Maybe if I played them backward.

The second drawer was for socks, mostly ragg wool and
white cotton. There was nothing under the socks except
more socks. There was nothing in the third drawer except
underwear. Coyote wore briefs.

In the bottom drawer there were flannel work shirts,
neatly folded and arranged in two stacks. I lifted the stacks
and felt the wooden drawer bottom but nothing else. I
dropped the shirts back in, thumbing through them as I
went. It was in the second stack that I heard something. Or
felt something. A crinkle.

I felt between the shirts until I heard it again, then felt
it. The shirt was on the bottom. It was black and tan and
looked old. I slid it out and felt again and reached into the
pocket. And pulled out a folded twenty-dollar bill.

Coyote's mad money? A bill that had gone through the
wash? I looked at the twenty. It didn't appear faded, the
way paper money does after a few turns in the spin cycle.
It was crisply folded. I opened it up and held it under the
light. One side was normal. Someone had written something on the other.

Bernie. Please take me with you. Luv ya. Tanya.

Bernie? Coyote didn't seem like a Bernie.

But if he was, in fact, Bernie, I had just learned one
thing. Tanya loved him or at least at one time had said she
did. And she had expensive letterhead.

I folded the bill and put it back in the pocket of the shirt.
The shirt, I folded the best I could and slid back in the

drawer. The stack of shirts went on top of it. I closed the drawer and looked over the rest of the room. There was a stack of folded dungarees on the floor by the door. I checked the pockets but didn't find any money, inscribed or otherwise. Next to the dungarees were two pair of work boots, one black, one brown. There was nothing in the shoes. Nothing up my sleeve. Presto change-o.

I went back to the kitchen and up the stairs.

The stairs were narrow and steep, like stairs on a ship. I walked up slowly and quietly and stood in the center of the master bedroom, the honeymoon suite. There were windows on three walls and a crude skylight fitted into the sloping roof. Drywall had been hung on two-thirds of the ceiling but there was one section where the foil backing of the insulation showed. The place was not plush.

Bobby and Melanie slept on a double-sized futon on the floor. There was a puffy black quilt folded neatly on the end of the futon, and the sheets were arranged neatly, too. Next to the bed were shoes, his and hers. There were books in wooden crates, two crates on Melanie's side and one on Bobby's. I scanned the titles. Melanie read books about holistic health and herbal remedies, and travel books, which seemed odd. Europe on a budget, Australia's Barrier Reef, backpacking in Thailand. Bobby read spy novels and, curiously enough, a book about "maximizing your assets."

The first step was to go to Lewiston and get the guy who was holding some of your assets to cough them up. The rest was easy.

I played the light across the room. Along one wall there were hooks that held pants and shirts, all lined up like raincoats at the fire station. Boots and shoes and sneakers on the floor along that wall. A small, beat-up bureau, painted blue. I pulled on the top drawer and it stuck, so the whole thing started to topple. I caught it. Turned the light out and listened. Turned the light back on and eased the drawer open.

It was women's underwear, mostly cotton, mostly white, with some black mixed in. I overcame my embarrassment and burrowed my hand under the pile. Pulled out a tube of something and it wasn't toothpaste. Feeling like a pervert, I put it back.

The next drawer was for her socks. The one below that was for Bobby's boxers, mostly dark colors. The bottom drawer held his socks. Nothing more.

I stood for a moment and gave the room a last glance. Looked back toward the books. Bobby's. Melanie's. There was one in one of her crates that looked like a journal. I walked over and bent down and pulled it out. It was a small photo album, one picture per page.

A younger Melanie with long shaggy hair and bangs, standing in front of a stoop. A younger Bobby with hair longer than Melanie's. He was wearing mirrored sunglasses and sitting on a motorcycle. An old Honda. A big one. Two pictures of a little kid. Stephen with a plastic tricycle. Stephen just standing there, hands hanging down in front of him, looking lost. Melanie and Bobby, arm in arm, and Stephen off to the side, as if he'd snuck into the picture. The same faraway eyes. I looked at them.

Then heard something.

Outside.

I turned off the light and listened. Couldn't hear anything. I went down the stairs in the dark, eased my way into the kitchen and waited. Still nothing. Then a rattling. Chickens clucking.

The back door was off the kitchen. I went to it and slid the latch up. It was open. I stepped out and closed it behind me. Stood there and watched. Listened. The chicken house was off to my left. I walked to that corner of the house and peered out. They were still clucking but I didn't see anybody. I went as far as the front of the house and stopped again. There was no one in sight. No vehicles. No lights. Just the amorphous blackness. I walked toward the driveway. Something moved in the brush to my right and I jumped.

A raccoon. The chickens clucked.

"Sorry, girls," I said. "You're on your own."

●　　●　　●

I walked up the road in the dark, watching the woods and thinking. I considered why it was I had come here. I was looking for something, anything, that would tell me that Bobby and Melanie weren't what they seemed: a couple of small-time pot growers, maybe not as naive as I'd thought at first glance, but likable in other ways. Bobby, up here in the woods but still running on streetwise chutzpah. Melanie, small and resilient, living without electricity and running water, independent of everything but her husband. Stephen, misplaced and resentful, being groomed for a career as a jungle sniper.

And, of course, Coyote—Bernie to his friends—living in exile in the Maine woods, getting his big-city fix by reading classified ads in the *Boston Herald*.

Were they all what they seemed? Or when I started knocking on doors in Lewiston, would I uncover yet another layer?

I walked faster, silent as I stepped from rock to rock. Missing a rock, I stumbled and considered turning the light on. Then there was a pale shadowed opening up ahead and I could see the space that was the road. I went off the road to the left and got in the truck and rolled the window down and waited. There were no lights showing, and on this stretch of road you could hear a car a mile away. I didn't want to be caught in Melanie's headlights. For that matter, I didn't want to pass her on the road.

I'd have to find another route home, I thought as I eased the truck out of the woods. Maybe over to Farmington, then east on Route 2, south to Fairfield and Waterville. If I was going to Lewiston anyway, maybe I'd drive down to Portland and spend the night with Roxanne, wake up fresh and—

Headlights came out of nowhere and lit up my rearview mirror. Then they wigwagged and a blue light blipped on.

"Shoot," I said.

I pulled the truck over, and the lights hung behind me, close, and then more lights shot out of the darkness in front of me. They rushed toward me and I squinted against the glare and doors began opening. First theirs. Then mine.

"Out of the vehicle," a voice shouted, behind me, to my left. "On the ground. Hands above your head."

"Hey, I don't know what—"

"Out of the truck and down, please," the voice shouted again and I swung my legs out and saw a guy in jeans and a dark windbreaker that said "MAINE DEA" in stenciled white. He was holding a gun, on his right side, pointed at the ground.

His hand grabbed my shoulder and he guided me to the pavement and I said, "Hey, come on," but put my hands against my ears as hands ran across my back, my legs, fingers muscled down inside my boots.

"Thank you," the guy said.

"He's clean," a voice said, and another voice said, "Okay, sir, we'd like you to stand up."

I stood and they were on each side of me, two cops, one young and thin with a month-old beard and very light blue eyes and another, older, big and thick and sort of pudgy. The older one was wearing a jacket, too. His face was flushed.

"I'm going to ask you to come this way, sir, and get in this vehicle," he said.

"Who the hell are you?"

"Special agent. Maine Drug Enforcement Agency."

"Let me see a badge or an ID or something."

He hesitated, then fished inside his jacket and pulled out a leather wallet and handed it to me. I opened it up. Inside was a gold badge that said, "Maine Drug Enforcement." It looked real. So did he. I handed the wallet back to him and he shoved it back inside his windbreaker. Then he told me to come with him, so I did.

I followed him and went and sat in the front passenger seat of his truck, a red and white Chevy Blazer with New York plates. When he got in, he put his police radio on the dash. There was no police radio in the truck and the blue light was on the floor, connected to the cigarette lighter by a cord.

"You have some ID, sir?"

I took out my wallet and handed it to him. He opened it and my driver's license flopped out. He studied it for a moment. Outside, the younger guy was looking inside the cab of my truck with his flashlight. The cops behind my truck had gotten out of a black van and were shining their lights into the back window of the camper cap.

"This isn't a Ranger," I heard one of them say.

"It's red, though. Black cap," the other one said.

"What about the warrant?"

The older guy handed me my wallet. I held it in front of me on my lap.

"You're a long way from home, Mr. McMorrow."

"You're Johnston."

"Small world," he said.

"No, just a small town."

"I thought you didn't want to come all the way to Somerset."

"Something unexpected came up," I said.

He looked at me. I looked back at him. He had gray in his sideburns. Broken blood vessels near his cheekbones.

"You got the wrong guy, didn't you," I said.

"Yup."

"Your search warrant is for somebody else, a different truck."

"Yeah, but I'm going to ask you for permission to look through yours."

"Go right ahead. All I've got is empty beer cans."

"Have you been drinking?" he asked.

"You've got to be kidding."

He picked up the radio from the dash and said, "Go ahead. And kill all those lights."

The headlights went out, replaced by the glow of orange parking lights and fingering flashlight beams. I saw the back window of the cap swing up, heard the tailgate creak.

"So what's the deal, Sergeant?" I said.

"We're involved in an active investigation."

"Beats an inactive one."

"How 'bout you, Mr. McMorrow. What are you doing up this way? You don't have to tell me."

"I know that."

"I thought you knew that," he said.

"I'll tell you anyway. Just like I said. I'm reporting. Doing a story on the marijuana legalization movement up here. For the *Boston Globe*."

He looked at me. The look in his eyes told me to prove it.

"Oh yeah?" he said.

"Oh yeah," I said.

"What's your editor's name?"

"Tom Wellington. New England editor."

"Where's he work?"

"The *Globe*'s main office. Dorchester."

"You got his phone number?"

"Matter of fact, I do. I'll give it to you. You can call him. Tell him I deserve more money."

"Anything else?"

"No, just tell him the story's going well and—"

"No, do you have anything else you can show me?" Johnston said.

"An old press pass."

"Could I see it?"

I took it out of my wallet and handed it to him. While he put a light on it, I dug out the scrap of paper with Wellington's number. I handed that to him, too. He turned the press pass over and read the back. Then looked at the front one more time.

"*New York Times*?"

"Five years ago."

"You got more miles on you now, huh?"

He looked at me, his eyes glancing over the long scar on my cheek.

"Where'd you get that? Covering a war?"

"In Kennebec County."

"Your name's starting to sound familiar," he said.

He handed the card back to me, then rubbed his nose. The younger cop who had been with him walked up and Johnston hit the button and his window zipped down.

"Nothing," the younger cop said.

"No shit," Johnston said. "Mr. McMorrow's a reporter.
Boston Globe."

"Just a freelancer," I said. "I live in Waldo County."

I tried to look harmless. The younger cop was not reassured.

He looked at Johnston. Johnston stared straight ahead.
The younger cop looked at me.

"How ya doin'?" he said.

I reached into my jacket pocket and took out a notebook
and pen.

"Just fine," I said. And I grinned.

The younger cop sat in the backseat. I sat with Johnston in
the front. The van that had pulled me over left, heading
north where there was nothing but woods and darkness.
After a few minutes, Johnston turned on the heater.

They said they had information from a confidential informant that a load of marijuana was to be taken by truck
from this property sometime this week. The pot was supposed to be in a load of vegetables bound for a farmers'
market. The vegetables were supposed to be in the back of
a red Ford Ranger pickup or similar pickup with a black
aluminum cap. My truck was a red Toyota and the cap was
dark blue.

Close enough in the dark.

"How much pot?" I asked.

Johnston shrugged.

"A few pounds. We wouldn't sit up here for a couple
ounces. We have information that people up here are moving moderate amounts, mostly to buyers down south."

"And I didn't even have a rutabaga."

"Nope. But I'm still going to ask you some questions,"
Johnston said.

"Likewise, I'm sure."

He asked me how I knew the Mullaneys and I told him.
He asked me if I had any knowledge of marijuana being
grown in the area and I said I wouldn't comment on that.
He asked me if the Mullaneys were home and I said no.
He asked me if I knew where they were and I said Melanie

had gone to get her son at school but she'd be home soon.
He asked me what I was doing at the house and I said,
"Nothing."

My turn.

I asked him how many cops he had working this part of
Somerset County and he said a few. Scrawling in my notebook, I asked him how this area compared with others in
the state in terms of marijuana growing and he said it was
probably the most active, but not for long. I asked him why
he said that and he said police had turned the heat up in
Somerset County.

"So you arrest a few?"

"And some of the others decide it isn't worth the risk.
The hard-cores just move."

"Why Maine?"

"Look around you, McMorrow. This is one of those
places where you can do just about anything and nobody's
gonna notice."

"And the ones who do leave you alone," I said.

"Right. The law up here is something very far away."

"But you're here."

"Now we are. But when we first started doing operations
up here, turning informants, some of these people we arrested couldn't believe it. It was like we had no right to
enforce the law here."

"You believe in what you're doing?"

He paused, his eyes narrowing.

"Yeah, I do."

"Why's that?"

" 'Cause I've seen what drugs can do to people."

He paused, staring off through the windshield. I waited.
Waited some more. I could feel it coming and it did.

"I'm gonna tell you something before you go out making these people out to be a bunch of hippies. Peace, love
and all that. My father was a drunk. My oldest son ended
up in a friggin' rehab hospital. He's a great kid but he
started getting high in high school, and he liked it and that
was it. Quit football, had to repeat tenth grade. Then he
started doing coke and it just latched right onto him like I

don't know what. Something about his chemistry, you know? Body chemistry or something. He just couldn't shake it. It was like this thing eating him up inside.''

He stopped. The cop in the back was frozen in his seat, listening. I scrawled in my notebook.

''So what happened?'' I asked.

''He went through hell. The family went through hell. He's okay now but I don't know for how long. Once that stuff has its claws in you, it never lets go.''

''But that's not marijuana.''

''It's the same friggin' thing,'' he exploded. ''Same idea. You take a drug to go somewhere else from where you are, from reality, the real world. The pot didn't ruin David but it sure as hell started him down the road. Like I said on the phone, this goddamn bullshit about nature and all this sacred herb shit. Poison ivy's an herb, for God's sake. Heroin comes from goddamn flowers. Pot wasn't good for him. He didn't learn. He didn't talk. He threw away all the things he'd been working on for so long.''

I waited a moment as his mind raced through the past.

''But what about tobacco? Alcohol? They do more damage.''

He looked at me. Hard.

''I can't do anything about that, Mr. McMorrow,'' he said. ''They're not against the law.''

We sat there for a minute in awkward silence.

''I'd like to use that,'' I said, finally.

''No names,'' he said. ''Just 'one police officer.' ''

''I don't even know your name.''

''Fine.''

He looked toward the Mullaneys' driveway.

''So Batman and Robin aren't in there, huh?''

''Nope. Not that I could see.''

''You know who his sidekick really is?'' he asked.

''Coyote? No.''

''We don't either. But we're gonna find out.''

Twelve

THE ROAD FROM Florence to South Portland was a long dark strip that meandered through blackened woods, past blank shadowed fields. The woods were interrupted by sudden little towns. A cluster of streetlamps, a store with a neon beer sign, light flickering dimly in the windows of houses and trailers like candles in sod houses. And then there was more road and the tunnel chiseled out of the dark by the headlights as if everything else had been taken over for the night by birds and bugs and animals.

I drove in silence, fighting off the urge to stop in one of the outpost stores for a beer. In between fighting, I replayed the events of the day over and over in my mind. Melanie. Stephen's room. Johnston and his son. Over and over, and then I got on the interstate at Gray and ten minutes later a gray glow began to appear in the sky to the south, and then, out of nowhere, there were the lights of Portland, shimmering like Las Vegas.

It was seven-fifteen when I crossed the bridge into South Portland, circled back to the harbor and pulled up in front of Roxanne's condo. Her Subaru wagon was there. Her lights were on. I went to the front door and rang the bell, then unlocked the door and went in.

"Honey, I'm home," I called.

"I'm up here," Roxanne called back.

I went up the carpeted stairs two at a time, turned left and right and into the bedroom.

"What?" I said. "No negligee?"

"You should hope not. I didn't know you were coming."

"You could get gussied up every night. Just in case. You know, those high heels with the little puffy things on them."

"A cold day in hell . . ." Roxanne said.

"Where's your sense of romance?"

"Where's my glass of wine?"

Roxanne was sitting cross-legged on the bed. She was barefoot, wearing jeans and a plain white T-shirt, and there were legal pads and official-looking documents scattered all around her. I went to her and she leaned toward me and we kissed.

"Wine me," she said.

I went down to the kitchen and opened a bottle of California merlot from a winery I'd never heard of. The label was very pretty. I glanced at it, then filled the biggest wineglass I could find, and took a sip. It wasn't bad but the label was better. I took a Shipyard ale out of the refrigerator and headed for the stairs, then stopped and turned around and got another one, just in case.

Me and the Scouts.

Back upstairs. Roxanne hadn't moved. I handed her the glass and, shoving some papers aside, sat on the edge of the bed.

"What's all this?"

"Those two kids I was telling you about."

"The one with the kid who went to get Cheerios for his sister?"

"And the mother who keeps forgetting to come home," Roxanne said. "I'm getting the petition ready."

"Petition saying what?"

"That we want to keep the kids. They're in temporary foster care now."

"Mom's memory isn't improving?"

"She's burnt."

"And still burning?"

"Word is she's discovered crack now."

"Not exactly on the cutting edge, is she?"

"This is Maine," Roxanne said.

"The way life should be," I said.

I picked up the closest paper. It was a psychological evaluation done by an outfit in Portland. At the top it said it was confidential and privileged, to be interpreted by "a competent clinician only."

"What'd they find out?"

"I can't tell you," Roxanne said.

"If you could tell me, what would you tell me?"

"That it says he's developing a psychotic condition."

"At nine years old?"

"Yup."

"From being left alone?"

"He was abused by his father when he was little," Roxanne said.

"He's still little."

"That's right."

I read on and shook my head. Impulsiveness. Low frustration tolerance. Angry. Defiant.

"Hypervigilant style. What's that mean?"

"He doesn't trust anybody so he doesn't ever let his guard down," Roxanne said.

"Nine years old. God. What about the little sister?"

"She's better but give her time."

I put the paper down. Roxanne sipped her wine.

"Sometimes I wonder how you can do this," I said.

"Sometimes I wonder how people can't."

"And you keep coming back for more."

"Speaking of which," Roxanne said.

I looked at her.

"More wine?" I asked.

This time, it was her turn to shake her head.

• • •

The papers were in a pile on the floor. My boxer shorts were missing in action. Roxanne's clothes were scattered around the room as if the house belonged to Auntie Em.

We ended up with our feet at the head of the bed. My heart was pounding and my head still spinning with images of Roxanne. Laughing, moving, pushing, devouring, slamming and then coming to a screeching halt.

Literally.

"You're gorgeous," I said, running my hand down her side, from her shoulder to her knee. And back.

"You're not so bad yourself."

"Pretty of you to think so."

"Where's that come from?" Roxanne asked, her head back, her breasts poised. I looked at her.

"Yike," I said.

"Yike?"

"Oh. No. That's Hemingway. The end of *The Sun Also Rises.*"

"Which comes from the Bible."

"Ecclesiastes," I said. " 'All the rivers run into the sea; yet the sea is not full.' "

"I love it when you quote Scripture."

"I love you all the time."

"And I love you all the time," Roxanne said. "Why don't you move in and be my concubine?"

"My funny concubine. That's a song, isn't it?"

"But if you keep that up, I'll have to gag you."

"Oh boy," I said. "Just don't lose the key to the handcuffs. I've got places to go, people to see."

"Name one."

"Well, tomorrow I have to go to Lewiston and look up a guy named Paco."

"What for?"

"Oh, well. It's sort of a long story."

Roxanne turned toward me.

"So go ahead," she said.

"Well, you know those pot guys you liked so much?"

"Yup."

"They're missing."

"What's the bad news?" Roxanne said.

I started with the phone call from Melanie. From there, I went on to coffee at the restaurant in Madison, my inspection of the Mullaneys' abode, and sitting in the undercover Blazer while Johnston told me abouthis son's drug problem.

Roxanne, still naked, had hoisted herself up on one elbow.

"You're nuts," she said.

"No, it'll be a good story. Better than just dueling propagandists from the two sides of this marijuana thing. Write about the nitty-gritty. The trail of the drug trade."

"Is littered with dead people."

"Not in Lewiston, Maine. This isn't New York."

"You think this Paco guy is going to be sitting on the porch saying 'Ayuh'?" Roxanne said.

"No, but—"

" 'Sure, Mr. Reporter. Come on in. I'll tell you what it's like to be a drug trafficker. It all started when I was three . . . ' "

"Rox—"

"Jack, I can't believe you're going to do this. Looking for guys who didn't come back from some drug deal?"

"It isn't a kilo of cocaine."

"It's drugs. It's money. It's a lot of money. It's people who go to prison if they get caught. It's people who carry guns."

"So I'll bring Clair."

"Jack."

She pulled herself up and knelt, facing me, her face flushed but this time for a different reason. I swung my legs over the edge of the bed.

"Don't go there," Roxanne said.

"Roxanne, you do more dangerous stuff every time you go to a house to ask about some kid being beat up."

"No, I—"

"It's true. I'm not taking kids away. I'm just asking if they've seen Bobby and Coyote. They say, 'No, never heard of 'em,' I'm out the door. I don't even have to go in the door.''

"Do you think they're going to tell you?" Roxanne asked. "Like, 'Yeah, they were here but we didn't have the money so we killed them. Any other questions?' "

"Roxanne," I said. "I just want to see it."

"Why?"

"Because it's real. And I need to get back into it once in a while. I don't cover wars. I don't cover gangs. I don't ride around Manhattan with a photographer and a police radio anymore. I want to write a good story. Make 'em sit up at the *Globe*. A good, real raw story. I'm sorry but that's the way I feel. It's what I do and if I can't keep pushing toward something then . . . then what am I doing?''

She looked at me, her eyes full of worry. Then she got up and went to the closet and took out a bathrobe, whipping the tie around her waist. At the door, Roxanne paused.

"You take care of yourself, because I love you," she said, without looking at me.

"You do the same," I said. "For the same reason."

So we had cheese and crackers and carrots and celery in front of the big window in the dining room, and watched the traffic on the ship channel. The *Scotia Prince* ferry was lit up like Disney World, and cars were loading into the bow for the overnight run to Halifax.

"We should do that sometime," I said.

"Yeah," Roxanne said, dressed now, her feet up on the coffee table.

"We could have dinner and a drink and then retire to our cabin."

"To read," she said.

"Twin beds."

"Of course."

"Do you think we'd rock the boat?"

"I doubt it," Roxanne said. "Our rocking would be countered by somebody else rocking the other way on the other side of the ship."

"If the ship is rocking, don't come knocking. Remember the last time? When we had Skip's sailboat?"

"Yeah."

She smiled softly.

"I think they picked us up on loran," I said.

"Was that the white thing that spun around, way up high?"

"No, I think the white thing was radar. But I'm not sure."

"Good thing we never left the dock," Roxanne said.

"Good thing."

I put my left arm around her shoulder. With my thumb, I could feel a pulse near her heart. I counted the beats, watched the cars roll up the ramp and onto the ferry like hippos onto Noah's Ark.

"They have slot machines on there," I said.

"What a waste of time and money."

"I know. But some people just love to gamble."

"I don't," Roxanne said.

I looked at her. Her face was in resigned repose.

"No more than I have to," she said.

I didn't say anything.

"You know why? Because I couldn't stand to lose. I wish you weren't going down there."

"I know."

"It doesn't seem worth it."

"Three hundred bucks? Maybe if I had one of those cushy state jobs . . ."

"You know what I mean. Those people just don't seem worth it. Thirty years old and all they care about is sitting around and getting stoned. Why don't they just grow up?"

"I don't know. I kind of admire them in a way. The woman with the MS. They're willing to fight for what they believe in. There's something sort of naive about them. It's like they think the government is corrupt and out to get them, but they haven't given up. They're not totally cynical. They believe they can change something they think is wrong."

Roxanne's eyebrows flickered skeptically.

"They should channel all that energy into something real instead of just getting high. Volunteer in a hospice. Work with kids. Cook in a shelter. I mean, get a life."

"I take it you still don't want to sign a petition."

"Just one to keep you here with me," Roxanne said, turning to me.

"I'll be back tomorrow night. What do you want to bet? I'll give you odds."

Roxanne just shook her head and looked out at the ferry and the lights and the red and white running lights of a sailboat, motoring toward the slips.

"There are some things you don't joke about," she said. "Losing you is one."

Roxanne was up at five to go over her documents one more time. I lay in bed and watched her for a while and then rolled out of bed. When I came out of the shower, I pulled on my jeans and sat on the edge of the bed again.

"I hope it goes well for you," I said.

"Thanks. I hope it goes well for them."

"They couldn't be in better hands."

"We'll see."

"Maybe I'll come back and help you celebrate."

Roxanne, still in her robe, smiled. A rueful smirk.

"The first time I did this, I had to go take the child. Me and another guy and a deputy. The little guy had been beaten and locked in a closet and all this horrible stuff but still, there he was hanging on to his mother's leg, sobbing. I got home, I just lost it. I cried all night."

Her eyes misted at the thought.

"But it's for the best."

"I need you to keep telling me that. I need you to be here to keep telling me that."

She reached out and took my hand.

"Be careful."

"You, too," I said. "Fight the good fight."

"Don't you."

"Don't worry. I'll call you. Or I'll just show up."

"I'd like that," Roxanne said, and she kissed me and then her face jelled, from soft to hard. As she got up and headed for the shower, she already had her armor on and was ready for battle.

She was a tough act to follow.

We drove out together, past the now empty ferry terminal, over the crest of downtown Portland and down the other side. I swung onto the interstate ramp and beeped once. Roxanne kept going up Forest Avenue. She beeped twice. I caught a last glimpse of her hand as it waved.

I drove north with Mozart on the radio, cranked up to be heard over the whir of the knobby tires. After ten minutes, the din became unbearable and I turned Mozart off. That left me with my thoughts of Roxanne, how lucky I was to have found her, how lucky I was to know her. I wondered where she got her resolve. From her father, a workaholic surgeon who died of a massive coronary while she was in college at Dartmouth? From her mother, who six years later still hadn't forgiven the God who took her husband away? What kept Roxanne on the front lines of this war to save children? The same need that was sending me to Lewiston?

I'd asked her, more than once, and the only answer I'd gotten had something to do with her father dying.

"Since Dad, I decided I had to make every minute count," Roxanne had said.

So she had been out there fighting for four years. Her colleagues had fallen away, burned out and worn out. But Roxanne didn't allow herself even that much self-pity. She didn't allow herself any at all.

Roxanne was a rush of focused, directed energy. When it was aimed at her job, it made her relentless. When it was aimed at me, as it had been the night before, it did the same.

I smiled, remembering. And a blast from the truck coming up beside me sent me back into my own lane.

So for the next hour, I tried to keep my mind off of Roxanne and on the road and the task at hand. It wasn't easy, but that was why they paid me the big money. Three hundred bucks to drive around the far reaches of Somerset County, to trek to Lewiston in search of Bobby and Coyote. But they weren't paying me for that one. That one, I'd throw in for free.

And I was excited about it, Roxanne's concerns notwithstanding. I didn't dismiss these people as easily as she did, but then I didn't spend my days the way she did. They were likable, except for Coyote of course, and even he was intriguing. I liked sitting in the Blazer with the cop. I even liked being patted down, as long as they didn't take my Swiss Army knife.

I didn't know that I'd learn anything knocking on doors in Lewiston, but I'd be out there. I'd be in the midst of the tumult, the whirling, twirling, wheeling, dealing that was life on this particular edge. I would be in the thick of it. Again.

I drove north to Augusta, over the black ribbon of the Kennebec River and up Route 3 toward Belfast. On Route 3, I followed the slow-moving foliage fans from New York and Pennsylvania until the turnoff in Palermo, where I swung west through the forgotten Waldo County hills toward the hollow that was home. When I turned onto the dump road in Prosperity, I almost hit Clair's big green Ford head-on.

He swerved, stopped and backed up. I did the same.

"Goddamn flatlander," Clair said.

"Sorry. I can't drive and listen to opera on public radio at the same time."

"Should've blown up the bridge at Kittery a long time ago. This state's going straight to hell."

"We'd sneak around and come in from the north at Jackman," I said. "What're you up to?"

"A run to the store in Albion. Ran out of shingle nails."

"I've got some."

"Ran out of shingles, too. Doing the back of the barn."

He pushed his John Deere cap back and smoothed his silver hair. The motor in the big Ford thumped dependably, like a dog's wagging tail.

"Where you been?"

"Roxanne's."

"I figured. What a fine girl like that sees in you is beyond me. One of life's eternal mysteries."

"You've said that."

"Have I?" Clair said.

"Once or twice."

"Must be getting senile."

Clair smiled and put both of his big hands on the steering wheel and stretched, his muscles like taut cords below the rolled sleeves of his flannel shirt.

"Gonna be around?" he said. "I'd let you hammer a few shingles, just so you don't forget what working is altogether."

"What do you mean? I'm working hard right now."

"You hide it well."

"Thank you."

"So you're not going to be around?"

"I just stopped to pick up clothes and a notebook and stuff. I've got to go to Lewiston."

"What's in Lewiston?" Clair asked.

"It's kind of a long story," I said, once again.

Clair reached over and put his truck in gear.

"I got time," he said, and pulled the Ford over to the side of the road. I backed up behind him and we shut our motors off and got out. We stood there under a two-hundred-year-old maple, with pale yellow leaves falling occasionally like flurries from the flat blue sky, and I told him my story.

Hat pushed back, hands in the pockets of his jeans, Clair listened until I was finished. And then he studied me for a moment.

"You're nuts," he said.

Clair wanted me to stay and help shingle his barn. Then he wanted to come with me and bring his Mauser deer rifle. Then he wanted to come without the Mauser. Then he said I was nuts, again.

"You're just gonna walk up and knock on some crazy druggie's door?" Clair said, as I came down the loft stairs, changed into jeans and a dark blue chamois shirt but not shaved.

"Right," I said.

"Just show him your reporter's card?"

"You've been talking to Roxanne."

"You ought to start listening to one of us."

"I do listen. And then I ignore what you say."

"Leave me the address. In case somebody wants to know," Clair said.

I took the paper out of my wallet, scrawled the address on a page of reporter's notebook and handed it to him.

"Amazing how far some people will go to avoid honest work," Clair said.

"About sixty miles," I said.

It turned out to be sixty-six, from my house to the Lewiston line, the other side of a town called Greene. After an hour and ten minutes of woods and farms, used-car lots and mini-malls, I slowed as I descended the Androscoggin River Valley and headed into the big city.

Somewhere in the back of my mind a voice said, "You're nuts."

I ignored that one, too.

Thirteen

LEWISTON WAS A tired mill city, home to forty thousand hardworking, clean-living people who went to work every morning, came home every night, had supper with the family and a big dinner after Sunday Mass in one of the big stone cathedrals that loomed over the narrow streets like castles.

I wasn't looking for those people.

The Lewiston street map in my atlas showed Poplar Street as being off Park Street, which ran one block above Lisbon Street, which was off Main just above the canal and the mills. I drove past the quiet neighborhoods east of the center of the city, in the direction of downtown. Suddenly the signs said I was on Main Street, which poured down toward the river like a sluiceway. The plain Victorian houses turned to law offices and medical buildings and then there was a big brick hospital on my right and as I stared up at it, I almost ran into a meter maid driving a three-wheel scooter.

Meter maids. The big city.

I missed Lisbon Street and swung left at the next street, Canal. I drove slowly, staring across the canal at the sprawling red brick mills. They had made shoes here. Blankets.

Bedspreads and towels. An entire city had grown up around churning machinery driven by the cold current of the Androscoggin River. With ornate clock towers and finely arched windows, the mills were graceful, dignified monuments to the industrial revolution.

Soon to be tombstones.

In cities like these across New England, people in government and business struggled to keep the few mills still operating. Others looked, mostly in vain, for uses for massive antique buildings that stretched for miles along riverfronts. This was an uphill battle because the mills had long ago outlived their usefulness. There was no reason to make things in Maine, New Hampshire, Massachusetts or Connecticut when you could make them far cheaper in Guatemala, the Dominican Republic or the Republic of China.

Nobody needs a Maine river to make shoes. They just need a hundred hardworking Koreans.

Times changed, turning cities into museums populated by those who could still make a decent life and living, but more and more by people who had given up on the idea or had never had it at all.

And here they were.

As I swung up onto lower Lisbon Street, I was hit by a blast of déjà vu. Men stood in clumps of two or three outside bars with blacked-out windows. A tired hooker clip-clopped down the sidewalk in heels, stockings and a black leather skirt. When she walked by me, I could see that her hair was dyed red with a gray band of roots. She looked like somebody's grandmother, playing dress-up.

There were pawnshops and porn shops. A sign that advertised peep shows and adult videos, Triple X. A guy wheeled out of a bar with empty beer cases on a dolly, and headed for a beer truck to reload. Just up the block, a guy in a fatigue jacket and big basketball shoes stood with his hands in his pockets and rocked back and forth. Walked ten feet and stopped and rocked some more, looking up and down the street.

He was a lookout. This was New York, in miniature.

I drove up the street and slid the truck into an open space. Ahead of me, I could see the meter maid chalking tires, leaning out of her scooter with a stick. Did they give parking tickets in Gomorrah? I put a quarter in the meter just in case and headed back down the street.

I peered into the darkened bars, where you could spend an hour just waiting for your eyes to adjust. The porn shop door was open, too, this being a beautiful sunny autumn day, and inside I could see men drifting down aisles of videos, lost in their fantasies. I window-shopped at a pawnshop, which seemed to specialize in biker stuff and guns. There was a great deal on a right-side ankle holster but I decided to pass. After I got a look at Poplar Street, I might be back.

Poplar was up the hill a block and over three. I stayed on Lisbon and the guys outside the bars gave me the once-over. Did I want coke? Did I want sex? Did I want to put them up against the wall and arrest them? It was so hard to tell these days. They turned away and let me pass.

I turned off two blocks up and started up the hill. The street was steep and lined with four-story apartment blocks, hung with wooden fire escapes. The houses crept up the hill and I did, too, past blank vinyl-sided walls, gravel parking lots clogged with junked Monte Carlos and Mustangs. One sign said unauthorized vehicles would be towed at owner's expense.

You couldn't find an emptier threat.

I continued up the hill to Park Street, but took a left instead of a right, procrastinating but chalking it up to reconnaissance. I passed women smoking on their front porch, cars up on blocks in the yard infront of them. Farther along, scrawny cats were eating from ripped trash bags along the curb. At the next house, an obese young woman in sweatpants and sweatshirt stood in a doorway and screamed at toddlers, who were foraging in the dirt like chickens.

"These effing kids," she called to a guy hanging out a window across the street. "I'm about to give 'em away."

Go right ahead, I thought.

I looked over and one of the toddlers, a little girl with dark curls and filthy pants, said, "Hi." It was a high-pitched cheep, like a bird, and I smiled and said hello. The mother looked at me and then at the girl.

"I told ya," she snarled. "Ya don't talk to strangers."

I shook my head.

Where was Roxanne when ya needed her?

The streets were named after the usual trees—Spruce, Maple, Oak—which were, in this neighborhood, endangered species. I made my way up the hill and the houses began to lose their raggedness. Trash gave way to neat tenements with white sheer curtains and bare square yards, tended like cemetery plots. The people walking were old, women with shopping bags and men wearing caps. The first two women who passed me were speaking French and the two after that. Then a white-haired man, small and stooped, wearing a tweed sportcoat.

"*Bonjour,*" I said.

He smiled.

"*Eh, comment ça va?*" he said. "You have a good day, uh?"

This was the old way, salvation after life on dirt-poor Quebec farms. A steady job in the mill and a paycheck every week. An apartment with heat and running water. Food on the table and a future for all the little ones gathered around it. Walk to church. Walk to work. Walk to the corner market. Stop on the sidewalk and gossip. Get home and read the paper. Make sure the kids do their homework.

Fifty years ago, that was the good life on these streets. Now it was going, if not fast, then steadily, as modern times, modern values crept up the hill like encroaching vines. Gang graffiti. Kids who had fathers but no dads. People who didn't need cars, not because they walked to work in the mill down the hill, but because they didn't work at all and didn't need to go anywhere.

Except to buy beer.

It was sad, this passing of an era. I thought this as I made my way down the next block, past the towering cathedral of Saints Pierre et Paul. I stopped and looked up at the rose window above the door, the twin towers topped by four spires, reaching up to heaven. The church was quiet but one of the massive front doors was propped open for some reason. I considered going in, at least to sit and look, if not to pray. But then I knew that I was doing everything but what I had come to do.

I kept walking, back into the tattered part of the neighborhood, two blocks down and one block over and back down Lisbon Street to my truck. I circled the block again, drove past the mill and up the hill to where Poplar Street was supposed to be.

And there it was.

It was a short street, on the right, lined with dingy apartment houses that overlooked a drab vacant lot. Number 17 was on the left, three houses in. It was mostly yellow with the word "Satan" spray-painted near the front door. Other than that, there had been no attempt to gussy the place up.

There were three floors, with wooden stairs running up the side. The staircase was roofed with green corrugated plastic. There were mailboxes on the wall at the bottom of the stairs and I got out of the truck and walked over to them. Of the six boxes, three had names scrawled on them. None of them was Paco.

I looked up the stairs and took a deep breath. Then began the climb.

At the second-floor landing there was a windowless steel door. It was a good heavy door, because someone had tried to kick it in and had given up. Probably the wicked wolf. Looking to do a story on three little pigs. Who sold cocaine.

At the landing, I paused to admire the view of the house across the way and then kept going. Six steps to the landing, where there was a broken Budweiser bottle. Six more steps to the door, which was gray steel and dented.

And unlocked.

"Damn," I said.

I eased it open slowly, not knowing whether it opened into a hallway or a living room.

It was dark. It was a hallway.

I went in, leaving the door open a crack behind me. The hallway was lit by a single bare bulb. There was stuff strewn on the floor: beer cans, fast food cartons, an empty bottle of cheap vodka. The carpeting was dirty gray, and where there was no trash, it was gritty, like a floor mat in a dirty car. This drug business was all glamour.

There were two doors on my end and presumably two on the other. I stopped in front of the first two and listened.

Nothing.

I started down the hall and immediately I could smell it. Pot.

And then I could hear voices.

A woman laughing.

I kept walking and the smell was stronger. The woman was talking. I heard a guy's voice, then the woman again, then a second guy's voice, lower than the first. I got to the door and stopped.

The door on the right. Cheap unpainted wood. No name. No number. It could have passed for the broom closet, if the place had ever had a broom. I stood outside it for a minute and listened, simply because listening was easier than knocking. I heard the voices, the woman give a little shriek that sounded almost coquettish, the guys laughing now.

They were in a good mood. I knocked.

The apartment went dead. There was no sound at all, then footsteps that came toward the door and stopped.

"Hello," I called.

I heard a chair scrape and a door slam but I didn't hear a shotgun being racked. I wouldn't have heard a knife coming out of a sheath, but I tried not to think about that.

There were more footsteps. I waited and was about to call again when a voice, the woman's voice, said, "Yeah?"

"I'm looking for Paco," I said through the door.

I heard her whisper, "Somebody's looking for Paco."

"Who is it?" she said.

I hesitated. Crunch time.

"My name's Jack McMorrow."

"What do you want?"

"Just to talk to Paco. That's all."

"What for?"

" 'Cause I'm looking for a guy named Bobby Mullaney. Another guy named Coyote."

"You a cop?"

"Nope."

I heard more whispers.

"What are you?"

"A reporter," I said, continuing my dialogue with the door. "I'm writing about Bobby and Coyote. About marijuana. I need to find them and somebody told me they were coming here. Bobby's wife sent me. She's looking for him, too."

More whispers. Then the woman again.

"Paco ain't here."

"Where can I find him?"

"He ain't here."

"I got that part. Can I give him a message or something?"

"I don't know where he is."

"How 'bout Bobby and Coyote?"

"Never heard of 'em."

"You sure about that?"

No answer.

"Hey, I just need to talk to Paco. If he doesn't know where they are, that's fine. I'm outta here."

"He ain't here."

"Who's on first?" I said.

"What?"

"Never mind. Listen. Can I slide my ID under the door or something?"

They conferred.

"Go outside. Out back. Look up at the third floor. Take off your shirt so we can see if you're wired."

"Take off my shirt?"

"Or hit the road," the woman said.

I looked down at my hunting coat. It was warm outside but it wasn't that warm. What if I just signed an affidavit?

"Okay," I said.

I went back down the hall slowly, then just as slowly down the outside stairs. When I got to the bottom, I walked toward the back of the building and looked around the corner. There was a small overgrown yard, with a mound of demolition debris in the center. The debris backed up to some brush. There was nobody around. I walked out into the yard and turned and looked up. The windows of the apartment in question were covered with blankets. As I watched, one of the blankets moved.

I pulled my chamois shirt and T-shirt out of my pants. Eased my jacket off and then unbuttoned the chamois shirt and slid it off my shoulders. I lifted my T-shirt up to my neck. The air was cool on my chest. I dropped the T-shirt back down.

"Turn around," the woman called, her voice muffled behind the window.

I did, lifting the T-shirt again. And as I bent to pick up my jacket, they came around the corner.

Fourteen

I WHIRLED. THEY came at a trot. One taller. One bearded. The tall guy had a piece of pipe.

"Hey," I said, but I was already backing up, and the guy with the pipe had it back and he was swinging and my jacket went out in front of me and the pipe grazed my hands and hurt but then the other guy, the one with the beard and the clenched jaw, had me by the upper arm, the left arm, and he was holding me while the pipe went back again. I spun and moved the bearded guy in front of me and he was grunting and the guy with the pipe stopped and looked for another opening.

The bearded guy let go with one hand and started to cock it back and I ran right at him, my left forearm up in his face, and he wasn't strong enough to hold me so he fell backward and I drove into him until he went down. I went right across him, low, feeling his face under my boot and his grunt as I started to run. But the pipe slammed into my back and I pitched forward, scratching on all fours to keep moving, my jacket in my left hand, my shirttails out, and the taller guy was trying to grab them. I pulled and kept running and then a third guy came around the corner of the building and he wasn't a cop.

He had a piece of wood and he held it in both hands, turning his body like it was a cricket bat. I dodged left, hacked at the guy's hand on my shirt and broke loose and ran for the truck but then realized the keys were in my jacket someplace and I couldn't stop so I kept going, down Poplar on the edge of the street, across the next road, and I could still hear footsteps.

I glanced back, at a full run, and the taller guy was in front, the pipe held close to his chest like a baton. He was twenty yards back and the other two were twenty yards behind him as I sprinted down the street, looking for somebody, anybody, but there was no one. I kept running and there was a car but it turned ahead of me and drove away, so slow I thought I could almost catch it but then it was gaining on me and was gone.

Still running, the taller guy staying with me, I stayed in the street and then there was the church, the towers and steps and I sprinted up them and went through the door, which, miraculously, still was propped open.

It was cool inside and vast and empty and I started up the center aisle, my boots pounding on the marble floor. The sound echoed through the hollowness of the big empty place and then something the nuns had drummed into me in first grade must have kicked in, and I stopped running and just walked quickly toward the front of the church, where I looked behind me.

They weren't there.

I got to the front of the aisle, and it must have been the nuns again because, for the life of me, I genuflected as I crossed in front of the altar. I went to the right, where there was another door and a stairway, but when I hit that door, which was a slab of oak, it was locked. I walked to the corner, beside the red-curtained confessional, and pressed my back against the wall.

And waited.

For ten minutes, I stood still. I looked at my hand, which was scraped from the wrist to the first knuckles but not deeply. I flexed it gently and it started to bleed.

That done, I started cataloguing the sounds, all of which were outside. Horns beeping. A siren that got my hopes up because it seemed to be coming closer but then it grew fainter and disappeared altogether. Motors revving and gears grinding and children calling back and forth and a dog barking. And, of course, the heavy, stultifying sound of silence.

I listened. Shifted on my feet. The movement of my boots made a scritching sound that wafted into the air, hanging under the vaulted ceiling like smoke. Clear your throat in this place and they'd hear it in Portland. To sneak up on me, the guys from Poplar Street would have to be ghosts.

After ten minutes, I eased my head out past the edge of the confessional, just far enough to look down the church toward the door. At some point, preferably before the seven o'clock Mass the next morning, I was going to have to make a break for it. It was 12:20. I had lots of time. Then again, maybe I should just stay and go to Communion.

Leaning back against the church wall, I looked around. It was a magnificent church, but a little frayed at the edges. There were brown water stains on the ceiling, one big one that ran down the wall opposite me, next to one of the stations of the cross. The station was a faded fresco of Jesus carrying his cross. It was too far away to read the writing but it looked like Jesus was being harassed by the centurions and the cowardly rabble. I leaned out and looked up, to my right, and saw Jesus limp and pale and wounded on the hands and feet. The lettering said, *"Jésus est mis dans le tombeau."*

The bastards.

I looked down the church toward the door. There was no sound, no movement. Above the door was a choir loft, railed with ornately carved oak. Above the loft was an organ and above the organ was a round stained-glass window, twenty feet across, glowing deep rose in the afternoon sun. Above the round window were smaller windows in pink and blue and purple.

There were worse places to be cornered.

If that was the case.

I supposed that the three of them could have jogged back to the apartment. While I leaned against a confessional in an empty cathedral, they were watching reruns of *I Love Lucy*. When I went back to pick up my truck, they'd wave from the window.

Or they could be waiting outside, but for how long? Guys like that usually didn't have a lot of patience. That was how they got to be guys like that. Prisons were full of guys who couldn't sit still in class.

But how long could I stand still? I leaned back again. This wasn't what I had planned, but then, I hadn't planned much. Come down here and knock on doors and see what happened. I could write a story that said the trail of Bobby Mullaney ended in a backyard in Lewiston. I'd write around my ignominious flight. In any event, my report to Melanie Mullaney was going to be short and sweet.

It was 12:31. I told myself I'd give it five more minutes and then see if there was a door somewhere beyond the sanctuary. If I could get out without being arrested for burglarizing the sacristy, then I could figure out how to get my truck. Maybe take a cab so I'd have a witness in case—

Steps.

At the door.

The one that was locked. On this side.

I weighed bolting for the back of the church but then there were more footsteps. The other end of the church.

The footsteps behind the door were closer. Someone coming upstairs. The footsteps at the back of the church had stopped. I didn't look because my head would hang out there like a flag. Then the door rattled and I slipped to my left and pushed past the red curtains. Inside, it was dark. I heard the door open.

There were two narrow strips of light at each side of the curtain. I peered through one and heard steps, then saw a man walk along the altar rail. From the rear, I could only see that he was tall and narrow, wearing jeans and a black leather jacket. His hair was tied in a short ponytail. When he reached the center aisle, he didn't genuflect.

I watched as he looked at the altar, then turned. He looked young. Early twenties. As he got closer, I could see that he was smiling. Maybe smirking. When he was ten or so pews from the front, he sat down.

"You wanted Paco, here he is, man," he called. "At your service."

I watched.

"Hey, man, you want to talk. Got some questions. This is, like, your chance, man. Me and you. My friends'll stay outside. I'll just sit here and pray or something."

I didn't answer. Paco put his arms on the back of the pew, looked straight ahead.

"Okay. You don't want to talk, fine. I thought you, like, really wanted to talk to me. Hey, I'll count to ten, man. Then I'm outta here. You can get your truck anytime. Like, no hard feelings."

He paused.

"One . . . two . . . three . . . four . . . five . . . Halfway there, man. Six . . . seven . . ."

I pushed through the curtain.

We sat side by side. If there was anyone at the back door, I didn't see him. It was just the two of us, and whoever else inhabits such a place.

"Nice church," Paco said. "But the friggin' roof leaks. They oughta do something about that."

"You come here often?"

"Right. I sing in the choir. So what is it?"

"I'm looking for Bobby Mullaney. And a guy named Coyote."

"Who the hell are you?"

"Jack McMorrow. I'm a reporter. I'm doing a story on Mullaney and his friends in Maine. Marijuana people. Legalization and all that. Then Mullaney and Coyote didn't come home. Mullaney's wife, her name is Melanie, I got to know her a little. She asked me to see if anybody down here had seen them. She didn't feel like she could call the cops."

"No doubt. How'd you get my name?"

"The wife gave it to me. Bobby told her he was coming down here to meet you."

Paco looked toward the altar. He looked younger than I'd thought. Not long from high school, assuming he'd ever gone.

"Why the friggin' hell would I want to talk to you?" he said.

"Because I asked so nicely."

"Oh, yeah?"

"Because your buddies came at me with a pipe."

"That right?"

"And maybe I should just go to the cops with the whole thing."

"What if you're a cop already?"

"If I was a cop, you think your boys would have chased me down the street with a pipe? Cops stick together. Even drug cops wouldn't let me get my head broken. Where do you pick your friends, anyway? If I was DEA they'd be sitting in Androscoggin Jail."

Paco didn't answer. The church was as still as ever. Maybe it was time for somebody to check on the priest.

"Let me see your wallet."

"My wallet?"

"Hand it over. I'll give it back."

I looked at him. Slowly reached for the right hip pocket of my jeans and pulled the wallet out. Handed it to him. Paco flipped through it. Looked at the photos on my driver's license and *Times* ID. Glanced at me. Glanced back at the photos. I considered him. He seemed pretty smart. Pretty cocky, at least on his square foot of turf.

Paco handed me my wallet.

"What if I still don't believe you?"

"What if I walk past the altar and start screaming for somebody to call nine-one-one? At this point, it doesn't matter to me. What if I tell the cops everything I know? They'll hassle you for months. Or you can just tell me the little bit I need to know so I can go back to Melanie Mullaney and tell her something. Your choice."

"What if you, like, don't make it out of here?"

"What if I do?" I said.

Paco scratched his earlobe, which was scarred where an earring had been ripped off. He had long thin fingers. A tattoo of a skull on the front of his right hand.

"Open your shirt up," he said.

I hesitated, then unbuttoned it. Four buttons. Paco reached over and slid his hand across my chest, under both arms.

"Lean forward."

He slid his hand across my back, first at the shoulder blades, then lower, then across my waist. Then he felt the tops of my thighs and, matter-of-factly, my groin.

I didn't flinch. He sat back.

"You can button your shirt again," Paco said.

"Thank you, Doctor."

"Yeah, right."

He took a deep breath. The pews were hard. The church was peaceful.

"I'm gonna tell you what I heard," Paco said. "General talk about nobody in particular. I'm gonna tell you this and then I'm gonna walk out of here and I'm never gonna see you again."

"Uh-huh."

"I heard this guy you're talking about came down here looking for another guy. The other guy owed the first guy, your guy, money."

He wet his lips. Continued.

"But the other guy owed him this much money before, like for a lot longer. And this guy you're looking for never got too worried about it."

Paco looked at me and smiled.

"That's what I heard."

"On the street," I said.

"Right. So your guy gets all friggin' wound up about it. I mean, he's right out of his tree. I heard this. I mean, is he friggin' crazy? Doing bad drugs, doing crack and Jack? He shakes this other guy down. Way too hard, you know?"

He gave me the look again.

"You heard."

"Right. I have no firsthand knowledge of any of this."

"Right."

"So," Paco said, "I heard this guy really pushed. This laid-back hippie guy came on, like, real hard. And the guy he was pushing told him he didn't have the money, that the money was like the product. It was in the pipeline. Still in the pipeline."

"The product went down the pipeline but the money hadn't come back yet?"

"Right. That's what I heard."

"On the street."

"Right. I mean, these things take time. This is retail. A retail business. There's, like, this collection aspect to this. That's what I've heard."

"So what happened then?"

Paco fingered his phantom earring again. His jacket smelled like a saddle. Or maybe it was his jeans.

"So I heard that this guy pushed real hard. Like he wanted to talk to the manager, you know? You go in a store or a restaurant and the meat ain't cooked or something and the chump behind the counter don't give you any answers so you say, 'Listen, shithead. Let me talk to the manager.' You know what I'm saying?"

I nodded.

"So he went to talk to the manager?"

"He wanted to," Paco said. "But he got lucky, I guess."

"How's that?"

He smiled. He had smoker's teeth.

"The manager happened to be in town. When he heard that the guy wanted to talk to him, he came right over. When he heard how wound up the guy was over this thing, he wanted to talk to him. The manager, I mean."

"How come?"

"I don't know. Seemed screwy."

"What seemed screwy?"

"Getting all bent like that. And when somebody's acting screwy, sometimes there's a reason, you know what I'm saying?"

"Like he's been turned," I said.

"I wouldn't know about that."

"Then what?"

"I don't know that, either. I ain't heard nothin'."

"Was a guy named Coyote in on all this?"

"Not that I heard. I heard the first guy was alone."

"Where'd they go? The guy and the manager?"

"They left. I heard."

"This manager from around here?"

Paco shook his head.

"I heard out-of-state."

"Which one?"

He looked away.

"South," he said.

"Mass.?"

Paco shrugged.

"Where in Mass.?"

He smiled, still looking away.

"When I was a kid, they used to make me sing in school, you know? To punish me. Make me stand in front of the class and sing. This old bitch. She's probably dead. But it didn't bother me, 'cause I liked to sing. I used to get right down. I remember the song, even. 'Down in the Valley.' "

He sang it and when he paused, the last note floated there in the air for a moment.

Paco turned to me.

"Had to pull me back to my desk. I wouldn't stop singing. 'Down in the Valley.' "

I got it. Valley, Mass. Another mill town, a lot like this one.

We sat there in the stillness. Suddenly I felt oddly like a priest. A confessor. Maybe it was the setting. The red velvet curtains.

"Why are you telling me this much? Of what you've heard, I mean."

Paco looked up at the altar, at the statuary that rose to the high ceiling, staring empty-eyed figures stacked atop each other like dolls on a toy store shelf.

" 'Cause if I'm right about you, you'll be my witness. If I'm wrong about you, that's not so bad, either, if things went the way they could've."

"And what way's that?" I asked him.

Paco started to stand, then paused, still looking away from me, straight ahead.

" 'Cause I don't want nobody's blood on my friggin' hands."

I looked down at the scrapes on mine.

"Yeah, well," Paco said. "If you're who you say you are, sorry about that."

I got up, too.

"Tell your buddies, next time they should just say, 'No comment.' "

Fifteen

THE PHONE WAS in the glass-lined hallway at the Windham McDonald's. It was a little after two and I'd come directly from Poplar Street, where I'd found my truck right where I'd left it and my welcoming committee nowhere to be seen. I'd driven fast down Lisbon Street and out of town, my conversation with Paco playing over and over in my head, and then I'd realized there was no real reason to rush because Roxanne didn't get home for three or four hours.

I had time to kill. Which was exactly what I figured had happened to Bobby Mullaney.

The restaurant was mostly empty. The hallway smelled like french fries but it was quiet. I dialed the Mullaneys' number, back in the woods in Florence. It rang three times, four times, and as my hopes lifted, Melanie answered and brought them crashing back down.

"Hi, Jack," she said. "Find out anything?"

"Yeah," I said, bracing myself. "I found Paco."

"And?"

"Well, he said Bobby was here."

"Was?"

"He left with another guy. From Massachusetts."

Melanie didn't say anything but I could hear her exhale, something between a gasp and a sigh.

"Paco said Bobby was mad about the late payment. Wanted the money. The next guy in the pipeline happened to be in Lewiston."

"Where is he from?" Melanie said quietly.

"Who?"

"The next guy."

"I think Valley. He didn't say that but—"

"Oh, my God," Melanie moaned, "Oh, my God."

I felt my teeth clench.

"Oh, my God, they'll kill him. Oh, my God, they've probably already . . . Oh, my God."

"Who?"

"They're killers. Down there, they're all killers. They'll just kill him. You don't know. Oh, my God, he's gone. Oh, my Bobby, oh my baby."

Melanie sobbed. An old couple squeezed by me and went into the restaurant. I covered the receiver as the door hissed shut.

"Oh God, oh God . . ."

"Well, maybe not," I began. "This guy Paco could be full of it. We don't know that it's true, even what he said."

She coughed.

"Well, he wouldn't just make it up, would he? Do you think he was making it up?"

"I don't know."

"What's your gut?"

I hesitated.

"Tell me, Jack."

"That he's telling the truth. Or close to it, as far as—"

Melanie interrupted with a guttural moan that feathered upward into something like a bird's cry, like one of the keening sounds a crow makes. It seemed out of character, coming from her, but then I'd only seen her hard shell. And underneath every hard shell, somewhere, was soft underbelly.

"Hey, but that doesn't mean that something's happened to him. He's from there, right? And Paco said there was no sign of Coyote."

"The bastard probably coughed him up," Melanie cried. "The bastard probably set him up. Oh, my God, I can't believe this. I told him. This is gonna lead to trouble. There's no safe way to do this, not even up here. I told him and he said, 'Mel, stop nagging. It's just a little pot.' Goddamn pot, goddamn pot, goddamn it all to hell pot."

I waited for her to stop yelling and lapse back into crying. She did.

"Listen, I'll make some calls down there. Maybe he got busted or something in Massachusetts. Maybe they haven't given him a phone call. I don't know. It could be anything. Maybe's he's sick in a hospital. Maybe he was in a car accident. It could be anything. Really, I'm not just saying that. I really think you're really getting upset about something that might not have happened."

"Oh, you don't know those people, you don't know how they are, they just kill you, like it's nothing, like it's nothing, no big deal, nothing."

"But wouldn't Bobby know that?"

"Oh, Bobby, he's so cocky."

She sobbed. The old couple came back out and stopped in front of me. The man looked in his bag and told his wife he was going back for ketchup. The wife looked at me and backed up against the wall.

"He's not afraid," Melanie was saying. "He thinks everything's fine and I told him it wasn't. I told him, I said, 'Don't do this. Stay up here. Don't get involved with those people again.' I told him that and now, oh, my God . . ."

"Maybe it's time to go to the police," I said. "Speaking of which, you know the DEA was working your road Tuesday?"

"How do you know that?"

"I just know."

The old woman looked at me and turned and went back inside.

"Oh, no," Melanie said. "I can't go to them. And tell them? Tell them all of it?"

"Yeah."

"They'd kill me."

"Melanie, I don't think it's like that. This Paco guy was a lightweight. I mean compared to what you're talking about. And some of his buddies went after me and they weren't much better. They couldn't find Florence if you drove them to the town line."

I heard her sigh.

"Jack, this is what Bobby told me. He told me the Valley guys were setting up in Lewiston for crack. Too many cops in Massachusetts. The people who actually do the dealing are Dominicans. The ones with the money are Colombians."

"Then why are they fooling with—"

"It was just a side deal or something. Pocket change. They were up here anyway."

"You seem to know more about it than I thought you would."

"Bobby told me that much. And I told him, 'These guys are too rough. Let's stay away from them.'"

"Which brings us back to the cops."

"Jack, I don't know. Who'd take care of Stephen?"

"If what?"

"If something happened to me. If I went to jail. I mean, I can't leave him here alone. There's nobody else but me. Oh, Jesus Christ, almighty God, oh, God . . . Oh, here he is."

In the background, a door banged.

"Stephen, I've got to talk to you," I heard Melanie say.

"Mom, this sucks," I heard him reply.

I waited. The old couple came out, the man first, giving me a hard look, the woman staying behind him, as if I might grab their Big Macs.

"Sorry," Melanie said.

"Okay," I said. "How 'bout this. I'll make some phone calls down to Valley. See if he's turned up down there. If I don't find out anything in a day or two, I think you should go to the cops. Unless you think there's a chance he just, I don't know, sort of took off."

"He wouldn't do that. He's got plants to tend up here."

And promises to keep. No doubt.

• • •

The restaurant was across the street from the McDonald's.
The sign outside said there was karaoke on Saturday nights.
This was Wednesday so they just served beer.

I had my choice of tables so I sat down near the back.
The waitress, a solid and energetic young woman in a short
black skirt, popped out from behind the bar and offered me
a menu but I declined and ordered the beer instead. They
were cheap so I ordered two. The waitress hustled off and
then hustled right back and put both glasses on the table.

"Hard day at the office?" she said.

"Something like that," I said, raising my scraped hand
to take a swallow of the first beer.

The waitress grimaced.

I switched hands and smiled disarmingly.

"Got hit with a pipe," I said.

"You a police officer?"

"No, a plumber."

She looked at me funny and fled to the kitchen. I had
the place to myself.

I sipped the beer, which was standard-issue Budweiser
served very cold. The bottom of the glass felt good on my
knuckles. The beer felt good everywhere else.

In the dim light, I became the observer again. It was
easier.

I scribbled in my notebook as fast as I could recall, trying
to get every utterance, every monosyllable down on paper.
The woman speaking through the door on Poplar Street.
Descriptions of the three guys in the backyard. Every word
that I could remember Paco saying.

It came in jumbles, out of order.

"Was a guy named Coyote there?"

*"Not that I heard. I heard the first guy was by him-
self."*

"Where did they go? Bobby and the manager?"

"They just left. I heard."

"Where's the manager from?"

"I heard he was from out of state."

"Which state?"

"I remember the song, even. 'Down in the Valley.' "

"I heard this guy came here came here looking for another guy. The other guy owed him money.

"But the other guy owed him as much money as this before, for a lot longer. And this guy you're looking for never worried about it.

"This guy's all wound up about it. Right out of his tree. I heard this. I mean, is he nuts? Doing bad drugs, crack and Jack? He shakes this other guy down too hard."

"If I'm right about you, you'll be my witness. If I'm wrong about you, that's okay. If things went wrong.

"I don't want nobody's blood on my hands."

Was that right? Or was it anybody's blood? Close enough for my purposes, whatever they were.

The reporter Jack McMorrow could write that Bobby Mullaney was last seen in Lewiston, Maine, where he was said to have gotten into a dispute over payment for a load of marijuana. The seller was a young man who gave his name as Paco.

Would I have to slip into first person? The *Globe* wouldn't go for it. I'd have to write it straight.

In an interview in a church in Lewiston last week, Paco said Mullaney demanded to see another drug seller from another state. That drug trafficker happened to be in Lewiston, Paco said, and a meeting was arranged.

Paco said that was his last contact with Bobby Mullaney.

Or maybe I wouldn't use his name. Change it to something else? Use the real names and burn Melanie and Stephen but have a better story by far. And what about my

conversation with Melanie? Was that privileged? Off the
record? I mulled it for a moment, then bent to my notebook.
It was easier.

"Oh, my God, they'll kill him. Oh, my God, they've
probably killed him already by now. Oh, my God."
   "Who?"
   "They're killers. Down there, they're killers. They'll
just kill him. You don't know. Oh, my God, oh, my
Bobby, oh my baby."

"What are you writing?"
I looked up and there was a little girl. A round-faced
blond little girl who looked to be about four. Maybe older.
She was standing a few feet away to my left, eating some
sort of candy. She sidled closer and I could see that there
was pink drool at each corner of her mouth, which was
smiling. Her teeth were very small.
"You doing your homework?" the girl said, chewing.
I smiled.
"Sort of. I'm writing some stuff down so I don't forget
it."
"Why don't you want to forget it?"
I considered her. She was doing a little dance in place,
her high-top sneakers crossing in front of her.
"Because I might have to write it in a story later," I
said. "Are you a dancer?"
"Yes. I go to Miss Flossie's. I don't go today. I go on
Fridays. Today me and my mom are here to pick up her
check. It's on Friday we go to Miss Flossie's."
"Is that a dancing school?"
"Yes. Miss Flossie's really nice."
"You must be a good dancer."
"I am. I do tap and ballet but tap's too loud."
"All that tapping, huh?"
"Yeah. I like ballet 'cause it's quieter. You wear ballet
shoes. Can you read this writing?"
She fingered the scrawled page of my notebook. Her
hand was sticky and left a smudge the same color as the

drool at the corner of her mouth. The sticky passage was Melanie saying her husband had been killed.

"Sometimes," I said.

"Do you write books?"

"No, I write stories in the newspaper."

"Why do you do that?" she said.

She looked up at me. I could see that her eyes were blue. When she smiled, her cheeks dimpled and her eyes smiled, too.

"Because it's what I do," I said.

"Why is it what you do?"

She giggled. She was teasing me now.

"Because it's my job. I write stories. I write them down and they put them in the newspaper."

"Why don't you just tell your stories out loud?"

"Because . . . because nobody would hear them."

The girl chewed and did her little two-step. A woman appeared at the far end of the restaurant.

"Hillary. Come on, babe," she called.

"See ya later, alligator," the girl said, and then the sneakers thumped across the fake wood floor and I was, once again, alone.

I looked down at my notes and I knew the complete, unexpurgated answer to her question. I was clinging hard and fast to my reporter's role. I was the observer, back from the war, the poverty, the starving children and bloated infants. As long as I had this notebook, I was detached, safe from the clinging tentacles of real emotion. File my story and go home. At various times during my determined climb to the *Times*, and the top, it had struck me that I was dodging life, evading something. Well, there was no evading this.

Bobby probably dead. Melanie already grieving. Coyote gone. The Mullaneys' peculiar misfit of a kid wandering the woods with his rifle. And me, caught in the middle of it all, wrestling a story that didn't want to stay on the page, that wanted to suck me in, yank me out of my easy chair and pull me through the TV screen and into the show.

I drained my beer and threw money on the table.

Maybe now the *Globe* would go to three-fifty.

Sixteen

I WAS SITTING in my truck in the dark when Roxanne's car swung down the drive and pulled in and parked. The door popped open, the dome light came on and there she was, turning to me, getting out of the car, coming across the little parking lot, running in that short-stepped way that women run when they're wearing heels.

As I fumbled with the door, Roxanne pulled it open from the outside. I slid off the seat and into her arms.

"Baby," she whispered, holding me tightly.

"Hey, hon," I said.

I could smell her perfume, somebody's cigarette smoke in her hair. Her face was against my neck and I felt her breathe in and then out in a long sigh that ended with a barely perceptible tremor.

"I . . . I'm just glad to see you," Roxanne said, leaning back and scanning my face, as if to make sure it was all there. I held her by the waist.

"I'm glad to see you, too. How'd you do today?"

Her face fell.

"Oh, so-so. Not so good, I guess. It was, well, it's a long story. How 'bout you?"

"I guess I did so-so, too."

"You didn't find him?"

"No, but I did find people who had seen him."

"So they were okay? You look fine."

Roxanne scanned my face again. I kept my hand on her back.

"They told me what I needed to know, I guess. After a while."

"You charmed them," Roxanne said.

"Oh, yeah. They wanted me to stay for dinner, smoke a few bowls, meet the wife and kids, but I said I had a date."

"You do, huh."

"With a strikingly beautiful woman."

"Who's ready for a glass of wine."

"And I brought a bottle of the good stuff."

"My connoisseur."

"Mais, oui."

I reached into the truck and pulled out a bottle in a bag.

"And what made you select this particular vintage, Monsieur McMorrow?" Roxanne said, slipping the bottle from the bag to read the label.

"It was five dollars," I said. "And the four-dollar one had a screw top."

The heels were catapulted across the living room rug. The briefcase thunked onto the kitchen chair. Roxanne took off her blazer and tossed it over the banister to be brought upstairs. I opened the wine and poured two glasses and brought them to the living room, where Roxanne had flopped on the couch. She sat up, putting her stocking feet together primly, and took the glass and sipped.

"Mmmm," she said. "Worth every penny. And I don't suppose you're going to tell me what you did to your hand."

"I didn't do anything."

"I thought you said you charmed them down there."

"I didn't say it was instantaneous. There was a feeling-out period."

"What'd they feel you out with?"

"Nothing much."

I sat down beside her. Roxanne eyed the scab on my hand disapprovingly.

"It's healing as we speak. You want to talk about court?"

"Oh, gee, I don't know. It was just sad."

"They all are, aren't they?"

Roxanne sipped her wine. Her earrings swung gently.

"This one was harder because I think the kids were really ready to make the break. After a week in a normal house, they know what they're missing."

"Toys?" I said.

"Meals. An adult who answers when they call. They know something's wrong. Really wrong. At least the older one."

"Were they there?"

"Waiting in a conference room. Mom showed. She even looked sort of straight. Put her hair up in barrettes and everything. She brought a counselor who said she'd come to her for help."

"Well, that's good, isn't it?"

"Won't last. She'll be back at it, partying all night. I give it a day or two. She's an addict. You can see it in her eyes. The distraction. It'd take months for her to really clean up."

"So what happened to the kids?"

"They went home with her," Roxanne said.

"Were they crying?"

"No, but I was."

"Really?"

"Close as I get. It just got to me. The little girl turned and gave me this little wave. Oh boy . . ."

"What do you do now?" I asked.

"Follow up on her. Wait for the cops to call again."

"Stinks."

"Yup," Roxanne said. "I'm going to go over there tomorrow and follow up. And tomorrow night. Don't worry. I'll bring a cop."

"The cop can bust her for crack and you can grab the kids."

"If this were a perfect world . . ." Roxanne said.

I took a sip of wine. It wasn't perfect, either.

"This must be one of those where you wish you could just grab them."

"But I can't. I have to play by the rules."

"And stay in there swinging."

"On to the next windmill, Pancho," Roxanne said. She smiled.

"So, dear," Roxanne said. "Tell me about your day. What did you do in Lewiston?"

"I went to church."

"How was the sermon?"

"The gospel according to Paco. That's where I met him. It was pretty interesting. And the church is beautiful. But after that I had to call Melanie."

"And tell her what?"

"That her husband might be dead."

"Are you serious?"

"Yeah."

"What did she say?"

"She cried. Sobbed and cried."

Roxanne looked somber and concerned.

"What did you tell her then?"

"I said I'd make some calls and see if he's turned up in Massachusetts."

"Massachusetts?"

"That's where Paco said the guy Bobby was with may have brought him."

"His body, you mean?"

"Maybe," I said.

Roxanne grimaced, then fixed her narrowing gaze on me. I sipped my wine.

"I hope you don't get any ideas about going down there," she said, her legs tucked under her.

"Why would I want to do that?"

"Why do you do anything, Jack?"

"Can we make this a take-home test?" I said.

"No."

I sipped, then shrugged.

"It's going to be a pretty good story. From the hippies at the fair in Maine to the mean streets of Massachusetts."

"But it's just a story. It isn't worth it."

"If I thought that, I'd never write another word," I said.

"Can't you write about something else? These people are drug dealers," Roxanne said.

"I know, but it isn't so black and white. Melanie isn't a bad person and even Bobby, he's sort of engaging, in a way. Anyway, there's a lot of hypocrisy out there. Booze is a multibillion-dollar industry but these people get called drug dealers. I don't know. One man's drug is another man's cocktail."

"God, Jack," Roxanne said, swinging her legs down and getting up from the couch. "There's hypocrisy everywhere."

"But don't you think it should be unmasked?"

"Sure. Politicians who talk about helping kids and then give the money to their pals. These bozos in Congress who go around saying they have no money for your program but then turn around and give millions to these filthy dictators. I don't know. It just seems you have to pick your battles, Jack."

Sitting there gripping the stem of the wineglass, I could feel myself hardening.

"I have, Rox," I said. "You pick your windmills and I'll pick mine."

Dinner was stir-fried vegetables, prepared and eaten in silence. Roxanne picked and then got up and left. I put the dishes in the dishwasher and wiped the wok and half watched the news on the little television on the kitchen counter. It was mostly reports of problems without solutions, the decline of societies and economies, currencies and cultures. Pick one of those battles, why don't you?

I sat for a while and then put water on for tea and went upstairs to find Roxanne. I found her laid out on the bed in her blouse and skirt, a magazine on her chest, her breath making a faint rustle as she slept. For a minute or so I looked at her. She was such a strong woman but something about her was still childlike. Skin like snow. Dark hair gathered at the back of her graceful neck. Lips and eyelashes and feet in stockings snuggled together.

Smiling grudgingly, I took a goose-down comforter off of the blanket chest and put it over her. Roxanne was reason to be careful.

So I went downstairs and made tea and put on my jacket and went down to the dock behind the condo complex. The few sailboats left were jostling in their slips, their rigging ringing like wind chimes in the breeze. I sat on a bench in the dark and watched the clouds race past the stars, a tugboat huff out of the harbor and blinking jets bank and take aim for the Portland airport. As I watched, I thought about Roxanne and her kids and Melanie and her son and Bobby and his wacky confidence and where it had gotten him. And I thought that it was all such chaos, everything, all around us, that the only recourse was to try to make a small part of it good, or to chronicle the chaos so at least there was a record to provide a scant semblance of order.

If Roxanne had been there, she would have asked me which I thought I was doing. And I would have said I was doing a little of both. I hoped.

When I came in, Roxanne had awakened enough to get out of her clothes and into a flannel nightgown. She was asleep again and I got undressed and climbed in beside her and then the alarm was cheeping on her side and she was lurching toward the shower. I fell back into a thick tar pit of sleep and then felt her lips on my cheek, smelled her smell.

"I love you, I really do," she said, bending over me.

"I love you, too," I mumbled, and before I was conscious, Roxanne was gone.

After an eternity that was really an hour, I rolled out of the bed and into the shower. I used Roxanne's herbal revitalizing shampoo, her soap that squirted out of a little white bottle. The soap stung the gash on my hand. The white plastic razor I left alone.

Breakfast was a raisin bagel and a glass of juice. I took my last clean shirt from Roxanne's closet and made a mental note to replenish the stock. By the time I went out the front door, the mental note had been erased. I bought a large tea at the Dunkin' Donuts in Portland, and was on the interstate by eight-fifteen.

It was sunny but still windy and much colder and the truck seemed drafty. It was also very loud from the tires and the wind, and only one speaker was working on the stereo. Other than that, I traveled in style.

The southbound lanes were full of Saabs and Volvos driven by southern Maine commuters, but by the time I hit Brunswick I had the road to myself. It stayed that way until Augusta and then thinned out again on Route 3 heading for Belfast. I took the turnoff, and wound my way west between the windblown yellow-and-orange trees and back into the hills, and at 9:40 sharp I was home in Prosperity.

And ready to man the phones.

The first call was easy. I dialed Roxanne's office and a woman answered and said she was on the phone. I asked her to ask Roxanne to call me when she got a chance, but told her it was nothing urgent. Then I dialed directory assistance for Massachusetts and asked for the number of the Valley Police Department. The operator said I had the wrong area code and gave me the right one. I tried again and the next operator asked me if this was an emergency. I said, no, not yet, and after a couple of clicks an alien recorded voice gave me the number. I wrote it down.

I was rolling.

The first time I called, the number was busy. I hit redial and waited and it rang. Once, twice . . .

"Valley Police Department. May I help you?"

It was a man's voice. A very faint Latino accent.

"Yeah, this is Jack McMorrow. I'm a reporter up in Maine and I'm looking for some information."

"And what kind of information is that, sir?"

"I'm looking to find out whether a man I'm writing about has turned up in your area. He's sort of missing up here and there's reason to believe he may have gone to Valley."

There was a pause. A long one.

"I'll give you detectives," the man said. "You said you're a reporter?"

"Right."

The phone clicked and rang again and a woman answered. She said, "Yeah?"

I gave her my spiel. She paused, too.

"What'd you say your name was, sir?"

"Jack McMorrow."

"And you're a reporter? For what?"

"I'm a freelancer. I'm doing a story for the *Boston Globe*."

"But you're in Maine?"

"Right."

"And what does this have to do with Valley again?"

"The guy I'm writing about has disappeared and I was told he may be in Valley."

"What, he doesn't want to be written about?"

"No," I said. "He wants to be written about. Him disappearing didn't have to do with the story."

"Huh," the detective said.

She did not sound impressed.

"Why're you writing about him?"

Oh boy, I thought. Here we go . . .

"He's involved in the marijuana legalization movement in Maine. That's what I'm writing about."

"What's that got to do with Valley?"

"He used to live in Valley," I said. "He may have gone back there."

"Well, sir, that's his right, right? I mean, I don't know what the police department is supposed to do about—"

"Excuse me, but I just want to know if something's happened to the guy. I'm calling for his wife. She's worried."

"Why doesn't she call?" the detective said.

"She's sort of upset. She thinks he might be dead."

"And tell me why she thinks that, Mr.—what was it?"

"McMorrow."

"Okay, why does she think this marijuana guy might be dead? How long has he been gone?"

"Two or three days."

"Two or three days? Listen, sir, I've got cases piled up on my desk a foot high. I mean, I don't mean to be rude but I've got serious felony crimes here I can't even get to. All I can tell you is to contact the appropriate law enforcement agency in your area and they'll handle it according to—"

"His name's Bobby Mullaney. He may be with a guy named Coyote. Heard of them?"

"Nope. And like I said—"

"Both white males, around six feet. Coyote has long dark hair. Says he's Native American but I don't think so."

"Nope."

"No dead bodies like that kicking around down there?"

"No, and I've got a call on the other line."

"What'd you say your name was, Detective?"

"Detective Martucci," she said. "Have a good day, sir." And she hung up. I did, too.

But being a dogged journalist, I kept trying. I called directory assistance and got the name of the Valley hospital. It was Valley Hospital. I called there and was quickly put through to something called patient information. A guy there asked me who the patient was and I said his name was Bobby Mullaney but I didn't know if he was a patient. Actually, the guy at patient information was rather impatient and almost hung up before I could ask if Bobby was on the patient directory.

"And who are you?"

"My name's Jack McMorrow. I'm a reporter. I'm calling from Maine."

"Sir, all press inquiries are handled by the public information office. This is patient information. I'll transfer you."

And he did. And a woman answered. I did it again, with feeling, and she interrupted me and said the public information director was Roger Valdez and Mr. Valdez was out of the office.

"But I just want to know if somebody I know is in the hospital," I said. "I mean, what if my brother were in an accident and I wanted to know whether he was in your hospital? What would I do?''

"Where was this accident?'' she said.

"There wasn't one. That was a hypothetical situation. I just want to know how to find out if this guy is a patient in your hospital.''

"What's your brother's name?''

I stopped. Took a deep breath. Let it out.

"His name's Bobby Mullaney.''

"But that wasn't the name you gave me,'' the woman said. "You said your name was Mc-something.''

"McMorrow,'' I said. "Bobby's my stepbrother. Is he in your hospital?''

"Well, I don't know. I'll give you back to the operator. She can have him paged.''

There was a click. A buzz.

And a dial tone.

I sat back in my chair for a moment, then dialed again. This time the phone rang twice. A woman answered, sounding harried.

"Please give Roxanne Masterson a message,'' I said. "Tell her Jack said to be careful.''

Seventeen

I SPENT THE morning on the phone or standing near it, hands on my hips, wondering whom to call next.

There were four hospitals within twenty-five miles of Valley. Each hospital had a public relations department, none of which did much relating. I called as Jack McMorrow, reporter looking for information. I called as Jack Mullaney, looking for his missing brother. At one hospital, a woman said there was no record of any Bobby Mullaney being admitted to the hospital, but if there were, she couldn't tell me. At another hospital, a man named David something-or-other cited laws regarding patient confidentiality. I asked how long they would hold my brother incommunicado. He said he would have his supervisor call me.

At ten o'clock, I still was waiting.

At ten-fifteen, I had tea and changed tacks. There had to be a newspaper in Valley, so I called the police department again. The dispatcher answered and asked if it was an emergency and I said no, and she put me on hold. I waited for three long minutes and then the dispatcher came back on and I asked her my question.

"The *Chronicle*," she said, and hung up before I could thank her. I called directory assistance and got the number of the *Valley Chronicle* and hit the button and dialed. A man answered and asked how he could direct my call. I asked for the newsroom and the phone rang again and a younger-sounding man answered breathlessly, the way somebody in a real newsroom should.

I had to smile.

"Could I have the city desk?" I said.

"They're in the late-news meeting," he said.

He was all business. His accent was Hispanic.

"Is there a police reporter there?"

"That's Patty. She's out of the office."

"Are you a reporter?"

"Yeah. Well, I'm an intern," the guy said. "Who's this?"

I told him my name. I said I was a freelance reporter looking for information.

"Yeah, well, we're kind of—"

"I want to know if a guy's been killed."

Melodramatic but it got his attention.

"Killed how?" he said.

"I don't know. Murdered. Car accident. Anything."

"You mean you have a specific guy in mind?"

"His name's Bobby Mullaney. Heard of him?"

"Nope."

"Who's your city editor?"

"Robert."

"Robert who?"

"Robert Hood."

"And his merry men?" I said. "You think he'll be out of the news meeting soon?"

"I don't know. But after that, we'll be right on deadline so he'll be pretty busy. Maybe you could call back later. I really got to go, too."

"This a p.m.?"

"Uh-huh."

"You on deadline?" I asked.

"Yeah," he said, his voice filled with the sense that deadlines were sacred and making them was a religious obligation. I remembered that feeling. Like a nostalgic agnostic, I remembered what it was to truly believe.

"What are you working on?" I said.

"What am I working on? Oh, it's just a story on this car accident. Tractor trailer flipped on Route Three. Spilled, like, tons of potato chips. Tied up traffic for a couple of hours."

"How many tons?"

"I don't know. I don't know if it even was tons. Maybe a truckload of potato chips just weighs pounds."

"You should find out. And ask if there were pretzels or tortilla chips mixed in. Those kinds of details make a story like that. Anybody hurt?"

"No."

"You get a byline?"

"Well, I haven't yet. They said—"

He caught himself.

"What'd you say your name was?"

"Jack McMorrow."

"You've been a reporter?"

"Oh, yeah."

"Where?" the young man asked.

"Oh, here and there."

I called back but Robert Hood was in a meeting. Then he was out of the office. Then he was somewhere in the building but they didn't know where. I asked for the intern but they said he'd gone home for the day. I asked his name and they said it was Joe Mendoza. I asked for Patty the police reporter and they said she'd gone home, too, that she worked from five a.m. to two p.m. but she'd left early because she hadn't felt well. I asked with whom I was speaking and the last woman I talked to said she was a newsroom assistant. In the background, I heard someone say, "Is it that weird guy from Maine again?"

But I didn't feel weird. Mostly I felt frustrated.

After a morning on the phones, I knew that Bobby probably wasn't on the front page of the Valley newspaper tomorrow, that he might be in any of several hospitals, that he hadn't been killed in such a dramatic way that his death had been brought to the attention of one Detective Martucci.

Yet.

Of course, Bobby could be on the bottom of some river, or stuffed inside a car trunk, or left in a vacant apartment or dumped in the woods on a median strip. And where was Coyote, last seen leaving Florence, Maine, in Bobby's company? Why wasn't he with Bobby when they met Paco in Lewiston?

I sat there and stared out the window. The wind had picked up even more and the sun had disappeared, replaced by a woolly bank of gray clouds, rolling in from the northwest. The pale yellow leaves on the poplars looked panicky, twisting and writhing as if they were trying to flee. There was rain coming but it was still in the distance, in the clouds, and even through the window I could feel the damp breath of the wind. I felt a pang of isolation, a tremulous shifting, as if the center of my universe had been moved from this forgotten hollow in Prosperity, Maine, to another place. But I hadn't been told where the other place was. I was still in Prosperity, left behind, marooned, forgotten and uninformed.

With a shiver, I got up from the chair. I walked to the window to shake it off, then walked back to the chair. I looked at the phone, then picked it up and started to dial Roxanne's office again. After four numbers I hung up. I knew then that I couldn't finish this story, project, whatever it was, from here.

"I hope you don't get any ideas about going down there," Roxanne had said.

But I just had to see it. The city. The police station. The newspaper. The television news. I reached for the phone.

It rang.

"Thought maybe you'd died and gone to purgatory," Clair said.

"What do you mean, purgatory?"

"I'm giving you the benefit of the doubt."

"Thanks, I think."

"What are you doing for dinner?"

"I don't know. I might be heading south, again."

"You fly south more than the birds," Clair said. "Where to this time?"

"A place called Valley, Massachusetts."

"Some kind of armpit place, ain't it?"

"More or less," I said. "I think it's sort of an abandoned mill town, from what I've heard. A little city built around mills on the Merrimack River. Then the mills pulled out and the place was left to its own devices."

"What devices?"

"Drugs, I think. It's a big stop on the cocaine pipeline."

"So, why are you going there, Jack?"

"Because some of them dabble in marijuana."

"What, like a hobby or something?" Clair said.

"Helps them unwind after a hard day dealing crack."

"That's nice."

"I knew you'd understand."

"Yeah, I understand this Valley is a pretty rough place."

"You're a walking encyclopedia since you got that satellite dish," I said.

"I try. So you're really going down there?"

"I think so."

"For how long?"

"A day. A night, maybe. I just want to see it. Get a feel for the place."

"How was Lewiston?"

"Okay. Pretty interesting."

"You find the druggies you were looking for?"

"Yeah, I did, actually."

"What'd they say?"

"A couple of 'em didn't say anything. They were too busy trying to hit me with a pipe."

"You all right?"

No more joking.

"I'm fine. They weren't very good hitters. Benchwarmers."

"But these guys in Massachusetts are a different league, aren't they?"

"A step up. Maybe two. Actually, the Massachusetts guys were in Lewiston."

"What were they doing?" Clair asked. "Scouting?"

"Probably bringing up some coke and heroin. While they're up here, they pick up a little pot to sell down south."

"They tell you that?"

"A guy named Paco did," I said.

"Is he the guy with the pipe?"

"No. He called them off. We had a good talk. In a church."

"Then maybe it *will* be purgatory," Clair said. "What'd you talk about?"

"This Mullaney guy. From Florence. This guy Paco said he made a big stink out of not getting paid for his pot. Mullaney did, I mean. He wanted to see somebody higher up and the somebody higher up happened to be in town."

"So?"

"So the guy who was higher up left and took Mullaney with him."

"And went to this Valley place."

"Where Mullaney used to live," I said.

"So it all fits together."

"I guess. But I'm not quite sure exactly how."

"How 'bout I ride along this time? Just so there's somebody to notify the next of kin."

"That's just Roxanne," I said.

"Good. It won't take long."

"I don't know. What's Mary going to say?"

"She's in North Carolina visiting Susan."

"She is? When did she go?"

"Yesterday," Clair said.

"You didn't tell me that."

"You haven't been around."

"Why didn't *you* go?"

"Oh, I figured a girl has to just be with her mother, sometimes. And Larry would just want me to play golf."

"That'd be like you dancing in the ballet."

"I'd take the dancing, tell you the truth. Last time he wanted to loan me a pink sweater and these goddamn white-and-black saddle shoes," Clair said.

"Did you punch him?"

"He's my son-in-law."

"Did you play golf?"

"Hell no. He went and played golf and I put in a couple of those garage door openers. Some yahoo tried to do it and got it all bunged up."

"Larry?"

"Yeah. He's a nice kid but he doesn't know much. So what time we leaving?"

"How 'bout in an hour. Get down there in time to catch the night's first drive-by shooting. Speaking of which . . ."

"What?"

"You probably shouldn't bring the Mauser. Massachusetts has nasty gun laws."

"Goddamn uncivilized place," Clair said.

"Well, we won't stay long. Interview a few drug lords, find Bobby Mullaney and be home in time for cocktails tomorrow."

"But we'll take a real truck. I like you okay but I'm not sitting on your lap."

"Story of my life," I said.

So by one o'clock we were on the road in Clair's big Ford. We had a thermos of tea and a thermos of coffee. A bag of apples. Our duffels were in plastic garbage bags in the back, in case of rain, which didn't start until somewhere around Biddeford. Clair clicked on the wipers and the truck lumbered along at a regal pace as we sat high above the traffic, peering down into passing cars.

"You think we should have told Mary and Roxanne we were going?" I said.

"Just get 'em all worried," Clair said. "Hell, a man shouldn't have to check with the old lady every time he blows his nose."

"Right."

I looked out as a Mercedes swished by.

"But Roxanne may have had a hard day. I think I'll call when we get there," I said.

Clair looked at me and grinned.

"Yeah. Me, too."

So we drove down the interstate, with country and western playing softly on the radio and the heat on just enough to offset the dampness and chill. Just south of Kennebunk, Clair reached for the case on the floor and took out a folder. From the folder he took out a cassette tape and put it in the radio. A man's voice said, "Chapter twenty-four. 'The Sharpsburg Campaign.'"

"Most people know it as Antietam," Clair said.

And then the narrator began, reading his story about Mc-Clellan and Lee and Joe Hooker and Stonewall Jackson.

"More Americans killed that day than any other day in history," Clair said quietly. "Twenty-three thousand casualties."

"Insanity," I said.

"No, not really. It's just that people are sort of short-sighted. One action leads to another. That one leads to something else. Before you know it, you're into some pretty horrible situations. You don't know how you got there. You don't know the way back out."

"It was like that in your war, wasn't it?"

"Oh, yeah," Clair said quietly. "One dumb move leads to another."

I thought for a moment.

"This pot story's like that," I said, as the wipers waved. "One thing led to another. Sort of snowballed. Out of control."

Clair looked in the side mirror and pulled out to pass a semi-trailer.

"I don't know," he said, glancing in the mirror to pull back into his lane. He reached out and ejected the Civil War tape.

"Tell me about this one again. Start at the beginning. Don't leave anything out."

I didn't. I told him the whole story, from the fair to Stephen and Melanie. When I forgot something, I went back and retrieved it. Tromping through the woods to see the bushy green plants, with their rose-tinted buds. Melanie calling me, asking for help. Going through their drawers. Finding the name Bernie. Going to Lewiston. Sitting in the cathedral with a drug dealer.

When I was done, Clair reached for his thermos and filled his cup with coffee.

"I don't know," he said. "It seems like there's a straight line that runs right through the whole thing. It's like there's a hook in you and every little while the line gets reeled in a little more."

"But I picked them out," I said. "I was the one who initiated the whole thing. They didn't even know me."

Clair sipped his coffee.

"But they didn't waste any time bringing you into the fold," he said.

"They want some sympathetic press."

Clair sipped again.

"I don't know," he said. "I don't know much about it, but seems to me, for drug dealers, they're awful chatty."

"I can't help it if I inspire confidence."

"When did you start doing that?" Clair said.

Eighteen

AS WE CROSSED from New Hampshire into Massachusetts on Route 495, the woods became more scrubby, more temporary, as if they could be mown anytime, should the right deal come along.

We drove in silence, listening to the accounts of long-ago battles for pastures and cornfields. The light faded, but the rain continued, and finally we crossed a highway bridge over the Merrimack River. The river was wide and skimmed smooth by the rain and I looked beyond it and saw the mills, sprawling red brick buildings that stretched far into the distance.

I elbowed Clair but he'd already seen them and he slowed the truck. The buildings closest to the highway had graceful arched windows, some without glass, some plugged with plywood. The complex looked vast and abandoned, a massive undertaking that had seen its purpose flow by like the waters of the river itself.

"Jesus," Clair said. "Looks like some goddam Mayan city, doesn't it?"

"The ruins of the industrial age."

It did look like ruins, standing there empty and grand. Then the mills were gone and we were still heading down the highway and I reached for the map. Two exits up, we turned off and headed north on a two-lane road that passed scrubby lots and then dingy plazas, linked by lines of small square houses. The houses were drab, with porches on the front, one after another, and then there was a faded white wooden sign that said we were entering the city of Valley, Massachusetts.

The sign promised nothing else.

We stopped at the first light, the truck towering over the car in front. The car was small, a Honda or Toyota, and there were little kids in the backseat. They turned and stared at the truck and at us, and then the woman in the front passenger seat turned and stared, too.

"We must look like a couple of lost lumberjacks," Clair said.

"So much for undercover."

"I thought you were just gonna look in the Yellow Pages under D for drug dealers."

"Let's look under M for motel," I said.

"Isn't exactly a tourist trap."

"Yeah, but people must stay the night here sometime."

"Yeah, when their cars are stolen," Clair said.

"And the rental place is closed."

The light changed and we followed the traffic as it made its way into what must have been downtown Valley. The truck idled along in the line of Toyotas and Nissans and I looked out the window. A stone church with a high stone wall around it, statues peeking out timidly. A huddle of kids in hooded football jackets, standing on a corner that was as close to a football field as they'd ever get. An insurance office in a storefront barricaded with heavy wire mesh. A used-car lot lit brighter than Fenway Park, ringed by a chain link fence, which was topped by glistening razor-wire loops. A fortified shop that cashed checks and sold beepers. A sporting goods store that probably sold banana clips for AK-47s.

"The American dream," I said.

Clair looked out at the brick and concrete.

"You know, we turn up our noses but a big chunk of the world would kill to live in a place like this," he said, his big arm slung over the steering wheel. "Running water, toilets that don't dump on the ground. Medicine and schools."

"Hope, you mean."

"A lot of places, there isn't any. People come here from these dirt-poor countries and they work their asses off. After five years, they're out of here. Fifteen years, their kids are in graduate school. Places they come from, it can't be done. Once you're born, that's it. A few people get lucky, get born rich. The rest crapped out and they have the rest of their lives to think about it."

"And the ones who don't want to work their asses off can deal drugs."

"And if they get caught they get a free lawyer," he said. "Like I said, a great country. Where to?"

We decided to look for a place to stay, but on the first pass through the main drag, didn't see anything remotely resembling a hotel. Beyond the little business district, the street went over a little drab green bridge and then passed into the half-light between two brick mill walls. We peered up like explorers eyeing the jungle along the Amazon. The mills were four stories high, broken windows on each floor. Pigeons huddled on the granite sills, a couple of winos on the sidewalks below them. Gang graffiti was painted on the walls like petroglyphs. "MLA . . . Cookie . . . TZT." A graceful brick tower loomed above it all, with a clock in it that had once kept the workers punctual.

The clock said it was eleven-thirty. These days, that was close enough.

Then the mill walls ended and there were empty lots and more drab little houses. One had a sign advertising for rooms by the day, week or month.

Clair slowed.

"Naah," I said.

"Naah," he said.

Clair took a right and the houses closed in.

The street was narrow, the tenements right on the sidewalk. The big Ford seemed to take up both lanes and the first oncoming car went up on the sidewalk to pass us. Two young women pushing baby carriages stared. At the corner at the end of the block, there was a store with boarded-up windows. The sign said "*Eglisia Pentecostal. Soldados de Jesus.*" A bunch of guys stood in a knot on the sidewalk out front. Hooded jackets. Hard stares as the big truck with Maine plates rolled slowly by.

"We could stop but they'd probably try to convert us," I said.

"They may have been *soldados* but I don't think they were with Jesus."

"Hey, the Lord works in mysterious ways."

We worked our way through the neighborhood back toward the downtown. The signs in the stores were in Spanish. The bakery was Dominican. In the window of the Spanish video store was a poster of Arnold Schwarzenegger holding a big pistol. The store sat at a square named for somebody called Thomas Kelly, who was probably long dead, his progeny scattered to the suburbs. In their wakes were women, hurrying to the store where the sign advertised *chuleta de cerdo.*

"How's your Spanish?" Clair said.

"Somewhere between rusty and nonexistent."

"Me, too. Between the two of us, we ought to be able to communicate at least the basics. If they speak English."

"Like, 'Have you seen a guy named Bobby Mullaney?' "

"Right," Clair said. "And, 'Which way to the Holiday Inn?' "

"I think the nearest one's in Boston. Let's try the police station, first."

"What do we do there?"

"Ask if they've seen Bobby Mullaney," I said.

"I thought you already asked them that."

"I did, but you get different answers when you're standing right in front of somebody."

"You hope," Clair said.

"I hope."

Clair tossed our duffel bags in the truck cab and locked it. The truck was parked in front of a meter on a triangular common at the center of the downtown. Valley City Hall was across the common. A guy on a street corner had told us the police station was out back. He looked like he would know. And he did.

The Valley cruisers were black and white and so was the paddy wagon that pulled up to a side door as we passed. The cops got out and yanked the back door open and said, "Watch your step, ladies," and several women of indeterminate age but very determinate profession teetered out.

"What time is it?" I asked Clair.

"Five-thirty," he said.

"Things get rolling early here."

"Maybe they never quite stop," Clair said.

"It's the crack."

"No rest for the weary," he said.

Which I was feeling myself, but we followed the women into the police station and down a flight of stairs. They went through a door, ragged models heading for the runway. The door closed and we stood there, looking at the empty seat behind the bulletproof information window. Police, uniformed and detectives, went by us going both ways. They all looked busy and my mission seemed suddenly trivial, but I shook it off. I followed a detective down the hall and Clair followed me.

Twenty steps down the hall, the detective turned.

"Can I help you?" he said.

"I'm looking for Detective Martucci."

He was chunky, gun high on his right hip, folder in his left hand. Young but tough beyond his years.

"Who are you?"

"I'm a reporter."

He looked at Clair, big and hard in his green canvas jacket and work boots.

"He's with me," I said.

"I figured that. She isn't here."

"Is she gone for the day?"

"No, she's out."

"You expect her back soon?"

"I don't know. She's on a homicide."

"Oh, wow."

His look said no wow was necessary.

"What sort of homicide was it?"

"The kind with a stiff," he said.

"Stiff wasn't named Bobby Mullaney, was it?"

The detective looked at me. While I had his attention, I quickly explained.

"Never heard of him," he said. "But I've only been here three years. Came from Methuen. You came all the way from Maine to find this guy?"

I shrugged.

"I got a bridge in New York I want you to look at."

"Only if Bobby Mullaney's floating under it," I said.

The detective looked at Clair.

"What're you? The photographer?"

"Chaperone," Clair said.

He smiled as he looked down on the detective. The detective didn't know whether to smile, so he didn't, but something in Clair connected with him.

"You hunt?" the cop said. "I bet you hunt."

"Oh, yeah. Waldo County's chock-full of deer."

"Last year I went up, I didn't even see one. Froze my butt. This year I may say the hell with it."

"You gotta let 'em come to you," Clair said. "Know where they spend time and go there and wait."

"Hey, I don't have the patience."

"That's hunting. It isn't chasing animals through the woods. Hell of a lot more relaxing. Know your prey and let it come to you."

"Well, maybe I'll try it," the detective said, and with that he walked down the hall and through an unmarked door. It closed behind him. We stood there.

"If you're all through male bonding, maybe I could ask some questions," I said.

"He never heard of him," Clair said.

"I wanted to give him my name, in case he came across him."

"What're you gonna do? Have him call you on the car phone?"

"I don't know."

"I think you're reporting like he hunts. Let's go find a hotel and a TV and a couple cold beers. See if this Mullaney guy's on the local news."

I looked at him. A uniformed cop came by and gave us a suspicious look. I smiled at her and it was enough to keep her moving.

"I thought I was in charge here," I said to Clair.

"Where'd you get that idea?"

"I don't know. It was my idea to come down here. It's my story."

"And my truck. Let's go."

"Once an officer, always an officer," I said.

"Goddamn right. Ain't often I get outranked."

"And she's in North Carolina."

"Right."

"Let's find a room and a phone," I said. "You can go first."

"Chicken," Clair said.

Mary told Clair to be careful. Then she put his daughter on and his voice softened even more. He asked Susan if she was getting enough rest and he asked what the baby did that day. Then, sitting there on the edge of the motel bed, he smiled and said, "Hey there. You let your mama get some sleep, you hear me? Or I'll have to come down there and pummelize you. Yeah. That's what I'll have to do. Yeah."

He paused and smiled deeply and said his goodbyes.

It was my turn.

I got Roxanne's answering machine, which could have meant she was in the tub, in a courtroom, putting out the trash, or facing down some bullying scumbag parent. I told the machine I was in Valley, staying at the renowned Route

293 Motel. In fact, I was the only person staying in the renowned Route 293 Motel. I gave the number and I said I was with Clair, which would reassure her. I said we'd stop on the way back tomorrow and I said I loved her. As I hung up, Clair handed me a beer.

He turned on the TV and found the local news. The newscasters, a daft-acting man and woman, were chuckling over what was apparently a private joke. When they were through laughing, they reported that asbestos had been found in a Valley elementary school, causing the place to be shut down, maybe forever. Then they laughed some more. Finally they said it was going to be clear and cool on Friday but before that, police were investigating a possible murder-suicide on Lawrence Street in Valley. A man had killed his wife and himself, in that order. There were no names available but the man and wife were in their seventies.

And then the newspeople took a breath and laughed some more.

"Doesn't sound like Bobby," I said.

"Nope. Let's go eat."

"After I call Melanie."

"Break the good news?"

"Make sure he hasn't come straggling home, tail between his legs. Wouldn't that be funny?"

"We could relax and take in the sights," Clair said.

"What sights?"

"Don't be such an uptight Anglo. Let's find a good Dominican restaurant. Or Cambodian. I thought I saw a Cambodian place when we were downtown."

"Let me call Melanie," I said. "See if she can give us anybody to talk to."

Clair opened two more beers and handed me one. I put it next to the first, on the phone table, and took out my notebook. I found Melanie's number in Florence and dialed, charging the call to my number in Prosperity. The phone rang and then there was a click. A long pause.

"Hello?" I said.

"Yeah," a voice said.

It was Stephen.

"Stephen. This is Jack McMorrow. How're you doing?"
There was a pause. He grunted.

"Is your mother home?"

"No, she's out."

"How 'bout your . . ."

I stumbled. Dad? Stepfather? I liked it better in the days
of the traditional nuclear family.

"How 'bout Bobby? Has he been back?"

"No," Stephen murmured.

Then stopped.

Poise himself. Maybe I should have inquired about his
ammo supply. I wasn't sure what to say, didn't know how
much he knew.

"Listen, Stephen," I began. "I'm in Valley. I just
wanted to let your mother know that. I just thought
I'd—"

"What're you doing there?" he blurted.

"Well, I thought I'd see if he'd been arrested or something down here. Hurt or something. I tried over the phone
but it—"

"So you're down there?"

He sounded anxious, upset. Maybe he hadn't known.
Maybe I was bringing bad news, or at least foreshadowing
it.

"Yeah," I said. "I thought I'd look around. See if anybody had seen him. I thought I'd talk to the newspaper
people down here, see if—"

"Jesus," Stephen said.

And he hung up.

I sat there with the phone in my hand.

"Whoa," I said. "What's his problem?"

"Was he upset?" Clair said, sitting back in a chair, beer
on his lap.

"I don't know. I guess. I don't know. He seemed surprised to hear I was here, in Valley. And when I was telling
him what I was going to do, ask around a little, all that, he
just said, 'Jesus,' and hung up."

Clair sipped his beer.

"Maybe he thinks the only news from down here would be bad news."

"Maybe he didn't know Bobby was down here at all," I said.

"Maybe you should call back."

I did. The phone rang twice. Melanie answered.

"Hi," I said. "I think I upset Stephen."

"Where are you?"

She sounded tense.

"Valley. The Route Two-ninety-three Motel. I tried getting answers over the phone but I kept getting put on hold so I zipped down."

"So what are you going to do?"

You're welcome, I thought.

"Ask around some. I talked to some cops already but they haven't seen him down here. Not that they know of."

"What are you gonna do now?"

Jeez, I thought. Is it okay if I go to the bathroom?

"I don't know. I'll probably stop by the paper in the morning. Try to talk to the police reporter. Wander around some, I guess. Get somebody to ask around for me. Who would Bobby see if he was down here? Relatives? Old friends?"

"There's nobody," Melanie said flatly.

"Nobody? How long did you guys live here?"

"Long enough. When we left we burned up the bridges behind us."

"All of them?"

"Some of 'em we didn't want."

"What do you mean? You got chased out of here?"

"Something like that, I guess. I mean, we didn't leave our address."

"And Coyote?"

"He didn't, either," Melanie said.

"So have things cooled down or what?"

"I don't know. I guess a lot of the people from back then are dead. Or in jail."

"What about the guy Bobby left with? Was he from the old days?"

Melanie hesitated.

"I hope not," she said.

Downtown was a half-mile from the motel as the crow
would have flown had there been any in Valley. For us,
half lost, circling in the dark, it was a couple of miles and
then we pulled up on the main drag. There was a restaurant,
Restaurante Dominica, just behind us, between a bank and
a department store. Clair locked the truck and we walked
back. I was reading the menu in the window when Clair
tried the door. It was locked.

"Must be a lunch hour place," Clair said.

"It sounded good," I said.

We kept walking.

There was a Christian Science Reading Room, but that
was closed, too. Another bank, then a storefront display of
the Valley mills in their heyday. Sepia photographs of
poker-faced young women in front of long rows of spinning
machines. Poker-faced guys with mustaches, standing beside the women.

"There must be a museum in this place," Clair said.

"We'll find it tomorrow. I'm starved."

So we walked down the block, then took a left. Walked
down that side street and took a right. A sign way down
the block said, "Phnom Penh Gardens."

"Yes," we said in unison.

Phnom Penh Gardens was open. Better than that, it was
almost empty. We had three hovering waiters, all young
men, none of whom spoke much English. I counted five
more people in the kitchen.

"How does a place like this support so many people?"
I said.

"They don't have American expectations."

"A lot of money?"

"For very little work, in the shortest possible amount of
time," Clair said.

"You think they'll catch on?"

"The ones who do join gangs."

"Trade in their Old World values for new ones," I said.

"Everybody else has," Clair said.

Dinner was hot-pot vegetables, simmering in electric cook-pots on the table, with raw seafood on the side. We cooked the shrimp and scallops, mussels and clams, holding them in the steaming broth. It was very good and the beer was cold. I noticed that Clair handled chopsticks as well as he handled a chain saw, which was very well.

"You look like you've done this before," I said.

"I loved Asia. In peacetime, it's paradise."

"And in war?"

"It's like every other place in war."

We ate with purpose, then drank tea as the waiters stood around us like servants in livery. The one who spoke the most English told us to have a nice night. I thanked him and paid the bill. Clair left a big tip.

"Sign of a tourist," I said.

"Industry should be rewarded," he said.

Outside, it was quiet and dark but on the next block there were lights and people on the sidewalk.

"Let's see what's down there," I said.

Clair nodded and we walked. The lights turned out to be bars, one on our side of the street, two on the other. As we got closer, I could see that the people on the sidewalk weren't directly outside the bars, but a little distance away, walking, leaning against the brick walls. Cars passed and they moved to the edge of the street.

I could see they were mostly women.

"The red light district," Clair said.

"I think I'll try to talk to them."

"Talking doesn't pay their bills."

"Their bills are for heroin and cocaine," I said. "They never get paid."

We slowed as we approached. Two women leaning against the wall looked at us warily. A guy was leaning against the door of an idling Toyota. The Toyota had fancy wheels and blacked-out windows. The driver was a shadow in the seat. The guy who was leaning gave us a long look,

then turned back to his conversation. I felt like a conven-
tioneer stepping out.

"You boys need a date," a woman said, coming from
one of the doorways.

She was small and young, dressed in red heels and a
black skirt that was very short and was not real leather. Her
sweater was white and fuzzy and barely buttoned.

I tried to look paternal.

"You could get hypothermia out here dressed like that,"
I said.

"You know what you could get?"

Her accent was city. She came close and took hold of
my arm. Her hair was dyed an odd shade of orange. Her
face was clumsily made up, so she looked like a little girl
playing dress-up. She might have been pretty but between
the red stuff on her cheeks and the red stuff on her lips was
sallow junkie pallor.

"You guys have a car?" she said. "We got a two-for-
one special I think you'd like."

I shook my head. Clair was on my left, closer to the
street. His face was full of pity.

"No, we're just walking," I said. "But I do have a question for you."

She sidled closer.

"You want to talk," she breathed huskily. "I'm good at
talking. Ten minutes. Twenty bucks."

"I'd like to talk to you but that's not—"

"I make that phone stuff look like baby talk, I'm telling
you."

"I'm sure," I said, "But I'm looking for somebody. A
buddy of mine. His name's Bobby. Maybe you've seen
him. You or one of your friends."

"Maybe," the woman said.

She held out a hand with long red nails, palm up.

"Talk's talk," she said

I hesitated, then took out my wallet and slipped out a
twenty. I put it in her hand and it disappeared inside the
waistband of her skirt.

"His name's Bobby Mullaney," I said. "He's about my height, a little skinnier. Dark curly hair, talks a mile a minute. He's from Maine."

The woman shrugged. Another woman, who had been watching our transaction, walked toward us. She was bigger, older, black hair and a short black dress.

"Your friend here, he need a date, too?"

Clair shook his head slowly. The woman went to him to try the next phase of persuasion. He stood there, impassive and immobile, probably thinking about his daughter.

My friend still had me by the arm.

"You heard of him? Bobby Mullaney?"

"Uh-uh."

"I'll give you another twenty if you walk along here and ask these people."

She looked doubtful.

"Come on. Twenty bucks for two minutes. Think of what you have to do normally to make forty dollars."

"I don't—"

"And he may be with a guy named Coyote. Really tall and thin. Long hair down his back. Black, black eyes. Says he's an Indian. Real spooky-looking."

I took out a ten and held it out. Her hand came up and snatched it like a frog snagging a fly.

"Ten more if you look like you made a good effort."

"I'll be right back," she said.

She moved up the sidewalk. The car still idled and the two guys were still talking. When the woman walked away, the guy outside the car stopped talking and looked at us. We looked back at him. Clair hadn't blinked since we'd stopped.

With him as my backup, I walked over to the two men. I smiled and said hello. They were young but not children. Handsome faces sharp as knives. Dark hair swept back to small tails. The guy in the car was wearing a football jacket and batting gloves. Cross-training. The guy closest to me was wearing a fatigue jacket and a baseball hat on backward.

They looked at me as though I hadn't spoken.

"I'm looking for a guy," I said.

No reaction.

"He's from Maine. His name's Bobby Mullaney. He may be with a guy named Coyote. Both around thirty. Bobby's got curly hair, talks a lot. Coyote's tall and skinny. Hair real long. Says he's an Indian."

They looked at me like I was a museum specimen, behind plate glass.

"I'm down here for the guy Bobby, his wife. She's afraid he might get whacked."

Two sets of eyes were fixed to mine. That much I knew.

"He left Lewiston, Maine, with a guy from Valley who does business up there. More than just a runner."

The guy in the car moved his lips. I was getting through.

"If anybody's seen these guys down here, I'd sure like to know and so would Bobby's wife. I'm sure she'd make it worth your while. She's pretty worried. I'm staying at the Two-ninety-three Motel. Jack McMorrow."

I reached into my pocket. The guy in the car reached under the seat and back up before I could take out my pad. He had something in his lap and it wasn't a map. And fifty bucks said the safety was off.

Very slowly, I wrote my name and Bobby's name. Then I wrote the hotel name and phone number on the pad. Just as slowly, I extended the paper to the guy in the fatigue jacket.

He looked at me.

Looked at the paper.

It fluttered like a hankie. Fluttered again and then just hung there.

He took it.

"Cop?" he said.

"Reporter."

"Who's that one?"

He looked toward Clair, who I sincerely hoped was still behind me.

"A friend."

He looked at Clair and then back at me. The guy in the car was still as a mannequin.

"You guys are from Maine?"

"Yeah."

"You must be nuts. Loco."

"I don't know. You get used to the winters. Mud season's kind of a drag and then there are the blackflies . . ."

I let it trail off. The fatigue guy looked at me as he slipped the paper inside his jacket pocket.

"You better watch your goddamn ass down here, man," he said. "You just used up a big chunk of luck."

He turned away and we did, too. The woman came back and said nobody had heard of Bobby Mullaney. She held out her hand and I put a ten in it. She asked if I was sure I didn't want a date. I said I was and took out my pad and wrote the names and number again. She took it and read it, which took her a long time, as if I'd written her a long letter. Then she stuck the paper in the front of her skirt and did a little gyration.

"You sure?"

"I'm sure," I said.

We walked up the block to the next intersection, where cars were crossing and we stopped.

"I'm impressed," Clair said.

"Reporters in New York talk to people like that every day. Alone."

"No, I mean how you memorized the phone number of the motel."

He grinned.

"Superior intellect," I said.

"This guy's wife really putting up money?"

"I made that part up."

"Smart. You think this direct approach'll work?"

"I don't know. It's really a pretty small place. We do this a few times and the word will get around."

"And then what?"

"I don't know. If that doesn't work maybe we could get one of those planes that tow the signs behind them. 'Seen Bobby Mullaney? Call 677-7866.' "

"How 'bout milk cartons?"

''That's good. And posters on all the telephone poles.''

''Maybe Bobby would see them,'' Clair said.

The cars passed. We stepped out.

''Oh, yeah. I guess I keep forgetting that he could be out there.''

''Alive,'' he said.

We walked up two blocks, over one. On that block was another tavern with several cars parked outside. Across the street, a half-dozen women stood. We approached and were received just as warmly as before. Different faces. Same misery.

A white blond woman wearing a long black leatherette coat latched on to me and I gave her my pitch. She opened the coat to show me she was wearing only underwear, and when I still didn't bite, she grudgingly took my ten dollars and went to ask her colleagues my question.

The woman stopped at each woman. A couple, she queried two at a time. At the far end of the sidewalk, I couldn't hear what she was saying. I saw heads shake no. Then she made her way back, still walking her swinging, hooker's walk.

As she drew closer to us, she stopped at a woman she'd already polled once. I heard the woman say, ''Cops?''

Our woman said, ''Nah.'' Then said something quickly in Spanish. I caught the words ''Mullaney'' and ''Maine.''

''*El indio?*'' the other woman said.

Her voice became almost angry. Or afraid.

''No *indio*. No, no,'' and she gave the first woman a little shove and hurried away.

I started after her.

And headlights came on.

They glared from the end of the block, beyond the women. The women turned to look and then lights came on behind us and they were hurtling forward and a loud-speaker voice was saying, ''Police. Stay where you are.''

''The other ten, quick,'' the woman said.

I had it in my hand and I put it in hers as a spotlight lit the sidewalk.

"You," a voice said. "Hold it right there."

The woman scuttled away on her heels. Across the street, a guy had his hands on a car roof, a cop in a blue raid jacket already patting him down. More headlights were coming down the block. I saw the paddy wagon come around the corner. Two cops were coming toward us.

"Which one?" they called back to the car.

"The younger guy. Soliciting. Saw cash."

"Damn," I said.

"John law," Clair said.

"Okay, Jack," one of the cops said. "Put your hands on that wall there and spread 'em."

I did.

"What's your name, sir?" he asked, patting me down.

"Jack," I said.

"Hey, you wanna play games? I'll play games."

"Play 'em by yourself," I said. "My name's Jack McMorrow."

Nineteen

THE COP WHO frisked me put me in the back of an un-marked car. The women went in the black and white van. Clair was halfway up the block on the way back to the truck when I went by in the car. He looked calm and not the least bit surprised.

That made one of us.

My hands were handcuffed behind me and I was belted in. It was a different cop and he drove fast, whistling softly to himself.

"Where you from, sir?" he said suddenly.

"Maine," I said.

"Looking for a little action in the big city?"

He said it without judgment.

"No, I was looking for some information."

"Oh, yeah. How's that?"

"I'm a reporter. I'm trying to find a guy. He's in the story I'm working on."

"What's his name?"

"Bobby Mullaney. Another guy named Coyote."

"Don't know any Coyote. You really a reporter?"

He said that without judgment, too.

"Yeah."

"What paper?"

"Freelance. Doing a story for the *Globe.*"

"No kidding."

"No, really."

"Hey, I do a little writing myself. I'm taking a course at U Lowell. Expository writing. You do a lot of writing in this job but most people, they don't know that. They think you just ride around looking for bad guys, you know? But it's a lot of desk work. Killer desk work. But this writing class, I think my reports are better already. I mean, I know what to put first and then second and so on. Before, I just sort of upchucked it all out there, you know what I mean?"

I said I did know. I also knew the handcuffs hurt, and my triceps were cramping from having my arms behind my back. The cop pulled up to the back of the police station and stopped, then backed up and stopped and got out.

He opened the door and helped me out, too.

"So you know Bobby Mullaney?" I said, as soon as I got to my feet.

"I don't know. Maybe," the cop said. "I mean, the name sounds familiar. I'd have to check. But I can't check now 'cause we gotta get you processed."

Then he walked me to a door that hissed open, like the door to a supermarket. We went inside, into the same hall where Clair and I had spoken to the detective. It looked different with cuffs on.

"Maybe crystal meth, a few years ago," the cop said, as we walked down the hall. "That's what comes to the top of my brain. They had a few little labs here. Bikers mostly. These guys bikers?"

"More like hippies. But people change."

"You think so?" the cop said, pushing open a door. "I don't know. I think they change the looks, the wrapper, but they stay pretty much the same underneath. Maybe I'm wrong but that's what I think. Now, let me ask you something. When you write, do you write up, like, an outline or do you just have the outline in your head?"

• • •

The room was small like a chapel and filled with metal folding chairs. I sat there alone with a surveillance camera peering at me and then the door opened and four of the hookers came in, but not the woman who had said *"el indio."* The four women sat down wearily in their short skirts and heels, like movie extras after a long shoot. Whatever little allure they might have had was washed away by the fluorescent lights.

I turned but none of them looked at me. Then the door opened again and a cop and my friend and her friend were led in. They sat down without acknowledging me. I got up and moved three seats over and sat down next to the woman who had said she'd seen Coyote. She was small and thin and hollow-eyed but her legs were crossed primly, as if to preserve at least that much dignity. Her eyes were runny and so was her nose. She kept rubbing the side of her face.

"El indio," I said. *"Dónde el indio?"*

She didn't laugh at my Spanish but she didn't answer, either. Her foot jiggled nervously and her shoe slid off enough to show a hole in her black stocking.

"Dónde el indio?" I repeated.

My flasher friend looked over from two seats down. She shrugged and the thin woman blurted something to her in Spanish.

"She wants money," my friend said.

"All I have is twenty," I lied.

"That's good."

I looked around and took out my wallet again. I gave the hollow-eyed woman the bill and she shoved it in her shoe.

"So what else does she know?"

The hollow-eyed woman looked at my friend, not me. Spoke low and fast.

I caught the words *"Él busca cadáver."*

I waited.

"She says she heard he was looking for a body. The body."

"Bobby Mullaney's?"

A side door opened. A matronly woman cop came in and the women all pulled themselves to their feet and headed for the front of the room. Some dug in their clothing for cash. A bald man in a jacket and turtleneck came in and opened a blue plastic folder.

"Hello, ladies," he said. "You know the drill, let's keep it orderly and we can all go home early."

The women put down cash and filled out a form. Then they moved over and were fingerprinted by the uniformed cop, who then stepped over and snapped a Polaroid on a tripod. The class picture: Valley High.

They went out the door, one by one, first my friend and then the hollow-eyed woman. Damn, I thought. I quickly stepped up and the bald guy looked at me.

"Soliciting. Class E misdemeanor. Where you from, Mr. McMorrow?"

"Prosperity, Maine," I said.

"What you doing down here?"

"Working on a story. I'm a reporter."

"You got ID that says so?"

"Sort of."

I dug out my wallet and my *Times* press card. My driver's license and two credit cards. The bald guy looked at them.

"But you live in Maine?"

"I freelance."

"Ever been picked up for this before?"

"Nope."

"You make a habit of these fine ladies?"

"No. I was just trying to talk to them. Wrong place, wrong time, I guess."

He looked at me.

"What are the chances of you coming back to appear in court?"

"Hundred percent," I said.

"I'm gonna make your day, Mr. McMorrow. I'm gonna issue you a summons. It says you'll be required to appear in Valley District Court November seventeen at nine a.m. If you don't show, that means we put out a warrant for your arrest. You could go to jail. Let me tell you, it'd be a lot easier to just show up."

"I know that."

He slid the summons toward me. I hurriedly signed at the bottom and he took two of the three copies and handed the third to me. I thanked him. I'd thank him more if I caught up with the women.

"You can thank me by showing up in court."

"I will."

"And if I were you, I'd choose my company more carefully next time. Me, I tell you guys right out. I got no sympathy for johns myself. I figure you're sort of an enabler. Like with booze. If there weren't any johns, there wouldn't be any hookers."

"I suppose," I said.

"And you know what else bothers me?"

I shook my head. Precious seconds went by.

"The johns have a choice, you know. They're just horny and lazy and scumbags. These girls are desperate. Coked-out crackheads. Heroin addicts. They've got less choice."

"I was just doing my job, asking questions. These are the people who might have the answers."

"Did they?" the cop asked.

"I think so. One or two."

"What's your story about?"

"Marijuana. Mostly in Maine."

"That right? Well, let me tell you something. You better watch your step down here. This isn't Maine. Fifteen-year-old kid'll blow you away and go have pizza. Not even think about it."

"I'll keep that in mind."

"They're like goddamn reptiles. They don't blink when they look at you. No conscience. No nothing. You got that in Maine yet?"

"No," I said. "Our kids just started wearing their baseball hats backward. Give us time."

Clair was standing in the hallway inside the door.

"Against the law to talk to a prostitute?" he said, pushing the door open.

"Did they come out this way?"

"Three or four of 'em did. Got in a cab."

"The skinny one?"

"Yup."

"Let's try to find them."

"You a slow learner or what? You want to get picked up again?"

"No, I want to talk to that thin woman again. She said she saw Coyote. She called him *el indio*."

"She didn't see the other guy?"

"No, but she said she heard '*el indio*' was looking for a body."

"Sure it wasn't 'buddy'?"

"No. It was Spanish. *Cadáver*."

"Bobby's?"

"That'd be my first guess," I said. "Maybe he knows more of what they're dealing with down here."

"What are you going to tell the wife?"

"Nothing yet."

"Why do today what you can put off till tomorrow?"

"Right. And besides, I don't really know anything."

"Well, I'll tell you what," Clair said, unlocking the truck door. "If you want to bet that this Mullaney'll turn up safe and sound and cocky, I'll take that bet. And I'll give you odds."

"I'm about to start hedging," I said, and I swung up into the seat.

We cruised the downtown but didn't see any prostitutes, at least not on the streets. I poked my head into one smoky barroom while Clair waited outside in the truck.

"It was all guys," I reported, climbing back in.

"Friendly?"

"Cozy. I would have stayed if I'd been heavily armed."

"No women?"

"A couple but you wouldn't want to fight 'em."

So we crisscrossed the streets, working our way south. The main drag led to a bridge across the black murky river. On the other side was a housing project, with rectangular brick buildings and small trees broken off waist-high. We drove through and saw more of the little cars with black

windows and fancy wheels. Clair's big truck was from another culture, and when we pulled up to a light where a
knot of kids stood on the corner, the kids turned and stared
as if we were riding a float from the Macy's Parade.

I stared back at their baby faces and feral eyes.

"I was talking to a patrolman while I was waiting for
you," Clair said. "He said the new weapon of choice for
these kids is a machete."

"It is a jungle out there."

"And a machete doesn't violate the gun laws."

"So they have to lop off a hand instead of blowing somebody away," I said. "A small price to pay."

I looked out at them. Their faces were without expression.

"There's a hole in them somewhere," I said. "That
look."

"You know where you see that? In places where kids
grow up in wars."

"What's the war about here?"

"We're fighting ourselves," Clair said, putting the truck
in gear as the light changed. "It's coming apart from the
inside. The core is starting to rot. No religion. No family.
No rules. No hope."

"Thank you, Pollyanna."

Clair smiled.

"Don't mention it."

We doubled back over the bridge and through the downtown, where the sidewalks still were empty, save for a couple of street people in winter hats. They moved in their
perpetual shuffle and we swung onto the road that took us
across a canal and onto the street that led to the motel.

Like bunkmates at summer camp, I sat on the edge of
my bed and Clair sat on his.

"Too bad about this soliciting thing," he said.

I shrugged.

"No big deal. If I write this first-person, like for the
Globe magazine, it'll add to the spice."

"Maybe you should've taken a swing at the cops. Spice it up with a night in jail."

"I can always come back and do that later, if they don't go for my query letter."

"A hard-bitten journalist," Clair said.

"Only on the outside," I said.

Clair took off his shirt and yawned and stretched. He was muscular beyond his years.

"What do you think of this cadaver thing? Think she just wanted some money?"

"No. It was too spontaneous. I think she heard something. But you don't know for sure that *el indio* is Coyote."

"No. And why would Coyote be so sure Bobby was dead?" I said.

"He knows these people better than we do."

"Why would he hang around? Just to bring back the body? If somebody you were with had been killed, wouldn't you run?"

"Plains Indians would do anything to retrieve the bodies of fallen warriors," Clair said.

"I don't think he's a Plains Indian. I think he's Italian or Armenian or something."

"Maybe he wants to make sure Bobby gets a proper burial, instead of going in some incinerator."

"I've got to find that woman again."

"I'm sure it's the most sought after she's been in years," Clair said.

And then he said he was tired and, like a soldier who had gone without sleep in the past, conked right out. I locked and chained the door, opened a warm beer from my bag and sat on the bed to do my notes before the memories faded. I described everything and everybody. What the women looked like. What the cop said in the patrol car. What it was like to be picked up for soliciting. What the prostitutes looked like, sounded like, acted like. I wrote two pages describing this ruined little city. And I wrote what I'd learned about Bobby's disappearance, which was that this city was dangerous beyond its size, that he was still gone and his friend was asking if anybody had seen a body.

I sat there and considered how to phrase it to Melanie. Then I decided the best solution was to just call Roxanne instead. As I reached for the phone, it rang.

"Jack, it's Melanie. Have you, well, have you found anything?"

Oh, no, I thought. I reached for my beer.

"Well, not really. Well, I *have* found something."

"What?"

Her voice was expectant, as if she were clinging to hope.

"Well, I found a woman. A prostitute. She said she saw Coyote. Or overheard him or something. At least by my description. *El indio,* she called him."

"She was Hispanic?"

"Yeah."

"Where is he?"

"I don't know. She didn't—I didn't get to ask her that."

"But—"

"The police came and swept the street where these prostitutes were. She got away from me at the police station."

"And you can't find her?"

"I couldn't tonight. I'll try to track her down tomorrow, I guess."

"What was he doing? Was Bobby with him?"

I took a long pull on the beer.

"No," I said. "He—I'm not sure how to put this. She said, this woman, I mean. She said Coyote was . . . was looking for a body."

There was silence.

And then a weary moan, a soft uttering.

"Oh, my God," Melanie Mullaney said.

Twenty

"TELL ME AGAIN," Melanie said.

I'd told her four or five times but I told her again. She wanted to know what street the woman was on, what she looked like, exactly what she said. After I'd told her everything I knew, two and three times over, we came back to the same point, which we left unsaid.

That it was likely that Coyote thought Bobby was dead. That he was looking for his body or at least someone who knew where Bobby might have been dumped. Maybe there'd been a rumor. A guy hassled so-and-so and he was killed. Word was that he'd been left . . .

"I think you should come back," Melanie said suddenly.

"Well, I will. After I ask around some more. Tomorrow I thought I'd see if I could find her, see where she saw Coyote, if it was really him. If I get something pretty positive, I think I should go to the police here."

"I can't do time," Melanie said. "If I'm inside, what about Stephen?"

Inside, I thought. Is that the way they talk in Florence, Maine?

"You should come back. I should never have gotten you into this, but God, I didn't know you'd go down there. What if you get hurt or something?"

"I won't."

"But you might. I know what it's like down there. That's why we left and that was years ago. Now it's like that times a hundred."

"I'll be fine," I said. "I have reporter's immunity."

"You're gonna write about what you find down there?"

I paused.

"That was the deal. That was the deal we made."

"Right," Melanie said, as if she'd forgotten. "Well, I just don't want you getting hurt. I'd feel responsible, you know? I think you should come back in the morning."

"I'll look around some more tomorrow. And I'll call you."

"Oh . . . Well, okay. I mean, take care now."

And she hung up. I did, too, and sat there.

Something had jarred me. Melanie had said she didn't want me to get hurt. She'd said she hadn't known I'd go down *there*. But how could she have known? When we'd talked, when I'd agreed to ask around, it had been to ask around Lewiston. Had she known then that the trail would lead to Valley? Was she more than a bystander to the marijuana deals?

I mulled it some more, sitting there as Clair slept. I sipped the beer, which was even warmer. Then I made notes of that conversation with Melanie, before it slipped away. The notes ended with a question: What did Melanie know and when did she know it?

Clair slept and I sat. When I finished that beer, I opened another one and sat some more. The questions whirled around inside my head. Did I really know these people? I'd known they probably weren't exactly what they pretended to be, but had I misjudged even that? Were they something altogether different? Was there a layer to them I still hadn't seen?

I sipped and thought and listened to Clair's slow breathing. Then at eleven o'clock, I called Roxanne. Her answering machine clicked on and I winced, hoping she'd pick up, then sat up as I realized it was a different message.

"Hi," Roxanne's voice said. "J.M., if this is you, that matter we talked about needed some more observation. Don't worry. I'm fine. I'll be back by one. Call me in the morning. Please."

I put the phone down. She was tromping around Portland probably checking on those kids. Would she have a cop with her? One of her patrolman friends? A detective? She wouldn't just wander around those apartment buildings by herself? I reached for the phone to call and leave her a message saying to be careful. And then I realized it was too late.

I slid out of my jeans and lay back on the bed. It was a long time before I slept. And then a rattle woke me.

It was gray light. Dawn. I looked to my right and saw Clair's shadowy figure sitting up. He looked at me and put a finger to his lips. I heard a scraping sound outside. Then I heard the storm door squeak open. A whisper. More scraping at the doorjamb.

Clair eased out of bed and I did the same. He shoved the pillow into his sleeping bag and silently fluffed it up. I leaned over and piled my blankets. Then we padded to the side of the door. Clair was in front.

There was scraping at the jamb, then a click. The door eased open and the jaws of bolt cutters appeared at the chain. The jaws closed and the chain separated. There was a soft jingle.

Then silence.

The door pushed open. A leg stepped out. A basketball shoe on it. A black basketball shoe. Black sweatpants. The barrel of a shotgun. Short.

Clair hit the door with his shoulder, came around with his right forearm and lifted the kid off the ground by the throat. There was an "ooof" and the kid's head hit the wall by the door and Clair had the gun out of his hands and tossed back on the bed.

I turned the door bolt. Someone said "Shit" outside and there was a bang, like somebody's shoulder slamming the door. Clair had the kid by the throat with both hands and then the kid's right hand dropped to his sweatshirt pocket and I grabbed that arm just as the knife was coming out. Clair's big right arm pulled back and then shot out like there was a giant spring in it. His fist drove into the kid's mouth and nose, and the kid's head hit the wall again and blood spurted from his face like juice from a splatted orange.

The knife fell from his limp hand and I grabbed it. The shoulder hit the door again and I yelled, "Shoot through the door," and somebody said "Shit" again and then there were footsteps and a car motor revving and tires scrabbing on pavement.

"Call nine-one-one," Clair said, staring into the kid's face.

I went to the phone, picked up the receiver.

Put it back down.

"What's the matter?" Clair said.

"I don't know. Do we want to do that?"

"What?"

"Get involved with cops again. We'll be stuck here all day."

"What the hell else are we gonna do with him?"

"Bring him into town and dump him."

"At forty miles an hour," Clair said.

"And I want to talk to him."

"Should have told me that a couple of minutes ago."

"Glass jaw?"

"I guess. These kids are used to getting shot at but they never get punched."

"You hit him hard enough."

"You want a knife stuck in your side up to your aorta, be my guest."

"No thanks. But maybe we should clean him up a little."

"And then we better get out of here," Clair said. "The other guys probably went to get the rest of the club."

He was still holding the kid up against the wall. The kid's eyes were vague, his head weaving on his shoulders, blood running out of his nose and mouth and off his chin like drips off an icicle.

"I'll get a towel," I said.

I went to the bathroom, ran a hand towel under cold water and wrung it out. I came out and handed it to Clair and he clamped it over the kid's face as if I'd soaked it in chloroform.

It came back red. He put it over the kid's face again and pinched the kid's nose. He took the towel off and then pinched again. And then he led the kid over to the bed. I picked up the shotgun and Clair sat him down.

The kid was young, maybe sixteen, my height but thirty pounds lighter. He was dark and had even, almost handsome features and a wisp of a mustache. A tattoo on his hand was three letters, "TZT." His eyes were beginning to focus.

"Can we help you?" I said, still holding the shotgun, the barrel pointed at the floor.

He looked at me and made ready to spit. Clair smacked him on the side of the face with his left hand, lightly, with his open palm. The kid's head rolled and then snapped back. He stared at the space between us.

"Mind your manners," Clair said.

"What do you want?" I said.

The kid stared.

I repeated the question.

He took a deep breath.

"You're both dead," he whispered.

"What do you want?" I said.

He stared.

"Get the knife," Clair said.

"What?"

"Just get it."

I'd left it in the bathroom, by the sink. I went and got it, handed it to Clair. It was a wicked-looking combat knife, with a six-inch blade and holes for four fingers in the grip.

Clair handled it like a commando.

He grabbed the kid's left hand and jerked it toward him, shoving the blade between the kid's middle fingers. The knife was in a position to pare them off.

"Ten seconds," Clair said.

I looked at him.

"Nine, eight, seven . . ."

The kid's eyes began to widen. His breathing came faster.

"What do you want?" I said.

"Six, five, four, three—"

"The money," the kid blurted, his eyes on the knife.

Clair stopped counting.

"What money?"

"The money. The money for the buy."

"Who told you we were here for a buy?"

"Somebody."

"Who?" I said.

"Somebody. A friend of mine."

"Who?"

"A guy."

"A guy you know?"

He nodded, his eyes still locked on the knife.

"A guy from here?"

"Yeah."

"A guy you've known a long time from here?"

He nodded again.

"How much?"

"Thirty thousand."

"For coke?"

He nodded.

"Who told your buddy?"

"I don't know," the kid said.

"Should he start counting again?"

"Oh, no. I don't know, man. I don't know. They don't tell me that."

"What if he starts counting again?"

"I'll have to make it up," the kid said. " 'Cause I don't know."

I looked at Clair.

"Let's get out of here," he said.

The kid sat on the bed while I pulled on my clothes and stuffed both of our duffels. Clair stood with the shotgun hanging at his side. When I was done, he handed me the gun.

"Be careful with that thing. It's a piece of junk."

"You mean this isn't a sporting piece?" I said.

"For jacking drug dealers and storekeepers."

"And other sitting ducks."

"Which we'll be if this kid's frat brothers come back."

He grabbed his jacket from the hook by the door and put it on. I handed him the shotgun, and put my jacket on. The kid on the bed hadn't flinched.

I opened the door a crack and looked. This end of the parking lot was empty except for Clair's truck. I watched for another moment and then turned and grabbed both duffels. I went quickly to the side of the truck and tossed them in. Clair came out with the kid in front of him. I opened the passenger door and got in. Clair opened the driver's door and shoved the kid up and in. The gun was at his side.

He climbed in after the kid and shoved the kid's head forward so his forehead pressed against the dash. Then he handed me the gun. I held it on my right side, pointed forward. The motor started with a throaty rumble and Clair backed up and then forward and we bounced out of the parking lot and headed south for the interstate.

"We'll circle around," he said.

We got on the highway and headed east. Two exits up, we got off again and doubled back toward Valley. The kid looked straight ahead and didn't say a word.

When we got close to the city, Clair slowed and pulled into a strip mall. It wasn't much of a strip: a convenience store, a pizza shop and a hair salon. The pizza shop was closed so we pulled up there, then turned so the front of the truck was pointing out. We waited for a lull in the traffic and then Clair shoved the kid's head forward again. I handed him the shotgun, which he kept on the seat, pointing toward the kid. Then I opened the door and got out.

"Your only way out of this is to get some education," Clair told the kid. "Go back to school. Move away. It's your only chance. Get out."

Wordlessly, the kid slid across the seat and out onto the pavement. There was crusted blood under his nose, and both of his lips had ballooned. Worse than that, he'd lost considerable face.

The kid started walking, across the parking lot toward the city. I jumped back in the truck and Clair started off, away from the city. Five hundred yards down the road, he pulled into a vacant lot and, with the motor idling, picked up the gun and broke the barrel open and dropped out the shell.

"Junk, huh?" I said.

"Doesn't even deserve to be called a gun," Clair said.

We started again and a few hundreds yards farther Clair pulled off and eased up to a mailbox with one of those drive-through snouts. I grabbed a dirty pad from the glove box, pulled off a page and wrote, "Deliverto Valley P.D. Gang weapon. TZT." Clair took out his handkerchief and wiped the gun down, then the knife. Then he pulled the mailbox door open and dropped both of them in. They made a muffled thump.

"Special delivery," I said.

We drove away from the city, back to the interstate. One ramp said west, and one said east. West was Valley. East was home.

"Which way?" Clair said.

"I think we've worn out our welcome."

"Or used up our luck."

"Go east, young man," I said.

He did.

We'd driven five miles before either of us spoke. I broke the silence.

"You wouldn't have hurt that kid, would you?"

"When he was holding that shotgun, I would have killed him dead."

"But the thing with the fingers?"

"A bluff," Clair said.

"You scared the hell out of him."

"No easy task."

"You looked like you'd done that before."

"Yeah. Well, they called them insurgents back then."

I looked at him.

"I don't think I could do that. Even just bluffing."

"When a man's sole purpose in life is to kill you, you can do a lot of things," Clair said.

I thought for a moment.

"You know," Clair said. "you could probably save that kid. Take him away from that place. Deprogram him."

"You don't think it's too late?"

"No. Did you see his eyes? There was something left in there. I'd say he has six months. A year."

"If they don't dust him for screwing up."

"Goes without saying," Clair said.

We drove in silence for five more miles. My back was damp with cooled perspiration. I looked out at the gray nondescript sky and woods and highway. Clair turned on the radio. It blared news of traffic jams and other sporting events.

"We forgot our garbage bags," he said.

"I forgot my toothbrush."

"So what do you think that was all about?"

"I don't know," I said. "Maybe if two guys from Maine come down and start rummaging around Valley, it can only be for one reason."

"And it isn't to look for some lost soul."

"Probably we're an anomaly."

"I hate that word," Clair said. "It's hard to say. Like anemone."

"You get the feeling we made an anemone or two?"

"Well, we didn't make many friends, did we?" he said.

"But somebody got the idea we were carrying thirty grand."

"Pretty specific."

"Maybe they just told the kid that so he wouldn't chicken out," I said.

"I doubt it. They go in looking for something. We offer 'em forty bucks and change and it's our fingers under the knife."

"Maybe they were looking for two other guys from Maine, driving a big Ford four-wheel-drive."

"Good-looking guys, you mean."

"Right. Or maybe we just don't know what's going on. Maybe we were in over our heads down there."

"When you don't truly understand your enemy, you're always at a disadvantage," Clair said.

"Thank you, Mr. Military History."

"It's true."

"I know," I said. "But I figured—"

Clair held up his hand, then reached for the radio and turned it up.

"The investigation is being handled by the Valley Police Department and Massachusetts State Police," a radio voice intoned. *"A police spokesman said the body was discovered early this morning, in the burned remains of a car. The fire was reported at three-eleven a.m. in a deserted area behind the former E. E. Wooling Mill in Valley. Firefighters extinguished the blaze and discovered the man's body in the backseat.*

"The body was reportedly burned beyond recognition and has been taken to the state coroner's lab for identification and determination of cause of death. Police said the car was a white Subaru station wagon with Maine license plates. It was not known if the death was drug-related. And that's it for News Central Ninety-eight. Tune in at nine-oh-eight this morning . . ."

"They killed him," I said. "I can't believe it."

Twenty-one

VALLEY WASN'T A model city but some things it did very well. Cleaning up dead bodies was one of them.

By the time we found the Wooling mill, the body was gone. So was the car. So were any interested bystanders, assuming there had been any.

The scene was behind the mill, a monolithic building with gaping windows. The car had burned on a rocky slope that ran down to a canal, where water trickled through black muck littered with rusting iron shapes that leaned here and there like the remains of a sea battle. An industrial Truk Lagoon.

A Valley police cruiser sat idling at the top of the slope. The spot where the Subaru had been was looped with crime-scene tape. In the center of the loop was a chunk of melted tire and gashes in the gravel, probably from when the car had been yanked onto a ramp truck.

We parked behind the cruiser and got out. The cop buzzed his window down. He was bald with glasses. When we got closer, I could see a book on his lap, his hand on his gun.

"Can I help you?" the cop said.

"This where they found the body?" I said.

"Yup."

"White Subaru wagon with Maine plates?"

"It was. Isn't anymore."

"I think I know who was in it," I said.

The cop looked at me.

"Who are you?"

"Jack McMorrow."

"The guy from Maine?"

"Yup."

He reached for the microphone on his shoulder.

"Stay put," he said.

The detectives pulled up within ten minutes. There were two of them and one was Detective Martucci, whom I'd spoken with on the phone. This time she didn't have a call on the other line.

Clair went with the other detective, a small gray-haired guy. They went and stood at the rear of the unmarked car. I saw Clair reach into his wallet for his ID.

I stood by the hood of the cruiser with the patrol cop and Martucci. She was tall and thin and was wearing jeans and a tweed blazer. At first glance she looked like a fortyish mom, but up close there was a hardness in her gaze, a feeling that she was driven to do her job. She looked at my ID and didn't give it back.

"Okay, McMorrow," Martucci said. "Sorry about the brush-off before but this place is crazy, you know? Start at the beginning. Tell me what the hell you're doing down here."

I did, right from the beginning. Martucci took notes on a tiny pad. The fair. Florence. Bobby's marijuana plots. The legalization movement. Melanie in the restaurant. The people in Lewiston. What Paco said in the church.

"So he squawked and they whacked him?" Martucci said.

"I don't know. What do you think?"

"I think maybe your buddy—"

"He isn't my buddy. Wasn't, I mean."

"Whatever. Your source may have been up in the woods too long. Maybe he didn't know that they play a little rougher down here than they did ten years ago.''

"I've seen that."

"How so?"

I told her about the kid in the motel. I told her about the gun in the mailbox. I didn't tell her about the knife and the fingers.

"That's pretty stupid and you're pretty lucky. How'd your buddy get to be so tough?"

"He's an ex-Marine, and he's from Maine," I said. "The kid never knew what hit him."

"You can ID him?"

"You can't miss him. He's the one with the smushed face."

"We could charge you for putting that gun in the mailbox. Why didn't you call?"

I shrugged.

"I guess we just wanted to get out of here."

"Just turn the kid loose?"

"What would you have done with him?"

"Charged him with attempted armed robbery."

"And then turned him loose," I said.

She ignored that one.

"Why'd they think you were here to make a buy?"

"I don't know. A pretty big one, too."

"Thirty thousand isn't big around here," Martucci said. "It's on the small side of medium."

"So they took us for a couple of nickel-and-dimers?"

"Easy marks, maybe. Home invasion at a motel. Couple of hicks. Easy money."

"Which doesn't tell us what happened to Bobby Mullaney," I said.

"I don't have a Bobby Mullaney yet," Martucci said. "I got a burnt body in the back of Mullaney's car."

We followed Martucci and the other detective to the police station. When we got there, we were put in separate rooms with pads of paper that said "Official Statement" on the top. We were told to write what we'd told the detectives. Clair finished first and was waiting in the hall when I came out. We were standing there with our statements when Martucci came out of a door across the hall.

"We've got to be able to find you guys," she said.

"That's easy. Just come to Prosperity, Maine, and ask."

"How do we find Prosperity?"

"Head for Belfast and take a sharp left," I said.

"I'd rather you both stayed here," she said.

"We've got things to do in Maine. Speaking of which, have you called his wife?"

"Last time I checked they hadn't reached her. No answer at the residence."

"She may not be shocked," I said. "She's been expecting this ever since I told her Bobby had gone to Valley."

"She pretty together?" Martucci asked.

"I'd say so. Maybe a little pushed around by him. I think he went off on these adventures and she trailed along. Not entirely, but a little of that."

"So you said she expected her husband to be killed?"

"Yeah. In fact, last time we talked she said, 'Oh, my God, they've killed him.' Something like that."

"She know who 'they' were?"

"I don't know. It was hard to tell."

Martucci stood there for a moment, looking away, her hands inside her blazer pockets.

"So the wife feared the worst and got it. And the pot-grower husband was sort of naive, just bopping around?"

"Yeah, I guess. He was very cocky, very persuasive. Made a good argument for legalization and rallied the troops pretty well. I don't know. He really had some charisma."

"But was he dumb enough to think he could screw around with the bad guys down here?" Martucci said. "I mean, these guys don't take any shit. And if you're a problem—big problem, little problem, in-between problem—they kill you."

"Saves a lot of hemming and hawing," Clair said.

"Sure does. So what made him think he could rattle their cages down here and walk away? Was he suicidal or something?"

"I don't know," I said.

Martucci looked to Clair.

"Maybe he was just stupid," Clair said.

"Maybe he thought he had Coyote covering him," I said.

"Maybe it was Coyote in the car," Martucci said.

"How long for an ID?" I asked.

"A couple of days anyway. It's gonna be a dental job. We have to get the records from the guy's dentist in Maine or wherever the hell it is. That's why we need to talk to the wife right away. Find out the name of his dentist."

"If he had one."

"Oh, he had one. We peeked. Mouth full of silver."

"That's the thing about his generation," I said. "Never learned to floss."

Martucci very much wanted to keep us in town. She said she could hold us for putting the gun in the mailbox, which a detective had retrieved. Martucci said they were federal crimes: tampering with the mails, using the mails to transport firearms, possession of a sawed-off shotgun. I said the feds could find us in Prosperity. She said if we stayed she'd get the soliciting charge dropped. I said I'd take my chances. She gave me back my driver's license. I said she should call a Maine DEA guy named Johnston. She said she would.

Martucci went back through the door. We walked toward the exit and stopped at the door to the dispatcher's area. I stood for a moment, then knocked on the Plexiglas. A very blond woman appeared.

"I'm a reporter," I said. "I need to look at the arrest records from last night."

She frowned.

"You're a reporter?" she said, her voice muffled through the glass.

"Yeah, but they're public record, aren't they? I could be anybody and I'd still have a right to see them."

She frowned again. Disappeared to our left.

"Pushy, aren't you?" Clair said.

"Should have seen me in my prime," I said.

The woman came back with a mimeographed sheet and shoved it through the hole in the window. I looked at it. Arrests and summonses. There were seventeen names. Drugs, drunk driving, domestic assault. And the six women and me.

We stopped at a pharmacy and bought a street map of the city. I thought the woman we wanted had been in the middle of the line when we were being processed. I found the street listed for woman number four. It was across a highway, near the projects. Clair drove and I navigated, peering at the map and directing. In ten minutes, we were in front of the house, on a short grimy block next to a big garage and a fenced lot full of delivery trucks. The house was mostly pale green. The address didn't list an apartment number. There were many to choose from.

We parked in front and went to the front porch. There were several doorbells but they were painted over and stuck. The door was locked.

I went around back, and found a backyard full of brush and sumac and trash, and another door. That door was open and I went in and there was a stairway, lit by glaring bare bulbs. Two doors on each floor. I listened. Heard a television, somewhere. I knocked on both doors on the first floor and waited.

Nothing.

I went up the stairs and knocked on two more. I waited, then heard a door open. Downstairs.

"Day late and a dollar short, aren't you?"

I came back down the stairs. An old, red-faced man stood by his open door. He was wearing slippers and baggy slacks and a white T-shirt. The T-shirt had a stain on the front like a birthmark.

"You guys didn't find her dead someplace?"

"Who?"

"Jasmine."

"What makes you say she's dead?"

"Don't play games. She ain't dead, is she?"

"Not as of nine last night. Why would she be dead?"

He looked at me slyly.

"When cops come knocking, I figure it ain't to give her a civic award."

"You know her?"

"Oh, yeah. We talk. She likes me 'cause I'm too old to put the boots to her. I'm a nice change of pace."

"You watch out for her?"

"I keep my ears open. Eyes, too."

He gave me a sly leer.

"I don't miss much."

"She does a lot of business here at home?"

"When she can."

"Beats the backseat of a car, huh?" I said.

"Safer, 'cause we got a code. Three quick raps on the floor, then two, and I call nine-one-one. There's a lot of goddamn crazies out there. I guess you know."

"Yeah, I do."

"You watch the guys come and go?"

"Oh, yeah. I write down their descriptions. I'm retired. I got nothing else to do."

There was a step outside; then the door opened and Clair appeared.

"He with you?" the man asked.

"Yeah."

"Little long in the tooth, ain't he? What about twenty years and out and all that?"

Clair looked at me quizzically.

"Some people just have it in their blood," I said.

I looked at Clair.

"This gentleman said Jasmine didn't come home last night. Is that her real name, sir?"

"Jasmine? Nah, that's her stage name. Street name."

"Because the woman who was picked up last night was named Dora Santos."

"I call her Jasmine. What'd she get picked up for?"

"Loitering for prostitution."

"You guys ought to give her a break. She's just trying to live, put food on the table. Why don't you catch some real crooks? Catch these goddamn gang kids and these god-damn druggies.''

"Jasmine isn't a druggie?"

"Hell no. I mean, she might smoke a little pot now and again but none of this goddamn needle crap. Crack and all that. Those people are animals. Goddamn animals.''

"You speak Spanish, sir?"

"A little. You pick it up, you know. I'm a Scotsman.''

"Jasmine ever talk to you about a guy she called *el in-dio?*"

"Why don't you ask her? You got her in jail.''

"She was released on bond. Nine o'clock last night.''

"Then where the hell is she?"

"I don't know," I said.

"This *indio* got her?"

His face hardened with concern.

"You ever see this guy? Very tall and thin. Long black hair, way down his back. Sometimes it's in a braid. Black eyes set deep. Eyes are really black. You can't forget his eyes."

The old man rocked on his slippered feet.

"Kind of a bony face?"

"Yeah."

"Yeah, I seen a guy looked like that," he said. "He waited in the car. A couple days ago."

"Who was he with?"

"This girl. A girl like Jasmine. I've seen her here a couple times. She stops. You know. Says hello.''

"He just stayed in the car?"

"Sat there. He didn't know I was watching him from the window. He just sat there in the driveway. It was dark but I was right in the window, the kitchen. I could see him. I figured he was a pimp or something. Not going in, I mean.''

"What kind of car was it?" Clair said.

The guy looked startled. He looked at Clair, then at me.

"It was a little station wagon," he said. "Foreign job. It was white. I think it was from out of state.''

Twenty-two

"SO COYOTE WAS in the car and then the car ended up burned with a body in the backseat," I said.

"Maybe it's Coyote who's dead. Maybe he looked for Bobby too hard."

"But if it's Bobby, then Coyote found him and then he was killed after that. So what happened to Coyote?"

"Probably nothing good," Clair said.

We were sitting in the truck down the block from Jasmine's house. There was a mill tower visible in the distance, a package store on the corner, some sort of fortified apartment building across the street. A guy stood outside of each.

"They sure stand around a lot down here," Clair said.

"I'd sure like to find Jasmine again."

"If she doesn't want to be found, you could look for her around here for a month."

"And find later that she was in Boston or Hartford."

"Or East Overshoe."

I looked at Clair.

"You're ready to get out of here, aren't you?"

"It isn't that I don't enjoy your company," he said.

"Or the stench of urban decay?"

"That's been fun, too," Clair said. "But I think I'm a country mouse. It's time to go home."

"Then let's go. I can do a lot over the phone. If I need to come back—"

"Don't call me, I'll call you."

Clair smiled and put the truck in gear and we rolled up to the light. The men stared at us impassively from their respective corners on this dirty forgotten street in a dirty forgotten city. Even more than some grimy New York neighborhood, which at least was connected to something bigger and grander than itself, Valley seemed to have no purpose. It seemed a hopeless place to live a life, a pointless place to die.

I looked at the man on my right and nodded. He didn't even flinch.

Clair drove in the direction of the highway that would take us south to the interstate. The streets were lined with triple-deckers, some ornate, some plain, all grim. There were bodegas with barred windows, an insurance office with heavy steel mesh over the door. What? Was somebody going to break in and steal actuarial tables?

I thought about Bobby and Coyote and the old man and Jasmine. I wondered who the woman was whom Coyote had been with. How did he know her? From his days as a biker with a crystal meth factory? What was he doing down here? For that matter, what was he doing in Florence? What were any of them doing in Florence?

At some point, I had to call Melanie. I had to call Roxanne. I could do it from a rest area on the interstate. Clair wouldn't want to stop any sooner.

We drove out onto a main thoroughfare, past a brick church with a walled courtyard. There were more people walking. Several women carrying lunch baskets, going to or from a mill that still had jobs. A guy wearing a hard hat turned backward, carrying a cooler. So maybe all wasn't lost here. There were people working, people performing a task in return for a paycheck. When we got back, that's what I would have to do. I started to reach for my notebook and there he was.

The kid.

I saw him and he saw us. He was riding in the passenger seat of a silver Toyota sedan and he turned and looked right at us. I could see his swollen mouth. Then I saw the Toyota brake and whip around so fast it slid sideways. Then it was three cars behind us and closing.

"You see that?"

"Yup," Clair said.

"They're coming after us."

"Should never have mailed that gun."

"Too late now," I said.

"Maybe you can throw your notebook at them."

"Maybe we can hail a passing cop."

"You know what they say," Clair said, accelerating as the car in front of us turned off. "Where are they when you need one?"

We were doing fifty, the big tires drumming the pavement. The Toyota passed a van and was only two cars behind us. I could see the two figures in the front seat, two more in the back. A gang car pool.

A car pulled out in front of us and we slowed. It was an old beat-up junker trailing a plume of blue smoke and it lurched along. The Toyota was edging over the center line to pass the car behind us.

"You think they'll just start shooting right in the road?" I said.

"Probably won't be the first time."

"We've got to do something. We're just sitting here in this traffic. Turn off and double back and maybe we can get headed for the downtown. They won't shoot us in front of the police station."

"Maybe," Clair said. "Maybe not."

He yanked the wheel and the truck squealed around a corner to the right. The street was narrow and there were cars parked on both sides. A small pickup was coming the other way and Clair floored it and the truck pulled over and stopped, the driver giving us the finger as we passed. Clair slammed around the next right, downshifting, the big motor roaring. There was no sign of the Toyota and Clair bounced through an intersection, and down another narrow sluice of a street.

The Toyota appeared, just making the first right.

"We gained on 'em," I said. "Take another right and get back on the main drag."

Clair hit the brakes and the rear end slung around and he hit the gas again and then stomped the brakes hard.

"Whoops," I said.

It was a dead end, like a court with houses on all sides, the back of a brick building straight ahead, nobody around. Clair drove into a driveway behind a car and jumped out, saying, "Lock the hubs."

I jumped out, too, and turned the dial on the front wheel on my side, locking the wheel for four-wheel drive. We scrambled back in and Clair ground the gears into reverse and roared back out. We ended up facing the open end of the street. Clair pushed the lever for four-wheel low.

We sat. Waited.

And then the Toyota started to go by the street, skidded to a stop and backed up. The car turned into the court.

It accelerated and then slid to a halt, facing us, fifteen feet away. I could see the guys smiling and then both doors popped open. The kid had a handgun. The driver, older, had a handgun, too. They had their hoods up and they trotted toward us, guns low by their thighs. Clair tromped on the gas and the truck roared forward. The older guy stopped and turned, as if to run to get his car out of the way, but it was too late and the truck hit the Toyota head-on, the steel plow frame crumpling the car with a sound like balling-up paper.

The two guys were still in the back and I could see them covering their faces with their arms. The kid was behind us somewhere and I heard a shot, then another, then the transmission whining, the motor roaring and all four tires scrabbling on the pavement, driving the car forward like a rushing football lineman. The truck started to climb the hood and Clair kept the power on and the windshield shattered in front of us and then the car was flatter and wasn't rolling but was scraping on the street. The two guys were hunched in the back, all arms and shoulders. The car suddenly slid sideways and Clair could have turned away and around it but he didn't.

He turned with the car, so he had it broadside, and it was sliding and then the front of it hit the curb on the right and it spun and rolled over and it was still rocking on its roof when we turned the corner and Clair slowed, shifted from low to high and the motor stopped roaring.

"Can't beat these old Ford three-sixties," Clair said. "Gobs of low-end torque."

We drove in silence, back through the downtown, down the highway south of the city and onto the interstate. After two or three miles, my heart stopped pounding. Clair pulled into the breakdown lane and we got out and released the hubs by turning the dials on the front wheels. Clair surveyed the damage.

The plow frame was scratched. The right headlight was cracked. There were two bullet holes in the tailgate.

"I'd say they got the worst of it," Clair said.

"Ayuh," I said.

We got back in and drove up Route 495 to Route 95, then got off the highway in Hampton, New Hampshire, to avoid scrutiny at the toll station.

"You think they'd call the cops? What are they going to say?"

"Somebody else might," Clair said.

"In that neighborhood?"

Clair thought for a moment.

"Naah, you're probably right," he said.

But we stayed on Route 1, just to be on the safe side. In twenty minutes we were in Portsmouth, where Clair pulled into a Dunkin' Donuts so we could use the phone on the wall outside. I went in and bought coffee, tea and muffins while he called Mary.

"Love you, too," I heard him say as I came back.

Clair hit the button and handed me the receiver.

"They're fine?" I asked.

"Safe and sound."

"You tell Mary what we've been doing?"

"I told her we've been doing some research."

"At the public library."

"Right," Clair said. "I don't know why I even bothered to come along."

"I told you I'd be fine."

"Right. You're a grown man. You can bail yourself out."

"Damn straight," I said.

The phone booth had obscenities gouged in its burnished metal with a knife or a nail and they stared me in the face as I dialed Roxanne's number, then punched in the number of my credit card. I waited. It rang. Rang again.

"Hi," Roxanne's voice said. "J.M., if this is you, that matter we talked about needed some more observation. Don't worry. I'm fine. I'll be back by one. Call me in the morning. Please."

I banged the receiver down and dialed Roxanne's office number, my credit card number again. Waited again. It was busy.

"Damn it," I said.

Clair was sitting in the truck. I dialed the office number. Again it was busy. I dialed Roxanne's number and got the recording again so I told the machine I was fine and on my way back to Maine. I was in Portsmouth and Clair was fine, too, I said, and I hoped she was okay. It was a little after eleven and I'd be in Portland by one.

And then I got back in the truck and started to worry.

We stayed on Route 1, crossing the Piscataqua River on the old bridge so we could bypass the tolls at Kittery. It started to rain and I looked out at the strip malls full of factory outlets and the shoppers trotting from store to store like looters.

"You okay?" Clair said, as we pulled up to a red light.

"Fine. You?"

"Can't complain. Doesn't do any good anyway."

"Sorry to drag you into all this."

"Beats watching the TV," Clair said.

I looked out the window.

"I hope Roxanne's all right."

"She's a big girl," Clair said.

"Yeah, but she was going out late to check on this drugged-out mother. See if she was leaving her kids alone."

"She knows what she's doing."

"I know, but she didn't change the message."

"Maybe she's been busy."

"That's what I'm afraid of," I said.

We rolled north with the traffic, through Kennebunk, where the gentry lived, on to Biddeford, where they didn't. The river in Biddeford had a different name but the mills were the same, big and brick and still.

"So what if they're both dead?" I said. "Coyote and Bobby."

"Then you can write about their demise."

"It's not the story I thought I'd be doing."

"You didn't know where it was headed, did you?"

"I thought it was just going to be the world of these backwoods hippies. Instead, it's this. A line right to the hard-core drug trade. And you know what?"

"What?"

"The common denominator isn't drugs. It's money."

"Easy money."

I thought for a minute.

"That's what doesn't add up," I said. "These people— the Mullaneys, I mean—they didn't seem to care about money. I mean, if you want to make a lot of money you don't live in Florence, Maine."

"You don't choose to live in Florence," Clair said.

"I don't think they chose it. I think they were running from something."

"But they didn't stay hidden, if they were doing all this pot stuff," Clair said. "Recruiting at fairs and all that."

"Maybe whatever they were hiding from went away. Somebody died. The statute of limitations ran out. I don't know."

"So they get back into it? Start selling pot and getting back in with the drug types in Massachusetts?"

"But you know what?" I said. "If they knew the drug types, why would they go plunging right in there? Bobby, I mean. The guy wasn't stupid but you go rousting these major dealers, you'd better have an army behind you."

"And he had one guy."

"Coming along behind him. Looking for his body."

"Doesn't seem very helpful," Clair said.

We were in South Portland by quarter to twelve. Clair pulled in at Roxanne's condo but her car wasn't there. I scrawled a note on a piece of notebook paper and unlocked the door and started to stick it inside. I started to leave and then stopped.

I walked into the hall, then into the living room. The air was still. There was no odor of her. No lingering dampness from a shower. No waft of stale morning coffee. I went up the stairs two at a time.

There was a black skirt on the bed. Stockings and a red blouse. Her shoes were kicked off on the floor. The bed was made.

Roxanne had come home and changed her clothes. She hadn't slept here.

I hurried back downstairs and went to the phone and hit the playback button. The tape rewound with a high-pitched whine and slammed to a stop. It hissed, then beeped.

"You bitch."

A woman's slurred, sobbing voice.

"I hope you die, you bitch. I hope you break your neck. I hope you get pregnant and you have a baby and your goddamn baby dies. You bitch, I want you to know what it feels like, you goddamn bitch, you goddamn dirty bitch. I'll kill you. Give me my kids or I'll kill you. You're gonna die, bitch. I hope you die. I'll kill you. I'll find you and I'll follow you and I'll kill you dead. I'll come in your house and cut your throat, you bitch."

There was a click. Dial tone. The machine stopped, and I popped out the tape.

I grabbed the phone and dialed Roxanne's office. The number was busy. I dialed again. Busy. I tried a third time. A fourth. It rang.

"Child Protective."

"Roxanne Masterson, please."

"I'm sorry but—Is this Jack?"

"Yeah."

"Jack, this is Kathy. We haven't met but I've heard lots about you. Well, Jack, Roxanne's in the hospital. She's in Maine Med."

Twenty-three

WE LEFT THE truck illegally parked, took an elevator up and looked for room 305. It was on the end. The door was closed. There was a Portland patrolman sitting in a chair beside it.

I started to explain.

"Jack, is that you?" Roxanne called.

The patrolman put his head in.

"Go ahead," he said.

She was on the bed. Her left thigh was in a cast. There was an intravenous tube in her right arm, a bag of clear liquid hanging from a hook.

Roxanne turned her head.

"Hey, baby," she said.

"Playing hooky, huh?"

She smiled weakly.

"How are you doing?" I said.

"Okay. I'm all doped up. Hi, Clair."

"Hello, Roxanne," Clair said.

"How'd you guys do in Massachusetts?"

"Better than you did in downtown Portland."

Roxanne looked down at her leg.

"Yeah, well, I'll set off airport metal detectors now. They put pins in my leg."

"What happened?"

"Oh, I don't know. Knocked on the wrong door, I guess."

"Looking for the mother?"

"Yeah. Me and a detective. We found the kids alone, again. We wanted . . . we wanted to catch her in her altered state."

"Did you?"

"Oh, yeah. And four guys doing coke."

"And they did this to you?"

"They went down the stairs and took me with them. They thought it was a drug bust."

"What about the detective?"

"She shot one of them."

"My God."

"Oh, yeah. You want to interview me? The *Press Herald* has been calling. Channel Thirteen. Oh, I'm quite the celebrity."

"Was the guy killed?"

"No. I think he's in here somewhere."

"I'll go strangle him."

"I think he has a cop, too."

"Deluxe service."

"Nothing but the best."

She smiled, her lips dark against pale skin. I took her hand. Clair stood back shyly.

"Is it a bad break?"

"Yeah. I got knocked down the stairs and sort of trampled. They said the femur was broken and then probably stepped on. They did surgery. This morning, it was."

"We should leave."

Roxanne squeezed my hand.

"No, you shouldn't," she said. "No, you shouldn't."

"You sure?"

She nodded.

"They broke your collarbone, too?"

"I guess. It's all kind of a blur. Happened fast."

"When was this?"

"About one-thirty, I think."

"Where's the mother now?"

"Last night she was in jail, but she probably got out this morning. They don't like keeping women in."

I hesitated.

"We stopped at your place on the way up," I said.

"Oh?"

"There was a message on your machine. I was worried so I played it."

"TV people?"

"No, I think it was the mother. She made threats."

"She's full of it," Roxanne said.

"I don't know about that. She sounded pretty serious."

"But was she drunk and stoned?"

"Probably."

"The hell with her."

"I'm going to tell the police."

"Fine. We'll get her for criminal threatening, too. That's good for the kids."

"How were they this time?"

"Hungry and dirty and the little one had two black eyes and handprint bruises on her backside. It could have been the mother, it could have been some other burnout. I think we got them just in time."

"You're pretty amazing."

I held her hand. Clair discreetly stepped out.

"So," Roxanne said softly. "Will you still make love with me with screws and bolts in my leg?"

"Even if I have to bring my toolbox."

"I'm going to have a scar on my thigh."

"My bionic woman."

"The Bride of Frankenstein."

"Lucky him."

"Will you still love me all busted up?"

"You're not busted up. You're gorgeous."

"But will you still love me?"

"Even more," I said. "And that's saying something."

I kissed her.

"Now sleep."

I told the patrolman that there had been threats on Roxanne's life. He was young and solid and serious and I felt, when I left, she was in good hands.

We went out to the truck and drove downtown and out Forest Avenue to Roxanne's office. Clair waited in the truck while I went in. I told the receptionist who I was and what I wanted and he looked concerned and hurried me back between the fabric partitions to a glass-walled office. A silver-haired woman was sitting behind a desk. The receptionist showed me in and introduced me. The woman behind the desk came around and clasped my hand in both of hers.

"We're all so sorry," she said. "We're going over this afternoon. It's just terrible. Roxanne is so dedicated and so wonderful."

"Yeah, well, I guess there's a dissenting opinion on that."

I handed her the tape.

"It's from Roxanne's answering machine. I think it's the mother. I figured you'd be the one to take it to the police."

"Is it threatening?"

"Yeah. I don't know that she'd ever follow through."

"You never know," the woman said. "We take all threats seriously and prosecute them to the fullest extent possible. We'll go after her on this."

"Will this keep the mother away from her kids longer?"

"It'll help. Depending on what she said."

"She said she wanted to kill Roxanne."

"She belongs in a rehab hospital," the woman said.

"Roxanne said she was getting into crack."

"We're seeing more and more of that, but you know, it's worse because it completely consumes people, but drugs are drugs. Crack, coke, pot, alcohol. It's all a variation on the same old theme. They take you somewhere else when you should be right here, taking care of your kids."

I looked at her. Nice tweed suit. Hair just so. And a fire burning inside her.

"You ever get sick of doing this?"

"I'm always sick of doing this, Mr. McMorrow. But I'm never sick enough of it to stop. Things like this, with Roxanne, push me close."

"She's okay. She was sleeping when I left."

"The doctor this morning said she's going to have a long road back. Physical therapy and all that."

"She'll get through it," I said, managing a smile. "She's tougher than she looks."

Roxanne was still asleep when we got back to the hospital. I wanted to stay but Clair needed to get back to Prosperity and I did, too, at least to get clean clothes and my computer. Clair pointed out that this might be the time to go, while Roxanne had visitors and would be sleeping a lot anyway.

So we drove north on the interstate to Augusta and then on up Route 3, back to Waldo County. After Massachusetts and Portland it was like driving back in time, trading malls and parking lots and frantic traffic for the lonely, bristling, dappled hills.

I wouldn't be staying long.

Turning off Route 3, we began to get the nods and waves that were rites of passing in central Maine. A log truck driver who recognized Clair's truck and waved as he passed. A white-haired woman coming out of the Prosperity road in a small black pickup. A game warden in his green state truck on the edge of town. On the end of the dump road, an older guy named Percy who'd just lost his wife of fifty years. He was on his front lawn with his remaining companion, a poodle. The college kids from up the road went past, banging along in their Jeep.

Waves. Nods. Beeps. Signs of community.

"Up here we wave," I said. "Down there they have gang colors."

"Maybe we ought to get some of those colors for Prosperity."

"Anything in mind?"

"I don't know," Clair said. "Is green taken?"

I smiled.

"It's good to be back."

"I'm ready to hide away," Clair said.

"Yessuh," I said. But I knew the time for hiding had passed.

Clair dropped me off and headed down the road, the bullet holes showing in his truck tailgate as he pulled away. I went across the road to the mailbox and pulled out a sheaf of stuff I didn't need. Then I went inside and tossed my bag on the kitchen floor, the mail on the counter, and hit the button on the answering machine, which now didn't seem so harmless.

It whirred. Beeped.

"Mr. McMorrow. This is Joe Mendoza. *Valley Chronicle*. I'd like to talk to you about the body found in the car here. My number is . . ."

Another beep.

"Mr. McMorrow. Joe Mendoza calling. Could you please call me at the *Valley Chronicle?* I really need to talk to you. The number is . . ."

Beep again.

"Mr. McMorrow. Could you please call me? Joe Mendoza. The number is . . ."

I could run but I couldn't hide. I dialed and the receptionist connected me to the newsroom. I asked for Joe and the phone clattered and clicked and Joe answered.

"Newsroom. Joe Mendoza."

"Jack McMorrow."

"Jesus, man. I gotta talk to you."

"About what?"

"About the body. The body in the car."

"What about it?"

"This was the guy you were looking for, right? I told my editor I talked to you and he told me it was page one. The same guy, right?"

"I don't know. You tell me. Who was it?"

"I don't know yet. But the car was registered to that guy you were looking for. Mullaney. Robert Mullaney."

"I know."

"So it is the same guy?"

"Is this on the record?"

"Well, yeah. Is that all right?"

I thought for a moment. Felt myself slip into his cub reporter's shoes.

"Yeah, I guess. But you shouldn't ask if it's all right. You should ask why I wouldn't want it to be. Sound a little surprised that it would even be a question."

"I think you're evading the question," Joe Mendoza said.

"You might be right."

"So it is the same guy, right? The guy you were looking for?"

"It's his car."

"Who is he?"

"The guy I'm looking for is Bobby Mullaney. I don't know who the guy in the car is."

"A crispy critter," Mendoza said. "You see him?"

"No. The car was gone."

"So what can you tell me about this guy?"

"What do you know?"

"I don't know anything. Zero."

I thought. Considered my own story. If my story for the *Globe* tracked Bobby from Florence, Maine, to Valley, Massachusetts, from activist to "crispy critter," what should I tell the *Valley Chronicle?* How much was too much?

"I've got a deal for you," I said. "I'll give you stuff from my end. But you've got to give me what you know from down there. Deal?"

Mendoza didn't answer.

"I don't know. I don't know if I'm supposed—"

"If there's no deal, I don't say another word."

"Okay."

"Mullaney's from a little town called Florence in western Maine. Northwest Maine."

I heard the sound of tapping on a keyboard.

"What's he do?"

"Not much."

"How'd you get onto him?"

"He's a legalize-marijuana type. Goes around collecting signatures on petitions."

"That big up there?"

"Not really. But it's growing. A lot of old hippies live up here. A lot of locals grow it. Drug cops came in and started hitting these little places pretty hard. People got pissed off. People in Maine question authority anyway."

"Mullaney married?"

"Yup."

"Kids?"

"One step."

"Doesn't work? What does he do? Deal dope?"

"I don't know. He cuts wood. Works here and there. A lot of people do that up here. They build their own houses, have a garden, raise pigs. They're homesteaders. They don't need forty hours a week in an office."

"What was he doing down here?"

"I don't know."

"He's from here, right?"

"Where'd you hear that?"

"A cop."

"Where'd he hear it?" I asked.

"From you."

"Busybody."

"So is he from here?" Mendoza said, still tapping on the keyboard.

"He told me he lived there years ago. Maybe ten years ago. I'm not sure."

"Why'd he leave?"

"I don't know."

"And you don't know why he came back?"

"Nope."

"Not even hearsay? Rumor?"

"Nope."

Mendoza paused. He thought I was lying. I was. That was tough.

"Okay, now, Mr. McMorrow. Let me ask you a couple of questions about yourself."

"You can ask them. A couple."

"You string for the *Globe*?"

"Sometimes."

"Other places?"

"Magazines."

"Where do you live?"

"Maine."

"Where in Maine?"

"I'd rather not say."

"Why not?"

"I'd rather not say that, either."

"I can find out through the phone number. The exchange."

"I can't stop you from doing that."

"But you won't tell me?"

"Nope."

"So what's the problem?" Mendoza said.

"No problem."

"You worked for newspapers? I mean, full-time."

"Yeah, I did."

"Where?"

"All over the place."

"Where most recently?"

"A weekly in western Maine. You never heard of it."

"Before that?"

"Here and there."

"Like where?"

I hesitated.

"New York Times."

"No shit?"

"Nope," I said.

"And then you went to a weekly?"

"Yup."

"You got a drinking problem or something?"

"No more than most people."

"So where'd you first meet Mullaney?"

"In Maine, when he was passing out pot petitions."

"What's your story about?"

"I don't know yet."

"Why'd you come down here looking for him?"

"Because I couldn't find him in Maine."

"How'd you know he was in Valley?"

"I still don't know he was in Valley."

"What?"

"I just know his car was in Valley."

"It didn't get down here by itself," Mendoza said.

"Nope."

"And it was found with a man's body in the backseat."

"Was it a man?"

"I, um, I thought it was a man."

"Did they say that yet?"

"They didn't say anything yet. They have to compare the teeth and all that."

"So they don't know?"

"I guess not."

"I wouldn't assume anything, if I were you," I said.

"Why not?"

"Because good reporters don't."

"Yeah, well, I'm not even a reporter, really."

"You're doing pretty good so far."

"You really think so?"

"Yeah."

"What should I do next?"

"Stay with the coroner's office. Check around down there and find out who Mullaney was down there. Police record. Family."

"How do I do that?"

"Go to the courts. The cops. Call every Mullaney in the phone book. Find high school yearbooks from years he would have been in."

"You think I should call his wife?"

"What do *you* think?"

"I guess I should. But I hate that."

"What?"

"Calling dead people's families."

"But you don't know he's dead."

"Who the hell else could it be?" Joe Mendoza asked.
I didn't answer.

Twenty-four

I BEAT JOE Mendoza to it.

"Hello," Melanie Mullaney said. Her voice was distant, weak with defeat.

"It's Jack."

"Oh, hi."

"They called you?"

"The police did. From down there."

"So what happens now?"

She breathed slowly, almost a sigh but not quite.

"I don't know. I guess I have to call a funeral home. I don't know. What is it you do when somebody dies? I mean, I've never had to be the one to do all this."

"But they haven't identified the body, have they?"

"No. They asked me who Bobby's dentist was. They were gonna call and get X rays or whatever it is."

"But they haven't done that yet?"

"I don't know. But I've got to get going with the arrangements, I guess."

"But Melanie," I said. "What if it isn't him? What if he isn't dead?"

"McMorrow, don't do this to me," she shrieked. "He's dead. They killed him, he's dead, he's gone."

She started to sob.

"I'm sorry, but what if—"

"What if nothing. He's gone. His car. His rings. His size. I mean, I can't sit here and torture myself. Bobby's gone, goddamn it. Goddamn it all to hell."

She cried. I waited.

"But Melanie, listen. Just listen. I was down there."

"I know. And Coyote was looking for the body. I haven't heard from him. They'll probably find him next. They probably killed both of 'em. Why did we leave there? To get away from those people. It was getting bad back then but now, jeez, they just kill people. They just killed . . . Bobby. I got to start to deal, you know? I mean, I've done this denial shit before. Makes it friggin' worse, kidding yourself, like he's coming back, it was a homeless guy, sure it was, and Bobby's gonna come through the door any goddamn minute and—"

"Melanie. Coyote had the car."

She didn't say anything.

"I talked to a guy. This old guy. He kind of looked out for this hooker. The hooker who talked about Coyote looking for the body. This guy saw Coyote with the car."

"What car?"

"Your car. The Subaru. It came to the house once. This guy's an eagle eye, peeking out the windows and writing stuff down. He said the guy in the car looked like Coyote. The face. The hair."

"So?"

"So if Coyote was driving around in the car, without Bobby, and now the car's found with the . . ."

I hesitated.

"With the body, then maybe Bobby wasn't in the car. Maybe it was Coyote. I don't mean to say that would be good news, but it would be different news. Maybe it was somebody else."

"No. No way. I'm not gonna do that to myself. I'm not. How can you do this to me? He's dead. Dead, dead, dead. The car. His rings. McMorrow, don't do this. You son of a bitch, how can you do this? You talk to some old guy and he comes up with some bullshit story about—Goddamn you, McMorrow. Why can't you just leave me the hell alone?''

And she hung up.

It was good work, if you could get it. Raising grieving widows' hopes. Spinning hypothetical webs, little rungs that the red-eyed women could hitch themselves up, hand over hand, out of the depths of despair, toward the tiny window of light, following the direction of Jack McMorrow's pointed finger. See it? See the light? All isn't black. Bobby Mullaney might be on the other side of that window. Your husband, who police think probably was burned into a charred bundle of potato-chip flesh and crumbling bones, might be sitting out there. He might be just fine. Sipping a beer, smoking a joint, moving to the reggae music, mahn, as alive as you and me.

I stood there at the counter. Closed my eyes and hung my head. Was I wrong? Was I holding out false hope for Melanie Mullaney? Was it cruel, what I had just done? Was I preying on this poor woman, exploiting her for a news story and a week's pay, playing a sadistic game in which her hopes were stretched farther and farther until they were near the breaking point and she screamed?

No.

No, I wasn't.

There was still reason to think the body might not be Bobby's. There was no positive ID. There was a guy who might have seen somebody else with the car. There was the unknown quantity, Coyote. Where was he? Why hadn't he called Melanie? Was he dead? Had he set Bobby up? Who the hell was he, anyway?

I turned to the refrigerator, took out a Ballantine. I opened it and walked to the back window. It was after three and the light was starting to fade, turning the sky a darker gray. The trees waggled their leaves scoldingly. With a twinge of guilt, I thought of Roxanne in the hospital, realizing I'd forgotten her for a few minutes.

Make one woman cry. Leave the other one, who loves you, alone and forgotten in a hospital room. And, oh yeah. Get picked up for soliciting a prostitute.

Nice guy, McMorrow, a voice in my head said. Yeah, I am, another voice said back.

Because I was right.

A guy disappears, turns up in a city seventy miles from home. He's following up on a soured drug deal and one of the dealers says he was last seen in the company of some higher-level traffickers from one of the drug armpits of New England. The implication is that the traffickers from the armpit city weren't happy. The guy's sidekick turns up in the armpit looking for a body. Then the guy's car turns up burned, and sure enough, there's a body in it, albeit a trifle overdone.

But who is it?

A homeless person, crawled into the car for the night? One of the bad guys, who underestimated Bobby and got killed? Coyote, who asked too many questions? Some kid who stole the car? A police informant? A junkie who overdosed?

Or Bobby?

If Melanie wanted to think the worst, that was her problem. I could wait. In Portland.

I emptied my dirty and bloody clothes into a laundry bag and took my duffel up to the loft. I refilled it with jeans and shirts and shorts and came back down the stairs. Opening the refrigerator, I took out tomatoes, a cucumber, a cabbage, some cheese and a plastic container of refried beans. I put the food in a paper grocery bag and took out the remaining four cans of ale and put them in, too.

I unplugged my computer and keyboard and printer and brought them out to the truck, one by one, and put them on the seat on the passenger's side. Then I went to the drawer by the sink, reached under the dish towels and took out a box of Winchester .30-30 shells. The shells went in the bag. The rifle I took from the closet.

That went in the gun rack.

• • •

It was the only gun rack in Roxanne's parking lot. When I pulled in, there was a man getting into his car in the next space. The guy was wearing round gold-rimmed glasses and his car had a bicycle on the roof. I shut off the motor in the truck. He looked over at the truck and me and the rifle.

I smiled and gave him a little salute. His doors locked with a thunk.

I took my duffel and groceries and the rifle out of the truck and went inside. If I'd brought a gas mask, I could have held off the state police for a week.

It was almost six and the condo was quiet and dusky dark. I flicked on the hall lights and listened. It was quiet.

I shut the door behind me and put the duffel and the rifle by the foot of the stairs. I listened again, then took the bag of groceries to the kitchen and put the stuff in the refrigerator alongside Roxanne's grapefruit and yogurt. The shells didn't need to chill. I took them out of the bag and went back to the hallway and, sitting on the bottom stair, loaded the rifle.

I was home.

Leaving the rifle leaning next to the door, I went back out to the truck and brought in the computer and printer. I set those on the dining room table, then went to the living room and looked at the answering machine. The light was flashing furiously. I hit the button. The machine whirred and beeped.

The first message was somebody from Channel 13. The second was from Channel 8. The third was from the *Portland Press Herald* and the fourth was the mother.

"Where are they? Masterson, you're dead. I'll find them and I'll find you. You better stay in that hospital the rest of your friggin' life, lady, 'cause you're dead. I'll kill you right there. I'll be the night nurse. Think about that. 'Cause you're dead, lady. Give me my kids. You can't take my kids, you can't, I'll kill you, I'll friggin' kill you.''

Five calls from her. All in a row, all expounding on the same theme. Between threats, she took a swallow of something that probably wasn't Pepsi. Her voice became more

and more hysterical until, in the last call, she started to sob
and then lapsed into a long wail.

A mother in drunken mourning.

I popped the tape and grabbed the phone book and
looked up the number of the Portland police. I asked the
dispatcher for somebody assigned to the assault on Roxanne Masterson, the Human Services social worker. He told
me to hang on and I did for a long minute.

"Detective Briggs," a man's voice said.

I told him who I was. I told him what I had.

"I need that tape, Mr. McMorrow."

"I'll bring it to you."

"I'm going home at six," he said. "You can put it in
an envelope with my name on it and leave it with the dispatcher. Tell him it's evidence. I'll tell him to expect you."

"You're going home?"

"Yessir. I'm going home. I've been here fourteen hours.
I've got a wife and kid who forget what I look like."

"Well, where's the mother?"

"She was released on personal recognizance bail this
morning at ten o'clock."

"But these calls were made sometime this afternoon.
What were the conditions of her bail?"

"No contact with victim."

"So pull her back in. This is contact."

"We're already looking for her. The DHS area supervisor gave us the tape from earlier in the day."

"So what's the problem?"

"We can't find her."

"You can't find her? She's a stumbling-drunk crackhead
junkie. How hard can she be to find?"

"Hard," the detective said.

"Christ almighty, she's no rocket scientist. Knock on
some doors. Shake down some of her junkie friends. Put
somebody up against a goddamn wall and tell 'em to pro-
duce her or you'll put 'em away."

There was silence on the other end of the phone. He was
waiting for me to finish.

"I know you're upset, Mr. McMorrow."

"Of course I'm upset. This loony's threatening to kill somebody and you're waiting to pull her over with a tail-light out, for God's sake."

"No, we're not. There's a detective looking for her as we speak."

"I'll find her," I said.

"I wouldn't do that, Mr. McMorrow."

"Yeah, well—"

"Listen, Mr. McMorrow. I know how you feel. If it was my wife, I'd feel the same way. But let me tell you something. The best thing you can do for her is to present her with a calm and reassuring demeanor and leave the police work to us."

"They teach you that at the police academy?"

"Yessir."

"Well—"

"They teach you that because it's right," the detective said.

"Yeah," I said. "I suppose it is."

So I went out to the truck with the rifle held close to my left leg. I slid it into the slot in the back of the truck seat and drove downtown to the Portland police station. While I waited at the window, two patrolmen brought in a drunk driver. He swayed between them and they helped him through a door with benign detachment. The dispatcher finally looked at me and I explained who I was and what I had. I slid it through the dish at the bottom of the window and he put it in an envelope and wrote "Att: Det. Briggs" in black marker. Then he went to the wall and opened a locked metal cabinet and put the tape in.

I watched it disappear and left.

There was a different patrolman on duty at Roxanne's door. She was young and pink-cheeked and looked like she was dressed as a cop for the high-school Halloween dance. When I approached she stood and faced me and looked older. I told her who I was and she asked for ID. I supplied it and then she told me to stand against the far wall and spread my legs. She ran a metal-detector wand over me and it clicked like a Geiger counter on my keys. I took them out and she waved the magic wand again and then said okay and told me to wait. Then she went into the room and I stood there like a suitor and she slowly opened the door.

"This him?" she asked Roxanne.

"Yeah," Roxanne said, from the bed. "That's him."

"You can go in, sir," the patrolman said.

"Thanks," I said. "And I mean that."

She nodded.

I went in and pulled a chair up to the side of the bed. Roxanne looked up at me and smiled. Around the room, there were flowers on every available flat surface.

"How's things in the boonies?" Roxanne asked.

"Fine. How's things in the big city?"

"Fine. They all came from the office. You see the flowers? I feel like I'm at my own funeral. Lying in state."

"Don't talk like that."

"Oh, don't be so bossy."

"I'm not. I just don't like you to talk like that."

"What's the matter?"

"Nothing."

She looked up at me, big dark eyes against white sheets.

"How are your druggie buddies?"

I thought of the detective's textbook advice.

"They're fine, I guess. Valley was a different world, though. Small and cramped and sort of hopeless. Like people living among ruins. How are you feeling?"

"The same. My leg aches but they keep me supplied with narcotics."

"Drugs, drugs everywhere . . ."

"The universal desire to be opiated," Roxanne said. "Overwhelms even maternal instincts."

"You having some of those?"

She grinned.

"Not today. You're safe."

But was *she* safe?

"Don't try to talk them into dropping the guard," I said.

"Why?"

"Because your crazy lady is still calling. Sounds like she's losing it. And she's focused on you. I don't want to worry you but I guess you should know."

"Of course I should know."

"And they can't find her."

"As long as she stays high, she's no threat," Roxanne said.

"What about her friends?"

"I don't know," she said, looking, for the first time that day, a little concerned. "That, I don't know."

I sat there. Hesitated.

"I have to tell you," I said. "Things were a little crazy in Massachusetts."

"I figured that," Roxanne said.

"See right through me, huh?"

"I just know you."

"Some gang guys tried to stick us up for drug money."

"What?"

"Clair had to slam this kid pretty good. To get him to drop his gun."

"His gun?"

"It wasn't much of one. Cheap sawed-off shotgun. Kid didn't weigh a hundred and twenty pounds."

"Oh, Jack. So you're both okay?"

"Fine. But they found Bobby's car with a body in it. All burned up."

"God, Jack."

"But I don't know that it was him. It could have been somebody else."

"When will they know?"

"Tomorrow probably."

"How's the wife?"

"Prepared for the worst," I said.

"Well, that's good, I guess."

"I'm not so sure. I think it's sort of unnatural. Wouldn't you cling to the hope that somebody was alive?"

"I don't know," Roxanne said. "Not if I'd clung before and been disappointed."

•   •   •

So I clung there for three hours. Roxanne dozed and talked and dozed some more. I bought orange juice from a machine down the hall and ate fruit from Roxanne's basket. Two women from her office stopped at seven but Roxanne was sleeping. They added to the jungle of flowers and left.

At nine, the guard changed to an older patrolman with a gut and a paperback about World War II. I gave him a pear and an apple. He told me it was a wonder these social-worker girls didn't get in more scrapes, the scum they had to deal with. I didn't disagree.

At ten-thirty, Roxanne had been asleep for an hour. I told the patrolman I was going home to eat but I'd be back. He said to take it easy, that the little lady was in good hands. I didn't disagree with that, either.

The truck was at the far end of the parking lot. It was a cool night, still cloudy, no stars. I went to the truck, unlocked the door and felt for the rifle. It was there, cold and hard and reassuring. I paid the sleepy kid at the gate and drove through the city and down the hill to the bridge to South Portland. The water was shiny blue-black and as I looked out, I could see the lights of the condos in Roxanne's complex. Roxanne's place was dark when I pulled in, and it was still when, rifle in hand, I unlocked the door. I put the gun by the door, went to the refrigerator and got three cans of Ballantine ale. I sat down in the big chair that looked out at the water, and swallowed one can whole and drank the other. The third I sipped until my head went back and I was asleep.

And then it was light and my mouth was open and dry and my boots were still on. The half-empty beer was on the table in front of me and I was in an achy stupor. I looked at my watch. It was quarter to nine. The phone rang.

"Roxanne," I said, and heaved myself to my feet. I said "hello" a couple of times to get ready and then I was in the living room.

"Hello," I said.

"Jack."

"Clair."

"Hate to bother you but this reporter from the Valley newspaper, he called here a few minutes ago."

"He called there?"

"Persistent bugger. Called the town office and asked who you were close to in town."

"Not bad. What'd he say?"

"He said he needed to talk to you. Said it was urgent. I said, 'How urgent?' and he said, 'Very urgent.' He was all hot and bothered. Left me two numbers. Pager and all this stuff."

"Yeah?"

"Jack, he said they identified the body."

My stomach rolled.

"Who is it?"

"He wouldn't say."

Twenty-five

I DIALED THE *Chronicle*. Asked for the newsroom. They said Mendoza was out but he'd be back. I dialed the pager and left a message with Roxanne's number. I waited. Went and brushed my teeth and found some orange juice. Came back. Dialed the *Chronicle* again. Mendoza still wasn't there. Stood by the phone and drank the juice. Picked up the receiver and put it back down. Reached for it again.

It rang.

"Yeah," I said.

"Mr. McMorrow. Joe Mendoza. You got my message. Sorry to bother your friend but I called your house a bunch of times. I left messages. Don't you check your messages?"

"No. Who is it?"

"It's your man. Mullaney."

"Shit."

I felt myself wilt.

"Dental records. They FedExed them yesterday from Maine. Got them in late last night. I camped at the coroner's office. I was right there when they made the ID. Assistant who did the autopsy said they matched like fingerprints. It's him."

"Son of a bitch."

"You're surprised?"

"I don't know. I guess so. I just thought . . . I don't know what I thought. I just can't believe it's him."

"Start believing. I'm on deadline. I gotta get back and file the story for this afternoon's paper. I'm at the police station."

"Find out anything else?"

"Yeah, he had a record. Nothing too heavy. Possession of marijuana. Some bad checks. Worst one was eleven years ago. Got picked up with, like, eight ounces of coke. Pleaded to possession with intent to distribute. But he got thirty days' probation."

"They turned him?"

"Flipped him right over, I'd say."

"And he took off for the woods," I said. "To save his hide."

"Maybe he thought there was a statute of limitations for selling somebody out," Mendoza said.

"And there isn't."

"Depends on who you sell. Some people have memories like elephants, or their friends do."

"And the penalty is death."

"Well, these guys don't want to appear soft," he said.

"Heaven forbid," I said.

Mendoza had more questions but I was only half listening. He wanted more, any little shred I could give him. What was Florence, Maine, like? Was this guy like a guru to the others in the pot group? Could I give him some names of pot people in Maine to call?

I didn't give him much. I had my own story to write, my own living to make.

"Have they called his wife yet?" I interrupted.

"I don't know. I would think so by now."

"I gotta go."

"Hey, McMorrow. You really haven't given me squat."

"I'll call you," I said, and I hung up and called Melanie Mullaney.

• • •

Melanie's number was busy the first time but rang the second. I waited. It clicked. Stephen said, "Hullo?"

"Hi, Stephen. This is Jack McMorrow. How are you doing?"

"Pretty shitty," he said.

"I'm sorry."

"Yeah, right."

"I mean it."

"Whatever."

He didn't say anything.

"How's your mother?"

"Pretty shitty."

"She there?"

"She's outside."

Silence.

"Can I talk to her?"

"I don't know. I'll ask her."

The phone clattered like it had been thrown on the floor. I waited. Heard a door slam, Stephen's sullen voice calling, "Mom." His shoulder was not one you'd cry on.

I waited some more. Heard the door slam again. The phone clattered, more softly this time.

"Hello."

It was Melanie. Her voice was expressionless and dead.

"Hi, this is Jack."

"Yeah?"

"I'm sorry."

"Oh. Thanks."

"How are you doing?"

"Fine."

"You sure?"

"Yeah. It was no surprise."

"It was for me," I said. "I still, I don't know, I still can't believe it."

"Well, what are you gonna do? Shit happens."

"I guess."

"I know," she said.

I paused. Heard Melanie sniff behind her quavering bravado. I wondered if she was cried out yet.

"No sign of Coyote?"

"No. They probably killed him, too."

"How were the cops?"

"Fine," Melanie said. "I mean, what could they say? My husband was killed by drug dealers."

"Is that what they said?"

"More or less."

"Are they working on it? I mean, trying to find the guys?"

Melanie sighed.

"I suppose. But they've got a lot to do. I don't expect much. I don't even care, at this point. He's gone. They're not gonna bring him back so the hell with it. I just don't care, McMorrow. I really just don't care."

"I understand," I said. "But there are some holes still. I'm sorry, I shouldn't bother you now. But there are some questions still."

"No there aren't, McMorrow. No questions. No answers. No nothing. Just a memorial service."

"I'd like to come, if that would be okay."

"Sure. Hey, Bobby liked you. It's gonna be in Florence. The cemetery right up the road. Day after tomorrow. In the morning. Bobby was a morning person. The cremation is supposed to be tomorrow. Down there. We won't really have anything to bury, but I figure you've got to do something. One of the people here is making this wooden cross, and Kathy, you met Kathy, she's going to read something from the Bible."

"People pretty upset?"

"Yeah. People liked Bobby. Mr. Happy-go-lucky."

"He was a very likable guy," I said. "That's why I've never been quite able to figure out why he went to Lewiston like that. He could talk the fruit off the trees. Why get so wound up? And who was the Valley dealer who was in Lewiston? He shouldn't be too hard to find."

"Leave it, McMorrow," Melanie said. Her voice was hard.

"But Melanie, there should be some sort of justice done."

"Just leave it. Drop it. There is no justice. Bobby's dead. Leave it alone."

No way.

I felt for Melanie, even for Stephen, but their tragedy was my story. And my story still had holes. I had to fill them. It was what I did.

Still standing there in the living room, my back to Portland harbor, I took out my notebook and scrawled notes of my conversation with Melanie. Then I flipped through the pages and found the number of the Valley PD. I dialed it and asked for Detective Martucci. I waited and she answered.

My lucky day.

"I've been calling you, McMorrow."

"I haven't been home."

"I thought maybe you were hiding."

"Nope. I'm right here. And I wondered what you could tell me about Bobby."

"You took the question right out of my mouth."

"I asked first."

"I'm a cop."

"I'm a reporter. So I hear the teeth fit."

Martucci cleared her throat.

"Yeah. Like a glove. Good thing 'cause that was about all that was left of Mr. Mullaney."

"Was he dismembered?"

"Nope, but you're close."

"Busted up?"

"Arms and legs."

"Jeez. Dead before the car burned?"

"They think so. Maybe for some time."

"So they kept him around the house a while and then took him for a ride?"

"I don't know. Stranger things have happened."

"Maine dentist didn't waste any time. Where was it?"

"I don't know. Someplace up there in the woods. Hartigan? Addison?"

"Madison?"

"That's it. Dentists are usually glad to help out."

"Mainers are like that."

"Good," Martucci said. "Now it's your turn."

She asked me to start at the beginning and I did. The fair, Florence, the plants in the woods, the apartment in Lewiston, Paco in the cathedral, Coyote in Valley. The hooker, Dora, and the old man downstairs.

"I want Paco," Martucci said.

"Lewiston PD ought to be able to round him up."

"And I want Coyote. I want his real name."

"The name you can probably get. I think his first name is Bernie. But I talked to Bobby's wife this morning and nobody's seen him."

"I talked to her, too. I had to tell her the news, but I figured I'd have a little taste and wait a few hours before I started grilling her."

"I waited a few minutes," I said. "She said she hasn't heard from or of Coyote since they left."

"He's got to be someplace."

"Could be dead."

"That's why I need Paco," Martucci said. "I want to know who Bobby left with."

"So do I."

"And I'm gonna need you, too, McMorrow."

"I figured that."

"So can you come back down?"

"Well, I'm tied up here. While I was gone, a good friend had an accident."

"Oh?"

"Yeah, she's in the hospital and I'd really rather not leave right now."

"Good friend as in ladyfriend?"

"Yeah."

"What kind of accident?" Martucci asked.

"Well, she sort of got trampled. She's a social worker. Works with abused kids. Some people don't like to see her coming."

"Is she going to be okay?"

"Yeah. A broken leg and collarbone. And she's still being threatened, so I really can't leave."

"I thought Maine was this really peaceful place," she said.

"Only from a distance," I said.

When I got to the hospital the cop was gone. So was Roxanne. I went back to the nurses' station and asked where she had gone and the man there asked who I was. I told him I was Roxanne's friend, Jack. He said they'd brought her down to X ray. I asked if something was wrong and he said no, it was just that another surgeon had come in and he wanted more pictures. I asked the nurse if the cop had gone with her and he said he didn't know.

I said I sure as hell hoped so. He looked at me but didn't say anything.

So I sat in the room with the banks of flowers and waited. Roxanne was right. The flowers did make the room seem funereal, and the bed seem like a casket. I got up and looked out the window at the highway, the bank towers that sprouted from the jumble of brick buildings like trees from low shrubs.

There was a noise and I turned. A young guy, maybe twenty, was standing there with a flowerpot in his arms. The guy was chubby. The pot, pressed against his soft belly, was wrapped in green foil.

"Masterson?" he asked.

"Yeah."

He looked around for a place to put them.

"Just what you need, huh?"

"What's one more," I said. "I'll take it."

I took the pot and the guy left. There was a little space on the radiator next to the window if I shoved the other pots over. I did and put the new one down and peeled back the wrapping.

The flowers were carnations. They were black.

"Damn," I said.

I dug in the greenery for a card. It was in a small envelope. The envelope had "Roxanne" written on it in black marker. I started to rip it, then hesitated.

Should Roxanne open it? Should she have the choice?

I held the envelope by the edges, then looked at the tag on the flowers. The florist was on Forest Avenue, a couple of miles from the hospital. I went to the phone and called.

A woman answered.

I chuckled and asked her if she could tell me who sent the black flowers to the hospital. She chuckled, too, and told me she thought it was pretty hysterical. I agreed and said I thought I had an idea of which of our friends had sent the flowers but I just wanted to make sure. She said the guy didn't leave his name.

"Guy?"

"Yeah. He came in and the lady waited outside. They said it was an old joke. Since high school. They said you'd know."

"I think I do. But what did the lady look like?"

"Well, I didn't go out and stare at her. I don't know. Blond. Very blond. Hair pulled back. Actually, she looked kind of rumpled."

"Rumpled?"

"Kind of mussed up. No offense."

"The guy filled out the card?"

"Yeah, well, I don't know. He was okay. Leather jacket. Beard. Shades. I mean, I don't know what else to tell you."

"That's fine," I said, and I thanked her and hung up.

I looked again at the envelope. Squeezed it. There was something hard inside. I held it up to the light and could see something rectangular. I slit the envelope open and shook it upside down.

A razor blade landed in my hand.

I put it down on the radiator. Slipped out the card and turned it over.

Do it yourself or we'll do it for you!!!

Twenty-six

"SO WE JUST have to find Will and tell him to cease and desist," Roxanne said, smiling from the bed.

"I'd prefer to take him out and shoot him."

"They'd put you in jail."

"So?"

"And you'd never see me again. Except for through that glass."

"Okay. I'll have Clair shoot him."

"Oh, Jack, don't worry about it. And don't think you have to guard me. I've had this happen before. Once somebody mailed me a bag of, well, feces. I mean, these people are pathetic. They aren't going to really do anything. That's why they call on the phone. It's why they send silly flowers. They're weak. Cowards. That's why they abuse their kids."

"Police didn't think it was so harmless," I said.

"They think the worst of people. It's their job."

"And you don't?"

"Only when it comes to kids. You don't have to baby-sit me. I've got my gendarme. You don't have to be here twenty-four hours a day. You've got a life to live. And a story to write. When is that due?"

"Nag, nag, nag," I said. "I'll get to it."

"I think you should do it while it's all fresh. I could be in here for another week. You can't just sit here."

I looked at her.

"I don't know. The view isn't bad."

She smiled.

"Just don't forget what the full panorama looks like."

"Never," I said.

We talked for a while longer and then Roxanne's eyes began to unfocus and she lapsed back into her medicated sleep. I looked at her for a minute, then went out to the corridor where the cop was standing. It was the young woman again. She had seen the black flowers and the razor blade. She had not been amused.

"She's sleeping," I said.

"Okay."

"I'll be back in an hour. Keep a weather eye out."

"You can count on it," she said.

"I am," I said. .

I went downstairs to the truck and drove through the streets and down the big hill and over the bridge to Roxanne's. It was sunny and breezy, and the water was a shimmering green-blue and Roxanne was stuck in a hospital room thanks to some craven, weak-willed loser. Some nodded-out druggie. I looked at my notes, spread on the table beside my computer, felt my sympathy for the marijuana movement draining away. This wasn't going to make the story write any easier.

But I clicked on the computer and sat down. It whirred and I opened up the file, "Marijuana outline." I scrolled through the chronology, picked out the holes and looked through my notebooks. What had the banner said at Bobby's table at the Country Life Fair? What had the petition said? How many miles was Florence from Augusta or Portland or some other landmark that even readers in Boston would know?

I needed Bobby's rap sheet, not Mendoza's secondhand account. I needed to know the year that Bobby had gone to the high school and threatened to demonstrate. I needed the coroner's report so I could say how many broken bones he had, and which ones. I needed to know how many acres the Mullaneys owned. I needed to get back to Florence and get a reaction to his death from his pals in the pot movement and other people in town. Who was the dentist? What did he think when he got the call from the cops?

What was the rank of that DEA cop in Florence, the one with the son with the drug problem? What was his son's name? Where was Bobby born? Were his parents alive? Did they know what had become of their little boy?

I needed to talk to Melanie again, as a source. I needed to talk to the Valley police. I needed to talk to Mendoza, have him send me a copy of his story. I needed to talk to the *Globe* and tell Wellington that the story I was going to deliver was going to be more extensive than the one we had discussed. Maybe I'd pitch it to the *Globe* magazine.

All of this was going to be hard to do from Portland. Maybe I could bring Roxanne to Prosperity to recuperate. Clair could stay with her when I was gone. Mary could make her chicken soup. God, I really did have to get back to Florence. Maybe down to Valley again. Could I ask Clair to come to Portland?

I looked at my watch. My hour was almost up and I hadn't even made a phone call. I dug in my wallet and took out a folded piece of paper: the instructions for my answering machine. I went to the counter with a pad and dialed, punching in numbers as my own voice answered.

The messages played.

Joe Mendoza, times five. A couple of hang-ups. Wellington, from the *Globe,* asking me to call him. Another hang-up. Then a tentative man's voice, asking for Mr. McMorrow the reporter. He said his name was Sam and we'd met at the restaurant in Madison.

It was Sam, the pot guy with the son who thought his daddy was a criminal. He said he wanted to talk to me about Bobby, that they all did. He said they wanted to set the record straight.

"Police are gonna try to discredit him, I know, just like they try to discredit all of us and what we're working for,"

Sam said. "Please call because we think you'll try to tell the real story."

He left a number. I dialed it. Sam answered breathlessly, as if he'd been sitting by the phone for eighteen hours, awaiting my call.

"So like I said, we need to talk to you about Bobby. The police are going to turn this into a smear campaign and we've got to defend him and defend ourselves. I mean, this is a good man we're talking about."

"Running with the wrong crowd?"

"Exactly. The wrong place at the wrong time. I mean, Bobby was no more a drug trafficker than I am."

My eyebrows raised.

"So I can call everybody. We've been waiting to hear from you, and we can be at the restaurant in, let's say an hour?"

"Can't do it. I'm in Portland."

"Well, how 'bout an hour and a half?"

"Can't do that, either. I've got a friend in the hospital down here."

"Oh."

He seemed puzzled.

"You going to the service?" I asked.

"Oh, yeah. Of course."

"I'm going to try to make that. How 'bout we talk then?"

"Meet before?"

"What time's the service?"

"Ten o'clock."

"How would nine be? Same place in Madison."

"Good," Sam said.

"How's your son?" I asked.

"My son?"

"Yeah. You told me before he was upset. About the pot arrest."

"Oh, yeah. Well, he's more upset now."

"Why's that?"

"He called him Uncle Bobby."

• • •

So my hour was up and I went back to the hospital. The nurses smiled at me when I got off the elevator, and the cop was at the door. None of the flowers had exploded and Roxanne was beautiful in the bed, sipping a cup of coffee, her leg under a leg-sized pup tent.

We talked and sat and held hands and watched the jets coast by outside the window. I told Roxanne what I still had to do on the story and that I'd like to make a quick trip up to Florence in the morning. She said that was fine, because she had friends who wanted to come over and she wouldn't be alone. I said I wouldn't be too long and Roxanne said I ought to take a day off from her and wind up the research and then take another day off and write it. I told her I'd think about it and she said not to worry about her, and I said I'd do just that.

That was the way the day went, and Sunday, too. I went back to Roxanne's and called the *Globe* and told Wellington what I was up to. He was interested but said he didn't want to give the story to the magazine because he wanted it for his own section so screw them. I told him it would be three days, which would mean I would file by Tuesday night, which would also mean I would need more money. Wellington said he'd go as high as six hundred if the piece was as I'd described and I asked him if I'd ever led him astray before and he said no.

When I went back at six, Roxanne was gone.

The nurse said she'd been moved to another room, on the eighth floor, as a security precaution. I got on the elevator and went up and asked for Roxanne at the desk and a new nurse asked my name. I told her but then the older cop with the paperback book waved to me and told her I was okay. I walked down the hall to the room and the cop asked how I was.

"Fine. How 'bout you?"

"Great."

"Why'd they move her?"

"Routine."

"Because of the mother and the flowers?"

"Mostly because of the mother," the old cop said. "They can't find her."

That night we watched the news on the television hanging from the ceiling. One story said the attorney general's office was still investigating the shooting of a Portland man by a Portland police detective who was accompanying a social worker on a visit to a downtown apartment. The man, Mark Radcliffe, twenty-eight, was in stable condition at Maine Medical Center.

"The social worker, Roxanne Masterson, twenty-seven, of the state Department of Human Services, was also seriously injured in the fracas," the TV reporter said. *"Masterson was taken to Maine Med with multiple fractures. A hospital spokesman said the Portland woman was expected to be transferred to another facility for further treatment."*

"That true?" I said.

"Not that I know of," Roxanne said.

"Misinformation."

"You don't approve?"

"No, it's completely unethical. And they should have said you'd been taken to a special hospital in Ohio."

That night I left again when Roxanne slept. With a beer beside me, I called Mendoza, first at the paper, then at home. The woman who answered was older, with a stronger Latino accent. His mother. She said Joe was working, that he was always working, even on a Saturday night.

"He's a reporter," she said proudly.

"I know," I said. "So am I."

"You must be very proud, too," Mendoza's mother said.

"Sometimes," I said.

After that I called Martucci to see about the autopsy report and Bobby's sheet. Martucci wasn't in, either. Out of excuses, I called Melanie. Nobody answered. Good things come in threes.

So I worked until ten, then called Roxanne's floor. The nurse connected me and the phone rang and Roxanne answered, sounding groggy. I had awakened her. I told her I loved her, that she wouldn't remember me calling in the morning. She said she would, but the next morning she didn't.

"You don't remember any of it?" I said, standing by her bed.

Roxanne shook her head.

"You wouldn't believe some of the things you said. And with the nurses right there. I tried to urge discretion, but you wouldn't have any of it. They left when you started comparing me to Adonis. I think they were embarrassed."

She smiled wearily. I squeezed her hand and pulled up a chair.

Roxanne dozed. I sat. Nurses bustled in and bustled out, the way nurses do. One bearded guy called her Roxie and tugged on her IV tube. He said I didn't have to move, so I didn't.

People from her office came in after lunch. A couple of them, women in their fifties, hugged her. One started to cry. Roxanne said it was okay. The woman said she knew, but she clearly didn't.

More medication in the afternoon. An orthopedic surgeon who poked his head in, but saw me, and said he'd come back, just wanted to say hello. He seemed a nice fellow.

"I wonder if he shaves yet," I said.

Roxanne smiled, her eyes closed. She slept and then dinner arrived, in a covered tray. Beside it was a plastic container of what appeared to be tapioca pudding. I let her sleep, watched her mouth part. She started to snore, and I decided I wouldn't tell her. For a moment, I had a vision of her old, in a nursing home bed. I took her hand, and the vision slipped away, leaving an unsettling chill.

A teenage girl came in and stopped. Whispered, "Should I leave her dinner?"

I nodded, and she left. I sat. Roxanne slept.

It was after nine when two nurses, one with a beard, one without, came in with a cart full of stuff. They said they'd be twenty minutes or so. Roxanne stirred. I said I'd say goodnight. Roxanne smiled her woozy junkie grin. I kissed her cheek and left. The cop in the hall told me to have a good night. I wished him the same, but meant it more.

The next morning, I was on the road by six, tea in my mug and rifle in my rack. The sun came up beyond the bay and I drove north with it on my right and then swung north-west. The sunlight beamed in low and the day seemed charged with light, the trees golden and reflective. I took Route 4 north to Livermore Falls and Jay, where the paper mill's plume was clean and white against the blue sky. By seven I was in Farmington and then beyond it, into the forgotten hills, where it was a beautiful day to look back on Bobby Mullaney's life, and just as good a day to try to figure out, yet again, why he caused his own death.

But first another piece of the story. The local reaction.

On the western outskirts of Florence, a woman was walking across the road from her mailbox with her newspaper. I pulled over and got out. She was somewhere near eighty, wearing jeans and boots, and she gave me a hard look that dared me to try something funny.

Instead, I introduced myself and asked her if she knew Bobby Mullaney. She said no, and kept on toward her trailer. I asked her if she knew about the marijuana legal-ization movement in her town.

"You mean them friggin' potheads?"

"Yeah, I guess. I'm doing a story on one of them. He was killed this week in Massachusetts."

"Good."

"Good?"

"Goddamn right. Ought to haul the rest of 'em down there, too, and blow 'em to hell. Ruined this town, is what they've done. Now let me ask you a question there, Mr. Whatever-your-name-is. Why don't you do a write-up on somebody decent?"

My poll continued all the way into the center of Florence and out the other side. I asked everyone I saw. When I was done, Bobby Mullaney's death had been approved, three to two. One guy, who was in his dooryard clanking on the underside of his old truck, was undecided, not on Bobby Mullaney, but on whether he should let me leave on my own volition or set the dog on me.

I fixed my notes on the side of the road and headed east toward Madison. It was eight-fifteen when I passed the restaurant on Main Street and I didn't see any of Bobby's clan. I drove past the mill and up to the light and took a left. I was about to take another left and circle back when I saw a sign: "Lester Pelham, D.M.D." I drove on and pulled in.

It was an old Victorian house, olive green with a plywood wheelchair ramp nailed to the front. The dentist was on the left and an accountant's office was on the right. There were a car and a truck out front. I went up the ramp and opened the door.

A chime sounded when I stepped on the carpet. The waiting room was paneled and a big unshaven guy was sitting in one of the wooden chairs. I went to the counter and leaned. A matronly woman came from out back and gave me a friendly smile. I did the same and told her my name.

"I'm writing a story for the *Boston Globe* about a man who lived in Florence," I said. "I was told that his dentist in Madison helped police in Massachusetts identify his body. I just wondered if this might be the dentist. I don't know how many there are in town."

"Two," the woman said.

The look on her face said this was the one.

She asked me to have a seat so I did. The unshaven guy stared at me for a good thirty seconds before going back to his magazine. Not to be outdone, I picked up a magazine, too. I had read most of an article on manatees when the woman called pleasantly to the unshaven man. He heaved himself up and left.

Dr. Pelham appeared at my left shoulder.

I stood and we shook hands. He was fifty-five, maybe, with a silvery mustache and a kind, open face. I explained what I wanted to know and he looked intrigued.

"*Boston Globe?*"

"That's right. I string for them."

"You intend to put us on the map, huh?"

"I don't know about that. I don't even know if I have the right dentist."

"You do."

"So the Valley police called you?"

I slipped my notebook from my jacket pocket.

"Yes, they did. They asked if Bobby was a patient of mine. I said he was. We did whatever we could to help."

He paused, as if he thought his next comment might be quoted and he wanted to word it carefully.

"He was a very pleasant, very funny fellow and this is a terrible tragedy," Pelham said.

I did the obligatory scribble.

"So you sent the dental records to the Massachusetts police?"

"They were out of here within twenty minutes of the call."

"Yes, they told me you were especially helpful."

He seemed proud.

"Have you had to do this before?"

"You know, that's an interesting question," Pelham said, folding his hands across his white coat. "I've been in practice here for twenty-six years. I've been called on to help with identification of bodies seven times. Two were drowning victims whose bodies were in the river for several months. One was a man who died in a house fire. They pretty much knew who it was but they had to be positive. Smoking in bed. Terrible thing. One was a body they found up in the woods outside Caratunk. Man hung himself from a tree. Hunters found him two years later. Animals had scattered the bones pretty good but they found the skull. The skull and a belt buckle. Buckle was silver. With turquoise. One of those Indian ones."

"Did you identify him?"

"No. I helped unidentify him. He wasn't the man they thought he was. They never did figure out who he was, as far as I know."

"So this is almost routine for you?"

"Oh, yeah. I tell Carol, 'Pull the last X rays. Send them Federal Express.' She knows what to do."

"That's funny," I said, writing in my notebook. "I would have thought that something like this would be pretty unusual for a small-town dentist."

"Heck no. We tend to know everybody in town, of course. Everybody has teeth. Well, most people do. And small towns aren't the idyllic little places they're made out to be. Not to disappoint the readers of the *Boston Globe,* but small towns have many of the bad things you find in the city. Just in smaller numbers. Proportionate numbers."

I smiled and scrawled. It was his theory and it was well polished.

"You know this building was broken into this week."

"They broke in here?"

"No, next door."

"What is it? An accountant?"

"Yeah, they must have thought accountants have cash. These kids aren't all rocket scientists."

"They take much?"

"Some petty cash. A computer. A very nice laser printer."

"They get in here?"

"No, which is funny. People don't realize it, and this isn't for print, but dentists do use some pretty powerful painkilling drugs. In their work, I mean."

He grinned at his bit of humor.

"Can you develop a Novacain habit?" I asked.

"No, but there are other things we use that would have a street value. All they had to do was walk through that door."

Pelham looked toward a door on the side wall, behind the counter.

"It was unlocked," he said.

Twenty-seven

THEY WERE ALL there. J. C. and Darrin. Sue and Kathy. Roberta. Sam had brought his son.

We sat at the same big table where I had met with them before. With Melanie and Bobby and Coyote there, we'd been jammed in. Now we had room to sprawl.

I put my notebook and tape recorder on the table. The waitress poured coffee all around, except for Kathy, who asked for two cups, one with hot water, one empty. When they came, she took a plastic bag from her canvas tote, scooped some sort of herb stuff from the bag and dumped it in a small filter contraption with a handle. Everyone watched as she poured the hot water over the filter and herb stuff and steam wafted from the cup.

It smelled like air freshener.

I opened the notebook, hit the button on the recorder. Sam looked at the recorder, swallowed and started us off. It seemed he'd rehearsed.

"Bobby Mullaney's death is ultimately, um, prima facie evidence of the corruption that is the very foundation of the criminal justice system in this country. Bobby fought that corruption and he paid with his life."

"How was he fighting corruption?" I asked.

"Bobby Mullaney was not a drug trafficker," Roberta said, her walker parked next to her chair. "Bobby's growing marijuana on his very own private property was civil disobedience. You know. Gandhi and all that. Martin Luther King?"

"Thoreau and all that," I said. "I know. But you guys are losing me a little here. How is selling pounds of pot to drug dealers civil disobedience?"

"He gave his life," Kathy said calmly. "He attempted to right this terrible injustice and they took of his life."

Took of his life?

I looked at her.

"Like you know who?"

"I didn't say that. But the Lord Jesus was also branded a criminal by the authorities."

"Bobby Mullaney was fighting for me," Roberta said, suddenly angry, her open hand slapping the table. "He was fighting for my right to live in peace. He was fighting for my right to try to sleep for more than an hour at a time. And this is what they did to him."

"Who's they?"

"The system. The system in this country that has made this medicinal herb an outlawed drug," Roberta said. "They're in with the drug companies, they're in with the booze makers, they're in with big business. Who do you think elects the politicians in this country? Who elects the president?"

Sam held his hand up to get my attention.

"Mr. McMorrow, what would happen if cannabis was legalized in this country? What would happen to Budweiser's sales? What would happen to Gallo wine? You can go to the store and spend six bucks on a six-pack, or you can partake of a natural, native plant that is free and people have used for centuries. The choice is—"

"Big business does not want this to happen," Roberta interrupted. "And the system won't let it happen without a fight. That's what this drug war really is all about. They've got to lump us in with the cocaine and the heroin because if we win, big business loses. It's money, money, money."

"Makes the world go round, doesn't it?" I said.

They talked for forty minutes without coming up for air. The gist of their argument was that the system had banned marijuana and if marijuana hadn't been banned, Bobby wouldn't have been forced to sell to murderous drug dealers and if he hadn't been forced to sell to murderous drug dealers, he'd still be alive.

It was a bit of a reach but I could see what they meant, though if Bobby had chosen not to sell pot at all, he'd be just as alive, albeit still living in this far reach of the backwoods, with no electricity or running water, writhing under the tyranny of big business.

A minor flaw in the argument.

They talked as we left the restaurant, and talked as we walked to the cars. I got in my truck and followed them in their two cars, both beat up, and we drove to Florence, past the store and out to the cemetery just before the Mullaney driveway. We all got out and Sam opened the trunk of his white Ford and lifted out a simple white cross. It was three feet high and carefully constructed, notched together so the pieces were flush. Sam brushed it off with his hand and we started across the grass.

I didn't know where we were going but they did. I brought up the rear, pausing to read the lichen-crusted headstones. Most of them went back to the early 1800s. There were many children. Infants. Toddlers. Young mothers and older brothers.

"Blessed are the dead which die in the Lord," the inscription on one stone said.

I wondered what that meant for Bobby Mullaney.

They stopped near the rear of the cemetery under a massive old maple, which streamed orange-yellow foliage against the blue sky. Someone had already dug a small hole, like a hole for a fence post. We stood around it and were suddenly somber and quiet. Sam leaned the cross against the tree and we stood and waited and then there was a rumble from the woods, the squeaking of springs, and Bobby's truck jounced into view.

It pulled up on the grass fifty yards away. Melanie got out first, dressed in a denim skirt and a heavy black sweater. She came toward us, weaving through the stones, and Stephen finally got out and followed, grudgingly it seemed. He was wearing his customary camouflage.

It was only his stepfather.

The group greeted Melanie. I nodded. Kathy embraced her. Roberta, with her walker, clumped over and took Melanie's hand. Sam touched her shoulder shyly. Melanie looked drawn and drained. Stephen stood ten feet away, alone. His face was blank, without expression.

As they hugged and held, another truck pulled up, a Ford with a cap. A big bearded guy got out and strode toward us. He was wearing a worn tweed jacket over a sweater and green work pants. He was holding a black book. We all watched him and when he reached us, Melanie stepped forward and shook his hand.

"Let's begin," the guy said. "I'd like everyone to stand in a semicircle. And join hands."

I stood between Sam and Kathy. Kathy's hand was cold and Sam's was sweaty. The bearded guy was a minister or some rough equivalent and he stood and meditated for a minute while we stood and stared at the posthole as if it were Groundhog Day and we were waiting to see if the critter would appear.

The bearded guy opened his book and cleared his throat.

" 'Let not your heart be troubled. You believe in God, believe also in me. In my father's house there are many mansions. Were it not so, I should have told you, because I go to prepare a place for you. And if I go and prepare a place for you, I am coming again, and I will take you to myself; that where I am, there you also may be. And where I go, you know, and the way you know.' "

He paused.

"Amen," he said.

"Amen," we said back.

Stephen said nothing and looked away.

"You may get the cross," the bearded guy said solemnly.

Sam broke free and went and got the cross and walked over and thrust it into the ground, as if claiming the cemetery for Her Majesty, the Queen. Melanie stepped up to the cross and turned toward us.

"I'd just like to say that if Bobby were here with us today, he'd probably thank you for being so brave and sticking together and everything. And, um, you've been good friends to him and I'll never forget that. I really won't. So, thank you, I guess. And thanks for coming."

Kathy squeezed my hand, moved by the eulogy, if you could call it that. It was more like a going-away party, which was curious. But then Melanie hadn't been blessed with Bobby's gift of gab. If it had been Bobby up there in front of the cross, we'd have been there all morning.

The group stood awkwardly and there was a little more hugging and touching. Kathy had tears in her eyes but Melanie didn't. Roberta looked angry, her constant state. Sam knelt and pressed earth around the bottom of the cross and J. C. and Darrin, in their jeans and work boots, looked like they wanted to go home.

Stephen stood alone.

I walked over to him.

"How are you doing?" I said.

He looked at me.

"Great."

"I'm sorry."

"Gimme a break."

I looked at him. He stared straight ahead, his face fixed in a glare. Melanie looked over at him, and looked concerned.

"What are you and your mom going to do?"

Stephen still hadn't looked at me.

"Live friggin' happily ever after," he said, and he turned away and started for the road to the house.

I stood there alone for a moment, like a newcomer to a cocktail party. Sam and Kathy were by the cross, Kathy kneeling and praying and Sam inspecting his own handiwork. The minister, or whatever he was, got in his truck and left. Melanie saw Stephen leaving and started after him. I intercepted her.

"Melanie, I'm sorry," I said, falling in beside her.

"Thanks."

"I know this is a bad time, but at some point I'm going to have a few questions. Little things. Bobby's background and yours. What you're going to do now."

For a moment, she didn't say anything. Just kept walking through the gravestones.

"Yeah, okay. Maybe when my head's cleared a little."

"You may be hearing from a guy named Joe Mendoza. He's a reporter from Valley."

"He called last night. Stephen talked to him."

"Oh?"

"He swore at him and hung up."

"Oh, well," I said.

We came to the edge of the cemetery and stopped by Bobby's truck. Stephen had disappeared into the woods.

"So our deal still stands?"

Melanie stopped and looked at me.

"The story?"

"Yeah."

"Um, I guess. I don't know. Yeah, I guess so."

"I'd like to use names."

"What? Real names? Bobby's name?"

"Yeah. I pretty much have to, now. With what's happened."

Melanie thought.

"Everybody's gonna know now anyway," she said. "So what's this gonna be? The life and times of Bobby Mullaney?"

"Something like that. Does that bother you?"

She gave a little sniff.

"No. I mean, me and Stephen are leaving anyway. Go someplace and get a job. I can't make it out here all by myself. Don't like to admit it but it's true. Without Bobby, it won't be any good anyway. And we don't have anything. Bobby liked living hand to mouth, but I can't stand the stress. I've got to make some real money. You're not going to make him look bad, are you, McMorrow?''

"I'll just make him look like he was.''

"There was a lot of good in the guy. You talked to him.''

"Yeah.''

"I mean, he was very funny. All this energy. And coming up here, it was, like, it was this big adventure. When we first got here, we had some funny times. We were so big-city, trying to figure out the locals. I mean, some people, we couldn't even understand what they were saying.''

Melanie smiled.

"I heard about some of the things that happened before you came here," I said.

She turned, her mouth a hard straight line.

"It was a long time ago.''

"I know that.''

"Why do you have to bring that up?''

"Because it's part of the story. It's part of the story of who Bobby was.''

"It's a very small part.''

"I didn't say it wasn't.''

"Then why do you have to bring it up?''

"Because it's true. I can't leave it out.''

"It was ten years ago. That's gonna make everybody think—''

"That he was a drug dealer.''

"Yeah," Melanie said.

"By some definitions, he was. Selling pot. Arrested with eight ounces of cocaine.''

"That's ancient history, McMorrow. We were kids.''

"But it's part of *your* history.''

"Not anymore.''

"Is that why you came up here? To get away from the dealers down there?''

"We had to leave. I mean, it was either go or die. Half the people we knew from those days are dead now. I had Stephen. I had to—McMorrow, why do you have to trash him? He's dead, for God's sake.''

"I'm not going to trash him. I liked him in a lot of ways."

"But Jesus, going back ten years?"

"It's part of the picture. All the little pieces. On the way here, I stopped in Madison and talked to all these guys. They said good things about Bobby, about how he was really trying to help them, how he was a victim of the system. Roberta and her condition and all that. I stopped and talked to the dentist. He told me how many times he's had to do this. It all goes in. It's all part of—"

Melanie had looked away. She was swallowing hard, like her mouth was dry and gummy.

"You okay?" I asked.

"Yeah, sure. It's just—The dentist, McMorrow? I don't know. I've still got to go to him. He's gonna think I'm the worst—"

"No, he won't. He was a very nice guy. Very chatty. He didn't seem to be judging Bobby at all. We talked, he told me about how somebody broke into the office next door—"

Melanie's face suddenly paled. She turned and lifted herself up into the truck and said, "I gotta go," and started the motor. Then she turned the wheel hard and wrenched the truck through a U-turn and drove off. I walked to my truck and got in and sat there and didn't feel so good myself.

Twenty-eight

SITTING IN MY truck on the cemetery grass, I pictured it again and again. One moment Melanie had been holding her ground for Bobby, saying I shouldn't trash him, and then the blood had drained from her face like it had been sucked out with a syringe.

No, I had been talking about Sam and Roberta and the dentist when something had pulled the plug.

Melanie had been physically overcome, but not by grief. She seemed more concerned about preserving her husband's reputation than about mourning his death, or the last gruesome hours of his life.

Did they hold him down and break his arms and legs with a baseball bat? Had they strangled him and then beaten him? Did they pound him and then just toss him in the backseat and torch the car? Did Bobby scream and writhe in terror as the flames crawled over him?

If the answer was yes to any of the above, where was the horror? Why did Melanie act as though her husband had been hit by a truck while walking the dog?

I didn't know.

The funeral broke up like a softball game and everyone retreated to their respective nooks and crannies of Somerset

County, Maine. I drove east, up and over the hills and across the Kennebec River and back into Madison. At the light on the end of Main Street, I stopped and sat, my conversation with Melanie replaying in my mind.

I'd told her I'd talked to Roberta. I'd told her I'd talked to the dentist. Her mouth had gone dry.

The light changed and I turned left, drove as far as the dentist's building and pulled up across the street and stopped. The dentist's sign loomed over the sign for the accountant, which said, "Marion Toose, CPA." The accountant's sign was small and understated. Why would anyone break into an accountant's office? What small-town punk would have been in the accountant's office to know about a computer or a printer? Why haul all that stuff out and not even open the door to the dentist's office?

If that was true.

I drove down the block and turned around and headed back toward Main Street. On the right was a low brick building, the town office. A sign on the side said the police station was in the rear. I drove around back and parked and went inside.

There was a small silver-haired woman sitting at a desk behind a wooden Dutch door, the bottom of which was closed. Behind her was a display case full of drug paraphernalia. I said hello and she asked if she could help me and I said I was a reporter and I needed information on a burglary. She asked if I was from the *Bangor Daily* or the *Morning Sentinel* and I said, no, the *Boston Globe*. She gave me a closer look.

"You'll have to talk to the chief," she said.

"Is she available?"

I smiled. She looked even closer.

"He's on the road."

"Could you call him?"

"I think he's out of the car on an investigation. I could have him call you."

I thought for a moment.

"I'll be on my way back to Portland. Maybe you could just tell me something. Just to confirm what I've been told."

She didn't say yes but she didn't say no.

"The dentist. Dr. Pelham. He was telling me about the break-in at his building. How they broke into the accountant's office but didn't even come into his. Does that sound right?"

The woman wavered.

"I'm not going to quote you. I just don't want to quote him if he's got it all wrong. They took a computer. A printer."

"And some change," the woman said.

"But they didn't bother with the dentist's office?"

"That sounds right. But you didn't hear it from me."

"Of course not. That's fine, I just needed to know that he got it sort of straight. It's not that important. I was talking to him about something else and it came up. You know, crime in the small town."

"We keep busy. Chief's right out straight."

"I'm sure."

I turned to leave, then turned back.

"Does it seem funny to you that they wouldn't go into the dentist's office? I mean, looking for drugs or laughing gas or something?"

The woman looked at me. I gave her my best smile. She tried to bite her tongue, but couldn't.

"Chief had them count the drug bottles and all that. He thought it was funny. But Les checked everything."

"So maybe they chickened out before they got that far, huh?"

"Or maybe they went in and didn't find anything that interested them. I was kind of hoping they'd steal the bill for my husband's bridge, but no such luck."

I laughed. She smiled. I left, and pondered her joke all the way back to Portland.

It was a little before one o'clock when I parked in the Maine Medical Center lot. I hurried to the front doors, down the corridor to the elevators, and kept going.

To the telephones.

First I called Clair. The phone rang a dozen times. I waited, in case he was in the barn. On the fifteenth ring, he answered.

"Yeah, hello."

"It's me."

"Hey. This is your personal secretary calling. I oughta get paid by the call."

"How's one beer per message sound?"

"Sold. Call Detective Martucci."

"When did she call?"

"This morning."

"What's she want?"

"To talk to you."

"God, it's hard to find good help these days. About what?"

"She didn't say."

"She say anything at all?"

"To me she did."

"Like what?"

"It was personal and confidential."

"They're putting you in the witness protection program?"

"Yeah. I'm gonna be a brain surgeon in Spokane. And also they found the kid with the gun. They want us to ID him. You interested?"

"Not terribly. He say anything about who put him onto us?"

"Nope."

"They don't know the finger trick," I said.

"And I didn't tell 'em," Clair said.

"Our little secret."

So I hung up and called Mendoza at the *Chronicle*. At first they said he was out and then they said he was in and then he picked up the phone.

"Mendoza."

"McMorrow."

"Hey, man. What's up?"

"I just got back from Bobby Mullaney's funeral."

"No kidding. How was it?"

"Small. Seven or eight people. No body. Just a cross stuck in the ground."

"Where was this?"

"The cemetery in Florence."

"Today?"

I could hear his pen scratching paper.

"This morning. Ten o'clock."

"You talk to the wife?"

"A little. Did you?"

"Tried. Couldn't get past the son. I guess it was the son. He told me to eff off and hung up."

"He's like that."

"What is he? Some kind of backwoods psycho?"

"Some kind. I haven't figured out exactly which one. Your story run?"

"Coming off the presses shortly. Confirms the identity. Gives some background. You're mentioned briefly."

"Very briefly, I hope."

"You scratch my back or I'll put you in the lead," Mendoza said.

"You play rough."

"This is the big city."

"Well, big-city reporter, I need a favor."

"What is it?"

"I need you to check your police blotter. Find out if there have been any break-ins at dentists' offices around there in the past few days."

"Dentists' offices?"

"Right. You know. Cavities and all that."

"Why do you want to know?"

"I can't really say yet. It might not be anything."

"McMorrow, I don't know. You expect me to hoof it over to the police station and look through the complaints for you but you won't tell me why? What do I look like? A goddamn servant?"

"Come on," I said.

"Nope. You want the information, call the cops yourself."

"Will they really check for me?"

"Depends on who answers the phone," Mendoza said.

"I need to know for sure."

"I need to know why."

I weighed it.

"Can I tell you off the record? Just for now? It isn't anything yet anyway."

Mendoza's turn to weigh.

"Okay. For now."

"There was a burglary at this accountant's office in the town of Madison, Maine. It was a couple of days before the body was found."

"Uh-huh."

"The accountant is in the same building as the dentist. The offices are connected by a regular door. And it was unlocked."

"Is there a point here or what?"

"They took computers and stuff from the accountant. But nothing was taken from the dentist's office. The dentist thinks they didn't even go in."

"But?"

"But what if they did," I said. "What if they went into the dentist's office. That's where Bobby's dental records were."

"But they were still there. They sent 'em."

"I know."

"Well, they matched."

"They matched something. Somebody."

"You're thinking it wasn't Mullaney?"

"I don't know. I just think it's funny that burglars would completely ignore a doctor's office, with drugs and all that, and break into an accountant's office. Who breaks into an accountant's office?"

"Isn't even tax time," Mendoza said.

"It just seems funny."

"But you're making a pretty big jump to get to wherever it is you're headed. What does that have to do with dentists down here?"

"What if they switched the X rays? Took some from down there and brought them up here."

"Why?"

"So the body would be ID'd as Mullaney's."

"So he can be written off as dead? What for? And McMorrow, if it wasn't him in the car, who was it?"

"I don't know," I said. "Somebody whose dental X rays were in an office in Madison, Maine."

"All because the burglars didn't go into the dentist's office? You're reaching, man. I think Mullaney got in way over his head down here and they wasted him. End of story."

"Probably. But I'm not a hundred percent sure."

"You're gonna write this? And get it past a *Globe* editor?"

"Only if I can prove it."

"Must be nice, McMorrow. Sit around up there in the woods and think up this crazy stuff."

"It *is* nice. Will you check for me?"

"You're gonna owe me one."

"Can you check today?"

"Jeez, McMorrow. Need your shoes polished?"

"I don't own any. I just have boots."

"What a hick."

"And proud of it," I said. "Will you still be there at four?"

"Most likely."

"I'll call you."

The elevator hummed me up to the eighth floor and spat me out. The corridor was cool and dim and silent as a padded room. The cop was at the door. It was the woman. She looked up.

"Quiet morning?" I said.

"Well . . ." she said.

I stopped.

"She tried to get in downstairs."

"The mother? In the hospital?"

"She got in the hospital. But she asked at the information desk where her friend Roxanne was."

"Did they tell her?"

"They have her mug shot. They knew who it was. They pretended to check and called security. She spooked and took off."

"You have a mug shot?"

"Sure."

"Can I see it? I've never seen her."

She fiddled with the button on her front pocket and pulled out a folded piece of paper. I took it and unfolded it. It was front and side views, Portland Police Department case numbers held under her chin.

She was blond with black roots. Her face was long and plain and drawn and her eyes had that hopeless look of somebody who has given up.

"Did they catch her?"

Her face fell a little.

"No. They patrolled the area but she was gone. It's a big city."

"It isn't that big. How can she just disappear?"

"She could have gotten in a car. Probably somebody picked her up."

"That's great. What was she going to do?"

"They said she was carrying a paper bag. Who knows what was in it."

"She knows," I said. "Does Roxanne know?"

"I told her."

"How is she?"

She hesitated.

"Well, I'd say she's a little nervous. Tries not to show it."

"She's like that," I said, and pushed open the door.

Roxanne was in bed, surrounded by her flowers. She was asleep and the casket effect almost made me shudder. I turned away and got the chair from the foot of the bed and lifted it over to the side by Roxanne and sat down. When I did, she jerked.

"Whaaa."

"Easy, it's me."

Her eyes focused slowly.

"It's okay," I said.

"She was here. Did they tell you?"

"Yeah, they did."

"I'm sick of this. I want to get away from here."

"I don't blame you. What does the doctor say? When will your beautiful bionic body be ready to travel?"

"She says two or three more days."

"The orthopedic surgeon?"

"Yeah."

"Then you should come home with me. Recuperate in idyllic Prosperity, upper case. I'll cook for you."

"I may come in spite of that."

"It'd be a lot better than sitting in South Portland. I'm sure she couldn't spell Prosperity, much less find it."

"I may take you up on that."

"You could wear your johnny. I like the off-the-shoulder look. And Clair and Mary would be there. You could invite your work friends up to visit, bring us lots of presents."

"It's a deal," Roxanne said. "But enough about me. How did you spend your morning?"

"I went to a funeral," I said. "Sort of."

Sitting there, I told Roxanne about the service and the cross. I told her about the marijuana gang at the restaurant. I told her about the dentist. I told her about Melanie. And I told her about Mendoza.

She sat there thinking, her eyes narrowed. Our minds were different. Mine meandered. Hers churned like a computer.

"You know what I—"

A nurse knocked and came in on padded white shoes. Roxanne turned and said, "Hi."

"We've got to check that incision, change it up," the nurse said. "It'll only take a few minutes."

She looked at me and smiled.

"Would you mind?"

"I could use a drink," Roxanne said. "There's juice and soda somewhere down the hall. Orange juice?"

"Third door on the left," the nurse said.

"I'll be back," I said.

I went out and asked the cop if she wanted a drink and she said she'd take a diet Coke. I passed a couple of patients in the hall, shuffling in their slippers, and then found the room and the cups. I filled them and came back. The cop took her drink. The door was closed and I could hear Roxanne and the nurse talking. I walked down the hall and around the corner and there was a waiting room. The television was on but nobody was there. There was a telephone, too, and I decided to call my answering machine. I put Roxanne's juice down and dialed. It answered.

Clair had called and asked me to call him at home, which I'd already done. Somebody had called twice and hung up. Roxanne had called, just to hear my voice, she said.

And then there was another message.

"Mr. McMorrow, this is Tony Stone. I'm an investigator with the Mutual Insurance Group, based out of Worcester, Massachusetts. I'm doing the preliminary work on a claim resulting from the death of Robert V. Mullaney . . ."

Twenty-nine

I PASSED THE nurse in the hall. Then I passed the cop, standing up, sipping her Coke. I pushed the door open and Roxanne looked at me from the bed.

"You know who called me? An insurance guy. Bobby had life insurance."

Roxanne grinned.

"Then that's it."

"What's it?"

"Insurance," she said. "The insurance money."

I stood by the bed.

"No," I said. "No, they just aren't the type. An insurance scam? I mean, these are people who wouldn't buy vegetables from the supermarket because they don't trust them. They probably still boycott grapes. They live in that homemade house in the middle of nowhere and go on about big business and corporations. It just doesn't fit."

"Maybe they see it as some sort of terrorist act," Roxanne said. "Maybe they're exacting revenge on corporate America."

"I can see that, but the money? These are people who pride themselves on not needing any. The garden. Even the pot. Bobby told me how he traded pot for services. It's their own economy they've made.''

"Maybe this economy was a matter of necessity. You know. They were poor so they pretended to like it.''

"And cooked up this scheme?''

"Why not?''

"I don't know. It just seems sort of beneath them.''

"And selling pot wasn't? You don't do that for fun, Jack. You do it for money.''

"But it was like raising a pig and slaughtering it in the fall,'' I said. "They tended their plants and brought them to market.''

"Maybe they got sick of playing dirt farmer. You said the son wanted a house with a basketball hoop in the driveway, didn't you?''

"Yeah, but since when is he calling the shots?''

"You look disappointed, Jack,'' Roxanne said.

"I am, I guess.''

"People aren't always what they seem.''

"They never are. And I knew these guys weren't what they seemed,'' I said. "I just didn't expect them to be like this.''

Roxanne looked at me.

"Are you going to call the insurance guy back?''

I thought for a moment.

"Not yet,'' I said. "Not yet.''

And I didn't call Detective Martucci, either. But I did call Mendoza. Twice. The third time I left the number of Roxanne's room. And waited.

We sat there, side by side. Roxanne dozed off. The guard changed at the door and the older cop took over. He looked in, book in hand. I nodded and he saw Roxanne sleeping and held up his book apologetically and tiptoed out. I sat some more. Thought some more.

It could all fit. Plant phony dental records. Get the body identified as Bobby's. Collect the cash and split. But if it wasn't really Bobby, who was it? A mouth full of silver,

Mendoza had said. A crispy critter with a mouth full of silver.

I picked up the phone and my chair and moved away from the bed. Quietly, I called directory assistance, asked for Lester Pelham's number and dialed again.

He was with a patient, the receptionist said. I said I'd hold. She said it would be quite a while and asked my name. I told her and she put me on hold and then Pelham wasn't with a patient anymore.

"A small question, Doctor," I said. "I know it might seem like a picky detail but bear with me, please."

"I'll try."

"I know Bobby Mullaney was your patient for several years, but did you do a lot of work on him? I mean, were his teeth in pretty bad shape? If you had, I thought I could say something like, 'Dr. Lester Pelham had a lot of calls about Bobby Mullaney over the years, but never one like this.' Sounds corny but something like that."

"Well, I probably shouldn't say this, with confidentiality and all, but he had plastic teeth."

"Pardon me?"

"They weren't plastic but that's what I used to call them. I kidded him. We kidded back and forth. I said his teeth couldn't be real because they never decayed. I think he must have grown up with fluoridated water down south somewhere. Makes a huge difference. Like night and day. I see people here, grew up with well water and—"

"You mean he didn't have a lot of fillings and all that?"

"I think he had one. Maybe two. Teeth as hard as rocks."

I thanked him and hung up.

"A mouth full of silver," I said, and I called Mendoza again.

I waited. This time he answered.

"Can I get my coat off, McMorrow?"

"Sure. After you tell me."

"How 'bout I write it up and mail it to you."

"Saying what?"

"There weren't any break-ins at dentists' offices, per se. Not in Valley, anyway."

"But?"

"But there was one at a clinic sort of thing downtown. They do, like, pro bono work. Checkups. HIV testing. And they have a dentist."

"When was the break?"

"September second."

"What'd they take?"

"Some change from the secretary's drawer."

"That's it?"

"Pretty much."

"No drugs?"

"They're locked up. The report said they attempted to gain entry but were unsuccessful."

"So they took the money and left?"

"Yup."

"Screw around with the files?"

"It didn't say that."

"Who goes to this place? I mean, who are the patients?"

"Mostly the homeless," Mendoza said. "Some druggies. Junkies. Winos. People on the streets."

He paused.

"How's your theory doing, McMorrow?"

"I think it's holding up so far. What do you think?"

"It ain't dead yet," Mendoza said.

Roxanne slept. The nurses looked in. I was on the phone.

I called directory assistance for the Valley area code and asked for the office of the state coroner. The operator said there was no such listing. I asked for the state medical examiner and she said there was no such listing as that, either, and then she said no, she had a number for the chief medical examiner's office at the UMass Medical Center in Worcester. I took the number and dialed. Readied my take-no-prisoners voice.

A man answered.

"This is Jack McMorrow. *Boston Globe.* I have questions regarding the autopsy performed by your office on a man named Robert Mullaney."

I didn't say pretty please.

He put me on hold. I waited. Roxanne stirred but still slept.

"This is Joan Jackson, can I help you?"

"This is Jack McMorrow. *Boston Globe*. I have a question about the Robert Mullaney autopsy."

"Oh?"

"A source has told me there might have been something amiss in the identification of the body. That there is still some question as to whether the body really is Mullaney's. Is that true?"

"Um, what'd you say your name was?"

"Jack McMorrow."

"You're a reporter?"

"Right. I'm doing a story for the *Globe* on the events leading up to Mullaney's death. But now I'm told that your office may have made a mistake."

"Well, first I've heard of it. I can check and call you back—"

"I'll wait."

"It may be a few minutes."

"That's okay. I'll wait right here."

"Do you have a deadline, Mr. McMorrow?"

"Very much so," I said.

The phone clicked. I waited. It was 2:46. At 2:50, the phone clicked again. I hadn't flinched.

"This is Dr. Bayross," a man's voice said sternly. "Can I help you?"

I gave him my pitch.

"What source?"

"I can't divulge that."

"So you're out to blindside this office on some anonymous tip?"

"No, I just have a question. If you can't answer it, I'll ask somebody else."

"Well, there is no somebody else. I performed that autopsy. I made the identification. There was no question. It was a hundred and one percent positive."

"Nothing out of the ordinary? Dental records?"

"Perfect match. Those were the teeth of the guy we named."

"Mullaney."

"Right."

"Nothing out of the ordinary at all? Nothing?"

"Nothing you need to bother yourself with," the doctor said.

"Like what?"

"I don't know where you're getting your information, but the only thing even remotely out of the ordinary was that the X rays were backward."

"Backward?"

"Yes. You have four pictures. Right, left, up and down. Except right is left and left is right."

"It's supposed to be that way?"

"Yes. That's how the dentist views your mouth. Your right is on his left."

"And these were backward?"

"Right was right and left was left. The way you would think they go."

"If you weren't a dentist," I said.

"If you were a layman," the doctor said.

"These X rays permanently stuck to something? Or can they be taken out?"

"They come in standard sleeves. Four to a strip. Somebody probably slipped them out to look at them more closely and screwed up when they put them back in."

"Somebody."

"But that has no bearing on the identification of the body. If you write anything, you'd damn well better make that clear. The teeth in that body were the teeth in the X rays."

"I don't doubt it," I said.

"Then what's this all about?"

"Good question, Doctor. But nothing you need to bother yourself with."

I took notes on the medical examiner. The basics and three or four good quotes. Roxanne stirred and this time she opened her eyes. I went to her.

"Whatcha been doing?" she murmured.

"Working."

"Did you go out?"

"No, I was here. I was on the phone."

"I'm glad you didn't leave," Roxanne said.

I looked at her. Rubbed her shoulder.

"You're worried, aren't you?" I said.

"A little."

"Maybe more than a little?"

"Maybe a little more than a little."

She smiled. I leaned down and kissed her cheek. At that moment, the nurse came in.

"No hanky-panky," she said brightly.

The nurse had an electronic thermometer. She snapped a disposable cover on the wand and held it out to Roxanne.

"I've got some more calls to make," I said. "I'll be out by the desk. It's the older policeman now. He'll be right outside the door."

"We'll be here," the nurse said brightly. Roxanne stuck the thermometer in her mouth.

I went down the hall to the phone but wished I could keep on going, down on the elevator and out the door. The hospital was starting to seem surreal. The hum of the lights. The patients in their dragging slippers. The silent world seen only through the thick-paned windows. I needed to go for a walk but I couldn't leave. I wanted to be there if Mommy Dearest came through the door.

So I faced the door as I called home again and listened. Detective Martucci said she wanted to talk to me. Detective Martucci said she really needed to talk to me. Detective Martucci said to call her ASAP because they'd picked up Paco.

"He says he never heard of you or Mullaney. He's never been inside that church. Call me."

The next call was dial tone. And the one after that. And then I heard Melanie Mullaney's voice.

"McMorrow, I gotta see you. Something unbelievable has happened. My God, I can't believe it. Oh, man, just call me as soon as you can."

"McMorrow. Melanie. Call me."

"McMorrow. Call me, goddamn it."

I did. Melanie answered in one ring.

"It's me."

"Friggin' A, I've been trying to reach you. Something's happened. I mean the story, it's all changed. My life is totally—A guy called me."

"Yeah?"

"Some insurance guy. McMorrow, Bobby had insurance. Life insurance. Bobby."

"How much?"

"Three hundred thousand."

"You didn't know that?"

"Bobby? Life insurance? He didn't even believe in paper money. I'm friggin' blown away, I mean, Bobby? Went and did this? I still can't believe it. It's like somebody you think you know completely has this totally different side. I mean, what'd he do? Sneak off and sign all these papers?"

"Who gets the money?"

"Well, that's the thing. I mean, that's why I'm—"

"Who, Melanie?"

"It goes to a guy named Bernard Begosian."

"Coyote?"

"Coyote," she said. "McMorrow, I think Coyote must have killed my husband."

Thirty

MELANIE SAID SHE had never known Coyote's real name. She said the insurance guy told her Begosian was in Pennsylvania, staying with friends in Pittsburgh. She talked fast, blurting the words out.

"How'd he get there so fast?" I said.

"I don't know. I never even knew his name. McMorrow, do you think he killed Bobby?"

"No."

"Then who did?"

"I don't think anybody killed Bobby."

"But he's dead. They said so."

"I don't think so."

"Then where is he?"

"I don't know."

"You think he's alive?"

Her voice quavered with hope.

"I don't know. I just don't think he was in that car."

"Well Jesus, McMorrow. What do you mean?"

"I don't know. I don't know yet."

"Don't know yet? What is this shit? You can't just tell me that much. Is my husband alive or not?"

"I don't know."

"You can't do this to me. This isn't right."

"None of this is right."

"Do you know what I'm going through? I mean, do you know how this feels? I feel like I'm being ripped apart."

"I'm sure it's very hard."

"Has my husband left me? Is he dead? What the hell is going on? You owe me an explanation, McMorrow."

I turned. The nurse was listening closely.

"It's kind of hard to explain over the phone."

"I'll come see you. Where do you want to meet? You name it. Do these cops know? I'll talk to them. I'll talk to anybody. Come on, McMorrow."

I hesitated.

"Well, I'm in Portland right now. I really can't—"

"I'll come to Portland. The truck'll make it."

My gut said no, keep the two worlds apart: yours and hers.

"I don't think that would be a good idea. How 'bout—"

I paused.

"I don't mind. I'll go to friggin' Pennsylvania if I have to, to find out what that bastard's done. I never trusted him, never talking, pulling Bobby away from me and going off like they had these important secret things they did. Bernard Begosian. Jesus. After that insurance guy called, I went up and ripped his room apart, I mean, I had to find out something about the bastard. Son of a bitch. I got pictures of him. Old ones. You want 'em, McMorrow? Put those in your friggin' story. Coyote without the hair. He thinks he's so spooky, screw him, that bastard. You know he was in prison? Federal prison in Allentown, Pennsylvania. It was in his papers."

"What for?"

"I don't know. I didn't read all of it. You can have it, McMorrow. A whole box of it. I just want to know what he did this time. I want to know what he did with Bobby. What the hell did he do, McMorrow?"

"I'm not sure. I just think it may not be what it's set up to be. The drug dealer hit, and all that."

The nurse looked up, eyebrows up around her temples.

"I can be in Portland in two hours," Melanie Mullaney said.

"No, I'll meet you. It's three thirty-five. You've got a box full of stuff on Coyote?"

"He had it in this hole in the floor. I knew it was there but I never touched it before. It's, like, his personal papers. Pictures and stuff."

"Can you bring it?"

"Sure. Put his skinny face on the front page. This bastard . . . well, whatever it is he did. You really think Bobby might be alive? Really?"

"Yeah," I said.

"Where should I meet you?"

I thought. I couldn't leave Roxanne alone, even with the cop.

"Maybe I should just give this stuff to the police," Melanie said. "They'd know what to do with it. You could get the pictures from them."

"No, I'd like to see it. Let me think for a second."

I could meet her halfway. Gardiner? Augusta? Livermore Falls?

"I'll call you back. You're home?"

"Yup."

"Give me a minute."

I hung up. Dialed again.

"Hallo," Clair's voice rang out.

"Hey, it's me."

"Jackson. I'd given up on you. Figured you'd succumbed to the siren call of the big city."

"There *are* sirens. You hear 'em all night. Mary back yet?"

"Pick her up tomorrow noon. Down there."

"How'd you like to come down early?"

So at six-thirty, before visiting hours, Clair arrived with four jars of Mary's preserves—blueberry and raspberry—and a shock of nasturtiums. He left his rifle in the truck.

I said I'd be back by nine, ten at the latest. Roxanne's eyes told me to be careful. Sitting in the chair by the bed, Clair came right out and said it.

"Watch yourself now," he said.

"Will do."

"Where in Madison?"

"The restaurant right on Main Street."

"Call when you get there."

"Yes, Dad."

"And call when you're leaving."

"Okay."

"I'm serious."

"I am, too," I said.

On the way out the door, I nodded to the cop.

I'd told Melanie seven o'clock. Out of there by seven-thirty, I'd be back at the hospital by nine to relieve Clair. And Roxanne.

All the way up the interstate, I pictured the story, composed headlines in my mind.

Who killed Bobby Mullaney? Or did they?

The short happy life of Bobby Mullaney. Is it over?

Bobby Mullaney: A life gone to pot

It wasn't the story I'd set out to write, but they never were. This one was going to be especially tricky because it could be breaking as I wrote it. In the morning, I'd call Martucci. I'd call the insurance investigator. I'd tell them both about the X rays and all the rest. They could go to the dentist, talk to my old man in Valley, the hooker's buddy. When Bernard Begosian came to collect his cash, he'd have some talking to do.

I got off the interstate in Waterville and headed northwest, the shopping center lights a dim glow behind me. I took the back road through a little town called Norridgewock, where the lights had been turned out, and crossed the Kennebec River on a rickety one-lane bridge. The road was empty and the woods were black, and the truck was the only spot of light. After five miles, there were scattered houses and I was coming into Madison from the south instead of the east. I made one pass down Main Street, turned around and came back and parked.

Right out front.

I knew the restaurant was open because the front door wasn't locked. Inside it was harder to tell, but country music was playing and I sat down at a table by the front window and waited. After a couple of minutes, the kitchen door banged and a waitress, a small woman with big glasses and big hair, came out with a rack of glasses. She put the glasses down behind the counter and looked up and saw me and jumped.

"Oh, my God, you scared me," she said, slapping her hand on her chest.

"Sorry," I said.

She hurried over with a menu, napkin and utensils.

"My heart's still pounding."

"Mine, too," I said.

"Coffee, dear? Cocktail?"

"Tea, if you've got it."

"You want anything to eat?"

"I'm meeting someone. I'll wait."

So I did.

Cars and trucks passed every few minutes, the tractor trailers lumbering over the railroad tracks. A couple of drivers came in and sat at the counter, giving me a quick sideways glance as they mounted their stools. The waitress called out, "More tea?"

The truck drivers glanced over again. I waited.

An old woman came in and picked up an order to go in a white paper bag. The truckers looked at me one more time and left. It was 7:10 and no sign of Melanie. Florence time was probably a little slow.

At 7:20, I went to the men's room. At 7:30, I decided I'd better call her. I was on my way to the pay phone by the coatrack when a phone rang somewhere else.

The waitress appeared.

"You Mr. McMorrow?"

"Yeah."

"Phone call for you."

The phone was on the wall by the kitchen door and the receiver was swinging slowly on its cord. I picked it up.

"McMorrow."

"Yeah."

"I flooded the goddamn truck, goddamn piece of junk. I just tried it again and it flooded again and now I've got to wait ten minutes and try it again. Carburetor's junk. Sorry. Are they getting ready to close?"

"I don't know."

"They close at eight, but if it's slow, a little earlier."

I looked around. I was the only customer.

"Well, I can wait a little longer, I guess. What are the chances of the truck starting?"

"I don't know. Once it floods, it's a bitch to get it started again. I'm sorry. It almost caught and I was in a hurry and I pumped it a couple times and that was it. I knew it, too. I said, 'Oh no. Of all the times.' I'm sorry, you come all the way up here."

I thought. I wanted to get back. Clair was waiting.

"You have the stuff?"

"Coyote's stuff? Yeah."

I thought some more.

Fifteen minutes out there. Ten minutes on their goddamn road. An hour made eight-thirty. Hour and a half back made ten. I'd said nine.

"Listen, McMorrow. I'll wait ten minutes and I'll try it again. I'm sorry, I really am. Or I can mail it to you. I could mail it tomorrow and—"

Two days in the mail. A day or two to write. I'd be another week.

"Listen, I'll come out and get it. I'll be there in twenty minutes."

"You're sure? I mean, this thing might start. You never know."

"No, I'll just get the stuff and go."

"You're sure?"

"Yeah. I'll see you."

I left two dollars for the tea, went out to the truck and did a U-turn and headed across the bridge. I drove fast, wasn't happy. I'd had enough of bouncing around Florence. I was ready to write. I was ready to get the hell out of there.

There was no moon and the woods were a black-walled canyon along the road. It dipped and swerved and I followed the faint stabs of the headlights all the way to Florence, where the crossing that was the center of the town was dark and still. I rolled on through, took a left and wound the truck through the gears up the hill. The cemetery showed on my left and I slid to a stop in the gravel along the road and got out and locked in the front hubs. In four-wheel drive, I started down the Mullaneys' road.

It was like driving in a cave, and the headlights jounced up and down like the lamp on a spelunker's helmet. The trees were yellow and pale, twitching in the light, but beyond them was blackness. I clenched the wheel and lurched over the rocks, down the pitches, winding along in second gear.

A bird flitted across in the lights. A rudderless moth veered into the front of the truck. Eyes reflected red, low on the edge of the road, and then disappeared into the woods.

Skunk? Cat? Opossum?

Finally, I reached the upgrade to the right that led to the house. The truck came into the headlights, its hood up. As I passed, I could see that the air cleaner cover was off. Melanie knew the drill.

Lights were on in the house, with the yellow cast of kerosene lamps. I pulled up close to the door and got out and went up the steps. Before I could knock, the door swung open.

"Hey, McMorrow," Melanie said. "Sorry about this."

"It's okay."

"Come on in. I made you some tea."

She saw me wince.

"No, it's the real stuff. I remembered how you were trying to be polite with the Japanese green."

She turned and I followed. She was wearing jeans and a black sweater with lint on it and old wooden clogs. They clopped on the floor all the way to the kitchen.

"How 'bout something to eat?"

"No, I've got to go."

"You eat at the restaurant?"

"No, just had tea."

"I made muffins. They're warm."

She leaned over and opened the oven door and took out
a pan and put it on top of the stove, beside a steaming
kettle. Her face was intent as she pried the muffins out of
their little holes. They smelled good but I felt a little like
Hansel in the witch's house.

Melanie put the muffins on a tray and went to the refrigerator and got butter. She put it out on the table with a
knife and then put out two mugs. One was black and one
brown and the black one got the tea bag. Red Rose. Melanie
poured from the kettle and steam billowed up. She took a
muffin and broke it in half and buttered it and took a big
chomp.

"I've been eating a lot. Takes my mind off it. Whatever
gets you through the night, right?"

She shrugged.

"How's Stephen?"

"Pissed off but what else is new."

"Is he home?"

"Yeah. In the woods someplace. I can't deal with him
right now so it's just as well. Where he wants to be, anyway. Here, have a muffin. Beats eating french fries on the
turnpike. They're carrot and raisin. You want milk in your
tea?"

I said yes and she turned to the refrigerator. The door
was covered with posters and notices, mostly from the marijuana movement. They fluttered when Melanie closed the
door.

She put the milk in a small stoneware pitcher and I
poured some in my tea. I dipped the tea bag up and down
and tossed it in the trash. Melanie poured water through
her strainer thing into her mug. I took a muffin, buttered it
and took a bite.

Not bad. A little odd organic taste but not bad. Better
than the ketchup at the fair, I thought. I ate some more.

"So what's the deal, McMorrow?"

"Where's the stuff?"

"Is this some kind of trade?"

"No, but what you have about Coyote could have a bearing on what I know. It could change it."

"Fine." She turned and strode off.

"You want pictures? I got pictures. You want clippings? I got clippings."

Melanie went up the stairs. I waited. Waited some more. It was ten minutes before she came clopping back down. She was carrying a small metal strongbox. When she set it on the table, I saw that the top was gashed open.

"Where'd you find it?"

"In the floor. Just like this, except it was locked," Melanie said, flipping up the lid.

"What'd you use?"

"A hatchet."

She took out a stack of clippings and started tossing them on the table like she was dealing cards.

"Bernard Begosian goes to Walpole State Prison, in 1989. Four years for cocaine trafficking. Bernard Begosian gets married, 1983. Bernard Begosian gets divorced, 1985. Bernard Begosian gets six months for aggravated assault, 1987. Believed to be drug-related."

I scanned the yellowed clippings. The wedding photo in the *Lowell Sun*. Coyote had short hair but the same eerie deep-set eyes. Probably scared the photographer.

"You didn't know any of this?"

"Nothing. I just knew he was an old buddy of Bobby's. I figured he was running from some kind of jam. When I asked, Bobby said, 'You don't want to know.' Like I really didn't want to know. So I didn't ask. He was quiet. Didn't get in the way, helped out quite a lot. More than Bobby, really."

Melanie paused to pop the rest of her muffin in her mouth. I took a bite of mine, a swallow of tea. Another couple of bites.

The clips were great; it would raise my story to another level, adding some sort of solution to the mystery. Who is the mysterious Coyote? Bernard Begosian, small-time criminal on the lam. From dealing coke to collecting signatures.

To insurance fraud.

"Okay, McMorrow," Melanie said, as if reading my mind. "Your end now."

My end. What did that mean? I found myself turning the word around in my mind, then wondering why I was doing that. She wanted me to tell her what I knew, my end of the deal, the bargain.

"Come on, McMorrow. What's the deal? Is my husband alive or what?"

Or what? The words hung there, floating, and in the background was a faint hum, like an electrical transformer. I could hear myself breathing, but loudly, like there was a microphone down in there somewhere. I looked at the clippings and the words slipped away from me and there was Coyote's face, only it was Bernie getting married and this seemed preposterous, even funny, and I looked up and Melanie was staring at me and when she opened her mouth to talk I could hear her lips parting, see her tongue, hear the sticky saliva smacking and I pushed away from the table and turned and I had to get out of there because there was no air.

"No," Melanie said, and then she said, "Bobby," and I heard a bang and feet pounding and I had the front door open and I turned and there was Bobby and Coyote behind him, coming at me, blond as albinos.

Thirty-one

I SLAMMED THE door behind me and went down the steps headed for the truck but the truck wasn't there and I was running down the hill to the driveway and the darkness was thick, like black pond water, and my feet were floating in long soaring strides, from rock to rock.

And then I could hear them behind me and I swerved right and bent my head and the branches lashed at me but there was no pain, just noise, and I bent forward, low, and plunged deeper and deeper into the brush and then it opened up and I was still running, in darkness like I had my eyes closed.

I didn't stop, didn't slow, and a branch slammed my forehead and I could feel that one, and wiped my face and felt blood and kept going, now weaving between trees. I couldn't stop to listen for them, the albinos, so I kept running, downhill because it was easiest, and then the ground was soft and there was grass and then muck and water after that, quickly up to my knees and I had to go out, not back in, because mud would leave tracks so I had to go deeper and swim because swimming left no tracks, just ripples and who could see ripples in the dark?

But it never got deep enough to swim, just up to my waist, cold if I could feel it, but I couldn't, just in a distant sort of way. I waded and there was stuff on the bottom that caught at my boots, branches and maybe snapping turtles but they'd go into the mud to hibernate and I found myself stepping carefully because I didn't want to step on a snapping turtle, not when I was stoned like this.

I was very high, like a whopping THC high, maybe in the tea or in the muffin and my mouth was dry and I thought of all this water and I was thirsty and wasn't that always the way but I couldn't drink this water because it had algae in it and green scum and this was a swamp and there were water snakes and frogs and mosquito larvae. They still would be in here, even though it was September, they hatched even in the Arctic, in those little pools that were frozen at night, so they'd hatch here and I didn't want them in my mouth.

There were trees in this swamp, dead ones from before this water was here, and the trunks were bare of bark and silver like bones. I waded past them, looking up, and then I waded over behind one and stopped.

I listened. Heard my heart pounding, oompah, oompah, like a German band, and my rasping lungs, but I had to hear them, Bobby and Coyote, not crispy critters at all, just blond now, both of them, like David Bowie back when, I didn't know when it was, but it was back a ways and he had white hair slicked back. David Bowie, I thought. What a thing to think of, but you could see the progression, the thought process that brought it up, but I didn't have time now to think about that.

In the distance I could hear crunching and then Melanie's city-tough voice—she'd never lose that accent—carrying across the water, saying, "Did you get him?"

They didn't answer but the answer was no and I almost yelled it out but I caught myself. I was standing behind one of the trees and the water was still around my thighs and when I moved away from the trees, I slipped in up to my chest and for the first time I felt cold.

It wasn't me, it was somebody else, but I had to get out of the water soon and get warm, build a fire, but I couldn't because they'd see it. So I kept moving until I came to a bigger tree, a tree skeleton really, probably a spruce, I thought. It was thick with spiny branches and I grabbed hold and hoisted myself out of the water but the dripping sounded like drums and I held my breath until it stopped.

And then I climbed, one branch after another, up twenty branches or maybe it was fifteen and I'd counted the same ones twice as I put my left hand on, then my right. But I didn't think I'd done that, I thought, though I couldn't swear on it. Strange thing, to swear on it, like a Bible, but I had to be stoned to be thinking that and I couldn't think, I had to just hang on.

I did. Like a porcupine, a treed raccoon. I had a branch for each arm and each leg, a limb for each limb, I thought. I hugged the trunk and felt it against my cheek, rough and scaly. Tree-huggers, they called them. Goddamn tree-huggers. I had to be a tree-hugger or I'd fall out and impale myself or hit the water, kaboom, and they'd be sure to hear that one, and I wondered if they had guns yet. They could just shoot shotguns at the splash, fire a few rifle rounds in the general direction.

I hadn't seen guns, but Coyote right out of Walpole, not right out of but not that long ago, he had to have guns and Bobby, he was a dirtbag, too, as it turned out. Melanie, too. Calling for them, and them coming in, and "Is my husband alive?" when he was in the next room or out back or wherever he was, with his dyed blond hair, so different you wouldn't know him unless you really knew him but I didn't really know him, not now, maybe nobody did, except Melanie and Coyote, who was really Bernie Begosian, who got married but it didn't last long and I wondered why, pictured Bernie saying, "I do," and, "Till death do us part."

I sat there in the tree and somewhere on the shore I could hear branches snapping as they searched. They weren't like Stephen. Where was Stephen? They moved like elephants, very arrogant, a flaw in a criminal because criminals have to be realistic in order to outwit the system but then most criminals don't, at least not for long, because that's how you know they're criminals, because they get caught. Bobby and Coyote hadn't been that good at it because they hadn't even outwitted me, at least not yet. But then I wouldn't be back by ten like I'd told Clair and Roxanne and they'd be worried and I really had to get out of here, besides I was cold.

My teeth had started chattering, first a delicate buzz, like brushes on a snare drum, and then an uncontrollable chatter, like a real drumroll. I wondered if they could hear it, like a partridge drumming on a log, or if it was all inside my head, echoing inside my skull. I rubbed my thighs, my sodden jeans, but I was just cold, and there was a breeze up there in the tree and I could feel it like it was a million tiny needles and I pulled myself closer to the bone-smooth trunk. The thrashing in the woods was closer and I clamped my hand over my mouth to quiet my teeth.

"He must have gone into the water," I heard Bobby say.

"Then he's got to come out. Or freeze to death."

That was Coyote.

"We've got to find him, either way. We've got to know."

"You think he'd be across by now?"

"Shit no. You go across and wait. We'll wait him out."

But I couldn't wait, not with those needles blowing into me and my hands that seemed like somebody else's. I clenched and unclenched them on the branch, thinking of the brain cells saying to the nerves, contract, and the nerves telling the tendons, pull in, and the muscles saying, yessir, right away sir, contracting, all red bands of raw meat. I closed my eyes and my head was humming from inside and I knew I had to stop thinking like that or I'd be dead and floating someplace, in the swamp, in another world, on the other side, where the souls floated, little paper bags of thoughts, drifting—

"Stop," I hissed.

I had to stop it. I had to live. I had to get it out of me, streaming out of something in my stomach, the muffin, a lump of sodden muffin feeding my system with THC or LSD or mushrooms or whatever it was that was in me, that Melanie had put in me.

Branch by branch, I lowered myself down, feeling the hard bones under my boots, then the water up my legs, into my crotch like a cold snake. I stood for a minute, feeling myself start to sink into the muck, and then I turned to my left because Bobby was in front of me and Coyote somewhere behind me, I thought. I moved slowly like a big snail, like a swan boat full of little kids tossing popcorn. I glided toward the edge of the swamp in the darkness and the bottom was all branches and sticks and other things and it got shallower and my knees were out and then I was in the mud on my hands and knees.

I had to get it out, what was in there, I had to, so I took a fistful of watery mud, a fistful of stuff I couldn't see and I shoved it in my mouth and swallowed. I gagged but that was all and I took more of the slime and put it in my mouth, all cold and gritty but parts slippery like fish and I thought of millions of bugs and slugs and baby leeches and dragonfly larvae, with legs and long abdomens and I thought of them in there and liking it because it was dark and warm and there were places to explore, tubes and spongy organs and flesh to eat and places to attach with pincers and claws and—

I vomited.

Spat the black stuff out. Vomited again. Retched and tried to be quiet but it sounded like my guts were being torn like a sheet. Again, the black goo dripping out onto the ground. I thought I tasted muffin.

But I had to move away from the swamp, if they thought I was out there and they were waiting. I had to get up into the woods where it was dry and maybe I could roll in leaves or something and it would dry me a little so I wouldn't be so cold, or wrap myself in pine boughs or spruce branches. Hemlock would be softer but hemlock wasn't as thick so I'd have to have two layers maybe.

I gave my face a slap, tried to think straight, down a tunnel, not spinning off in any direction. I moved slowly on my hands and knees into the brush, like a sea turtle coming ashore to lay eggs, through brush that was thick and viny and tangled. After counting a hundred crawls, I stopped and listened.

Nothing. I kept crawling.

There were small trees and the brush thinned and I felt like I was moving deeper into the woods but which way? I tried to orient myself and I wondered why that word came to mean that. Oriental. Orientation. We three kings of Orient are . . .

No.

I snapped out of it and it seemed easier to pull myself back from the tangent. Which way? I'd come into the woods, gone straight away from the road and into the swamp. In the swamp I'd done an about-face and then I'd climbed down and turned . . .

I thought.

Left? So that meant I was going parallel to the driveway, back toward the house, past the house really, and away from the road. I wanted to get to the road. I wanted to get out of here. I wanted to get dry clothes and boots. Dry socks. I really wanted to get dry socks. I really wanted to find my truck and turn the heat on, turn it on full blast and load my rifle and shoot those bastards, all three of them, kaboom, kaboom, kaboom. Maybe not. Maybe just drive home.

What had they done with my truck? I hadn't heard it start so they must have just rolled it down the hill. That meant it was up there somewhere and who had the keys?

I felt the soggy pocket of my canvas jacket.

I had the keys, keys to the puzzle, key of C.

The trees were bigger now, maples and poplars and birches, their white trunks leaning like ghosts, the pale yellow leaves flashing like snowflakes in headlights. I moved in a crouch, stepping like the ground was broken glass.

But where was Melanie? If Bobby was on one side of the swamp and Coyote on the other, where was Melanie? Back home heating up some soup? I thought you boys would be cold. Have a muffin. She'd laced mine, which

was why I felt like this, but I felt a little better, could think
sort of straight if I really tried, or maybe I just thought I
was thinking straight and I wasn't really and there were no
trees and I had hallucinated the water and the cold, but I
didn't think so because I wasn't tripping, I was just buzzed
but if I could think that, maybe I really was getting better.

I stopped and listened again. Heard my teeth starting to
chatter again, doing their little drum solo. I clenched my
jaw to make them stop and they waited a moment and
started up again, sneaky little devils. I kept moving.

Up the hill was toward the house, or behind it. I thought
I'd cross below the house, see if my truck was somewhere
in the woods. If not, I'd go beyond the house and work my
way through the woods on the other side of the driveway
until I hit the road.

So that's what I did, staying very low. I bent and dug
beneath the leaves for some soil and smeared it on my
cheeks and forehead like an Army ranger, a Navy Seal. Did
the Marines have one? Or did the Navy work with Marines?
I couldn't remember. I'd ask Clair. Roxanne. Clair and
Roxanne. God, I had to get out of here. I had to go up the
elevator in the hospital and down the hall and into that nice
warm room. They'd wonder what I'd done to my face or
maybe Clair the Marine would know, just by looking at
me.

Semper Fi, he'd say. Semper Fi, I'd say back.

"Cut it out," I said. "Focus."

So I went on, my teeth keeping up their Latin beat, my
feet getting numb, my hands aching. I counted steps again,
and after a hundred and thirty-one I came out in a little
cleared area. It was the butt end of the driveway.

No truck.

Oh, man, I felt so alone. Clair was seventy-five miles
away and going nowhere. There wasn't another house for
three miles, probably wasn't a cop for fifty. I had cut the
cord this time, I was floating in space, on my own. I crossed
over and into the woods again, moving behind the house,
twenty feet in. The lights were on but I couldn't see anybody so maybe Melanie was out here someplace or maybe

she was lying down or in the bathroom. I stopped and watched the windows.

Nothing moved.

Now my teeth were chattering more and it probably was getting colder. I held my hands under my arms and watched and still there wasn't anybody in sight. I walked slowly to the back door, the one Bobby and Coyote had come in. If I could get to the phone. Call 911 and head back in the woods and wait an hour for the sheriff's deputy to come. Maybe a state trooper.

I stood by the door, looked in the window. Nothing.

Was Melanie around the corner? Was she waiting with her shotgun, thinking I might try this? My teeth clattered like somebody had me by the nape of the neck and was shaking me like a dog shakes a rat. It would be warm in there. A couple of minutes in there would be so . . . so warm.

I touched the latch. Eased it up. It moved stiffly, then slipped.

Clack.

I didn't breathe. Waited. Nothing moved so I eased the door open. It squeaked but faintly. I opened it enough for my body to slide through, then took two steps inside and froze.

Waited.

Listened.

The house ticked. The woodstove popped. I took two more steps. Where was the phone? I thought. Tried to picture it. I thought I remembered a black phone on the wall in the hallway past the kitchen, toward the front room where we sat and talked.

I took two more steps. My boots made a gritty sound on the wood floor. I waited. Took two more. The passage to the storeroom under the stairs was on my right. It was dark. She could be waiting there. I could step out and boom, she could blow my head off.

She didn't.

It was a straight shot now, ten feet along the wall and then reach around into the little indentation where the

phone was. The lights were on. Anyone outside would see
me clearly and I wouldn't see them. I'd be inching along
the wall and they'd be hurtling back to the house. It had to
be quick.

I hurried, four or five steps in the open, reached around
the corner and—

The receiver was gone. The bastards.

I turned and bolted out the way I had come, pausing to
ease the door shut and then moving into the woods, beyond
the house, uphill from the driveway. The high ground was
easier going but littered with branches and last year's dead
leaves, crackly maples and slippery silvery oaks. I moved
a hundred yards into the woods, climbed over a blowdown,
then slid down a pitch and landed on my back. I got up
and listened, my teeth chattering uncontrollably.

"You're gonna freeze to death out here," a voice said.

Thirty-two

HE WAS BEHIND and above me, squatting in a comfortable crouch. His rifle was across his knees.

"You're making a mistake," I chattered.

Stephen looked at me, his face blank.

"I ain't done anything yet."

"I've got to get out of here."

"No shit. You've got hypothermia. You know you can die in the summer from that, you get cold enough? Your body temperature drops and things start shutting down. When the brain gets chilled, it's sayonara."

"But . . . but they'll kill me."

He looked at me.

"Not if I don't let 'em. Let's go."

He made a little gesture with the rifle barrel.

"That thing loaded?"

"Always."

"What if I run?"

"They'll hear you."

I looked at him. His impassive enigmatic eyes.

The rifle motioned again.

"Up the hill," Stephen said.

• • • •

I went first. Stephen was behind me, moving almost silently. My feet were lumps. My hands numb. When I looked down at them, they were bleeding from scratches I hadn't felt. My head felt better.

We moved straight up the side of the ridge. I counted steps but gave up at three hundred. We reached the top of the ridge, zigzagging between the trees, and moved along the crest for a hundred yards.

"To your left," Stephen said, and I started down the other side, hanging on to saplings and trees. After twenty yards, he told me to go right again, to follow the ridgeline. I did and then he told me to stop. I did that, too.

I heard a rustling behind me, to my right. I turned and Stephen was crouched along the side of the hill. He moved some branches aside and there was a hole, like the entrance to a bear's den.

"Inside," Stephen said.

"You've got to be kidding."

"Nope."

The rifle waved in my direction. I looked at it and at him. I moved toward the hole, bent down and then dropped to my hands and knees. I crawled headfirst into the pitch-blackness. Stopped. The rifle poked me in the buttocks.

"Keep going."

I did and Stephen was behind me. I stopped again, felt something in the air that felt like a bigger space. There was a flick and flame and I saw earthen walls with roots looping through them. There was an old blue carpet on the floor. Plastic bags hung from the roots and there was a wooden platform with a sleeping bag on it. Next to the platform was a Coleman lantern. Next to the lantern was a Coleman heater. On the other end of the platform was a wooden crate, turned over, with magazines and books piled on it. There was a vent in the ceiling with a piece of stovepipe shoved into it, like a chimney.

"So," I said, "is this where those elves make the cookies?"

He didn't laugh.

"You can sit on the bed," Stephen said.

I did, and he moved with the lighter and lit the lantern. The mantle glowed white and light filled the room. Then he moved to the heater, pumped the lever four or five times and fired that up, too.

"In a minute this place will be seventy-five degrees."

"I've died and gone to heaven."

"Not yet," Stephen said.

"Which one do you mean?"

He shrugged. I sat.

The room warmed luxuriously and I held my hands out toward the heater. They began to sting and then pulse with stabbing pain. But pain meant nerves weren't damaged, that I'd just have to thaw out. I could take it.

Stephen fiddled with the lamp and the heater and then picked up the magazines and put them neatly on the ground and sat on the crate, the rifle still across his knees. His eyes were onyx black in the gaslight. There was a little stubble on his chin. I watched him through my fingers, outstretched toward the heat. I wanted to take my boots off but I didn't want to seem like I was ready to stay.

"Don't you ever put that rifle down?" I asked.

"Not much."

"Am I supposed to be your prisoner here or what?"

"I don't know. I haven't figured it out yet."

"You working on it?"

"I guess."

"Well, I'll tell you what I want to do. I want to warm up and then I want to walk out to the road and flag down a car and get the hell out of here."

"And never come back?"

"Something tells me I won't be invited."

"You gonna go back and write your story?"

He looked at me, watching for my answer.

"I don't know."

"You're lying."

"No, I'm not. I don't know if I'm going back, at this point. So I can't know if I'm going to write anything."

"If you get back to your house are you going to write something?"

I considered him. Decided to tell him straight.

"Yup. It's how I make my living."

"What are you gonna write?"

"About how Bobby and Coyote and your mother seemed to be idealistic marijuana activists and maybe they were but then they turned into plain old crooks, pulling a life insurance scam."

Stephen's eyes flickered but I couldn't tell with what emotion.

"You say what you think, don't you?"

"I wouldn't insult you by lying to you. That's the story. That's what this is about. That's why I'm here."

"And they're out there."

"Looking for me to kill me," I said.

He looked down. Ran his fingers up and down the blue-black gun barrel.

"They're not murderers. Not my mom. Not Bobby."

"Coyote?"

"I don't know. I've come close to popping him. He's a friggin' animal."

"Oh, yeah?"

"Yeah. He looks at my mother when she's not looking at him. Looks at her butt when she bends over and stuff. I hate his guts."

"But Bobby doesn't."

"Nope."

"Why not?"

"I don't know. They've known each other since they were kids. They, like, made this pact when they were, like, my age. Blood brothers and all that."

"Tom and Huck," I said. "That's sweet."

"Yeah, right. Now we can't get rid of the guy."

"Sure you can. You can get me out of here. Your mother testifies against Coyote and gets a reduced sentence. Maybe suspended. She was coerced, you know? Threatened if she didn't go along with the plan. Coyote goes away for a long time."

"And Bobby?"

"He goes, too."

"She won't do that," Stephen said. "I mean, she's married to the guy. She loves him or whatever."

"She loves you more. She wouldn't leave you."

"I don't know."

He scratched his head, fiddled with the heater again. I flexed my fingers and toes. The toes were just starting to hurt. When they were thawed a little more, I'd jump him first chance I got.

"I don't know, McMorrow," Stephen said suddenly. "This is a tough one."

"Yup."

"I get you out of here and you write this story, and jeez, just telling the cops. I mean, they all get busted. My mother. I can't let you hurt my mother. You understand what I'm saying?"

"Bobby and Coyote will be gone. Your mother won't be hurt by that."

"What'd they do with me if I stayed? Put me in a foster home?"

"Probably something like that. I have a good friend who does that. Works for the state. I could talk to her."

"Jeez, I'd be getting my own mother arrested. What kind of guy does that?"

"What kind of guy kills somebody? That's what somebody's done here, Stephen. There was a body in that car, you know. It wasn't Bobby but it was somebody. I don't think they dug it up in a graveyard."

He sighed. Looked at his boots. Knocked them together. My feet were feeling better. It was almost time.

"This is tough," Stephen said. "What if they put my mother in jail for ten years?"

"They won't."

"How do you know?"

"I've done this for a long time. I've seen a lot of deals worked out. She could do a deal easy. I'll testify for her."

"I don't know. I just don't know if I can let you go. Let me think."

Stephen thought. I waited.

"If I don't help you?"

"The thing unravels anyway. I told a reporter in Massachusetts about the whole scam. I told a buddy of mine where I was going when I came up here. They switched the dental records, Stephen. All the cops have to do is ask the dentist what kind of work he did on Bobby. He says little or none and they say, 'Then why does this X ray show a mouth full of fillings?' He says, 'Because it can't be Bobby Mullaney's X rays.' The whole thing comes crashing down. And if there's a murder tacked on the other end—"

"Yours?"

"Uh-huh. Then we're looking at life sentences. You'd never see your mom again, at least not without looking through an inch of Plexiglas."

"Friggin' A," Stephen said.

He had his hand on the butt of the rifle, down low. The other high on the barrel, stroking the barrel. The .22 was his worry beads.

"This really sucks. I mean, the other thing is you seem okay, McMorrow. I mean, I don't want you to write about my mom, but you seem like a pretty good shit."

I smiled.

"Thanks," I said, and I came off the bed, six feet through the air, and landed on him and the rifle, and the crate went over and Stephen's head hit the earthen wall and he said, "Ooooh," and we went down, him squirming underneath me, the rifle pressing against my crotch.

I had to keep him underneath me, use my weight, but he was wiry and slippery and strong and he wrapped his leg around mine and started to flip me over. I flashed back to Clair and got my right arm up and drove it down over and over. His mouth, his chin, his cheekbone, his eyes, over and over.

Blood spurted from his nose, but his teeth were clenched like he'd been beaten before and he could take it. He still had both hands on the rifle.

"Let go," I said, my jaw clenched, too, and I reached underneath me with my left arm and got hold of his hand,

which was on the trigger but he'd have to throw me off to
bring the barrel around.

I let go of his hand and wrapped that arm around his
neck so I could feel the stubble on his chin. I held him
close and kept the right going at his face, short hard
punches, over and over and over, and he couldn't move
and couldn't protect himself and I kept punching and suddenly I felt the arms beneath me relax and his head loll
back and my fist was raised.

And I stopped.

"Sorry, Stephen," I said. "I like you, too."

He looked up at me, bloody and woozy, and then his
eyes gradually focused.

And he started to cry.

Thirty-three

I LEFT STEPHEN hog-tied with his boot laces and gagged with my handkerchief. I couldn't have him screaming for help or running to get the others, but I did leave the heater on, and turned off the light. The gun and a box of .22 long-rifle ammo, I took with me.

When I crawled out of the cave, it seemed even darker outside and I crouched for a moment to orient myself. I didn't feel so stoned anymore, which was good, but I wasn't sure where the road was. I went over our walk again in my mind.

We'd followed the ridge that seemed to run at an angle away from the driveway. The driveway ran perpendicular to the road, sort of. But then the road veered to the north just below the Mullaneys' driveway. I could miss it and end up going west deeper into the woods. But then, the farther I went, the better off I was. If they were still waiting by the swamp.

I set off just below the ridgeline. I didn't want to be silhouetted or spotted moving up that high, if they had staked out the driveway down by the road.

The woods were fairly open here but the ground was strewn with branches that snapped, leaves that crackled. I tried to move quietly, remembering Clair's commando instructions, given to me when we tromped through the woods in search of deer.

You don't move in a straight line. You pick a spot for your foot before you plant it. You stop often and listen.

But that took patience and discipline, and part of me wanted to run pell-mell for the road, screaming at the top of my lungs. They couldn't catch up with me, unless they drove.

Patience won out.

I walked the ridge, very slowly and almost silently. When I stopped to listen I heard trees rattle and birds rustling on their roosts. I heard a rustle in the leaves and froze, then followed. It was a rummaging skunk.

My clothes were still soggy and I started to get cold but it didn't matter. I was close to getting out. I was close to living the rest of my life. I could feel the anticipation, could imagine the glorious pavement under my feet. I had to fight to keep from moving faster, noisier.

I heard a truck. It was coming from behind me, to my right.

The road was closer than I'd thought and the truck lights pierced the woods. I crouched low and the headlights pierced the woods. No, it was a spotlight. It flicked across the trees above my head.

I lowered myself to the ground, the rifle beside me. The truck came closer, the motor roaring in low gear, and then it passed and continued on. I watched and listened for it to reach the main road to see how close I was. It rumbled, rumbled some more, then stopped. I heard the motor move up to first, then second, then go quiet again.

It was on pavement.

I got up and started in that direction, but off to the left, away from the driveway. The woods were open here, more cut over, and I didn't want them to see me coming out. I needed to get back in the brush. I needed—

I heard steps.

They were behind me, not crashing but not commando-quiet, either. I couldn't tell how far but they were coming faster than my steps and whoever it was would be gaining on me. I turned off to my left, moved into the brush and crouched and waited.

The steps crunched closer and then I could see a figure. It came through the trees, pushing the brambles aside, walking.

Bobby.

In his right hand was a handgun. He was looking to his right, peering through the trees toward the driveway. Like a marsh bird, I froze in my crouch and waited. He was fifty yards away, then thirty, then coming close, his steps making a soft crunch in the litter on the ground. His hair was white blond. Eyebrows, too. His eyes were still black.

I held my breath as he passed, the safety off on the rifle. If he turned this way, I'd fire. If he saw me, I had to put him down and run for the road.

But he didn't. He moved past me and then his back was to me, the handgun swinging down low by his thigh. I waited until he was forty yards away and I followed, just to keep him in sight. I didn't want him waiting for me behind the next tree, circling around and shooting me in the back.

Bobby led me to the road, a couple of hundred yards away. He broke through first, and I waited, still in the woods, well above him. He moved down the road toward the driveway, walking on the gravel shoulder. In Florence, Maine, you could walk down the highway with a handgun and not raise suspicion.

I crouched in the brush and waited. Maybe a car would come by. I'd run out with my rifle and ask them to stop and give me a ride. In Florence, Maine, it actually could happen.

And then Bobby was talking. I could hear him but I couldn't hear any response. I moved closer, picking my way along the edge of a bramble where birds flitted away from me.

"... walk down and back up through the woods, see if I can flush him out. If he tries to cross here, you've got him. You seen Mel?"

I could see the back of the truck now, a blond head behind the wheel, an elbow out the open driver's window. I waited. Bobby glided away, into the opening of the drive-way. In the truck, Coyote waited, motionless. The truck, pulled off the road against the brush, wasn't running.

It was thirty yards away. I lay down on my belly, the rifle in front of me, the strip of brushy edge between me and the road. I couldn't come through it right next to him, but I couldn't break through yet. I had to be closer, close enough that I'd be below the truck when he looked in the mirrors. I crawled slowly. Sticks and roots tore up my shirt and scratched my belly. I ignored them and kept going until I could see the round hole in the end of the truck's exhaust pipe. And then I moved to my left.

There was a small opening in the vines and blackberry canes and I squeezed through. I heard Coyote sniff. I waited. He sniffed again. I waited some more.

For a moment, I might be visible in his right side mirror. I had to pray he wouldn't look. I'd be committed. I'd be lying on the ground. I'd be in a shoot-out.

I moved.

In the open and then behind the truck. Still on my belly. I waited. No sound. Then another sniff. I lay there, my heart pounding. Sniff again. Postnasal drip.

I had to get close to the driver's door. I let my breath go in and out silently and then inched my way under the truck bed, until I was behind the right rear wheel. I waited again, my face against the gravel. I couldn't wait, couldn't risk a car coming by, a driver leaning out and saying, "Hey, none of my business, but there's a guy under your truck and he's got a rifle."

Coyote sniffed. I moved the safety off. I counted to three. One, two, three . . .

I was up, two steps and the muzzle of the rifle was pressed against the side of Coyote's neck.

"Hi, Bern," I said. "Want to sign my petition?"

I pushed the muzzle against him hard, so it made a crater in his flesh. He didn't move.

"Don't give me an excuse. It won't take much. My nerves are on edge, if you know what I'm saying."

Coyote's face was impassive. A prison mask.

"Here's what I want you to do. If you don't do it, I'll shoot you and do it myself. Your choice."

No reaction.

There was a handgun, a semiautomatic something or other, on the seat next to him.

"Pick the gun up by the barrel and throw it on the floor. Over to the right."

He did. The gun hit the floor with a clunk.

"Reach over to the shifter and put it in neutral."

He did.

"Jiggle it back and forth so I can see it's out of gear."

He did that, too.

"Nice hair, Bernie. That look's very big in New York. Now keep one hand on the wheel and reach down and start it up. Don't flood it. If your hand moves one inch toward the shifter, I'll put a bullet in your spine. Go ahead."

He did. The starter motor growled and the motor coughed and then rumbled. He didn't rev it. Now I had to get the door open. Should I shove him over? But the gun was over there. Make him get out this side?

The motor idled. Coyote stared straight ahead.

"Turn your head toward me."

He turned, slowly. His eyes showed nothing.

"Open your mouth."

He didn't.

"I'll shoot you. I swear I'll blow your head off. I'm getting out of here, I'm telling you."

For the first time, Coyote looked at me. Slowly let his mouth gape open. I moved the barrel from his neck, put it inside his mouth.

"Bite down hard. I want to see your teeth."

He did it.

"Nice and white. You and Bobby must go to the same dentist. Now I'm gonna open the door. If I feel you loosen your grip, I'll pull the trigger. I hope to hell you believe me."

I reached down with my left hand and pushed the button.
The door latch popped. I eased it open. Coyote stared at
me, the rifle barrel clenched in his teeth like a big stogie.

"Now I'm gonna tell you to let go of the gun. Keep your
hands on the wheel. You move anything and you're gone."

I pulled the door toward me, the gun still through the
window.

"I'll tell you when, Bern. Don't do it until—"

"Drop the gun, McMorrow."

I didn't. I didn't even look toward the voice. Melanie's.

"Drop it, I said. Take it out of his mouth."

She was coming from the driveway. Moving tentatively.
She had a gun. I could feel it. I glanced, just my eyes.

The shotgun.

"Drop it, McMorrow. Put it down."

"Nope. You move you're dead, Bern. Not one friggin'
muscle."

Melanie was in front of the truck. The shotgun was
pointed at me. Coyote stared at me from behind the rifle
barrel.

"I'll kill you, McMorrow."

"Is that right?"

"Yeah, it's right."

Coyote didn't move. The door was half open. I let it
swing shut.

"Drop it."

"No way."

She took two steps closer.

"That's Stephen's rifle. Where's Stephen?"

"You toss the gun and we'll talk about it."

"Where is he, McMorrow? What'd you do to my son?
Oh, my God, what's that blood all over your face? What'd
you do? Where is he, McMorrow? Oh, you bastard, oh, my
God, where is he, you tell me or I'll kill you, you tell me,
McMorrow, where is he?"

Her voice was shrill, screeching, near hysteria.

"You kill me and I won't tell you," I said.

"Where is he? What did you do to him? You bastard,
how did you get his gun? Bobby. Bobby. Bobby, come
here."

Melanie was screaming. Coyote's black eyes stared into mine. His two front teeth rested on the metal of the barrel. The left one, left from my side, was discolored. Yellow.

"Don't move," I said.

"Bobby, come here, Bobby."

There was the sound of someone running on the driveway and the sound got louder and there he was, pistol down low, then out in front of him, clenched in two hands, pointed at me.

"He returns from the dead," I said. "How was it?"

"He's done something to Stephen. He's got his gun. He's got Stephen's gun. What'd you do with him, McMorrow? You bastard, if you hurt him, I'll kill you, I'll kill you myself."

"Put it down, McMorrow," Bobby said, moving behind Melanie, into the road.

"The bad news is this blood all over me. It isn't mine."

"My God," Melanie gasped.

"The good news is he's okay. For now."

"Where is he?"

"State secret. I'll tell you in downtown Madison."

"I'm gonna kill him," Bobby said, pistol still pointed at me.

"You do that, he's dead. You won't find him and he'll die of thirst or exposure or something like that. Shooting me is shooting him. It's true. He's hidden out in those woods and you could look for him for a week. So back off."

"Where is he?"

"I'll call you."

"You're not going anywhere, friend."

"Yeah, I am. I'm gonna get in this truck and go. You go back to the house and wait and I'll call and tell you where Stephen is. That means you'd better find the phone."

"No way."

"Yes way."

"You're not leaving, McMorrow," Melanie said. "Not until you tell us where he is."

"You're smarter than that."

"You're going nowhere," Bobby said.

"Oh, I don't know. I had a couple of rocky years, but now this freelance stuff is kind of taking off."

Bobby moved a couple of steps toward me.

"One more and he goes. I'll keep shooting and Stephen'll die. Back off."

Melanie looked at me. Coyote did, too. I could hear him breathing. The barrel was wet with his saliva.

"Do it, Bobby."

"He can't leave."

"We've got to have Stephen. We've got to find him. Is he shot?"

"He's dead if I don't tell you. Simple as that. Now here we go. I'm gonna open this door. You're gonna put your guns down and lie in the road. Don't you ever get any traffic around here?"

"No friggin' way," Bobby said.

Melanie looked at me. Slowly lowered the shotgun.

"What are you doing?"

"I've got to have Stephen."

"He's not gonna call. He's gonna call the cops. He goes, we're history. Are you crazy? We'd have to run so friggin' fast, shit, the place would be swarming. In an hour? Shit. He can't go."

"Stephen," Melanie said.

"He's not going. You're not going, McMorrow. You open that door, you're a dead man. I swear it, man. You touch that door, you're dead."

"And so's Stephen."

"Don't try it, McMorrow. You tell us where the kid is, you toss the rifle, you start hoofing it down the road. We boogie and we all live happily ever after."

"Nope."

"I gotta kill him."

"No, Bobby."

"I gotta."

"No."

"I'm not going back to the joint."

"They'd love your hair," I said. "Right, Bern?"

"You're not leaving, McMorrow."

"I'll call you. Wait by the phone. Have a muffin, they're killers."

"I'm gonna drop him."

"No."

"That gun's pointed at Stephen's head," I said.

"Don't move, McMorrow."

"Here we go, Bern. We're gonna go nice and easy. Show me those pearly whites. That's a good boy."

"Don't do it, McMorrow."

"Here we go, Bernie. Nice and easy."

"McMorrow."

"Bobby, don't."

"Don't move, McMorrow."

"Bobby. Bobby. Please."

"He shoots, say goodbye to your son, Melanie. He's gonna die slow."

"No, Bobby."

"I'm telling you, McMorrow. Drop it. I'm gonna do it. I'm gonna kill you. I'm—"

"You want these two or do you want Stephen? It's that simple."

"Last chance, McMorrow."

"No."

It was Melanie. She had the shotgun on Bobby. Pointed at the side of his head.

"What the hell are you doing?"

"You're not gonna kill my son."

"Christ almighty, what are you doing?"

"You're not gonna kill Stephen."

"He's already dead. Look at the blood on this guy. He killed him."

"I don't believe it."

"He's fine," I said. "The blood's from his nose."

"Bullshit," Bobby said.

"You're not gonna kill my son, Bobby."

"He's a nice kid, Melanie. He deserves a life."

"Shut up, McMorrow."

"I'll call you, Melanie. Put the gun down and you can even come with me. Drop me in Madison and I'll tell you and you can come right back."

"He's not leaving."

"Sure I am. Right now. Nice and easy."

Bobby's pistol was on me. Melanie's shotgun was on him. The rifle was in Coyote's mouth. I eased the door open. A truck came around the bend from the west.

"Shit," Bobby said, but nobody dropped their guns. The truck had two guys in it. It slowed and stopped in the road a hundred yards away, backed up and turned and roared off.

"Too late now," I said.

Coyote was on his feet, on the other side of the door.

"Don't friggin' move, McMorrow," Bobby said.

"Make a choice, Melanie. Your son or these two dirt-bags. Keep in mind that they're going away for a long, long time."

I pulled the door toward me so my back was to Bobby.

"Put both hands on top of the door."

Coyote did it.

"Now open your mouth, very slowly."

He did that, too. I eased the gun out of his mouth but kept it pointed at his face. Then I pulled it through the window frame and had it back on his face.

"Now keep your hands up and lie down on your face in the road. Right there."

"McMorrow," Bobby screamed.

Coyote stretched out on the pavement.

"Bobby, don't," Melanie said.

I waited for the blast. One gun or the other. Waited. Then turned slowly, so I had the door between me and the two of them. Melanie had the shotgun on Bobby. He had the pistol pointed at me. My rifle was pointed at Coyote.

"McMorrow," Bobby screamed, trembling.

"No," Melanie shrieked.

The pistol came up, pointed at my face.

"He's my son," Melanie screamed.

Bobby took a deep breath.

And ran.

Thirty-four

DURING THE RIDE to Madison, Melanie was quiet. I was, too. The rifle went in the gun rack. It was no longer needed.

On the Anson side of the bridge to Madison, I pulled the truck over. Melanie looked over at me, her face taut with worry.

"Who's the dead guy?" I said.

"Where is he, McMorrow?"

I looked at her. Slowly shook my head. I leaned over and opened the glove box and found a pink piece of paper, the back of a receipt. There was a pencil, too.

"You've got to be kidding," Melanie said.

"Nope. Who's the dead guy?"

Melanie looked at me.

"Goddamn you, McMorrow. Goddamn you to hell."

I wrote that down. Waited.

"How can you hold my son hostage to your goddamn story?"

"I'm doing what I set out to do. We had a deal, remember? You think I came all the way up here to visit? Now, who's the dead guy?"

Melanie looked at me.

"You son of a bitch."

I waited, pen on the paper. She looked away. I waited some more.

"He was some junkie. Coyote found him."

"When he was alive or when he was dead?"

"Dead."

I scribbled.

"Who killed him?"

"Nobody. He OD'd."

"And Coyote just happened to be standing there when he nodded out?"

"The word was out. Well, not really out. Coyote told a couple people we were looking for a body."

"And one just happened to fall into your lap?"

She shrugged.

"A body with a name and a dentist?"

"They all go to the clinic down there."

"Good luck explaining that to the cops," I said.

"Where is he?"

"Not so fast. What was I needed for?"

"Goddamn it, I want a lawyer."

"No you don't. You want your son. A lawyer isn't going to help you find him. Not in time, anyway. So let's hear it. Why bring me into it?"

Melanie swallowed, looked out at the falls tumbling past the brick walls of the mill. She looked jowly. She looked old.

"I'll sit here all day and all night," I said.

"We needed a third party. Somebody to say, 'Yeah. Bobby went to Lewiston to find a guy who owed him money for drugs.' We needed somebody who knew about it before. Somebody independent."

"And I fell into your lap."

"Yup."

"Except I wasn't supposed to chase him so far."

"Right. You weren't supposed to go all over friggin' New England. Now you got what you want? Where's my son?"

I filled the back of the paper and turned it over. It was a receipt for a tire. I wrote in the margin, down the sides.

"I'm not done. What'd you want the money for?"

"What'd we want the money for?"

"Yeah. You grow vegetables, don't even have electricity. What the hell you going to do with three hundred thousand?"

"It wasn't three, it was one. One for each of us. I was gonna take mine and take Stephen and go live someplace warm."

"The two of you?"

"You got it. The two of us."

"Did Bobby know that?"

"He never asked," Melanie said. "Now where's Stephen?"

I finished writing and put the piece of paper in my shirt pocket. Then I put the truck in gear. All the way to the Madison police station, Melanie called me names, said I was a double-crossing son of a bitch. This wasn't true, because I did tell her where Stephen was.

In the presence of a policeman.

Tom Wellington at the *Globe* liked that part of the story.

"'Go live someplace warm.' That says it all, doesn't it?" Wellington said, over the phone. "So much for the organic life. Bottom line is everybody wants to go to St. Thomas and drink rum. How the hell did you get her to talk to you like that?"

I looked over at Roxanne, sitting in the sun in the big chair by the window, her leg up on a wooden crate topped with a cushion.

"She just talked."

"It's a hell of a piece, Jack. I like the DEA cop talking about his son. The guy whose son was disillusioned. The dentist. Art is great, too. The mug shot, the family photo. And I don't say that easily. Don't suppose Mullaney and Begosian want to confess their sins."

"They've got lawyers now. I tried."

"They're gonna need 'em. Think they'll be able to convict them on the murder charge for the junkie?"

"I doubt it. But it's something to bargain with."

"And the wife is spilling her guts?" Wellington asked.

"That's what I hear. But I can't get it for the record. Mendoza at the *Chronicle* is in a better position to get that one. He's down there."

"Don't suppose we could get you down here, Jack."

"No, I've done that. And I like it up here."

"Prosperity, Maine. What the hell do you do all day?"

I moved to Roxanne. She was wearing running shorts over her cast, a tank top over her running shorts. I ran my hand up her good leg. She smiled at me lasciviously, licking her lips.

"Oh, I don't know. I've got friends here. I cut some wood, tromp around, read a lot. You know the raptors are migrating now?"

"Raptors?"

"Hawks."

"No kidding."

"No, I'm serious. So there's that, and I've got a good friend up here. She's sort of an invalid."

Roxanne punched me in the thigh.

"Yeah, she's really sort of a shut-in. So I feel an obligation to help her out."

She punched me again.

"What do you do? Bring her meals?"

"Yeah. Help her with her physical therapy."

I ran my hand up Roxanne's thigh. She pushed it away. Wellington said he guessed we were all set and the story would run that Sunday. I said I'd be looking for it and he said he'd call if he had any questions. He hung up and I did, too.

"A friend who's an invalid?" Roxanne said.

"Yeah, well, it's my way of giving something back to the community."

"A shut-in?"

"I'd like to shut you in."

"I'll bet you would."

I sat down on the arm of the chair and leaned over and kissed her. She was, as always, delicious.

"You know, you'd better not encourage me," I said. "I'll take advantage of your disability."

"I'm counting on it," Roxanne said. "Why do you think I agreed to come up here to the edge of civilization?"

"This isn't the edge. This is the last bastion."

Roxanne took my hand, looked up at me.

"So this last one didn't sour you too much?" she said.

"Did the loony mother sour you?"

"Hell no. We saved her kids."

"Right. So the supposedly naive old hippies turned out to be venal and greedy and conniving. And I liked someone who turned out to be using me for a scam. It isn't the first time."

"But you're not disillusioned?"

"Heck no. The rest of the crowd was pretty nice, and it's a good story. Besides, I have a new philosophy. I look for the good in people."

"Like what?"

"Well, Melanie chose her son over Bobby. And Bobby couldn't shoot me."

I smiled.

"So you don't feel burned? By Bobby?"

"No. Maybe a little singed. But that's what life does. You get singed, a little scorched, but you keep going. You know that as well as I do. So don't believe them when they say the world is going to hell."

"My positive thinker," Roxanne said.

"And you know what? I really like the lead. 'Bobby Mullaney thought growing and selling marijuana was a good way to make easy money. But then, police say, he thought of a better way than that.' It has a nice ring to it, don't you think?"

"Not bad."

"Hey, speaking of scorched, what time do you want to have dinner?"

"I don't know. What's my manservant cooking?"

"I thought I'd have Clair and Mary over. We could have chicken."

"Uh-huh."

"They were small, so I bought two. Little cute white fluffy ones. I went ahead and lopped their heads off because you were laid up."

Roxanne reached up and took my arm and pulled me toward her.

"Jack McMorrow," she said. "You'd better be kidding."

I kissed her for a long time, then smiled, looking into her eyes.

"About you?" I said. "I've never been more serious in my life."